Peering drunkenly about the crowded room, Harrington noticed for the first time that everyone's attention seemed to be focused toward the center. And there he recognized Nordgren. Damon thought he looked awful, far worse than earlier in the day. Shoving through to him, Harrington clasped hands.

Nordgren's handgrip felt very loose, with a scaly dryness that made Damon think of the brittle rustle of overlong fingernails. Harrington shook his hand firmly and tried to draw Nordgren toward him so they could speak together. Nordgren's arm broke off at his shoulder like a stick of dry-rotted wood.

Harrington just stood there, gaping stupidly. The crowd was silent. Then, ever so slowly, ever so reluctantly, as if there were too little left to drain, a few dark drops of blood began to trickle from the torn stump of Nordgren's shoulder.

The crowd's eyes began to turn upon Harrington.

MASTERS OF DARKNESS

# MASTERS OF DARKNESS

EDITED BY
## DENNIS ETCHISON

TOR
HORROR

A TOM DOHERTY ASSOCIATES BOOK

MASTERS OF DARKNESS

Copyright © 1986 by Dennis Etchison

First printing: August 1986

A TOR Book

Published by Tom Doherty Associates
49 West 24 Street
New York, N.Y. 10010

Cover art and text ornament by J. K. Potter

ISBN: 0-812-51762-8
CAN. ED.: 0-812-51763-6

Printed in the United States

0 9 8 7 6 5 4 3 2 1

# Acknowledgments

To
**KARL EDWARD WAGNER**

*who got to Powell Publications in time . . .*

*and*

*to*

**ANGELA TAYLOR BURGESS**

*literary godmother of us all*

# Contents

# PREFACE

*Masters of Darkness* is an "authors' choice" collection of works selected especially for this book by fifteen of the best writers currently practicing in the horror/dark fantasy field. In each instance I have asked the author to choose a personal favorite, to restore the text if necessary, and to provide a new commentary revealing as much as the author might care to share about how or why the piece came to be written. Several appear here for the first time in complete form, having been censored, abridged or otherwise altered without author approval in their earlier incarnations, and one has been newly revised for this edition. The book represents, then, the choicest work by writers at the top of their form, published here—and in some cases here alone—in their definitive versions.

Two entries come as genuine surprises. George Clayton Johnson has provided a full dramatic treatment rather than a short story, sold to Rod Serling but never produced for the original *Twilight Zone* television series. And Ray Russell has given us two poems, one of which makes its debut here. To these unusual contributions I direct your particular attention.

My labors have necessarily been limited to arriving at a final list of contributors, soliciting the manuscripts, and then commissioning the Authors' Notes. I have purposely avoided the temptation to influence the selection of pieces, since there are numerous existing reprint anthologies reflecting the idiosyncratic tastes of their various editors. Rather than add yet another point of view by imposing my own editorial preferences on an already confused readership, I have opted for the greatest possible degree of anonymity, preferring instead to offer a volume that should weather the vagaries of shifting critical fashion and earn a permanent place in any worthy library of the dark and fantastic.

It will be noted that *Masters* contains several names commonly associated with the field of science fiction. Since labels often function negatively by limiting an author's potential readership, I have attempted to cut across such boundaries by calling upon individuals whose darker works may not be as widely known as their more conveniently categorized writings. I have no interest in perpetuating the artificially imposed classes of commercial fiction. There are very few if any first-rate artists whose output falls neatly within the confines of a single camp. Science fiction, dystopian or otherwise, sometimes offers insights into our present condition that are not touched upon by the traditional horror story. On the assumption that there may be more frightening and immediate threats to modern life than haunted houses, werewolves or testaments secreted in musty attics, I have invited some of today's most gifted science fiction writers to participate, and I believe that their contributions are among the most disturbing and provocative to be found in the pages that follow.

Though the Table of Contents presents an impressive array of talent, not every important contemporary writer known to horror readers has been included. This is due solely to space limitations. I sincerely hope that they will be represented in a second volume—if your response to this first *Masters of Darkness* justifies publication of such a book.

—Dennis Etchison
July 1985

*The first reason for my selecting "The Dead Man" is* that it has rarely been reprinted and most of my readers hardly know of its existence. The second reason is that after all this time, the story seems to hold up. It was the result of a series of experiments I made with the right, middle, left or somewhere-in-between sections of my brain. Back in the early forties, I was just beginning to learn the secrets of writing. One of them most certainly was to tap the hidden stuffs put away where you don't even know where or how to find them. The best way, for me, was to make lists of nouns, to name subjects, and then sit down and write stories asking myself just why I had written out, as part of the list, The Night, The Wind, The Candle, The Trapdoor, or, as you will see here, The Dead Man. By relaxing into each of these Found Objects, as it were, the stories began to spill forth. When I began "The Dead Man," I hadn't the faintest idea how it would turn out. I simply had a strange lost creature on my hands, and

1

had to find a way to some proper finish for him. The story, from that point on, wrote itself. I went along on a trip around town with my sad gentleman to see what would happen. Now, it's your turn.

—Ray Bradbury

# THE DEAD MAN

## by Ray Bradbury

"That's the man, right over there," said Mrs. Ribmoll, nodding across the street. "See that man perched on the tar barrel afront Mr. Jenkins' store? Well, that's him. They call him Odd Martin."

"The one that says he's dead?" cried Arthur.

Mrs. Ribmoll nodded. "Crazy as a weasel down a chimney. Carries on firm about how he's been dead since the flood and nobody appreciates."

"I see him sitting there every day," cried Arthur.

"Oh, yes, he sits there, he does. Sits there and stares at nothing. I say it's a crying shame they don't throw him in jail."

Arthur made a face at the man. "Yah!"

"Never mind, he won't notice you. Most uncivil man I ever seen. Nothing pleases him." She yanked Arthur's arm. "Come on, sonny, we got shopping to do."

They passed on up the street past the barbershop. In the window, after they'd gone by, stood Mr. Simpson, snipping his blue shears and chewing his tasteless gum. He squinted thoughtfully out through

3

the fly-specked glass, looking at the man sitting over there on the tar barrel. "I figure the best thing could happen to Odd Martin would be to get married," he figured. His eyes glinted slyly. Over his shoulder he looked at his manicurist, Miss Weldon, who was busy burnishing the scraggy fingernails of a farmer named Gilpatrick. Miss Weldon, at this suggestion, did not look up. She had heard it often. They were always ragging her about Odd Martin.

Mr. Simpson walked back and started work on Gilpatrick's dusty hair again. Gilpatrick chuckled softly. "What woman would marry Odd? Sometimes I almost believe he *is* dead. He's got an awful odor to him."

Miss Weldon looked up into Mr. Gilpatrick's face and carefully cut his finger with one of her little scalpels. "Goldarn it! Watch what you're doing, woman!"

Miss Weldon looked at him with calm little blue eyes in a small white face. Her hair was mouse-brown; she wore no makeup and talked to no one most of the time.

Mr. Simpson cackled and snicked his blue steel shears. "Hope, hope, hope!" he laughed like that. "Miss Weldon, she knows what she's doin', Gilpatrick. You just be careful. Miss Weldon, she give a bottle of eau de cologne to Odd Martin last Christmas. It helped cover up his smell."

Miss Weldon laid down her instruments.

"Sorry, Miss Weldon," apologized Mr. Simpson. "I won't say no more."

Reluctantly, she took up her instruments again.

"Hey, there he goes again!" cried one of the four other men waiting in the shop. Mr. Simpson whirled, almost taking Gilpatrick's pink ear with him in his shears. "Come look, boys!"

*       *       *

Across the street the sheriff stepped out of his office door just then and he saw it happen, too. He saw what Odd Martin was doing.

Everybody came running from all the little stores.

The sheriff arrived and looked down into the gutter.

"Come on now, Odd Martin, come on now," he shouted. He poked down into the gutter with his shiny black boot-tip. "Come on, get up. You're not dead. You're good as me. You'll catch your death of cold there with all them gum wrappers and cigar butts! Come on, get up!"

Mr. Simpson arrived on the scene and looked at Odd Martin lying there. "He looks like a carton of milk."

"He's takin' up valuable parkin' space for cars, this bein' Friday mornin'," whined the sheriff. "And lots of people needin' the area. Here now, Odd. Hmm. Well, give me a hand here, boys."

They laid the body on the sidewalk.

"Let him stay here," declared the sheriff, jostling around in his boots. "Just let him stay till he gets tired of layin'. He's done this a million times before. Likes the publicity. *Git*, you kids!"

He sent a bunch of children scuttling ahead of his cheek of tobacco.

Back in the barbershop, Simpson looked around. "Where's Miss Weldon? Uh." He looked through the glass. "There she is, brushing him off again, while he lies there. Fixing his coat, buttoning it up. Here she comes back. Don't nobody fun with her, she resents it."

The barber clock said twelve o'clock and then one and then two and then three. Mr. Simpson kept track of it. "I make you a bet that Odd Martin lies over there till four o'clock," he said.

Someone else said, "I'll bet he's there until four-thirty."

"Last time"—a snickering of the shears—"he was there four hours. Nice warm day today. He may nap there until five. I'll say five. Let's see your money, gents. Or maybe later."

The money was collected and put on a shelf by the hair ointments.

One of the younger men began shaving a stick with his pocketknife. "It's sorta funny how we joke about Odd. We're scared of him, inside. I mean we won't let ourselves believe he's really dead. We don't dare believe it. We'd never get over it if we knew. So we make him a joke. We let him lie around. He don't hurt nobody. He's just there. But I notice Doc Hudson has never really touched Odd's heart with his stethoscope. Scared of what he'd find, I bet."

"Scared of what he'd find!" Laughter. Simpson laughed and *snished* his shears. Two men with crusty beards laughed, a little too loud. The laughter didn't last long. "Great one for jokin', you are!" they all said, slapping their gaunt knees.

Miss Weldon, she went on manicuring her client.

"He's getting up!"

There was a general scramble to the plate-glass window to watch Odd Martin gain his feet. "He's up on one knee, now up on the other, now someone's givin' him a hand."

"It's Miss Weldon. She sure got over there in a rush."

"What time is it?"

"Five o'clock. Pay me, boys!"

"That Miss Weldon's a queer nut herself. Takin' after a man like Odd."

Simpson clicked his scissors. "Being an orphan,

she's got quiet ways. She likes men who don't say much. Odd, he don't say hardly anything. Just the opposite of us crude men, eh, fellows? We talk too much. Miss Weldon don't like our way of talking.''

"There they go, the two of 'em, Miss Weldon and Odd Martin.''

"Say, take a little more off around my ears, will you, Simp?''

Skipping down the street, bouncing a red rubber ball, came little Charlie Bellows, his blond hair flopping in a yellow fringe over his blue eyes. He bounced the ball abstractedly, tongue between lips, and the ball fell under Odd Martin's feet where he sat once more on the tar barrel. Inside the grocery, Miss Weldon was doing her supper shopping, putting soup cans and vegetable cans into a basket.

"Can I have my ball?'' asked little Charlie Bellows upward at the six feet, two inches, of Odd Martin. No one was within hearing distance.

"Can you have your ball?'' said Odd Martin haltingly. He turned it over inside his head, it appeared. His level grey eyes shaped up Charlie like one would shape up a little ball of clay. "You can have your ball; yes, take it.''

Charlie bent slowly and took hold of the bright red rubber globe and arose slowly, a secretive look in his eyes. He looked north and south and then up at Odd's bony pale brown face. "I know something.''

Odd Martin looked down. "You know something?''

Charlie leaned forward. "You're dead.''

Odd Martin sat there.

"You're really dead,'' whispered little Charlie Bellows. "But I'm the only one who really knows. I believe you, Mr. Odd. I tried it once myself. Dying, I mean. It's hard. It's work. I laid on the floor for an hour. But I blinked and my stomach itched, so I scratched it. Then—I quit. Why?'' He looked at his shoes. '' 'Cause I had to go to the bathroom.''

A slow, understanding smile formed on the soft pallid flesh of Odd Martin's long, bony face. "It is work. It isn't easy."

"Sometimes I think about you," said Charlie. "I see you walking by my house at night. Sometimes at two in the morning. Sometimes at four. I wake up and I know you're out walking around. I know I should look out, and I do, and, gee, there you are, walking and walking. Not going hardly anyplace."

"There's no place to go." Odd sat with his large, square, calloused hands on his knees. "I try thinking of some—place to—go—" He slowed, like a horse to a bit-pull "—but it's hard to think. I try and—try. Sometimes I almost know what to do, where to go. Then I forget. Once I had an idea to go to a doctor and have him declare me dead, but somehow"—his voice was slow and husky and low—"I never got there."

Charlie looked straight at him. "If you want, I'll take you."

Odd Martin looked leisurely at the setting sun. "No. I'm weary-tired, but I'll—wait. Now I've gone this far, I'm curious to see what happens next. After the flood that washed away my farm and all my stock and put me underwater, like a chicken in a bucket, I filled up like you'd fill a thermos with water, and I came walking out of the flood, anyhow. But I knew I was dead. Late of nights I lay listening in my room, but there's no heartbeat in my ears or in my chest or in my wrists, though I lie still as a cold cricket. Nothing inside me but a darkness and relaxation and an understanding. There must be a reason for me still walking, though. Maybe it was because I was still young when I died. Only twenty-eight, and not married yet. I always wanted to marry. Never got around to it. Here I am, doing odd jobs around town, saving my money, 'cause I never eat, heck, I *can't* eat, and sometimes getting so discouraged and downright bewildered that I lie down in the gutter and hope they'll take me and poke me in a pine box and lay me away forever. Yet at the same time I don't want that. I want a little more. I know that whenever Miss Weldon walks by and I see the wind playing her hair like a little brown feather . . ." He sighed away into silence.

Charlie Bellows waited politely a minute, then cleared his throat and darted away, bouncing his ball. "See you later!"

Odd stared at the spot where Charlie'd been. Five minutes later he blinked. "Eh? Somebody here? Somebody speak?"

Miss Weldon came out of the grocery with a basket full of food.

"Would you like to walk me home, Odd?"

They walked along in an easy silence, she careful not to walk too fast, because he set his legs down carefully. The wind rustled in the cedars and in the elms and the maples all along the way. Several times his lips parted and he glanced aside at her, and then he shut his mouth tight and stared ahead, as if looking at something a million miles away.

Finally, he said, "Miss Weldon?"

"Yes, Odd?"

"I been saving and saving up my money. I've got quite a handsome sum. I don't spend much for anything, and—you'd be surprised," he said sincerely. "I got about a thousand dollars. Maybe more. Sometimes I count it and get tired and I can't count no

more. And—'' He seemed baffled and a little angry
with her suddenly. ''Why do you like me, Miss
Weldon?'' he demanded.

She looked a little surprised, then smiled up at
him. It was almost a childlike look of liking she gave
him. ''Because you're quiet. Because you're not loud
and mean like the men at the barbershop. Because
I'm lonely, and you've been kind. Because you're
the first one that ever liked me. The others don't
even look at me once. They say I can't think. They
say I'm a moron, because I didn't finish the sixth
grade. But I'm so lonely, Odd, and talking to you
means so much.''

He held her small white hand, tight.

She moistened her lips. ''I wish we could do
something about the way people talk about you. I
don't want to sound mean, but if you'd only stop
telling them you're dead, Odd.''

He stopped walking. ''Then you don't believe me,
either,'' he said remotely.

''You're 'dead' for want of a good woman's cooking, for loving, for living right, Odd. That's what
you mean by 'dead'; nothing else!''

His grey eyes were deep and lost. ''Is that what I
mean?'' He saw her eager, shiny face. ''Yes, that's
what I mean. You guessed it right. That's what I
mean.''

Their footsteps went alone together, drifting in the
wind, like leaves floating, and the night got darker
and softer and the stars came out.

Two boys and two girls stood under a street lamp
about nine o'clock that evening. Far away down the
street someone walked along slowly, quietly, alone.

''There he is,'' said one of the boys. ''*You* ask
him, Tom.''

Tom scowled uneasily. The girls laughed at him. Tom said, "Oh, okay, but you come along."

The wind flung the trees right and left, shaking down leaves in singles and clusters that fell past Odd Martin's head as he approached.

"Mr. Odd? Hey there, Mr. Odd?"

"Eh? Oh, hello."

"We—uh—that is—" gulped Tom, looking around for assistance. "We want to know if—well—we want you to come to our party!"

A minute later, after looking at Tom's clean, soap-smelling face and seeing the pretty blue jacket his sixteen-year-old girl friend wore, Odd Martin answered. "Thank you. But I don't know. I might forget to come."

"No, you wouldn't," insisted Tom. "You'd remember this one, because it's Halloween!"

One of the girls yanked Tom's arm and hissed. "Let's not, Tom. Let's not. Please. He won't do, Tom. He isn't scary enough."

Tom shook her off. "Let *me* handle this."

The girl pleaded. "Please, no. He's just a dirty old man. Bill can put a candle tallow on his fingers and those horrible porcelain teeth in his mouth and the green chalk-marks under his eyes, and scare the ducks out of us. We don't need *him!*" And she jerked her rebellious head at Odd.

Odd Martin stood there. He heard the wind in the high treetops for ten minutes before he knew that the four young people were gone. A small dry laugh came up in his mouth like a pebble. Children. Halloween. Not scary enough. Bill would do better. Just an old man. He tasted the laughter and found it both strange and bitter.

The next morning little Charlie Bellows flung his ball against the storefront, retrieved it, flung it again.

He heard someone humming behind him, turned. "Oh, hello, Mr. Odd!"

Odd Martin was walking along, with green paper dollars in his fingers, counting them. He stopped, suddenly. His eyes were blank.

"Charlie," he cried out. "Charlie!" His hands groped.

"Yes, sir, Mr. Odd!"

"Charlie, where was I going? Where was I going? Going somewhere to buy something for Miss Weldon! Here, Charlie, help me!"

"Yes, sir, Mr. Odd." Charlie ran up and stood in his shadow.

A hand came down, money in it, seventy dollars of money. "Charlie, run buy a dress for—Miss Weldon—" His mind was grasping, clutching, seizing, wrestling in a web of forgetfulness. There was stark terror and longing and fear in his face. "I can't remember the place, oh God, help me remember. A dress and a coat, for Miss Weldon, at—at—"

"Krausmeyer's Department Store?" asked Charlie, helpfully.

"No."

"Fieldman's?"

"No!"

"Mr. Leiberman's?"

"Leiberman! That's it! Leiberman, Leiberman! Here, here, Charlie, here, run down there to—"

"Leiberman's."

"—and get a new green dress for—Miss Weldon, and a coat. A new green dress with yellow roses painted on it. You get them and bring them to me here. Oh, Charlie, wait."

"Yes, sir, Mr. Odd?"

"Charlie—you think, maybe I could clean up at your house?" asked Odd quietly. "I need a—a bath."

"Gee, I don't know, Mr. Odd. My folks are funny. I don't know."

"That's all right, Charlie. I understand. Run now!"

Charlie ran on the double, clutching the money. He ran by the barbershop. He poked his head in. Mr. Simpson stopped snipping on Mr. Trumbull's hair and glared at him. "Hey!" cried Charlie. "Odd Martin's humming a tune!"

"What tune?" asked Mr. Simpson.

"It goes like this," said Charlie, and hummed it.

"Yee Gods Amaughty!" bellowed Simpson. "So that's why Miss Weldon ain't here manicurin' this morning! That there tune's the *Wedding March!*"

Charlie ran on. Pandemonium!

Shouting, laughter, the sound of water squishing and pattering. The back of the barbershop steamed. They took turns. First, Mr. Simpson got a bucket of hot water and tossed it down in a flap over Odd Martin, who sat in the tub, saying nothing, just sitting there, and then Mr. Trumbull scrubbed Odd Martin's pale back with a big brush and lots of cow-soap, and every once in a while Shorty Phillips doused Odd with a jigger of eau de cologne. They all laughed and ran around in the steam. "Gettin' married, huh, Odd? Congratulations, boy!" More water. "I always said that's what you needed," laughed Mr. Simpson, hitting Odd in the chest with a bunch of cold water this time. Odd Martin pretended not to even notice the shock. "You'll smell better now!"

Odd sat there. "Thanks. Thanks so very much for doing this. Thanks for helping me. Thanks for giving me a bath this way. I needed it."

Simpson laughed behind his hand. "Sure thing, anything for you, Odd."

Someone whispered in the steamy background,

"Imagine her and him married? A moron married to an idiot!"

Simpson frowned. "Shut up back there!"

Charlie rushed in. "Here's the green dress, Mr. Odd!"

An hour later they had Odd in the barber chair. Someone had lent him a new pair of shoes. Mr. Trumbull was polishing them vigorously, winking at everybody. Mr. Simpson snipped Odd's hair for him, would not take money for it. "No, no, Odd, you keep that as a wedding present from me to you. Yes, sir." And he spat. Then he shook some rose water all over Odd's dark hair. "There. Moonlight and roses!"

Martin looked around. "You won't tell nobody about this marriage," he asked, "until tomorrow? Me and Miss Weldon sort of want a marriage without the town poking fun. You understand?"

"Why sure, sure, Odd," said Simpson, finishing the job. "Mum's the word. Where you going to live? You buying a new farm?"

"Farm?" Odd Martin stepped down from the chair. Somebody lent him a nice new coat and someone else had pressed his pants for him. He looked fine. "Yes, I'm going to buy the property now. Have to pay extra for it, but it's worth it. Extra. Come along now, Charlie Bellows." He went to the door. "I bought a house out on the edge of town. I have to go make the payment on it now. Come on, Charlie."

Simpson stopped him. "What's it like? You didn't have much money; you couldn't afford much."

"No," said Odd, "you're right. It's a small house. Some folks built it awhile back, then moved away East somewheres; it was up for sale for only five hundred, so I got it. Miss Weldon and I are moving out there tonight, after our marriage. But don't tell nobody, please, until tomorrow."

"Sure thing, Odd. Sure thing."

Odd went away into the four o'clock light, Charlie at his side, and the men in the barbershop went and sat down, laughing.

The wind sighed outside, and slowly the sun went down and the snipping of the shears went on, and the men sat around, laughing and talking.


The next morning at breakfast, little Charlie Bellows sat thoughtfully spooning his cereal. Father folded his newspaper across the table and looked at Mother. "Everybody in town's talking about the quiet elopement of Odd Martin and Miss Weldon," said Father. "People, looking for them, can't find them."

"Well," said Mother, "I hear he bought a house for her."

"I heard that, too," said Father. "I phoned Carl Rogers this morning. He says he didn't sell any house to Odd. And Carl is the only real-estate dealer in town."

Charlie Bellows swallowed some cereal. He looked at his father. "Oh, no, he's not the only real-estate dealer in town."

"What do you mean?" demanded Father.

"Nothing, except that I looked out the window at midnight, and I saw something."

"You saw *what?*"

"It was all moonlight. And you know what I saw? Well, I saw two people walking up the Elm Glade road. A man and a woman. A man in a new dark coat, and a woman in a green dress. Walking real slow. Holding hands." Charlie took a breath. "And the two people were Mr. Odd Martin and Miss Weldon. And walking out the Elm Glade road there ain't any houses out that way at all. Only the Trinity Park Cemetery. And Mr. Gustavsson, in town, he sells tombs in the Trinity Park Cemetery. He's got an office in town. Like I said, Mr. Carl Rogers ain't the *only* real-estate man in town. So—''

''Oh,'' snorted Father, irritably, ''you were dreaming!''

Charlie bent his head over his cereal and looked out from the corners of his eyes.

''Yes, sir,'' he said finally, sighing. ''I was only dreaming.''

# FLASH POINT

## by Gardner Dozois

Ben Jacobs was on his way back to Skowhegan when he found the abandoned car. It was parked on a lonely stretch of secondary road between North Anson and Madison, skewed diagonally over the shoulder.

Kids again, was Jacobs's first thought—more of the road gypsies who plagued the state every summer until they were driven south by the icy whip of the first nor'easter. Probably from the big encampment down near Norridgewock, he decided, and he put his foot back on the accelerator. He'd already had more than his fill of outer-staters this season, and it wasn't even the end of August. Then he looked more closely at the car, and eased up on the gas again. It was too big, too new to belong to kids. He shifted down into second, feeling the crotchety old pickup shudder. It was an expensive car, right enough; he doubted that it came from within twenty miles of here. You didn't use a big-city car on most of the roads in this neck of the woods, and you couldn't stay on the highways forever. He squinted to see more detail. What kind of plates did it have? You're doing it again, he thought,

17

suddenly and sourly. He was a man as aflame with curiosity as a magpie, and—having been brought up strictly to mind his own business—he considered it a vice. Maybe the car was stolen. It's possible, a'n't it? he insisted, arguing with himself. It could have been used in a robbery and then ditched, like that car from the bank job over to Farmington. It happened all the time.

You don't even fool yourself anymore, he thought, and then he grinned and gave in. He wrestled the old truck into the breakdown lane, jolted over a pothole, and coasted to a bumpy stop a few yards behind the car. He switched the engine off.

Silence swallowed him instantly.

Thick and dusty, the silence poured into the morning, filling the world as hot wax fills a mold. It drowned him completely, it possessed every inch and ounce of him. Almost, it spooked him.

Jacobs hesitated, shrugged, and then jumped down from the cab. Outside it was better—still quiet, but not preternaturally so. There was wind soughing through the spruce woods, a forlorn but welcome sound, one he had heard all his life. There was a wood thrush hammering at the morning, faint with distance but distinct. And a faraway buzzing drone overhead, like a giant sleepy bee or bluebottle, indicated that there was a Piper Cub up there somewhere, probably heading for the airport at Norridgewock. All this was familiar and reassuring. Getting nervy, is all, he told himself, long in the tooth and spooky.

Nevertheless, he walked very carefully toward the car, flatfooted and slow, the way he used to walk on patrol in 'Nam, more years ago than he cared to recall. His fingers itched for something, and after a few feet he realized that he was wishing he'd brought his old deer rifle along. He grimaced irritably at that, but the wish pattered through his mind again and again, until he was close enough to see inside the parked vehicle.

The car was empty.

"Old fool," he said sourly.

Snorting in derision at himself, he circled the car, peering in the windows. There were skid marks in the gravel of the breakdown lane, but they weren't deep—the car hadn't been going fast when it hit the shoulder; probably it had been already meandering out of control, with no foot on the accelerator. The hood and bumpers weren't damaged; the car had rolled to a stop against the low embankment, rather than crashing into it. None of the tires were flat. In the woods taking a leak, Jacobs thought. Damn fool didn't even leave his turn signals on. Or it could have been his battery, or a vapor lock or something, and he'd hiked on up the road looking for a gas station. "He still should have ma'ked it off someway," Jacobs muttered. Tourists never knew enough to find their ass in a snowstorm. This one probably wasn't even carrying any signal flags or flares.

The driver's door was wide open, and next to it was a child's plastic doll, lying facedown in the gravel. Jacobs could not explain the chill that hit him then, the horror that seized him and shook him until he was almost physically ill. Bristling, he stooped and thrust his head into the car. There was a burnt, bitter smell inside, like onions, like hot metal. A layer of gray ash covered the front seat and the floor, a couple of inches deep; a thin stream of it was trickling over the doorjamb to the ground and pooling around the plastic feet of the doll. Hesitantly he touched the ash—it was sticky and soapy to the touch. In spite of the sunlight that was slanting into the car and warming up the upholstery, the ash was

cold, almost icy. The cloth ceiling directly over the
front seat was lightly blackened with soot—he scraped
some of it off with his thumbnail—but there was no
other sign of fire. Scattered among the ashes on the
front seat were piles of clothing. Jacobs could pick
out a pair of men's trousers, a sports coat, a bra,
slacks, a bright child's dress, all undamaged. More
than one person. They're all in the woods taking a
leak, he thought inanely. Sta'k naked.

Sitting on the dashboard were a 35-mm. Nikon SI
with a telephoto lens and a new Leicaflex. In the hip
pocket of the trousers was a wallet, containing more
than fifty dollars in cash, and a bunch of credit cards.
He put the wallet back. Not even a tourist was going
to be fool enough to walk off and leave this stuff
sitting here, in an open car.

He straightened up, and felt the chill again, the
deathly noonday cold. This time he *was* spooked.
Without knowing why, he nudged the doll out of the
puddle of ash with his foot, and then he shuddered.
"Hello!" he shouted, at the top of his voice, and got
back only a dull, flat echo from the woods. Where in
hell *had* they gone?

All at once, he was exhausted. He'd been out
before dawn, on a trip up to Kingfield and Carrabassett,
and it was catching up with him. Maybe that was
why he was so jumpy over nothing. Getting old,
c'n't take this kind of shit anymore. How long since
you've had a vacation? He opened his mouth to shout
again, but uneasily decided not to. He stood for a
moment, thinking it out, and then walked back to his
truck, hunch-shouldered and limping. The old load of
shrapnel in his leg and hip was beginning to bother
him again.

Jacobs drove a mile down the highway to a rest
stop. He had been hoping he would find the people

from the car here, waiting for a tow truck, but the rest area was deserted. He stuck his head into the wood-and-fieldstone latrine, and found that it was inhabited only by buzzing clouds of bluebottles and blackflies. He shrugged. So much for that. There was a pay phone on a pole next to the picnic tables, and he used it to call the sheriff's office in Skowhegan. Unfortunately, Abner Jackman answered the phone, and it took Jacobs ten exasperating minutes to argue him into showing any interest. "Well, if they did," Jacobs said grudgingly, "they did it without any clothes." *Gobblegobblebuzz*, said the phone. "With a *kid?*" Jacobs demanded. *Buzzgobblefttzbuzz*, the phone said, giving in. "Ayah," Jacobs said grudgingly. "I'll stay theah until you show up." And he hung up.

"Damned foolishness," he muttered. This was going to cost him the morning.

County Sheriff Joe Riddick arrived an hour later. He was a stocky, slab-sided man, apparently cut all of a piece out of a block of granite—his shoulders seemed to be the same width as his hips, his square-skulled, square-jawed head thrust belligerently up from his monolithic body without any hint of a neck. He looked like an old snapping turtle: ugly, mud-colored, powerful. His hair was snow-white, and his eyes were bloodshot and ill-tempered. He glared at Jacobs dangerously out of red-rimmed eyes with tiny pupils. He looked ready to snap.

"Good morning," Jacobs said coldly.

"Morning," Riddick grunted. "You want to fill me in on this?"

Jacobs did. Riddick listened impassively. When Jacobs finished, Riddick snorted and brushed a hand back over his close-cropped snowy hair. "Some damn fool skylark more'n likely," he said sourly, shaking his head a little. "*O*-kay, then," he said, suddenly becoming officious and brisk. "If this turns out to be anything serious, we may need you as a witness. Understand? All right." He looked at his watch. "*All* right. We're waiting for the state boys. I don't think you're needed anymore." Riddick's face was hard and cold and dull—as if it had been molded in lead. He stared pointedly at Jacobs. His eyes were opaque as marbles. "Good day."

Twenty minutes later Jacobs was passing a proud little sign, erected by the Skowhegan Chamber of Commerce, that said: HOME OF THE LARGEST SCULPTED WOODEN INDIAN IN THE WORLD! He grinned. Skowhegan had grown a great deal in the last decade, but somehow it was still a small town. It had resisted the modern tropism to skyscrape and had sprawled instead, spreading out along the banks of the Kennebec River in both directions. Jacobs parked in front of a dingy storefront on Water Street, in the heart of town. A sign in the window commanded: EAT; at night it glowed an imperative neon red. The sign belonged to an establishment that had started life as the Colonial Cafe, with a buffet and quaint rustic decor, and was finishing it, twenty years and three recessions later, as a greasy lunchroom with faded movie posters on the wall—owned and operated by Wilbur and Myna Phipps, a cheerful and indestructible couple in their late sixties. It was crowded and hot inside—the place had a large number of regulars, and most of them were in attendance for lunch. Jacobs spotted Will Sussmann at the counter, jammed in between an inverted glass bowl full of doughnuts and the protruding rear end of the coffee percolator.

Sussmann—chief staff writer for the Skowhegan *Inquirer*, stringer and columnist for a big Bangor weekly—had saved him a seat by piling the adjacent stool with his hat, coat, and briefcase. Not that it was likely he'd had to struggle too hard for room. Even Jacobs, whose father had moved to Skowhegan from Bangor when Jacobs was three, was regarded with faint suspicion by the real oldtimers of the town. Sussmann, being originally an outer-stater and a "foreigner" to boot, was completely out of luck; he'd only lived here ten years, and that wasn't enough even to begin to tip the balance in his favor.

Sussmann retrieved his paraphernalia; Jacobs sat down and began telling him about the car. Sussmann said it was weird. "We'll never get anything out of Riddick," he said. He began to attack a stack of hotcakes. "He's hated my guts ever since I accused him of working over those gypsy kids last summer, putting one in the hospital. That would have cost him his job, except the higher echelons were being 'foursquare behind their dedicated law-enforcement officers' that season. Still, it didn't help his reputation with the town any."

"We don't tolerate that kind of thing in these pa'ts," Jacobs said grimly. "Hell, Will, those kids are a royal pain in the ass, but—" But not in these pa'ts, he told himself, not that. There are decent limits. He was surprised at the depth and ferocity of his reaction. "This a'n't Alabama," he said.

"Might as well be, with Riddick. His idea of law enforcement's to take everybody he doesn't like down in the basement and beat the crap out of them." Sussmann sighed. "Anyway, Riddick wouldn't stop to piss on me if my hat was on fire, that's for sure. Good thing I got other ways of finding stuff out."

Jed Everett came in while Jacobs was ordering coffee. He was a thin, cadaverous man with a long nose; his hair was going rapidly to gray; put him next to short, round Sussmann, and they would look like

Mutt and Jeff. At forty-eight—Everett was a couple of years older than Jacobs, just as Sussmann was a couple of years younger—he was considered to be scandalously young for a small-town doctor, especially a GP. But old Dr. Barlow had died of a stroke three years back, leaving his younger partner in residency, and they were stuck with him.

One of the regulars had moved away from the trough, leaving an empty seat next to Jacobs, and Everett was talking before his buttocks had hit the upholstery. He was a jittery man, with lots of nervous energy, and he loved to fret and rant and gripe, but softly and good-naturedly, with no real force behind it, as if he had a volume knob that had been turned down.

"What a morning!" Everett said. "Jesus H. Christ on a bicycle—'scuse me, Myna, I'll take some coffee, please, black—I swear it's psychosomatic. Honest to God, gentlemen, she's a case for the medical journals, dreams the whole damn shitbundle up out of her head just for the fun of it, I swear before all my hopes of heaven, swop me blue if she doesn't. *Definitely* psychosomatic."

"He's learned a new word," Sussmann said.

"If you'd wasted all the time I have on this nonsense," Everett said fiercely, "you'd be whistling a different tune out of the other side of your face, *I* can tell *you*, oh yes indeed. What kind of meat d'you have today, Myna? How about the chops—they good? —all right, and put some greens on the plate, please. Okay? Oh, and some homefrieds, now I think about it, please. If you have them."

"What's got your back up?" Jacobs asked mildly.

"You know old Mrs. Crawford?" Everett demanded. "Hm? Lives over to the Island, widow, has plenty of money? Three times now I've diagnosed her as having cancer, serious but still operable, and *three* times now I've sent her down to Augusta for exploratory surgery, and each time they got her down on the table and opened her up and couldn't find a thing, not a goddamned thing, old bitch's hale and hearty as a prize hog. Spontaneous remission. All psychosomatic, clear as mud. Three *times*, though. It's shooting my reputation all to hell down there. Now she thinks she's got an ulcer. I hope her kidney falls out, right in the street. Thank you, Myna. Can I have another cup of coffee?" He sipped his coffee, when it arrived, and looked a little more meditative. "Course, I think I've seen a good number of cases like that, I *think*, I said, ha'd to prove it when they're terminal. Wouldn't surprise me if a good many of the people who die of cancer—or a lot of other diseases, for that matter—were like that. No real physical cause, they just get tired of living, something dries up inside them, their systems stop trying to defend them, and one thing or another knocks them off. They become easy to touch off, like tinder. Most of them don't change their minds in the middle, though, like that fat old sow."

Wilbur Phipps, who had been leaning on the counter listening, ventured the opinion that modern medical science had never produced anything even half as good as the old-fashioned mustard plaster. Everett flared up instantly.

"You ever bejesus try one?" Phipps demanded.

"No, and I don't bejesus intend to!" Everett said.

Jacobs turned toward Sussmann. "Wheah you been, this early in the day?" he asked. "A'n't like you to haul yourself out before noon."

"Up at the Factory. Over to West Mills."

"What was up? Another hearing?"

"Yup. Didn't stick—they aren't going to be injuncted."

"They never will be," Jacobs said. "They got too much money, too many friends in Augusta. The Board'll never touch them."

"I don't believe that," Sussmann said. Jacobs grunted and sipped his coffee.

"As Christ's my judge," Everett was saying, in a towering rage, "I'll never understand you people, not if I live to be two hundred, not if I get to be so old my ass falls off and I have to lug it around in a handcart. I swear to God. Some of you ain' got a pot to piss in, so goddamned poor you can't afford to buy a bottle of aspirins, let alone, *let alone* pay your doctor bills from the past half-million years, and yet you go out to some godforsaken hick town too small to turn a horse around in proper and see an unlicensed practitioner, a goddamn backwoods quack, an un*mit*igated phony, and *pay* through the nose so this witchdoctor can assault you with yarb potions and poultices, and stick leeches on your ass, for all *I* know—" Jacobs lost track of the conversation. He studied a bee that was bumbling along the putty-and-plaster edge of the storefront window, swimming through the thick and dusty sunlight, looking for a way out. He felt numb, distanced from reality. The people around him looked increasingly strange. He found that it took an effort of will to recognize them at all, even Sussmann, even Everett. It scared him. These were people Jacobs saw every day of his life. Some of them he didn't actually *like*—not in the way that big-city folk thought of liking someone—but they were all his neighbors. They belonged here; they were a part of his existence, and that carried its own special intimacy. But today he was beginning to see them as an intolerant sophisticate from the city might see them: dull, provincial, sunk in an iron torpor that masqueraded as custom and routine. That was valid, in its way, but it was a grossly one-sided picture, ignoring a thousand virtues, compensations, and kindnesses. But that was the way he was seeing them. As aliens. As strangers.

Distractedly, Jacobs noticed that Everett and Sussmann were making ready to leave. "No rest for the weary," Everett was saying, and Jacobs found himself nodding unconsciously in agreement. Swamped by a sudden rush of loneliness, he invited both men home for dinner that night. They accepted, Everett with the qualification that he'd have to see what his wife had planned. Then they were gone, and Jacobs found himself alone at the counter.

He knew that he should have gone back to work also; he had some more jobs to pick up, and a delivery to make. But he felt very tired, too flaccid and heavy to move, as if some tiny burrowing animal had gnawed away his bones, as if he'd been hamstrung and hadn't realized it. He told himself that it was because he was hungry; he was running himself down, as Carol had always said he someday would. So he dutifully ordered a bowl of chili.

The chili was murky, amorphous stuff, bland and lukewarm. Listlessly, he spooned it up.

*No rest for the weary.*

"You know what I was nuts about when I was a kid?" Jacobs suddenly observed to Wilbur Phipps. "Rafts. I was a'ways making rafts out of old planks and sheet tin and whatevah other junk I could scrounge up, begging old rope and nails to lash them together with. Then I'd break my ass dragging them down to the Kennebec. And you know what? They a'ways sunk. Every goddamned time."

"Ayah?" Wilbur Phipps said.

Jacobs pushed the bowl of viscid chili away, and got up. Restlessly, he wandered over to where Dave Lucas, the game warden, was drinking beer and talking to a circle of men. ". . . dogs will be the end of deer in these pa'ts, I swear to God. And I a'n't talking about wild dogs neither, I'm talking about your ordinary domestic pets. A'n't it so, every winter? Half-starved deer a'n't got a chance in hell 'gainst somebody's big pet hound, all fed-up and rested. The deer those dogs don't kill outright, why they chase 'em to death, and then they don't even eat 'em. Run 'em out of the forest covah into the open and they get pneumonia. Run 'em into the river and through thin ice and they get drowned. Remember last yeah, the deer that big hound drove out onto the ice? Broke both its front legs and I had to go out and shoot the poor bastid. Between those goddamn dogs and all the nighthunters we got around here lately, we a'n't going to have any deer left in this county . . ." Jacobs moved away, past a table where Abner Jackman was pouring ketchup over a plateful of scrambled eggs, and arguing about communism with Steve Girard, a volunteer fireman and Elk, and Allen Ewing, a postman, who had a son serving with the Marines in Bolivia. ". . . let 'em win theah," Jackman was saying in a nasal voice, "and they'll be swa'ming all over us eventu'ly, sure as shit. Ain' no way to stop 'em then. And you're better off blowing your brains out than living under the Reds, don't ever think otherwise." He screwed the ketchup top back onto the bottle, and glanced up in time to see Jacobs start to go by.

"Ben!" Jackman said, grabbing Jacobs by the elbow. "You can tell 'em." He grinned vacuously at Jacobs—a lanky, loose-jointed, slack-faced man. "He can tell you, boys, what it's like being in a country

overrun with Communists, what they do to everybody. You were in 'Nam when you were a youngster, weren't you?''

"Yeah."

After a pause, Jackman said, "You ain' got no call
to take offense, Ben." His voice became a whine. "I
didn't mean no ha'm. I didn't mean nothing."

"Forget it," Jacobs said, and walked out.

Dave Lucas caught up with Jacobs just outside the
door. He was a short, grizzled man with iron-gray
hair, about seven years older than Jacobs. "You
know, Ben," Lucas said, "the thing of it is, Abner
really doesn't mean any ha'm." Lucas smiled bleakly;
his grandson had been killed last year, in the Retreat
from La Paz. "It's just that he a'n't too bright, is
all."

"They don't want him kicked ev'ry so often,"
Jacobs said, "then they shouldn't let him out of his
kennel at all." He grinned. "Dinner tonight? About
eight?"

"Sounds fine," Lucas said. "We're going to catch
a nighthunter, out near Oaks Pond, so I'll probably
be late."

"We'll keep it wa'm for you."

"Just the comp'ny'll be enough."

Jacobs started his truck and pulled out into the
afternoon traffic. He kept his hands locked tightly
around the steering wheel. He was amazed and dis-
mayed by the surge of murderous anger he had felt
toward Jackman; the reaction to it made him queasy,
and left the muscles knotted all across his back and
shoulders. Dave was right, Abner couldn't rightly be
held responsible for the dumbass things he said—
But if Jackman had said one more thing, if he'd done
anything than to back down as quickly as he had,
then Jacobs would have split his head open. He had

been instantly ready to do it, his hands had curled into fists, his legs had bent slightly at the knees. He *would* have done it. And he would have enjoyed it. That was a frightening realization.

*Y' touchy today*, he thought, inanely. His fingers were turning white on the wheel.

He drove home. Jacobs lived in a very old wood-frame house above the north bank of the Kennebec, on the outskirts of town, with nothing but a clump of new apartment buildings for senior citizens to remind him of civilization. The house was empty—Carol was teaching fourth grade, and Chris had been farmed out to Mrs. Turner, the baby-sitter. Jacobs spent the next half hour wrestling a broken washing machine and a television set out of the pickup and into his basement workshop, and another fifteen minutes maneuvering a newly repaired stereo-radio console up out of the basement and into the truck. Jacobs was one of the last of the old-style Yankee tinkerers, although he called himself an appliance repairman, and also did some carpentry and general handywork when things got slow. He had little formal training, but he "kept up." He wasn't sure he could fix one of the new hologram sets, but then they wouldn't be getting out here for another twenty years anyway. There were people within fifty miles who didn't have indoor plumbing. People within a hundred miles who didn't have electricity.

On the way to Norridgewock, two open jeeps packed dangerously full of gypsies came roaring up behind him. They started to pass, one on each side of his truck, their horns blaring insanely. The two jeeps ran abreast of Jacobs's old pickup for a while, making no attempt to go by—the three vehicles together filled the road. The jeeps drifted in until they were almost touching the truck, and the gypsies began pounding

the truck roof with their fists, shouting and laughing.
Jacobs kept both hands on the wheel and grimly
continued to drive at his original speed. Jeeps tipped
easily when sideswiped by a heavier vehicle, if it
came to that. And he had a tire iron under the seat.
But the gypsies tired of the game—they accelerated
and passed Jacobs, most of them giving him the
finger as they went by, and one throwing a poorly
aimed bottle that bounced onto the shoulder. They
were big, tough-looking kids with skin haircuts,
dressed—incongruously—in flowered pastel luau shirts
and expensive white bellbottoms.

The jeeps roared on up the road, still taking up
both lanes. Jacobs watched them unblinkingly until
they disappeared from sight. He was awash with
rage, the same bitter, vicious hatred he had felt for
Jackman. Riddick was right after all—the goddamned
kids were a menace to everything that lived, they
ought to be locked up. He wished suddenly that he
*had* sideswiped them. He could imagine it all vividly:
the sickening crunch of impact, the jeep overturning,
bodies cartwheeling through the air, the jeep skidding
upside down across the road and crashing into the
embankment, maybe the gas tank exploding, a gout
of flame, smoke, stink, screams— He ran through it
over and over again, relishing it, until he realized
abruptly what he was doing, what he was wishing,
and he was almost physically ill.

All the excitement and fury drained out of him,
leaving him shaken and sick. He'd always been a
patient, peaceful man, perhaps too much so. He'd
never been afraid to fight, but he'd always said that a
man who couldn't talk his way out of most trouble
was a fool. This sudden daydream lust for blood
bothered him to the bottom of his soul. He'd seen
plenty of death in 'Nam, and it hadn't affected him

this way. It was the kids, he told himself. They drag everybody down to their own level. He kept seeing them inside his head all the way into Norridgewock—the thick, brutal faces, the hard reptile eyes, the contemptuously grinning mouths that seemed too full of teeth. The gypsy kids had changed over the years. The torrent of hippies and Jesus freaks had gradually run dry, the pluggers and the weeps had been all over the state for a few seasons, and then, slowly, they'd stopped coming too. The new crop of itinerant kids were—hard. Every year they became more brutal and dangerous. They didn't seem to care if they lived or died, and they hated everything indiscriminately—including themselves.

In Norridgewock, he delivered the stereo console to its owner, then went across town to pick up a malfunctioning 75-hp Johnson outboard motor. From the motor's owner, he heard that a town boy had beaten an elderly storekeeper to death that morning when the storekeeper caught him shoplifting. The boy was in custody, and it was the scandal of the year for Norridgewock. Jacobs had noticed it before, but discounted it: the local kids were getting mean too, meaner every year. Maybe it was self-defense.

Driving back, Jacobs noticed one of the gypsy jeeps slewed up onto the road embankment. It was empty. He slowed, and stared at the jeep thoughtfully, but he did not stop.

A fire-rescue truck nearly ran him down as he entered Skowhegan. It came screaming out of nowhere and swerved onto Water Street, its blue blinker flashing, siren screeching in metallic rage, suddenly right on top of him. Jacobs wrenched his truck over to the curb, and it swept by like a demon, nearly scraping him. It left a frightened silence behind it, after it had vanished urgently from sight. Jacobs pulled back into traffic and continued driving. Just before the turnoff to his house, a dog ran out into the road. Jacobs had slowed down for the turn anyway, and he saw the dog in plenty of time to stop. He did not stop. At the last possible second, he yanked himself out of a waking dream, and swerved just enough to miss the dog. He had wanted to hit it; he'd liked the idea of running it down. There were too many dogs in the county anyway, he told himself, in a feeble attempt at justification. "Big, ugly hound," he muttered, and was appalled by how alien his voice sounded—hard, bitterly hard, as if it were a rock speaking. Jacobs noticed that his hands were shaking.

Dinner that night was a fair success. Carol had turned out not to be particularly overjoyed that her husband had invited a horde of people over without bothering to consult her, but Jacobs placated her a little by volunteering to cook dinner. It turned out "sufficient," as Everett put it. Everybody ate, and nobody died. Toward the end, Carol had to remind them to leave some for Dave Lucas, who had not arrived yet. The company did a lot to restore Jacobs's nerves, and, feeling better, he wrestled with curiosity throughout the meal. Curiosity won, as it usually did with him: in the end, and against his better judgment.

As the guests began to trickle into the parlor, Jacobs took Sussmann aside and asked him if he'd learned anything new about the abandoned car.

Sussmann seemed uneasy and preoccupied. "Whatever it was happened to them seems to've happened again this afternoon. Maybe a couple of times. There was another abandoned car found about four o'clock, up near Athens. And there was one late yesterday night, out at Livermore Falls. And a tractor-trailer on Route 95 this morning, between Waterville and Benton Station."

"How'd you pry that out of Riddick?"

"Didn't." Sussmann smiled wanly. "Heard about that Athens one from the driver of the tow truck that hauled it back—that one bumped into a signpost, hard enough to break its radiator. Ben, Riddick can't keep me in the dark. I've got more stringers than he has."

"What d'you think it is?"

Sussmann's expression fused over and became opaque. He shook his head.

In the parlor, Carol, Everett's wife Amy—an ample, gray woman, rather like somebody's archetypical aunt but possessed of a very canny mind—and Sussmann, the inveterate bachelor, occupied themselves by playing with Chris. Chris was two, very quick and bright, and very excited by all the company. He'd just learned how to blow kisses, and was now practicing enthusiastically with the adults. Everett, meanwhile, was prowling around examining the stereo equipment that filled one wall. "You install this yourself?" he asked, when Jacobs came up to hand him a beer.

"Not only installed it," Jacobs said, "I built it all myself, from scratch. Tinkered up most of the junk in this house. Take the beah 'fore it gets hot."

"Damn fine work," Everett muttered, absently accepting the beer. "Better'n my own setup, I purely b'lieve, and that set me back a right sma't piece of change. Jesus Christ, Ben—I didn't know you could do quality work like that. What the hell you doing stagnating out here in the sticks, fixing people's radios and washing machines, f'chrissake? Y'that good, you ought to be down in Boston, New York mebbe, making some real money."

Jacobs shook his head. "Hate the cities, big cities like that. C'n't stand to live in them at all." He ran a hand through his hair. "I lived in New York for a while, seven, eight yeahs back, 'fore settling in Skowhegan again. It was terrible theah, even back then, and it's worse now. People down theah dying on their feet, walking around dead without anybody to tell 'em to lie down and get buried decent."

"We're dying here, too, Ben," Everett said. "We're just doing it slower, is all."

Jacobs shrugged. "Mebbe so," he said. " 'Scuse me." He walked back to the kitchen, began to scrape the dishes and stack them in the sink. His hands had started to tremble again.

When he returned to the parlor, after putting Chris to bed, he found that conversation had almost died. Everett and Sussmann were arguing halfheartedly about the Factory, each knowing that he'd never convince the other. It was a pointless discussion, and Jacobs did not join it. He poured himself a glass of beer and sat down. Amy hardly noticed him; her usually pleasant face was stern and angry. Carol found an opportunity to throw him a sympathetic wink while tossing her long hair back over her shoulder, but her face was flushed too, and her lips were thin. The evening had started off well, but it had soured somehow; everyone felt it. Jacobs began to clean his pipe, using a tiny knife to scrape the bowl. A siren went by outside, wailing eerily away into distance. An ambulance, it sounded like, or the fire-rescue truck again— more melancholy and mournful, less predatory than the siren of a police cruiser. ". . . brew viruses . . ." Everett was saying, and then Jacobs lost him, as if Everett were being pulled further and further away by some odd, local perversion of gravity, his voice thinning into inaudibility. Jacobs couldn't hear him at all now. Which was strange, as the parlor was only a few yards wide. Another siren. There were a lot of them tonight; they sounded like the souls of the dead, looking for home in the darkness, unable to find light and life. Jacobs found himself thinking about the time he'd toured Vienna, during "recuperative leave" in Europe, after hospitalization in 'Nam. There was a tour of the catacombs under the cathedral, and he'd taken it, limping painfully along on his crutch, the wet, porous stone of the tunnel roof closing down until it almost touched the top of his head. They'd come to a place where an opening had been cut through the hard, gray rock, enabling the tourists to come up one by one and look into the burial pit on the other side, while the guide lectured calmly in alternating English and German. When you stuck your head through the opening, you looked out at a solid wall of human bones. Skulls, arm and leg bones, rib cages, pelvises, all mixed in helter-skelter and packed solid, layer after uncountable layer of them. The wall of bones rose up sheer out of the darkness, passed through the fan of light cast by a naked bulb at eye-level, and continued to rise—it was impossible to see the top, no matter how you craned your neck and squinted. This wall had been built by the Black Death, a haphazard but grandiose architect. The Black Death had eaten these people up and spat out their remains, as casual and careless as a picnicker gnawing chicken bones. When the meal was over, the people who were still alive had dug a huge pit under the cathedral and shoveled the victims in by the hundreds of thousands. Strangers in life, they mingled in death, cheek by jowl, belly to backbone, except that after a while there were no cheeks or jowls. The backbones remained: yellow, ancient, and brittle. So did the skulls—upright, upside down, on their sides, all grinning blankly at the tourists.

The doorbell rang.

It was Dave Lucas. He looked like one of the skulls Jacobs had been thinking about—his face was gray and gaunt, the skin drawn tightly across his bones; it looked as if he'd been dusted with powdered lime. Shocked, Jacobs stepped aside. Lucas nodded to him shortly and walked by into the parlor without speaking. ". . . stuff about the Factory is news," Sussmann was saying, doggedly, "and more interesting than anything else that happens up here. It sells papers—" He stopped talking abruptly when Lucas entered the room. All conversation stopped. Everyone gaped at the old game warden, horrified. Unsteadily Lucas let himself down into a stuffed chair, and gave them a thin attempt at a smile. "Can I have a beah?" he said. "Or a drink?"

"Scotch?"

"That'll be fine," Lucas said mechanically.

Jacobs went to get it for him. When he returned with the drink, Lucas was determinedly making small talk and flashing his new dead smile. It was obvious that he wasn't going to say anything about what had happened to him. Lucas was an old-fashioned Yankee gentleman to the core, and Jacobs—who had a strong touch of that in his own upbringing—suspected why he was keeping silent. So did Amy. After the requisite few minutes of polite conversation, Amy asked if she could see the new paintings that Carol was working on. Carol exchanged a quick, comprehending glance with her, and nodded. Grim-faced, both women left the room—they knew that this was going to be bad. When the women were out of sight, Lucas said, "Can I have another drink, Ben?" and held out his empty glass. Jacobs refilled it wordlessly. Lucas had never been a drinking man.

"Give," Jacobs said, handing Lucas his glass. "What happened?"

Lucas sipped his drink. He still looked ghastly, but a little color was seeping back into his face. "A'n't felt this shaky since I was in the a'my, back in Korea," he said. He shook his head heavily. "I swear to Christ, I don't understand what's got into people in these pa'ts. Used t'be decent folk out heah, Christian folk." He set his drink aside, and braced himself up visibly. His face hardened. "Never mind that. Things change, I guess, c'n't stop 'em no way." He turned toward Jacobs. "Remember that nighthunter I was after. Well we got 'im, went out with Steve Girard, Rick Barlow, few other boys, and nabbd him real neat—city boy, no woods sense at all. Well, we were coming back around the end of the pond, down the lumber road, when we heard this big commotion coming from the Gibson place, shouts, a woman screaming her head off, like that. So we cut across the back of their field and went over to see what was going on. House was wide open, and what we walked into—" He stopped; little sickly beads of sweat had appeared all over his face. "You remember the McInerney case down in Boston four, five yeahs back? The one there was such a stink about? Well, it was like that. They had a whatchamacallit there, a coven—the Gibsons, the Sewells, the Bradshaws, about seven others, all local people, all hopped out of their minds, all dressed up in black robes, and—blood, painted all over their faces. God, I— No, never mind. They had a baby there, and a kind of an altar they'd dummied up, and a pentagram. Somebody'd killed the baby, slit its throat, and they'd hung it up to bleed like a hog. Into cups. When we got there, they'd just cut its heart out, and they were starting in on dismembering it. Hell—they were tearing it apart, never mind that 'dismembering' shit. They were so frenzied-blind they hardly noticed us come in. Mrs. Bradshaw hadn't been able to take it, she'd cracked completely and was sitting in a corner screaming her lungs out, with Mr. Sewell trying to shut her up. They were the only two that even tried to run. The boys hung Gibson and Bradshaw and Sewell, and stomped Ed Patterson to death—I just couldn't stop 'em. It was all I could do to keep 'em from killing the other ones. I shot Steve Girard in the arm, trying to stop 'em, but they took the gun away, and almost strung me up too. My God, Ben, I've known Steve Girard a'most ten yeahs. I've known Gibson and Sewell all my life." He stared at them appealingly, blind with despair. "What's happened to people up heah?"

No one said a word.

*Not in these pa'ts*, Jacobs mimicked himself bitterly. *There are decent limits*.

Jacobs found that he was holding the pipe-cleaning knife like a weapon. He'd cut his finger on it, and a drop of blood was oozing slowly along the blade. This kind of thing—the Satanism, the ritual murders, the sadism—was what had driven him away from the city. He'd thought it was different in the country, that people were better. But it wasn't, and they weren't. It was bottled up better out here, was all. But it had been coming for years, and they had blinded themselves to it and done nothing, and now it was too late. He could feel it in himself, something long repressed and denied, the reaction to years of frustration and ugliness and fear, to watching the world dying without hope. That part of him had listened to Lucas's story with appreciation, almost with glee. It stirred strongly in him, a monster turning over in ancient mud, down inside, thousands of feet down, thousands of years down. He could see it spreading through the faces of the others in the room, a stain, a spider shadow of contamination. Its presence was suffocating: the chalky, musty smell of old brittle death, somehow leaking through from the burial pit in Vienna. Bone dust—he almost choked on it, it was so thick here in his pleasant parlor in the country.

And then the room was filled with sound and flashing, bloody light.

Jacobs floundered for a moment, unable to understand what was happening. He swam up from his chair, baffled, moving with dreamlike slowness. He stared in helpless confusion at the leaping red shadows. His head hurt.

"An ambulance!" Carol shouted, appearing in the parlor archway with Amy. "We saw it from the upstairs window—"

"It's right out front," Sussmann said.

They ran for the door. Jacobs followed them more slowly. Then the cold outside air slapped him, and he woke up a little. The ambulance was parked across the street, in front of the senior citizens' complex. The corpsmen were hurrying up the stairs of one of the institutional, cinderblock buildings, carrying a stretcher. They disappeared inside. Amy slapped her bare arms to keep off the cold. "Heart attack, mebbe," she said. Everett shrugged. Another siren slashed through the night, getting closer. While they watched, a police cruiser pulled up next to the ambulance, and Riddick got out. Riddick saw the group in front of Jacobs's house, and stared at them with undisguised hatred, as if he would like to arrest them and hold them responsible for whatever had happened in the retirement village. Then he went inside too. He looked haggard as he turned to go, exhausted, hagridden by the suspicion that he'd finally been handed something he couldn't settle with a session in the soundproofed back room at the sheriff's office.

They waited. Jacobs slowly became aware that Sussmann was talking to him, but he couldn't hear what he was saying. Sussmann's mouth opened and closed. It wasn't important anyway. He'd never noticed before how unpleasant Sussmann's voice was, how rasping and shrill. Sussmann was ugly too, shockingly ugly. He boiled with contamination and decay—he was a sack of putrescence. He was an abomination.

Dave Lucas was standing off to one side, his hands in his pockets, shoulders slumped, his face blank. He watched the excitement next door without expression, without interest. Everett turned and said something that Jacobs could not hear. Like Sussmann's, Everett's lips moved without sound. He had moved closer to Amy. They glanced uneasily around. They were abominations too.

Jacobs stood with his arm around Carol; he didn't remember putting it there—it was seeking company on its own. He felt her shiver, and clutched her more tightly in response, directed by some small, distanced, horrified part of himself that was still rational—he knew it would do no good. There was a thing in the air tonight that was impossible to warm yourself against. It hated warmth, it swallowed it and buried it in ice. It was a wedge, driving them apart, isolating them all. He curled his hand around the back of Carol's neck. Something was pulsing through him in waves, building higher and stronger. He could feel Carol's pulse beating under her skin, under his fingers, so very close to the surface.

Across the street, a group of old people had gathered around the ambulance. They shuffled in the cold, hawking and spitting, clutching overcoats and nightgowns more tightly around them. The corpsmen reappeared, edging carefully down the stairs with the stretcher. The street was pulled up all the way, but it looked curiously flat and caved-in—if there was a body under there, it must have collapsed, crumbled like dust or ash. The crowd of old people parted to let the stretcher crew pass, then re-formed again, flowing like a heavy, sluggish liquid. Their faces were like leather or horn: hard, dead, dry, worn smooth. And *tired*. Intolerably, burdensomely tired. Their eyes glittered in their shriveled faces as they watched the stretcher go by. They looked uneasy and afraid, and yet there was an anticipation in their faces, an impatience, almost an envy, as they looked on death. Silence blossomed from a tiny seed in each of them, a total, primordial silence, from the time before there were words. It grew, consumed them, and merged to form a greater silence that spread out through the night in widening ripples.

The ambulance left.

In the hush that followed, they could hear sirens begin to wail all over town.

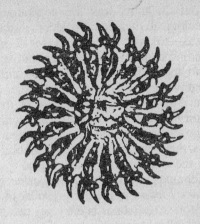

*It's hard to pinpoint the origins of a story so many* years after it was written, but I'll try. I'd just been to Skowhegan, Maine—where the story takes place—to visit an old army buddy of mine; that was one nub. When I returned, I was walking along 2nd Avenue in New York City one night when lines of dialogue began speaking themselves in my head, many of them actually used later in the story. So "local color" was important to the evolution of this story—I knew I wanted to set a story in Skowhegan, with the kind of people I'd met there, and I even knew the rough shape of what I wanted to say. Now I needed the armature of the plot. One nub of *that* was my continuing fascination with the idea of spontaneous human combustion, a subject I'd already done a good amount of reading about—while in London, a few years earlier, I'd had an idea for a story about spontaneous human combustion; I never wrote it, but no doubt the shards of it went into the subconscious melt for *this* one. Another nub was the dangers of bacteriological warfare research, something I also knew at least a little about. A third was the generalized concern about ecological dangers prevalent at the time. A fourth was—to wax pretentious for a moment—a long-standing concern of my own about spiritual isolation and the dangers of a lack of communication and empathy.

On the level of craft, a good deal of the structure of the story represented an attempt to adapt to my own purposes the narrative technique used in a series of stories that few people have probably ever even heard of these days: the "Mad Friend" stories that G. C. Edmondson ran in *The Magazine of Fantasy and Science Fiction* in the early 1960s. In the "Mad Friend" stories, Edmondson entwines two story lines, running simultaneously in a sort of contrapuntal fashion, using the up-front story line to distract you enough from the clues being planted throughout the course of the *secondary* story line so that the ending, when you reach it, comes as a surprise . . . even though you *have* been given enough information to have figured it out in advance, if you hadn't been distracted by the bells and whistles going off in the foreground. I admired this technique, and used a variant of it here.

It seems to me that the techniques used in "Flash Point" are one good way—among many others—to write a modern horror story. In recent years, people have taken to telling me that "Flash Point" is strongly reminiscent of Stephen King's work, some even accusing me of imitating King, even though the story was written long before I had ever even heard of Stephen King, let alone read anything by him. And no, I'm certainly *not* suggesting that King stole these techniques from *me*, either! The fact is that both of us—and several other writers as well—probably derived the tone and style of this kind of story indepen-

dently from the work of earlier writers, chief among
them Fritz Leiber, Theodore Sturgeon, and Ray Bradbury. In my case, there is probably a dash of Philip
K. Dick as well. There is also a stiff jigger of Edgar
Pangborn thrown into "Flash Point," as there is in
much of my work.

The incident with the gypsy kids in the jeeps actually happened, although in real life the kids were the
usual long-haired pseudo-hippies indigenous to the
times. In writing the story, I changed them into
skinheads, instead, which seemed a logical next swing
of the pendulum, and thus they became an early
prediction of the punk subculture, which was still a
few years down the road from when I was writing the
story, in 1972. The cathedral in Vienna with the huge
pile of human bones beneath it is also a real place,
and I have been there . . . and if there are any among
you who doubt the dreadful potency of biological
weapons, then I urge them to visit it as well.

—Gardner Dozois

# THE ANIMAL FAIR

## by Robert Bloch

It was dark when the truck dropped Dave off at the deserted freight depot. Dave had to squint to make out the lettering on the weather-faded sign: MEDLEY, OKLAHOMA—POP. 1,134.

The trucker said he could probably get another lift on the state highway up past the other end of town, so Dave hit the main drag. And it was a drag.

Nine o'clock of a hot summer evening, and Medley was closed for the night. Fred's Eats had locked up, the Jiffy SuperMart had shut down, even Phil's Phill-Up Gas stood deserted. There were no cars parked on the dark street, not even the usual cluster of kids on the corners.

Dave wondered about this, but for not for long. In five minutes he covered the length of Main Street and emerged on open fields at the far side, and that's when he saw the lights and heard the music.

They had a carnival going in the little county fairgrounds up ahead—canned music blasting from amplifiers, cars crowding the parking lot, mobs milling across the midway.

46

Dave wasn't craving this kind of action, but he still had eight cents in his jeans and he hadn't eaten anything since breakfast. He turned down the side road leading to the fairgrounds.

As he figured, the carnival was a bummer. One of those little mud shows, traveling by truck; a couple of beat-up rides for the kids and a lot of come-ons for the local yokels. Wheel o' Fortune, Pitch-a-Winner, Take a Chance on a Blanket, that kind of jive. By the time Dave got himself a burger and coffee at one of the stands he knew the score. A big fat zero.

But not for Medley, Oklahoma—Pop. 1,134. The whole damn town was here tonight and probably every redneck for miles around, shuffling and shoving himself to get through to the far end of the midway.

And it was there, on the far end, that he saw the small red tent with the tiny platform before it. Hanging limp and listless in the still air, a sun-bleached banner proclaimed the wonders within.

CAPTAIN RYDER'S HOLLYWOOD JUNGLE SAFARI, the banner read.

What a Hollywood Jungle Safari was, Dave didn't know. And the wrinkled cloth posters lining the sides of the entrance weren't much help. A picture of a guy in an explorer's outfit, tangling with a big snake wrapped around his neck—the same joker prying open the jaws of a crocodile—another drawing showing him wrestling a lion. The last poster showed the guy standing next to a cage; inside the cage was a black, furry question mark, way over six feet high. The lettering underneath was black and furry too. WHAT IS IT? SEE THE MIGHTY MONARCH OF THE JUNGLE ALIVE ON THE INSIDE!

Dave didn't know what it was and he cared less. But he'd been bumping along those corduroy roads

all day and he was wasted and the noise from the
amplifiers here on the midway hurt his ears. At least
there was some kind of a show going on inside, and
when he saw the open space gaping between the
canvas and the ground at the corner of the tent he
stooped and slid under.

The tent was a canvas oven.

Dave could smell oil in the air; on hot summer
nights in Oklahoma you can always smell it. And the
crowd in here smelled worse. Bad enough that he
was thumbing his way through and couldn't take a
bath, but what was their excuse?

The crowd huddled around the base of a portable
wooden stage at the rear of the tent, listening to a
pitch from Captain Ryder. At least that's who Dave
figured it was, even though the character with the
phony safari hat and the dirty white riding breeches
didn't look much like his pictures on the banners. He
was handing out a spiel in one of those hoarse,
gravelly voices that carries without a microphone—
some hype about being a Hollywood stunt man and
African explorer—and there wasn't a snake or a crocodile or a lion anywhere in sight.

The two-bit hamburger began churning up a storm
in Dave's guts, and between the body heat and the
smells he'd just about had it in there. He started to
turn and push his way through the mob when the man
up on the stage thumped the boards with his cane.

"And now, friends, if you'll gather around a little
closer—"

The crowd swept forward in unison, like the straws
of a giant broom, and Dave found himself pressed
right up against the edge of the square-shaped canvas-
covered pit beside the end of the platform. He couldn't
get through now if he tried; all the rednecks were
bunched together, waiting.

Dave waited, too, but he stopped listening to the voice on the platform. All that jive about Darkest Africa was a put-on. Maybe these clowns went for it, but Dave wasn't buying a word. He just hoped the old guy would hurry and get the show over with; all he wanted now was out of here.

Captain Ryder tapped the canvas covering of the pit with his cane and his harsh tones rose. The heat made Dave yawn loudly, but some of the phrases filtered through.

"—about to see here tonight the world's most ferocious monster—captured at deadly peril of life and limb—"

Dave shook his head. He knew what was in the pit. Some crummy animal picked up secondhand from a circus, maybe a scroungy hyena. And two to one it wasn't even alive, just stuffed. Big deal.

Captain Ryder lifted the canvas cover and pulled it back behind the pit. He flourished his cane.

"Behold—the lord of the jungle!"

The crowd pressed, pushed, peered over the rim of the pit.

The crowd gasped.

And Dave, pressing and peering with the rest, stared at the creature, blinking up at him from the bottom of the pit.

It was a live, full-grown gorilla.

The monster squatted on a heap of straw, its huge forearms secured to steel stakes by lengths of heavy chain. It gaped upward at the rim of faces, moving its great gray head slowly from side to side, the yellow-fanged mouth open and the massive jaws set in a vacant grimace. Only the little rheumy, red-rimmed eyes held a hint of expression—enough to tell Dave, who had never seen a gorilla before, that this animal was sick.

The matted straw at the base of the pit was wet and stained; in one corner a battered tin plate rested untouched, its surface covered with a soggy slop of shredded carrots, okra and turnip greens floating in an oily scum beneath a cloud of buzzing blowflies. In the stifling heat of the tent the acrid odor rising from the pit was almost overpowering.

Dave felt his stomach muscles constrict. He tried to force his attention back to Captain Ryder. The old guy was stepping offstage now, moving behind the pit and reaching down into it with his cane.

"—nothing to be afraid of, folks; as you can see he's perfectly harmless, aren't you, Bobo?"

The gorilla whimpered, huddling back against the soiled straw to avoid the prodding cane. But the chains confined movement and the cane began to dig its tip into the beast's shaggy shoulders.

"And now Bobo's going to do a little dance for the folks—right?" The gorilla whimpered again, but the point of the cane jabbed deeply and the rasping voice firmed in command.

"Up, Bobo—up!"

The creature lumbered to its haunches. As the cane rose and fell about its shoulders, the bulky body began to sway. The crowd oohed and aahed and snickered.

"That's it! Dance for the people, Bobo—dance—"

A swarm of flies spiraled upward to swirl about the furry form shimmering in the heat. Dave saw the sick beast shuffle, moving to and fro, to and fro. Then his stomach was moving in responsive rhythm and he had to shut his eyes as he turned and fought his way blindly through the murmuring mob.

"Hey—watch where the hell ya goin', fella—"

Dave got out of the tent just in time.

\*          \*          \*

Getting rid of the hamburger helped, and getting away from the carnival grounds helped too, but not enough. As Dave moved up the road between the open fields he felt the nausea return. Gulping the oily air made him dizzy and he knew he'd have to lie down for a minute. He dropped in the ditch beside the road, shielded behind a clump of weeds, and closed his eyes to stop the whirling sensation. Only for a minute—

The dizziness went away, but behind his closed eyes he could still see the gorilla, still see the expressionless face and the all-too-expressive eyes. Eyes peering up from the pile of dirty straw in the pit, eyes clouding with pain and hopeless resignation as the chains clanked and the cane flicked across the hairy shoulders.

Ought to be a law, Dave thought. There must be some kind of law to stop it, treating a poor dumb animal like that. And the old guy, Captain Ryder— there ought to be a law for an animal like him, too.

Ah, to hell with it. Better shut it out of his mind now, get some rest. Another couple of minutes wouldn't hurt—

It was the thunder that finally woke him. The thunder jerked him into awareness, and then he felt the warm, heavy drops pelting his head and face.

Dave rose and the wind swept over him, whistling across the fields. He must have been asleep for hours, because everything was pitch-black, and when he glanced behind him the lights of the carnival were gone.

For an instant the sky turned silver and he could see the rain pour down. See it, hell—he could feel it, and then the thunder came again, giving him the message. This wasn't just a summer shower, it was a real storm. Another minute and he was going to be soaking wet. By the time he got up to the state highway he could drown, and there wouldn't be a lift there for him, either. Nobody traveled in this kind of weather.

Dave zipped up his jacket, pulled the collar around his neck. It didn't help, and neither did walking up the road, but he might as well get going. The wind was at his back and that helped a little, but moving against the rain was like walking through a wall of water.

Another flicker of lightning, another rumble of thunder. And then the flickering and the rumbling merged and held steady; the light grew brighter and the sound rose over the hiss of wind and rain.

Dave glanced back over his shoulder and saw the source: the headlights and engine of a truck coming along the road behind him. As it moved closer Dave realized it wasn't a truck; it was a camper, one of those two-decker jobs with a driver's cab up front.

Right now he didn't give a damn what it was as long as it stopped and picked him up. As the camper came alongside of him Dave stepped out, waving his arms.

The camper slowed, halted. The shadowy silhouette in the cab leaned over from behind the wheel and a hand pushed the window vent open on the passenger side.

"Want a lift, buddy?"

Dave nodded.

"Get in."

The door swung open and Dave climbed up into the cab. He slid across the seat and pulled the door shut behind him.

The camper started to move again.

"Shut the window," the driver said. "Rain's blowing in."

Dave closed it, then wished he hadn't. The air inside the cab was heavy with odors—not just perspiration, but something else. Dave recognized the smell even before the driver produced the bottle from his jacket pocket.

"Want a slug?"

Dave shook his head.

"Fresh corn likker. Tastes like hell, but it's better'n nothing."

"No thanks."

"Suit yourself." The bottle tilted and gurgled. Lightning flared across the roadway ahead, glinting against the glass of the windshield, the glass of the upturned bottle. In its momentary glare Dave caught a glimpse of the driver's face, and the flash of lightning brought a flash of recognition.

The driver was Captain Ryder.

Thunder growled, prowling the sky, and the heavy camper turned onto the slick, rain-swept surface of the state highway.

"—what's the matter, you deaf or something? I asked you where you're heading."

Dave came to with a start.

"Oklahoma City," he said.

"You hit the jackpot. That's where I'm going."

Some jackpot. Dave had been thinking about the old guy, remembering the gorilla in the pit. He hated this bastard's guts, and the idea of riding with him all the way to Oklahoma City made his stomach churn all over again. On the other hand, it wouldn't help his stomach any if he got set down in a storm here in the middle of the prairie, so what the hell. One quick look at the rain made up his mind for him.

The camper lurched and Ryder fought the wheel.

"Boy—sure is a cutter!"

Dave nodded.

"Get these things often around here?"

"I wouldn't know," Dave said. "This is my first time through. I'm meeting a friend in Oklahoma City. We figure on driving out to Hollywood together—"

"Hollywood?" The hoarse voice deepened. "That goddam place!"

"But don't you come from there?"

Ryder glanced up quickly and lightning flickered across his sudden frown. Seeing him this close, Dave realized he wasn't so old; something besides time had shaped that scowl, etched the bitter lines around eyes and mouth.

"Who told you that?" Ryder said.

"I was at the carnival tonight. I saw your show."

Ryder grunted and his eyes tracked the road ahead through the twin pendulums of the windshield wipers. "Pretty lousy, huh?"

Dave started to nod, then caught himself. No sense starting anything. "That gorilla of yours looked like it might be sick."

"Bobo? He's all right. Just the weather. We open up north, he'll be fine." Ryder nodded in the direction of the camper bulking behind him. "Haven't heard a peep out of him since we started."

"He's traveling with you?"

"Whaddya think, I ship him airmail?" A hand rose from the wheel, gesturing. "This camper's built special. I got the upstairs, he's down below. I keep the back open so's he gets some air, but no problem—I got it all barred. Take a look through that window behind you."

Dave turned and peered through the wire-meshed window at the rear of the cab. He could see the lighted interior of the camper's upper level, neatly and normally outfitted for occupancy. Shifting his gaze, he stared into the darkness below. Lashed securely to the side walls were the tent, the platform boards, the banners, and the rigging; the floor space between them was covered with straw, heaped into a sort of nest. Crouched against the barred opening at the far end was the black bulk of the gorilla, back turned as it faced the road to the rear, intent on the roaring rain. The camper went into a skid for a moment and the beast twitched, jerking its head around so that Dave caught a glimpse of its glazed eyes. It seemed to whimper softly, but because of the thunder Dave couldn't be sure.

"Snug as a bug," Ryder said. "And so are we." He had the bottle out again, deftly uncorking it with one hand.

"Sure you don't want a belt?"

"I'll pass," Dave said.

The bottle raised, then paused. "Hey, wait a minute." Ryder was scowling at him again. "You're not on something else, are you, buddy?"

"Drugs?" Dave shook his head. "Not me."

"Good thing you're not." The bottle tilted, lowered again as Ryder corked it. "I hate that crap. Drugs. Drugs and hippies. Hollywood's full of both. You take my advice, you keep away from there. No place for a kid, not anymore." He belched loudly, started to put the bottle back into his jacket pocket, then uncorked it again.

Watching him drink, Dave realized he was getting loaded. Best thing to do would be to keep him talking, take his mind off the bottle before he knocked the camper off the road.

"No kidding, were you really a Hollywood stunt man?" Dave said.

"Sure, one of the best. But that was back in the old days, before the place went to hell. Worked for all the majors—trick riding, fancy falls, doubling fight scenes, the works. You ask anybody who knows, they'll tell you old Cap Ryder was right up there with Yakima Canutt, maybe even better.'' The voice rasped on, harsh with pride. "Seven-fifty a day, that's what I drew. Seven hundred and fifty, every day I worked. And I worked a lot.''

"I didn't know they paid that kind of dough,'' Dave told him.

"You got to remember one thing: I wasn't just taking falls in the long shots. When they hired Cap Ryder they knew they were getting some fancy talent. Not many stunt men can handle animals. You ever see any of those old jungle pictures on television— Tarzan movies, stuff like that? Well, in over half of 'em I'm the guy handling the cats. Lions, leopards, tigers, you name it.''

"Sounds exciting.''

"Sure, if you like hospitals. Wrestled a black panther once, like to rip my arm clean off in one shot they set up. Seven-fifty sounds like a lot of loot, but you should have seen what I laid out in medical bills. Not to mention what I paid for costumes and extras. Like the lion skins and the ape suit—''

"I don't get it.'' Dave frowned.

"Sometimes the way they set a shot for a close-up they need the star's face. So if it was a fight scene with a lion or whatever, that's where I came in handy—I doubled for the animal. Would you believe it, three grand I laid out for a lousy monkey suit alone! But it paid off. You should have seen the big pad I had up over Laurel Canyon. Four bedrooms, three-car garage, tennis court, swimming pool, sauna, everything you can think of. Melissa loved it—''

"Melissa?''

Ryder shook his head. "What'm I talking about?

You don't want to hear any of that crud about the good old days. All water over the dam."

The mention of water evidently reminded him of something else, because Dave saw him reach for the bottle again. And this time, when he tilted it, it gurgled down to empty.

Ryder cranked the window down on his side and flung the bottle out into the rain.

"All gone," he muttered. "Finished. No more bottle. No more house. No more Melissa—"

"Who was she?" Dave said.

"You really want to know?" Ryder jerked his thumb toward the windshield. Dave followed the gesture, puzzled, until he raised his glance to the roof of the cab. There, fastened directly above the rear-view mirror, was a small picture frame. Staring out of it was the face of a girl; blond hair, nice features, and with the kind of a smile you see in the pages of high school annuals.

"My niece," Ryder told him. "Sixteen. But I took her when she was only five, right after my sister died. Took her and raised her for eleven years. Raised her right, too. Let me tell you, that girl never lacked for anything. Whatever she wanted, whatever she needed, she got. The trips we took together—the good times we had—hell, I guess it sounds pretty silly, but you'd be surprised what a kick you can get out of seeing a kid have fun. And smart? President of the junior class at Brixley—that's the name of the private school I put her in, best in town, half the stars sent their own daughters there. And that's what she was to me, just like my own flesh-and-blood daughter. So go figure it. How it happened I'll never know." Ryder blinked at the road ahead, forcing his eyes into focus.

"How what happened?" Dave asked.

"The hippies. The goddam sonsabitching hippies."
The eyes were suddenly alert in the network of ugly
wrinkles. "Don't ask me where she met the bastards, I
thought I was guarding her from all that, but those
lousy freaks are all over the place. She must of
run into them through one of her friends at school—
Christ knows, you see plenty of weirdos even in Bel
Air. But you got to remember, she was just sixteen
and how could she guess what she was getting into? I
suppose at that age an older guy with a beard and a
Fender guitar and a souped-up cycle looks pretty
exciting.

"Anyhow they got to her. One night when I was
away on location—maybe she invited them over to
the house, maybe they just showed up and she asked
them in. Four of 'em, all stoned out of their skulls.
Dude, that was the oldest one's name—he was like
the leader, and it was his idea from the start. She
wouldn't smoke anything, but he hadn't really figured she would and he came prepared. Must have
worked it so she served something cold to drink and
he slipped the stuff into her glass. Enough to finish
off a bull elephant, the coroner said."

"You mean it killed her—"

"Not right away. I wish to Christ it had." Ryder
turned, his face working, and Dave had to strain to
hear his voice mumbling through the rush of rain.

"According to the coroner she must have lived for
at least an hour. Long enough for them to take
turns—Dude and the other three. Long enough after
that for them to get the idea.

"They were in my den, and I had the place all
fixed up like a kind of trophy room—animal skins all
over the wall, native drums, voodoo masks, stuff I'd
picked up on my trips. And here were these four
freaks, spaced out, and the kid, blowing her mind.

One of the bastards took down a drum and started beating on it. Another got hold of a mask and started hopping around like a witch doctor. And Dude—it was Dude all right, I know it for sure—he and the other creep pulled the lion skin off the wall and draped it over Melissa. Because this was a trip and they were playing Africa. Great White Hunter. Me Tarzan, You Jane.

"By this time Melissa couldn't even stand up anymore. Dude got her down on her hands and knees and she just wobbled there. And then—that dirty rotten son of a bitch—he pulled down the drapery cords and tied the stinking lion skin over her head and shoulders. And he took a spear down from the wall, one of the Masai spears, and he was going to jab her in the ribs with it—

"That's what I saw when I came in: Dude, the big stud, standing over Melissa with a spear.

"He didn't stand long. One look at me and he must have known. I think he threw the spear before he ran, but I can't remember. I can't remember anything about the next couple of minutes. They said I broke one freak's collarbone, and the creep in the mask had a concussion from where his head hit the wall. The third one was almost dead by the time the squad arrived and pried my fingers loose from his neck. As it was, they were too late to save him.

"And they were too late for Melissa. She just lay there under that dirty lion skin—that's the part I do remember, the part I wish I could forget—"

"You killed a kid?" Dave said.

Ryder shook his head. "I killed an animal. That's what I told them at the trial. When an animal goes vicious, you got a right. The judge said one to five, but I was out in a little over two years." He glanced at Dave. "Ever been inside?"

"No. How is it—rough?"

"You can say that again. Rough as a cob." Ryder's stomach rumbled. "I came in pretty feisty, so they put me down in solitary for a while and that didn't help. You sit there in the dark and you start thinking. Here am I, used to traveling all over the world, penned up in a little cage like an animal. And those animals—the ones who killed Melissa—they're running free. One was dead, of course, and the two others I tangled with had maybe learned their lesson. But the big one, the one who started it all, he was loose. Cops never did catch up with him, and they weren't about to waste any more time trying, now that the trial was over.

"I thought a lot about Dude. That was the big one's name, or did I tell you?" Ryder blinked at Dave, and he looked pretty smashed. But he was driving okay and he wouldn't fall asleep at the wheel as long as he kept talking, so Dave nodded.

"Mostly I thought about what I was going to do to Dude once I got out. Finding him would be tricky, but I knew I could do it—hell, I spent years in Africa, tracking animals. And I intended to hunt this one down."

"Then it's true about you being an explorer?" Dave asked.

"Animal trapper," Ryder said. "Kenya, Uganda, Nigeria—this was before Hollywood, and I saw it all. Things these young punks today never dreamed of. Why, they were dancing and drumming and drugging over there before the first hippie crawled out from under his rock, and let me tell you, they know how to do this stuff for real.

"Like when this Dude tied the lion skin on Melissa, he was just freaked out, playing games. He should have seen what some of those witch doctors can do.

"First they steal themselves a girl, sometimes a young boy, but let's say a girl because of Melissa. And they shut her up in a cave—a cave with a low ceiling, so she can't stand up, has to go on all fours. They put her on drugs right away, heavy doses, enough to keep her out for a long time. And when she wakes up her hands and feet have been operated on, so they can be fitted with claws. Lion claws, and they've sewed her into a lion skin. Not just put it over her—it's sewed on completely, and it can't be removed.

"You just think about what it's like. She's inside this lion skin, shut away in a cave, doped up, doesn't know where she is or what's going on. And they keep her that way. Feed her on nothing but raw meat. She's all alone in the dark, smelling that damn lion smell, nobody talking to her and nobody for her to talk to. Then pretty soon they come in and break some bones in her throat, her larynx, and all she can do is whine and growl. Whine and growl, and move around on all fours.

"You know what happens, boy? You know what happens to someone like that? They go crazy. And after a while they get to believing they really are a lion. The next step is for the witch doctor to take them out and train them to kill, but that's another story."

Dave glanced up quickly. "You're putting me on—"

"It's all there in the government reports. Maybe the jets come into Nairobi airport now, but back in the jungle things haven't changed. Like I say, some of these people know more about drugs than any hippie ever will. Especially a stupid animal like Dude."

"What happened after you got out?" Dave said. "Did you ever catch up with him?"

Ryder shook his head.

"But I thought you said you had it all planned—"

"Fella gets a lot of weird ideas in solitary. In a way it's pretty much like being shut up in one of those caves. Come to think of it, that's what first reminded me—"

"Of what?"

"Nothing." Ryder gestured hastily. "Forget it. That's what I did. When I got out I figured that was the best way. Forgive and forget."

"You didn't even try to find Dude?"

Ryder frowned. "I told you, I had other things to think about. Like being washed up in the business, losing the house, the furniture, everything. Also I had a drinking problem. But you don't want to hear about that. Anyway, I ended up with the carny and there's nothing more to tell."

Lightning streaked across the sky and thunder rolled in its wake. Dave turned his head, glancing back through the wire-meshed window. The gorilla was still hunched at the far end, peering through the bars into the night beyond. Dave stared at him for a long moment, not really wanting to stop, because then he knew he'd have to ask the question. But the longer he stared, the more he realized that he had no choice.

"What about him?" Dave asked.

"Who?" Ryder followed Dave's gaze. "Oh, you mean Bobo. I picked him up from a dealer I know."

"Must have been expensive."

"They don't come cheap. Not many left."

"Less than a hundred." Dave hesitated. "I read about it in the Sunday paper back home. Feature article on the national preserves. Said gorillas are government-protected, can't be sold."

"I was lucky," Ryder murmured. He leaned forward and Dave was immersed in the alcoholic reek. "I got connections, understand?"

"Right." Dave didn't want the words to come but he couldn't hold them back. "What I don't understand is this lousy carnival. With gorillas so scarce, you should be with a big show."

"That's my business." Ryder gave him a funny look.

"It's business I'm talking about." Dave took a deep breath. "Like if you were so broke, where'd you get the money to buy an animal like this?"

Ryder scowled. "I already said. I sold off everything—the house, the furniture—"

"And your monkey suit?"

The fist came up so fast Dave didn't even see it. But it slammed into his forehead, knocking him back across the seat, against the unlocked side door.

Dave tried to make a grab for something, but it was too late, he was falling. He hit the ditch on his back, and only the mud saved him.

Then the sky caught fire, thunder crashed, and the camper slid past him, disappearing into the dark tunnel of the night. But not before Dave caught one final glimpse of the gorilla, squatting behind the bars.

The gorilla, with its drug-dazed eyes, its masklike, motionless mouth, and its upraised arms revealing the pattern of heavy black stitches.

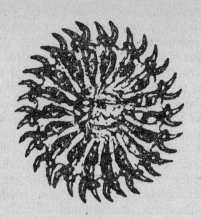

*Mother Goose said it first.*

*"There was an old woman who lived in a shoe
She had so many children she didn't know what to
do."*

Every writer knows the truth contained in this old
nursery rhyme. For the stories he creates are *his*
children, and when it comes to choosing between
them, quite frequently he doesn't know what to do.

Ignoring the somewhat-cynical possibility that the
old woman in the shoe had so many children *because*
she didn't know what to do, the fact remains that a
writer like myself, who seldom practices literary birth
control, is constantly forced to play favorites amongst
his offspring. Which one deserves reprinting—which
one should have an opportunity to travel abroad—
which one ought to make an appearance on television
or in a film—which one gets a pat on the head as the
best of the lot?

There are many factors influencing such decisions,
but in this case I had no problem selecting "The
Animal Fair" for inclusion here. Not only is it one of

my favorites—it also happens to be in need of tender loving care.

For this particular youngster of mine was a victim of child abuse.

In 1971 I sent it off, squeaky-clean and dressed in its Sunday best, to *Playboy*. And when it gained admission to the magazine's pages I was sure it had found a good home.

Nobody sent me any report cards or complaints about the kid, and it wasn't until I encountered him again in the May issue of the magazine that I discovered that he had been brutally attacked and physically violated.

Some moron had emasculated my child.

And there he was, exposed to all the world, with his ending cut off—only scar tissue remaining to show what a botched job had been made in an effort to repair the wound.

To this day I don't know who performed the stupid surgery. Usually, when an editor is dissatisfied with some aspect of a story, he notifies the author and makes suggestions for changes. In this case I wasn't offered this courtesy, and as a result both my child and I suffered the consequences.

And suffer we did. Because somebody decided in his infinite wisdom that he preferred a "more subtle" ending, he hacked away at my final paragraphs. As a result, the story attracted little attention from the readers of the magazine, and in the years that followed it was seldom chosen to appear elsewhere—even though I did manage to restore the original ending in a story collection of my own.

Now, once again, I have an opportunity to give the kid a break. He's still a favorite of mine, and I hope you like him, too.

—Robert Bloch

# THE END OF THE CARNIVAL

## by Chelsea Quinn Yarbro

*Radiation mama, shine your light on me, I
    said
Radiation mama, shine your light on me.
I need your loving, and I need it bad—
The hottest, longest, lastest love that I have
    ever had. I said
Radiation mama, shine your everlasting light
    on me.*

Big Hank Cassidy stood at the door of the Risen Sun and peered upward at the radiation symbol that was painted in the brightest Day-Glo colors with straight rays projecting around it like daggers. It was a couple miles out of town, this Risen Sun, a big lump of a house with nothing but room to recommend it to the fright-wigged woman who ran it. People in town preferred not to mention the Risen Sun, though it brought more than half the business done to the town: no one liked to admit it was a brothel that kept them alive.

There was a figure in the second-story window, a tall, angular creature like a mud-daubed scarecrow, who looked down at Big Hank. "We can't let you in yet. Becca isn't here!" The voice was raspy and gratingly loud, certainly not the soft and persuasive accents usually expected from a working whore, but those blandishments were not part of the Risen Sun, and no one expected them.

"How long do you think she'll be?" Big Hank shouted up at the window.

"Hard to tell. You know how folks are in Norlens. They don't take to her much." She waited. "You can keep on the porch, if you like. Elijah will bring you coffee, but it's extra."

"Fine with me," Big Hank said wearily as he stepped up to the elaborate screen door that was made to withstand much more than insects. He found a place on a small dusty bench and sat down.

Madame Becca rarely came into town, but when she did she was accorded a precise kind of courtesy usually reserved for those who are unwelcome. She was not deceived and occasionally admitted that she did not feel any more comfortable with the townspeople than they did with her. Even with her wig and half a mask on her face, there was no hiding what she was and nothing that would adequately disguise the extent of her deformity. Over the years, she had grown worse and her compensations more outrageous. Today she had donned a voluminous robe of metallic brocade that made her appear more enormous than she was and did little to conceal the wide swaths of scar tissue on her blotched arms. Her wig was a ridiculous shade of blue. The eyes behind her mask were intelligent and bright, more keen than compassionate, riddled with grinding pain.

"What can I do for you?" Mr. Taylor asked her when she came into his store. He kept his face averted from hers, addressing a shelf of canned goods instead of the middle-aged, deformed woman in front of him.

"You know what I always get, Taylor. I'll take the same thing." Her voice was harsh, more of a wheeze than speech.

"Sure," he said to let her know that he understood her. "Last week they said that you'd had another . . ."

"Accident?" she supplied when he faltered. "It was no more an accident than anything that happens at the Risen Sun. Nothing's an accident there."

"Unh . . ." was all the response he could manage. He looked at Madame Becca and tried to conceal his dislike of her, but there was a turn to his mouth or some other quirk that she could read, and she scoffed at him. He had the grace to look away.

"Mr. Taylor, if you like, I'll leave my wigs and dresses on the shelf and come here just the way I am. *Just* the way I am. Would you like that?" She grinned, showing her blatantly artificial teeth and laughing at the expression on Taylor's face.

"Miz Becca, I—"

"That's Madame Becca," she corrected him sternly. "Madame. That is my title because I run a whorehouse, Taylor." She picked two items off the shelves and held them out to him. "You better start ringing these things up, Mr. Taylor, sir, or you aren't going to get me out of here before sundown."

"That . . . sure." The prospect of having Madame Becca in his store any longer than absolutely necessary horrified him. "I'll just take your list while you—"

"And I'll want some of that good candy you stock. Lots of it. Some of my girls like candy. The drug list is at the bottom." She sighed. "We need more of those drugs, Taylor, but we can't let you . . ." It was rare that Madame Becca showed any emotion but scorn; now her face drooped near despair. "They keep promising to arrange for the drugs. Cat needs it, she needs it worse than ever, and those bastards don't know that she has to have it. They won't come to see us anymore, not now that we're making a little money. Look at what—" She turned abruptly as the door banged open.

"Saw your car, Becca," said the mayor, her moon face sweating from the effort of climbing three stairs. "I wanted to have a word with you."

"About what?" Becca demanded, her sarcastic smile once more affixed to her painted mouth. "We're gonna get hassled again?"

"No, I don't plan on it," said the mayor, her large, soft hands fiddling with the catch on her tiny purse. "I heard what you said about the drugs. I had to talk about that." She was embarrassed now, and motioned to Taylor to leave them alone.

"I can see you ladies want to be alone," Taylor said at once, grateful for the excuse to leave the room. Madame Becca was bad enough, but the mayor was infinitely worse.

"I been on the phone to that fool in Macon," the mayor said when the door to the back was firmly closed.

"You better talk low, Cindy. No telling what Taylor's doing back there, but I bet he's listening to us." Madame Becca pointed to a barrel of screws and nails. "Sit down. You look worn-out."

"I am," the mayor admitted. "The job's a killer. No one'd take it but me, and I got all of this to lug around with me." She sighed heavily and took her place on the barrel, hoisting her enormous thighs onto the uncomfortable surface with a resigned indifference.

"Now, what did you hear from Macon?" Madame Becca inquired. As she listened, she looked over the nearer shelves and occasionally took items from them to add to the pile on the counter.

"I heard that they're phasing out the drug program for the Swanee survivors." She did not mumble—it was not her style.

"Phasing out the drug program?" Madame Becca repeated. "Who're they kidding?"

"They say that there aren't all that many of . . . you left, and that local agencies can deal with . . . you." She gave a delicate little cough that seemed to come from some other, much smaller, body.

"You mean they're writing us off. They don't want to waste their time on us. We remind them of what happened just by breathing, and they don't like it, so they're setting us aside. Don't remind me it's happened before." She brought up her heavily-ringed hand and stared over at the mayor. "Is that it?"

"Aren't you going to say anything?" Cindy asked.

"What? What more is there to say? You've told me that my girls are being forgotten, and I'm doing what I can to—" She clapped her hands over her mouth as if she were about to vomit. "Oh, shit!"

"Becca," the mayor said, attempting to get down from her perch on the barrel. "What is it, honey?"

"Nothing. Nothing." She had regained control of herself. "Well. Local agencies, they say? What local agencies? We got any local agencies set up to deal with my girls?"

"No, we don't, and you know it," the mayor said. "The nearest local agencies are over two hundred miles away, and they're already too busy. I checked." She put her hands on her hips. "I'd like to find whoever made that decision."

"And what?" Madame Becca waited to hear.

"And *sit* on him!" This was no idle threat, since the mayor tipped the scales at over three hundred pounds.

"Wouldn't wish that fate on my worst enemy," Madame Becca said with a hint of jeering laughter.

"Well, I would!" the mayor insisted, then stared at Madame Becca.

"Don't, Cindy."

"You gonna be all right? I mean, you and the others?" There was real concern in her piggy eyes and she could not conceal her fear. "I told Pa that we'd stick together, and I won't go back on my word just because he's dead."

"I didn't think that you would." Madame Becca seized haphazardly on a few more boxes and two glass bottles.

"You tell me what you want me to do, sis, and I will." It was rare that either of them mentioned their relationship, but once in a great while, the words would escape them, and then both of them would be silent.

"What is there to do?" Madame Becca demanded of the air. "They don't want us around anymore, and so they . . . no more drugs and it isn't too long before the problem, the little reminder, disappears." She let one of the glass containers drop and there was a sudden, intense smell of old perfume.

"I'll find a way to stop this," the mayor said to Madame Becca. "There's got to be some way."

"What would you suggest? You read about how those other survivors committed suicide in a bunch. The authorities must have danced for joy over that one. Too bad that they killed themselves in public with half the cameras in the world covering it. That way, no one could pretend about them dying. But you can't tell me that they don't heave a sigh of relief every time one of us dies." She folded her arms as if to brace herself against onslaught. "I ought to get ahold of someone and . . ." She stopped. "That's what I ought to do, all right."

"Becca, what are you talking about?" the mayor asked, frowning with worry.

"I'm talking about getting even. If they're going to do this to us, we've got a right to fight back." She started down the aisle, then stalked back toward her sister. "I think I know a way. It will probably take a little time, but I can do it. If I have enough time, and if I can get some drugs from somewhere, just long enough to keep my girls going, then we could—"

"Could *what*?" the mayor exclaimed. "What are you talking about, Becca?"

"And they wouldn't have the chance to cover it up, not this time." She deliberately broke another two bottles of perfume, ignoring the overly-sweet stench that filled the room. "You know what they're like. They pretend that there was no real trouble when the plant failed, and when they couldn't pretend any longer, they said it didn't matter."

The mayor frowned at her sister. "You're not going to do anything . . . reckless, are you, Becca? I know what you're like when you get mad."

Madame Becca laughed, making a sound like a rusty saw on green wood. "What ever gave you that idea?"

> *You can close all the porno houses*
> *but the one in your mind;*
> *You can say that you're disgusted*
> *at the things that you find;*
> *You can say you're vindicated*
> *when they leave you behind;*
> *But the fires are burning closer.*

Inside the Risen Sun it was cool, not a degree over seventy. Nine of the women who lived and worked there lounged about in shapeless housecoats, their faces without adornment, the wreckage of their lives horrible and familiar.

Lucille, thirty-four and scarecrow-thin, was the least deformed of the group. She sat stroking an auburn wig in her lap as if it were a cat. On the floor, two of the women were measuring out pills into little paper cups, like children's party candy.

"Hurry it up, you two," said Jody, who was in pain more than most of them. "Can't wait much longer. It's bad today."

"You just take it easy there, Jody," Noreen told her as she concentrated on her counting. "You'll get your stuff in a couple minutes."

"I got to have it or I can't work," Jody reminded them.

"Yeah, well, who's any different?" Ellen said, nudging Lucille. "You notice that Big Hank Cassidy is outside? D'you reckon he wants to come in?"

"He calls Becca sometimes," Ellen said, then fell into brooding silence.

"Big Hank?" Lucille asked distantly. "I knew him in college. He got Ben's job." She fell silent, her hand still on the rich curls of her wig. "What's he doing here now? Why now?"

"Maybe he's tired of it all," suggested Jody in so resigned a tone that the rest of them were slightly embarrassed.

"Why else do they come, if they aren't tired of it all?" Noreen said, as if to restore a little lightness to them. "Who comes to the Risen Sun but guys who are—"

"Ready to check out," Sandra finished for her. She had been reading a book, paying no attention to

the work going on before her, as if she were unconcerned with what the others did. Many times the
women would do that, pretending that the drugs were
as important as extra vitamins—beneficial but not
essential.

"Becca should be back in another hour. We'll
know more then, I guess."

None of them responded to that, each of them
feeling too vulnerable. It was always frightening when
Madame Becca went to town, to find out about the
drugs and what might become of them. They were
nervous even at the mention of it.

"I think I'd like to have a go at Big Hank," Jody
said dreamily. "He was at the main office when the
plant went. A pity he wasn't . . ."

The others nodded. "I heard that he tried to get the
power company to provide maintenances for us,"
Noreen ventured.

"If he did, he sure as hell didn't succeed," Lucille
said, getting to her feet. "You gonna be all day with
that?"

Noreen swore as one of the cups overturned and
pills rolled across the faded carpet. "Almost done.
Anyone here need uppers or downers while I'm at
it?" She noticed that most of the women refused
these drugs, preferring to have their minds clear for
their work. "All right. Jody, you first. I put in a
touch of morphine for you."

"Thanks, Noreen." They all knew that she daily
used enough of the drug to kill a horse, but she had
developed a tolerance for it, and lived in dread of the
day that there would not be enough of it to hold her
pain at bay.

"We're gonna have Elijah bring in the tea now,
and we can get dressed when we're through." She

took up her own paper cup. "Well, here's to another day of harlotry."

The others copied her toast without irony.

Madame Becca got out of the battered old Plymouth station wagon that she had driven for the last nine years. There were large bags in the back of the car and she took two of them out before going up onto the porch.

"Afternoon, Becca," Big Hank said rather sheepishly from his seat.

"Madame Becca to you, Big Hank," she said stiffly as she tugged on the bell rope. "You here on official business?"

"No." He looked down at his hands. "I guess you might say pleasure."

"You might say," Madame Becca chuckled unpleasantly. "I hear that your company got its way at last. The mayor tells me that they're cutting off our drugs." She started through the door that Elijah held open for her, then looked back at the large man on the porch. "I don't imagine there's anything you can do about it, is there, Big Hank."

"I don't know, Madame Becca," he answered. "They don't pay much attention to me down at the office. Since the plant blew, well, you know what it's been like there."

Madame Becca handed the bags to Elijah. "I'll be in in a moment. You tell the girls to start getting ready." She gave her attention to Big Hank. "I don't have any idea what it's like at the plant. I haven't had since . . . it blew. I'll give 'em this: they stopped the meltdown, all right—with a blow-up. Fine planning there."

"Now, Becca . . . Madame Becca. You know there was no way for them to anticipate that," he protested, but his voice was a whine and he would not look at her.

"Sure, Big Hank. And we're all here because it's where we want to be." In disgust she went through the door and slammed it hard.

Elijah did nothing but shake his head: he had seen Madame Becca in these moods before and had learned to keep silent when she behaved this way. Without protest, he set about his work.

"Elijah," she said over her shoulder to him, "there are more bags in the car. You bring them in, will you? Part of it's groceries, but there are a few other items. I have to talk to the girls." With a wave of dismissal she headed for the back drawing room, trying to think of a way to tell the women what she had learned.

"It's Becca," said Noreen as the madame came through the door. "Glad you're back from town. How'd it go?"

"You might not be so glad when we're through talking," was her somber reply as she waded toward the flowered settee where Jody was just finishing her coffee. The discolorations of her ravaged face were less obvious because of the greater animation in her deep-set eyes.

"It's good you're here, Becca. The coffee's still hot. So's the tea."

> *The Risen Sun, come Mardi Gras*
> *Is shining, yeah, it's shining.*
> *There ain't no place, not near or far*
> *Shines out so bright at Mardi Gras;*
> *Makes fools forget what fools they are—*
> *The Risen Sun is shining.*

"What are we gonna do?" Lucille asked in dismay when they had all heard Madame Becca out. "What *can* we do?"

"Nothing, that's what; same as always," Jody answered with disgust. "They want us to die, and they're making it damned easy for us to do it. No more of this piecemeal shit, no sir, just the straight fun of radiation poisoning." She leaned her head back and laughed terribly. "I shouldn't've been so greedy about the morphine."

"Jody, you cut that out!" Noreen said sharply. "If they want us to die, then we got to find a way to stop that. There's got to be other ways to keep us going." She turned hopeful eyes toward Madame Becca. "You thought of anything yet, Becca?"

"Not yet." It had occupied her mind all the way back in the car, and now there was a tiredness in her face that appeared almost to be defeat.

"Can we keep going?" Jody asked. "Is there anything we can get, or do?"

"Not that I could find out about in town. . . . Well, it doesn't matter right away. So far as the mayor knows, there's nothing any of us can do, officially, and we'll have to fend for ourselves. That was the way the boys in the power company see it, and that's what they've got the government to believe, and that's the way we have to deal with it." She leaned back against the cushions as if ready for a nap.

"But how?" Lucille asked. She had put on her wig and now she fingered the tumbled curls as she had once done with her own hair. That had fallen out soon after the blow-up and she did not like to remember what it had been like not to be bald.

"That's what we have to figure out," Noreen said as reasonably as she could. "Isn't there anyone we can write to or call? There's newspeople, and—"

"They aren't interested in us anymore," Becca reminded the girls. "We're old news. And look what we're doing for a living. Why, one of those power company men could say a few words and make it look like we're nothing more than a bunch of greedy, crazy whores trying to take advantage of their generosity. You know what they did to that family in Coleville who tried to get their fields tested for contamination. By the time the power company got off the TV screen, those poor farmers sounded like the worst sorts of opportunists and zealots. They'll do the same to us if you let them.''

"No news, then. Besides, any of you want to see your faces on the news?'' Jody slapped her thigh at this and two of the women looked away from her.

"Jody's right,'' Lucille whispered. "The way I look now . . .''

"We've got to think of something,'' Noreen insisted, verging suddenly on tears. "There's more to . . .''

Elijah stopped in the door, clearing his throat before he spoke. "Beg pardon, Miz Becca, but Big Hank is getting terrible impatient. He's pacing around the porch.''

"You tell that man—''

Though Madame Becca was rarely interrupted, this time Jody cut her short. "Can't he wait to die? Can't he spare a few minutes for us to figure out a way to live?'' Jody pointed to a little case on the floor. "Hand me the makeup, will you, Sue?''

The girl did as she was asked, but kept her attention on Madame Becca. Sue was sometimes thought to be the most interesting of the girls at the Risen Sun because she occasionally glowed in the dark. She was soft-spoken and shy with people, wearing her contamination as a saint wears a halo. "Madame Becca, you'll find a way. You always have.''

Madame Becca swallowed back tears at Sue's faith and said with heroic nonchalance, "Why, sure we will, Suzy. We're not stupid women, no matter what the power company and the government think of us. We're not going to let them just forget about us."

"Damned right," Noreen muttered. "I figure we got enough drugs to get us through next week, and then we're going to be in trouble." She had not wanted to say this, but the knowledge burned in her with acid heat and she could not hold it back.

"So soon," Madame Becca said softly. "Then we got to work quick on this one." She knew as well as the others did that once the sustaining drugs were gone, there would be nothing they could do but suffer and die.

"They can wait us out," Noreen said. "It wouldn't take long. No phone calls for a couple of days, no letters read for a week, and they got no more troubles." Jody was hiding her fury under a predatory smile.

"Neither do we, for that matter," Lucille said. "Can't we just let it go? Or get some of that stuff they gave the survivors whose skin wouldn't grow back? They say it's quick and painless."

"But then they'd be getting *away* with it," Noreen protested. "Don't you know that?"

"Well, sure, but they're going to get away with it in any case." Lucille had tugged her wig askew and now busied herself in righting it onto her head.

"Not if I have anything to say about it. They got our men, and that's enough!" Madame Becca rose from the settee. "They gave my husband some of that stuff, and at the time I was grateful. He was out of his head with pain and he looked like he'd been dipped in sulphur. I thought it was mighty nice of them to help him end it. That was then. Now I know that they didn't do it for any decent reason like that. They wanted him out of the way, like they want us out of the way. We embarrass them." She folded her arms. "I won't go along with it. If any of you want to check out, that's all right with me. I don't blame you for wanting to, and I'll do what I can to make it easy for you. But if you want to fight them, then we got a lot of work to do and a real short time to do it in." She began to pace, glowering down at the carpet with its pattern of cabbage roses. "We have to think about what they want, and then we got to do what *we* want. Fast."

"But what do we want?" Jody asked. "I know I want out."

"Sure, Jody," Madame Becca said, stopping in front of the woman and reaching down to put a hand on her shoulder. "You got the best reason of any of us to do it. I'll see if the mayor will get us some of—"

"Thanks," said Jody, and went back to applying her garish makeup.

"The mayor's got her own worries," Sue cautioned them.

"Can the mayor help? Really?" Noreen asked. She was frightened enough to be skeptical, and blushed, being ashamed of her fear.

"The mayor'll help. She'll help." Madame Becca spoke with total confidence and the girls felt it come from her like heat. "You tell me what I should ask her to do."

"The drugs . . ." Noreen began.

"She'll be working on that already. If anyone can turn some up, she can." She could sense the doubt in her girls, but she said nothing more. "Not all fat women are lazy slatterns," she remarked with a nod toward Myra, who was even more enormous than the mayor, and who did all the carpentry around the Risen Sun when she was not tending to business.

"You know," Myra said in her thread of a voice, "I used to know Cindy pretty well, years ago. She's not the kind to say she'll do something and not do it." Myra did not often talk, as it was a tremendous effort for her as well as painful. When she did speak, it was usually only a word or two. The number of words she volunteered were eloquent testimony to her trust in the mayor's capabilities.

"Well, then, we'll let her get to work on that," Noreen said, nodding to the others.

Jody was half-done with her maquillage, and paused in the outlining of her scarred mouth to say, "I used to know a doctor in Fayette, a good man. Maybe I'll give him a call. He might know where we can buy supplies, temporarily."

"Thanks, Jody," Madame Becca said, and resumed her pacing. "There's two avenues already. You see, they aren't going to sweep us blow-up survivors under the carpet quite as easy as they thought they would."

"They're gonna try," Sue pointed out unnecessarily.

"But we aren't gonna let them," Madame Becca vowed.

"How?" Myra asked, and her question was echoed by the others.

"I don't know quite yet," Madame Becca admitted. "But we'll find a way. They killed our husbands and we are . . . what we are because of them and the blow-up. So we'll find a way. We'll get them where they live." She paused and her hard eyes grew thoughtful. "Where they live."

> Like Juliet and Isolde, girl, to love you is to
> die,
> And I'm searching for oblivion to end my pain,
> all right;

*So I'll tell you that I love you, babe, it's just a
   little lie
For the time we'll spend together for the carnival's last night.*

"They're gonna remember us," Madame Becca
promised Big Hank as they sat in the sunny morning
room, glasses of lemonade on the dainty round-topped
table between them. "If they don't, then it was all for
nothing, and those bastards will do it again."

Big Hank reached over and put his hand over
Madame Becca's. It was like covering a filet mignon
with a rump roast. "You know that they won't forget
you. You're letting all that scare talk fool you," he
said, trying to comfort her.

"Scare talk? Big Hank, Cindy knows they're doing
it. We all know they're doing it. They don't want
any more of us around, that's all. When the men
died, they were relieved, and you know it's true."

He met the challenge in her eyes with reason
tempered by fatigue. "Sure, they were relieved, because there weren't any more victims than—"

"Just what the fuck do you think *we* are?" Madame Becca demanded. "Because we weren't near
the plant when it blew, it doesn't mean that we
weren't victims of it, and you know that's the truth,
Big Hank." She pulled her hand away.

"But Becca . . ."

"*Madame* Becca," she corrected him at once.

"All right, Madame Becca," he conceded. "You
wives, you didn't know that it was so dangerous to
be with your men. No one knew."

"Want to lay a bet on that, Big Hank? I sure used
to think that, yes I did. But not anymore. Not since
they cut off our aid funds, and now with the drugs
. . . Why'd I have to start up this house, anyway?

Because there was no one who would let us work for them, that's why. We didn't have jobs, the insurances the power company provided did not cover deaths from nuclear accidents, such as explosions, and the pensions weren't available when less than the full term of employment had been served. No one in government would care for us unless we went into vegetable farms''—Becca winced at the current euphemism for mental wards even as she said it—''and none of us are ready for that. So what else was there? Most of spent what little money we had to make sure our kids were safe, the ones that weren't dead. We have to get by somehow, and Big Hank, there are a lot of men out there, believe it or not, who don't mind spending a lot of money to have one last night of love with one of my girls. We're getting by now, but without the drugs . . .'' She reached over and picked up her frosty glass of lemonade. ''I don't have to tell you what will happen when the drugs stop.''

''You can arrange something,'' he said with a hint of desperation in his tone now. ''You're not being fair to the power company, Madame Becca. You aren't trying to see what they want to do. They don't like to see you here, your girls, well, being whores. They were married to power company men, and it's . . .''

Madame Becca put her empty glass down so hard that the table rocked. ''It all comes back to embarrassment. The blow-up was an embarrassment. The deaths were an embarrassment. The drugs and publicity were an embarrassment. *We're* an embarrassment. And so something will have to be done to make them feel better.'' She shoved her chair back from the table with a sudden, abrupt motion. ''You listen to me, Big Hank. You were a good supervisor and I know that my husband respected you. It was just chance that you didn't end up the way he did, but that's how it goes. You came here because you want something, and I've listened to you, but if all they want is for you to try to get us to keep from *embarrassing* them again, you can tell them that they can forget it. We're a lot more than embarrassed, we're contaminated and dying. Our men weren't embarrassed, they were killed by massive doses of radiation. So it isn't my place to salve their consciences.''

"I didn't come here for them, not entirely,'' Big Hank said, staring down at his huge, meaty hands. "I felt real . . . rotten when the blow-up happened and my men all . . . died, and I wasn't there with them. I should have gone with them.'' He looked up at her quickly, then stared at the lace curtains where the sun came through them in a dappled pattern. "I've been trying to live with it for pretty long now. It isn't working, Madame Becca. I don't want to do it anymore. I just want to get away from it.''

Only the faint rattle of ice in their glasses disturbed the silence.

"You want to get away from it? Are you leaving town?'' She hardly dared to believe that Big Hank really wished that of her. "You're the only one from the power company who's kept in contact with me and my girls. I thought that it was on orders.''

"No. They don't know about it.'' He cleared his throat. "I hear that the girl to get is Sue, since she shines so pretty at night.''

"Sue.'' She nodded slowly. "You know what happens, don't you?''

"Sure. I get the sickness, just the way you've all got it. In a little while, my hair and teeth will fall out, I'll stop being able to eat and I'll die.'' He got up. "And you got those pills, to make it faster. The rumor is that there's a euphoric in the pills, to make it better while you're going.''

"Yeah. There's a euphoric." She started to leave the room, but Big Hank caught her by the wrist.

"Becca, if you got those pills, how come you and the girls don't take them? A lot of the other wives did.''

"I guess they weren't as mad as we are. I guess they wanted to forget as much as the power company wants us to forget." Their eyes locked, and he released her arm. "Sue will be ready in an hour or so. She's got the room on the third floor with the bay window. Think you can find it?''

It was the carnival week, Mardi Gras, and the Risen Sun was ready for it. Bunting and banners draped the front of the house like a muumuu on a dowager. Ribbons festooned the porch railings and sparklers marked the walkway. Speakers blared out taped music—few musicians came there willingly— and every window was shining with candles.

Madame Becca stood in the vestibule rigged out in her most outrageous clothes. Her towering wig was magenta and there were sequins pasted over the scars on her cheeks. Her wide smile seemed sincere enough and her manners were impeccable. "You did your job well, Big Hank," she said to the silent man in the wheelchair behind her. "You did a real, real good job for us.''

Big Hank did not reply. He had lost the ability to speak the week before but so far had refused that last, delicious pill that would bring him the oblivion he desired.

"You sure this is free?" asked one of the men in an undervoice as he took Madame Becca's proffered hand.

"You paid the initial fee, and that's it," she replied, beaming at the casually dressed young man. "You might have to wait an hour or two to be alone with one of the girls, but you can go into the drawing room. Ellen's serving tea and Myra is tending bar for the time being. Later, they'll trade off with the other girls." She beamed at him, showing her delight.

"You short-handed?" the man's companion asked, a bit surprised.

"Of course not," Madame Becca said, wagging an admonishing finger at the man who asked the question. "My girls work hard. They work real hard, and they've got the right to enjoy part of this carnival with you. Serving tea and canapés and drinks gives them a chance to socialize a little. And tell me the truth—wouldn't you rather that one of my girls wait on you, so you can have a look at her before anything more . . . involved happens, than have to look at servants in short jackets? Ellen likes a little conversation. Myra, though . . . she doesn't talk much."

Big Hank rolled his wheelchair back a few feet, out of the line of traffic. He had seen what he wanted to, and now he was ready to leave. He rang the bell hanging from the arm of the chair and attracted not only the notice of Elijah but of Madame Becca, who left her place at the door to come to his side.

"Oh, Big Hank, I am grateful to you. You've done so much." There were tears in her eyes, and she paused to blot them away before she bent down to kiss his cheek. "You done more for me, for all of us, than anyone ever did, and I hope, if there is a just God in Heaven, that He will take you and bless you for what you've given us." Her voice was more husky than usual.

Elijah came hurrying up to the two of them. "I heard the bell. You ready now, Mister Big Hank?"

Slowly, agonizingly, Big Hank nodded. It was all he could do to lift his hand a few inches to show he understood what Madame Becca had said to him.

"Good," Madame Becca acknowledged. "You go along with Elijah now, and spend a little more time with Jody. She's waiting for you, just for you. Elijah's got the pills, and it won't take too long for them to work. You . . . rest easy, Big Hank." She kissed his forehead, then turned away to greet the new arrivals.

"I'm so pleased you came," she said three hours later when the last of the invited guests arrived. "I was afraid that some of you might refuse, considering."

The young men exchanged doubtful looks. One of them tried to laugh. "Your place is pretty famous, Madame Becca. People talk about it. A lot."

"That's right," another chimed in. "When I started college last year, there were two songs about it already. You've got a famous place here." He gave one of his companions a shove in the arm. "I told my dad about the invitation, and he got mad about it, but . . . well, it *is* free, and it's worthwhile to come here, since it's so famous and all."

"I hope you won't be . . . disappointed," Madame Becca said, then turned as Noreen tapped her on the shoulder. "What is it?"

"There's a call for you—your sister." Noreen nodded toward the young men. "While Madame Becca is busy, will you let me take you in and buy you a drink?"

The young men exchanged nervous, eager glances and one of them said yes for all.

"Fine," Noreen said, and looped her arm through the elbow of the nearest of them. "You'll like Myra's way with bourbon."

\*      \*      \*

"What the devil is going on out there?" the mayor demanded of Madame Becca when she picked up the phone. "I been getting calls all evening."

"I'm holding carnival. It *is* Mardi Gras, isn't it?" She chuckled once, ending on a cough.

"Sure, it's Mardi Gras. You haven't done this before." The mayor's initial outburst gave way to worry. "Damn it, Becca, what are you up to?"

"Exactly what I told you I'd be up to," came the patient answer. "Who's called you, anyway?" She was pushing her luck with the mayor and knew it, but the victory was sweet and within her grasp.

"Mostly men from the power company." She paused. "They don't tell me much of anything, except that I've to close you down."

"And what have you told *them*?" Madame Becca asked, wishing they still had enough drugs to keep the pain away from all of them.

"You're not in town. There's nothing I can do. And the sheriff is fifty miles away." It was an uneasy answer.

"No, the sheriff is here. They can't reach him, even if they wanted to." Yes, the victory was good, she decided, in spite of the pain.

"They aren't upset about the sheriff," the mayor said decidedly. "Who else is there? Power company men?" Before Madame Becca could answer, the mayor went on. "No, of course not. They wouldn't come within a mile of your place, would they?"

"I don't think they would, no," Madame Becca said.

"Sis, will you tell me what's going on out there? And don't say Mardi Gras again, or I'll scream, so help me Jesus."

Madame Becca sighed. "I'm having a very select party. Everyone invited paid an initial fee of fifty dollars, and now everything here is free. Drinks, girls, pills, everything.'' She wheezed and her eyes watered. ''Big Hank got the names and addresses for me, from the power company.''

''But you just said that they're not . . .'' the mayor began, then fell silent.

''I had to think of some way to get back at them. They killed our men, they killed our kids, and they tried to forget about us. They just . . . threw us away with the rest of the contaminated garbage. Well, I couldn't bear it, Cindy. I couldn't. I told you. . . . You remember.''

''Yes, I remember.'' Her voice was soft now, and very kind.

''It was more than an insult, it was worse than death. They made us *worthless*. All right, then.'' Her voice got harder and louder as a burst of laughter erupted behind her. ''Listen to me, sis. Okay?''

''Sure, Becca,'' said the mayor.

''We got enough pills for all the girls. It won't matter that we're almost out of drugs, not after to-night, because we'll take them all. You know what will happen to the men here. I don't have to tell you about that. Well, it was the only thing I could think of, and with Big Hank's help . . .''

''You've got to have power company men out there, or government men, Becca,'' the mayor insisted. ''Who else?''

Behind Madame Becca, the party was growing rowdy, and she had to raise her voice.

''Not them—their sons.'' She laughed with an emotion that was too sad to be malice.

''Their sons?'' The mayor was horrified. ''But . . . God, why?''

''You know why,'' Madame Becca said just loudly enough to be heard over the din.

"But they'll die," the mayor protested.

"Yes. But they'll be famous, won't they? Remembered in song and story, honey. That's why they're here." And before the mayor could speak again, Madame Becca put the phone down and went back to the excitement and debauchery of her last Mardi Gras.

> *I said,*
> *Radiation mama, shine your everlasting*
>     *everloving*
>     *never-ending light on me.*

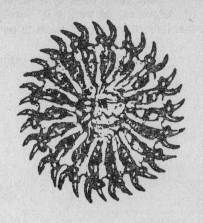

*"The End of the Carnival"* *stems in part from my* concern for the environment and the short-sightedness that all too often is characteristic of its use and abuse by industry and other corporate organizations. It also has resonances to my personal concern for the indifference that also all too often marks the dealing of large corporate entities with ordinary people. The women in this story are not abused in the active sense: they are neglected to death; it is a risk we all run in this magnificent, contaminated world where we all live, and where we all breathe the same air that was breathed by John F. Kennedy, Adolf Hitler, Leonardo da Vinci, Lady Wu, Gaius Julius Caesar, Tutankhamen, Nebuchadnezzar, Buddha, and all the rest of the people of this planet from the beginning of time. The women of the Risen Sun are worthy of mercy and pity, which they were not given in life. The lyrics that reoccur throughout their story show that they found more

sympathy in death than they ever discovered in life. For all our sakes, as well as (fictional) theirs, don't sell them short: we ignore them to our peril.

—Chelsea Quinn Yarbro

# DANCE OF THE DEAD

## by Richard Matheson

*I wanna RIDE!*
*with my Rota-Mota honey*
*by my SIDE!*
*As we whiz along the highway*

"We will HUG and SNUGGLE and we'll have a little STRUGGLE!"

> *struggle* (strug'l), n., act of promiscuous love-play; usage evolved during W.W. III.

Double beams spread buttery lamplight on the highway. Rotor-Motors Convertible, Model C, 1989, rushed after it. Light spurted ahead, yellow glowing. The car pursued with a twelve-cylindered snarling pursuit. Night blotted in behind, jet and still. The car sped on. ST. LOUIS—10.

"I wanna FLY!" they sang, "with the Rôta-Mota apple of my EYE!" they sang. "It's the only way of living . . ."

The quartet singing:

Len, 23.
Bud, 24.
Barbara, 20.
Peggy, 18.
Len with Barbara, Bud with Peggy.
Bud at the wheel, snapping around tilted curves, roaring up black-shouldered hills, shooting the car across silent flatlands. At the top of three sets of lungs (the fourth gentler), competing with wind that buffeted their heads, that whipped their hair to lashing threads—singing:

> *You can have your walkin' under MOON-LIGHT BEAMS!*
> *At a hundred miles an hour let me DREAM my DREAMS!*

Needle quivering at 130, two 5-m.p.h. notches from gauge's end. *A sudden dip!* Their young frames jolted and the thrown-up laughter of three was windswept into night. Around a curve, darting up and down a hill, flashing across a leveled plain—an ebony bullet skimming earth.

> *In my ROTORY, MOTORY, FLOATERY, drivin' machi-i-i-ine!*

> *You'll be a floater in your rotor-motor.*

In the back seat:
"Have a jab, Bab."
"Thanks, I had one after supper" (pushing away needle fixed to eyedropper).
In the front seat:
"You meana tell me this is the first time you ever been t' Saint Loo!"

"But I just started school in September."

"Hey, you're a *frosh!*"

Back seat joining front seat:

"Hey, *frosh*, have a mussle-tussle."

(Needle passed forward, eye bulb quivering amber juice.)

"*Live* it, girl!"

> *mussle-tussle* (mus'l-tus'l), n., slang for the
> result of injecting a drug into a muscle; usage
> evolved during W.W. III.

Peggy's lips failed at smiling. Her fingers twitched.

"No, thanks, I'm not—"

"Come *on*, frosh!" Len leaning hard over the seat, white-browed under black blowing hair. Pushing the needle at her face. "Live it, girl! Grab a li'l mussle-tussle!"

"I'd rather not," said Peggy. "If you don't—"

"What's '*at*, frosh?" yelled Len and pressed his leg against the pressing leg of Barbara.

Peggy shook her head and golden hair flew across her cheeks and eyes. Underneath her yellow dress, underneath her white brassière, underneath her young breast—a heart throbbed heavily. *Watch your step, darling, that's all we ask. Remember, you're all we have in the world now.* Mother words drumming at her; the needle making her draw back into the seat.

"*Come* on, frosh!"

The car groaned its shifting weight around a curve and centrifugal force pressed Peggy into Bud's lean hip. His hand dropped down and fingered at her leg. Underneath her yellow dress, underneath her sheer stocking—flesh crawled. Lips failed again; the smile was a twitch of red.

"Frosh, live it up!"

"Lay off, Len, jab your own dates."

"But we gotta teach frosh how to mussle-tussle!"

"Lay off, I said! She's my date!"

The black car roaring, chasing its own light. Peggy anchored down the feeling hand with hers. The wind whistled over them and grabbed down chilly fingers at their hair. She didn't want his hand there but she felt grateful to him.

Her vaguely frightened eyes watched the road lurch beneath the wheels. In back, a silent struggle began, taut hands rubbing, parted mouths clinging. Search for the sweet elusive at 120 miles per hour.

"*Rota-Mota honey*," Len moaned the moan between salivary kisses. In the front seat a young girl's heart beat unsteadily. ST. LOUIS—6.

"No kiddin', you never been to Saint Loo?"

"No, I . . ."

"Then you never saw the loopy's dance?"

Throat contracting suddenly. "No, I . . . Is that what . . . we're going to—"

"Hey, frosh never saw the loopy's dance!" Bud yelled back.

Lips parted, slurping; skirt was adjusted with blasé aplomb. "No kiddin'!" Len fired up the words. "Girl, you haven't *lived!*"

"Oh, she's *got* to see *that*," said Barbara, buttoning a button.

"Let's go there then!" yelled Len. "Let's give frosh a thrill!"

"Good enough," said Bud and squeezed her leg. "Good enough up here, right, Peg?"

Peggy's throat moved in the dark and the wind clutched harshly at her hair. She'd heard of it, she'd read of it but never had she thought she'd—

*Choose your school friends carefully, darling. Be very careful.*

But when no one spoke to you for two whole months? When you were lonely and wanted to talk and laugh and be alive? And someone spoke to you finally and asked you to go out with them?

"I yam Popeye, the sailor man!" Bud sang.

In back, they crowed artificial delight. Bud was taking a course in Pre-War Comics and Cartoons—2. This week the class was studying Popeye. Bud had fallen in love with the one-eyed seaman and told Len and Barbara all about him; taught them dialogue and song.

"I yam Popeye, the sailor man! I like to go swimmin' with bow-legged women! I yam Popeye, the sailor man!"

Laughter. Peggy smiled falteringly. The hand left her leg as the car screeched around a curve and she was thrown against the door. Wind dashed blunt coldness in her eyes and forced her back, blinking. 110—115—120 miles per hour. ST. LOUIS—3. *Be very careful, dear.*

Popeye cocked wicked eye.

"O, Olive Oyl, you is my sweet patootie."

Elbow nudging Peggy. "You be Olive Oyl—*you.*"

Peggy smiled nervously. "I can't."

"*Sure!*"

In the back seat, Wimpy came up for air to announce, "I will gladly pay you Tuesday for a hamburger today."

Three fierce voices and a faint fourth raged against the howl of wind. "I fights to the *fin*-ish 'cause I eats my *spin*-ach! I yam Popeye, the sailor man! *Toot! Toot!*"

"I yam what I yam," reiterated Popeye gravely and put his hand on the yellow-skirted leg of Olive Oyl. In the back, two members of the quartet returned to feeling struggle.

ST. LOUIS—1. The black car roared through the darkened suburbs. "On with the nosies!" Bud sang out. They all took out their plasticate nose-and-mouth-pieces and adjusted them.

> *Ance in your pants would be a PITY!*
> *Wear your noises in the CITY!!*

> *Ance* (anse), n., slang for anticivilian germs;
> usage evolved during W.W. III.

"You'll like the loopy's dance!" Bud shouted to her over the shriek of wind. "It's sen*saysh!*"

Peggy felt a cold that wasn't of the night or of the wind. *Remember, darling, there are terrible things in the world today. Things you must avoid.*

"Couldn't we go somewhere else?" Peggy said but her voice was inaudible. She heard Bud singing, "I like to go swimmin' with bow-legged women!" She felt his hand on her leg again while, in the back, was the silence of grinding passion without kisses.

*Dance of the dead.* The words trickled ice across Peggy's brain.

ST. LOUIS.

The black car sped into the ruins.

It was a place of smoke and blatant joys. Air resounded with the bleating of revelers and there was a noise of sounding brass spinning out a cloud of music—1989 music, a frenzy of twisted dissonances. Dancers, shoehorned into the tiny square of open floor, ground pulsing bodies together. A network of bursting sounds lanced through the mass of them; dancers singing:

*Hurt me! Bruise me! Squeeze me TIGHT!*
*Scorch my blood with hot DELIGHT!*
*Please abuse me every NIGHT!*
*LOVER, LOVER, LOVER, be a beast to me!*

Elements of explosion restrained within the dancing bounds—instead of fragmenting, quivering: "*Oh, be a beast, beast, beast,* Beast, *BEAST to me!*"

"How is *this*, Olive, old goil?" Popeye inquired of the light of his eye as they struggled after the waiter. "Nothin' like this in Sykesville, eh?"

Peggy smiled but her hand in Bud's felt numb. As they passed by a murky lighted table, a hand she didn't see felt at her leg. She twitched and bumped against a hard knee across the narrow aisle. As she stumbled and lurched through the hot and smoky thick-aired room, she felt a dozen eyes disrobing her, abusing her. Bud jerked her along and she felt her lips trembling.

"Hey, how about that!" Bud exulted as they sat. "Right by the stage!"

From cigarette mists, the waiter plunged and hovered, pencil poised, beside their table.

"What'll it be!" His questioning shout cut through cacophony.

"Whisky-water!" Bud and Len paralleled orders, then turned to their dates. "What'll it be!" the waiter's request echoed from their lips.

"*Green Swamp!*" Barbara said and, "*Green Swamp* here!" Len passed it along. Gin, Invasion Blood (1987 Rum), lime juice, sugar, mint spray, splintered ice—a popular college-girl drink.

"What about you, honey?" Bud asked his date.

Peggy smiled. "Just some ginger ale," she said, her voice a fluttering frailty in the massive clash and fog of smoke.

"What?" asked Bud and, "What's that, didn't hear!" the waiter shouted.

"Ginger ale."

"*What?*"

"Ginger ale!"

"GINGER ALE!" Len screamed it out and the drummer, behind the raging curtain of noise that was the band's music, almost heard it. Len banged down his fist. *One—Two—Three!*

> CHORUS: *Ginger Ale was only twelve years old!*
> *Went to church and was as good as gold. Till that day when—*

"Come *on*, come *on!*" the waiter squalled. "Let's have that order, kids! I'm busy!"

"Two whisky-waters and two green swamps!" Len sang out, and the waiter was gone into the swirling maniac mist.

Peggy felt her young heart flutter helplessly. *Above all, don't drink when you're out on a date. Promise us that, darling, you must promise us that.* She tried to push away instructions etched in brain.

"How you like this place, honey? *Loopy*, ain't it?" Bud fired the question at her; a red-faced, happy-faced Bud.

> *loopy* (loo pi), adj., common alter. of L.U.P. (Lifeless Undeath Phenomenon)

She smiled at Bud, a smile of nervous politeness. Her eyes moved around, her face inclined, and she was looking up at the stage. *Loopy*. The word scalpeled at her mind. *Loopy, loopy.*

The stage was five yards deep at the radius of its wooden semicircle. A waist-high rail girdled the circumference, two pale purple spotlights, unlit, hung at each rail end. Purple on white, the thought came. *Darling, isn't Sykesville Business College good enough? No! I don't want to take a business course, I want to major in art at the University!*

The drinks were brought and Peggy watched the disembodied waiter's arm thud down a high, green-looking glass before her. *Presto!*—the arm was gone. She looked into the murky green swamp depths and saw chipped ice bobbing.

"A toast! Pick up your glass, Peg!" Bud clarioned. They all clinked glasses:

"To lust primordial!" Bud toasted.

"To beds intemperate!" Len added.

"To flesh insensate!" Barbara added a third link.

Their eyes zeroed in on Peggy's face, demanding. She didn't understand.

"*Finish it!*" Bud told her, plagued by freshman sluggishness.

"To . . . u-*us*," she faltered.

"How o-*ri*-ginal," stabbed Barbara and Peggy felt heat licking up her smooth cheeks. It passed unnoticed as three Youths of America with Whom the Future Rested gurgled down their liquor thirstily. Peggy fingered at her glass, a smile printed to lips that would not smile unaided.

"Come on, *drink*, girl!" Bud shouted to her across the vast distance of one foot. "Chugalug!"

"Live it, girl," Len suggested abstractedly, fingers searching once more for soft leg. And finding, under the table, soft leg waiting.

Peggy didn't want to drink, she was afraid to drink. Mother words kept pounding—*never on a date, honey, never.* She raised the glass a little.

"Uncle Buddy will help, will help!"

Uncle Buddy leaning close, vapor of whisky haloing his head. Uncle Buddy pushing cold glass to shaking young lips. "Come on, Olive Oyl, old goil! Down the hatch!"

Choking sprayed the bosom of her dress with green swamp droplets. Flaming liquid trickled into her stomach, sending offshoots of fire into her veins.

*Bangity boom crash smash POW!!* The drummer applied the coup de grace to what had been, in ancient times, a lover's waltz. Lights dropped and Peggy sat coughing and teary-eyed in the smoky cellar club.

She felt Bud's hand clamp strongly on her shoulder and, in the murk, she felt herself pulled off balance and felt Bud's hot wet mouth pressing at her lips. She jerked away and then the purple spots went on and a mottle-faced Bud drew back, gurgling. "I fights to the finish," and reaching for his drink.

"Hey, the loopy now, the loopy!" Len said eagerly, releasing exploratory hands.

Peggy's heart jolted and she thought she was going to cry out and run thashing through the dark, smoke-filled room. But a sophomore hand anchored her to the chair and she looked up in white-faced dread at the man who came out on the stage and faced the microphone which, like a metal spider, had swung down to meet him.

"May I have your attention, ladies and gentlemen," he said, a grim-faced, sepulchral-voiced man whose eyes moved out over them like flicks of doom. Peggy's breath was labored, she felt thin lines of green swamp water filtering hotly through her chest and stomach. It made her blink dizzily. *Mother.* The word escaped cells of the mind and trembled into conscious freedom. *Mother, take me home.*

"As you know, the act you are about to see is not

for the faint of heart, the weak of will.'' The man plodded through the words like a cow enmired. ''Let me caution those of you whose nerves are not what they ought to be—*leave now*. We make no guarantees of responsibility. We can't even afford to maintain a house doctor.''

No laughter appreciative. ''Cut the crap and get offstage,'' Len grumbled to himself. Peggy felt her fingers twitching.

''As you know,'' the man went on, his voice gilded with learned sonority, ''this is not an offering of mere sensation but an honest scientific demonstration.''

''*Loophole for Loopy's!*'' Bud and Len heaved up the words with the thoughtless reaction of hungry dogs salivating at a bell.

It was, in 1989, a comeback so rigidly standard it had assumed the status of a catechism answer. A crenel in the postwar law allowed the L.U.P. performance if it was orally prefaced as an exposition of science. Through this legal chink had poured so much abusing of the law that few cared any longer. A feeble government was grateful to contain infractions of the law at all.

When hoots and shoutings had evaporated in the smoke-clogged air, the man, his arms upraised in patient benediction, spoke again.

Peggy watched the studied movement of his lips, her heart swelling, then contracting in slow, spasmodic beats. An iciness was creeping up her legs. She felt it rising toward the threadlike fires in her body and her fingers twitched around the chilly moisture of the glass. *I want to go, please take me home*— Will-spent words were in her mind again.

''Ladies and gentlemen,'' the man concluded, ''brace yourselves.''

A gong sounded its hollow, shivering resonance, the man's voice thickened and slowed.

*"The L.U. Phenomenon!"*

The man was gone; the microphone had risen and was gone. Music began; a moaning brassiness, all muted. A jazzman's conception of *the palpable obscure*—mounted on a pulse of thumping drum. A dolor of saxophone, a menace of trombone, a harnessed bleating of trumpet—they raped the air with stridor.

Peggy felt a shudder plaiting down her back and her gaze dropped quickly to the murky whiteness of the table. Smoke and darkness, dissonance and heat surrounded her.

Without meaning to, but driven by an impulse of nervous fear, she raised the glass and drank. The glacial trickle in her throat sent another shudder rippling through her. Then further shoots of liquored heat budded in her veins and a numbness settled in her temples. Through parted lips, she forced out a shaking breath.

Now a restless, murmuring movement started through the room, the sound of it like willows in a soughing wind. Peggy dared not lift her gaze to the purpled silence of the stage. She stared down at the shifting glimmer of her drink, feeling muscle strands draw tightly in her stomach, feeling the hollow thumping of her heart. *I'd like to leave, please let's leave.*

The music labored toward a rasping dissonant climax, its brass components struggling, in vain, for unity.

A hand stroked once at Peggy's leg and it was the hand of Popeye, the sailor man, who muttered roupily, "Olive Oyl, you is my goil." She barely felt or heard. Automatonlike, she raised the cold and sweating glass again and felt the chilling in her throat and then the flaring network of warmth inside her.

*SWISH!*

The curtain swept open with such a rush, she almost dropped her glass. It thumped down heavily on the table, swamp water cascading up its sides and raining on her hand. The music exploded shrapnel of ear-cutting cacophony and her body jerked. On the tablecloth, her hands twitched white on white while claws of uncontrollable demand pulled up her frightened eyes.

The music fled, frothing behind a wake of swelling drum rolls.

The nightclub was a wordless crypt, all breathing checked.

Cobwebs of smoke drifted in the purple light across the stage.

No sound except the muffled, rolling drum.

Peggy's body was a petrifaction in its chair, smitten to rock around her leaping heart, while, through the wavering haze of smoke and liquored dizziness, she looked up in horror to where it stood.

It had been a woman.

Her hair was black, a framing of snarled ebony for the tallow mask that was her face. Her shadow-rimmed eyes were closed behind lids as smooth and white as ivory. Her mouth, a lipless and unmoving line, stood like a clotted sword wound beneath her nose. Her throat, her shoulders and her arms were white, were motionless. At her sides, protruding from the sleeve ends of the green transparency she wore, hung alabaster hands.

Across this marble statue, the spotlights coated purple shimmer.

Still paralyzed, Peggy stared up at its motionless features, her fingers knitted in a bloodless tangle on her lap. The pulse of drumbeats in the air seemed to fill her body, its rhythm altering her heartbeat.

In the black emptiness behind her, she heard Len muttering, "I love my wife but, oh, you corpse," and heard the wheeze of helpless snickers that escaped from Bud and Barbara. The cold still rose in her, a silent tidal dread.

Somewhere in the smoke-fogged darkness, a man cleared viscid nervousness from his throat, and a murmur of appreciative relief strained through the audience.

Still no motion on the stage, no sound but the sluggish cadence of the drum, thumping at the silence like someone seeking entrance at a far-off door. The thing that was a nameless victim of the plague stood palely rigid while distillation sluiced through its blood-clogged veins.

Now the drum throbs hastened like the pulsebeat of a rising panic. Peggy felt the chill begin to swallow her. Her throat started tightening, her breathing was a string of lip-parted gasps.

The loopy's eyelid twitched.

Abrupt, black, straining silence webbed the room. Even the breath choked off in Peggy's throat when she saw the pale eyes flutter open. Something creaked in the stillness; her body pressed back unconsciously against the chair. Her eyes were wide, unblinking circles that sucked into her brain the sight of the thing that had been a woman.

Music again; a brass-throated moaning from the dark, like some animal made of welded horns mewling its derangement in a midnight alley.

Suddenly, the right arm of the loopy jerked at its side, the tendons suddenly contracted. The left arm twitched alike, snapped out, then fell back and thudded in purple-white limpness against the thigh. The right arm out, the left arm out, the right, the left-right-left-right—like marionette arms twitching from an amateur's dangling strings.

The music caught the time, drum brushes scratching out a rhythm for the convulsions of the loopy's muscles. Peggy pressed back further, her body numbed and cold, her face a livid, staring mask in the fringes of the stage light.

The loopy's right foot moved now, jerking up inflexibly as the distillation constricted muscles in its leg. A second and a third contraction caused the leg to twitch, the left leg flung out in a violent spasm and then the woman's body lurched stiffly forward, filming the transparent silk to its light and shadow.

Peggy heard the sudden hiss of breath that passed the clenching teeth of Bud and Len and a wave of nausea sprayed foaming sickness up her stomach walls. Before her eyes, the stage abruptly undulated with a watery glitter and it seemed as if the flailing loopy was headed straight for her.

Gasping dizzily, she pressed back in horror, unable to take her eyes from its now-agitated face.

She watched the mouth jerk to a gaping cavity, then to a twisted scar that split into a wound again. She saw the dark nostrils twitching, saw writhing flesh beneath the ivory cheeks, saw furrows dug and undug in the purple whiteness of the forehead. She saw one lifeless eye wink monstrously and heard the gasp of startled laughter in the room.

While music blared into a fit of grating noise, the woman's arms and legs kept jerking with convulsive cramps that threw her body around the purpled stage like a full-sized rag doll given spastic life.

It was nightmare in an endless sleep. Peggy shivered in helpless terror as she watched the loopy's twisting, leaping dance. The blood in her had turned to ice; there was no life in her but the endless, pounding stagger of her heart. Her eyes were frozen spheres staring at the woman's body writhing white and flaccid underneath the clinging silk.

Then, something went wrong.

Up till then, its muscular seizures had bound the loopy to an area of several yards before the amber flat which was the background for its paroxysmal dance. Now its erratic surging drove the loopy toward the stage-encircling rail.

Peggy heard the thump and creaking strain of wood as the loopy's hip collided with the rail. She cringed into a shuddering knot, her eyes still raised fixedly to the purple-splashed face whose every feature was deformed by throes of warping convulsion.

The loopy staggered back and Peggy saw and heard its leprous hands slapping with a fitful rhythm at its silk-scaled thighs.

Again it sprang forward like a maniac marionette and the woman's stomach thudded sickeningly into the railing wood. The dark mouth gaped, clamped shut and then the loopy twisted through a jerking revolution and crashed back against the rail again, almost above the table where Peggy sat.

Peggy couldn't breathe. She sat rooted to the chair, her lips a trembling circle of stricken dread, a pounding of blood at her temples as she watched the loopy spin again, its arms a blur of flailing white.

The lurid bleaching of its face dropped toward Peggy as the loopy crashed into the waist-high rail again and bent across its top. The mask of lavender-rained whiteness hung above her, dark eyes twitching open into a hideous stare.

Peggy felt the floor begin to move and the livid face was blurred with darkness, then reappeared in a burst of luminosity. Sound fled on brass-shoed feet, then plunged into her brain again—a smearing discord.

The loopy kept on jerking forward, driving itself against the rail as though it meant to scale it. With every spastic lurch the diaphanous silk fluttered like a film about its body, and every savage collision with the railing tautened the green transparency across its swollen flesh.

Peggy looked up in rigid muteness at the loopy's fierce attack on the railing, her eyes unable to escape the wild distortion of the woman's face with its black frame of tangled, snapping hair.

What happened then happened in a blurring passage of seconds.

The grim-faced man came rushing across the purple-lighted stage; the thing that had been a woman went crashing, twitching, flailing at the rail, doubling over it, the spasmodic hitching flinging up its muscle-knotted legs.

*A clawing fall.*

Peggy lurched back in her chair and the scream that started in her throat was forced back into a strangled gag as the loopy came crashing down onto the table, its limbs a thrash of naked whiteness.

Barbara screamed, the audience gasped and Peggy saw, on the fringe of vision, Bud jumping up, his face a twist of stunned surprise.

The loopy flopped and twisted on the table like a new-caught fish. The music stopped, grinding into silence; a rush of agitated murmur filled the room and blackness swept in brain-submerging waves across Peggy's mind.

Then the cold white hand slapped across her mouth, the dark eyes stared at her in purple light and Peggy felt the darkness flooding.

The horror-smoked room went turning on its side.

\*    \*    \*

Consciousness. It flickered in her brain like gauze-veiled candlelight. A murmuring of sound, a blur of shadow before her eyes.

Breath dripped like syrup from her mouth.

"Here, Peg."

She heard Bud's voice and felt the chilly metal of a flask neck pressed against lips. She swallowed, twisting slightly at the trickle of fire in her throat and stomach, then coughed and pushed away the flask with deadened fingers.

Behind her, a rustling movement. "Hey, *she's back*," Len said. "Ol' Olive Oyl is back."

"You feel all right?" asked Barbara.

She felt all right. Her heart was like a drum hanging from piano wire in her chest, slowly, slowly beaten. Her hands and feet were numb, not with cold but with a sultry torpor. Thoughts moved with a tranquil lethargy, her brain a leisurely machine imbedded in swaths of woolly packing.

She felt all right.

Peggy looked across the night with sleepy eyes. They were on a hilltop, the braked convertible crouching on a jutting edge. Far below, the country slept, a carpet of light and shadow beneath the chalky moon.

An arm snake moved around her waist. "Where are we?" she asked him in a languid voice.

"Few miles outside school," Bud said. "How d'ya feel, honey?"

She stretched, her body a delicious strain of muscles. She sagged back, limp, against his arm.

"*Wonderful*," she murmured with a dizzy smile and scratched the tiny itching bump on her left shoulder. Warmth radiated through her flesh; the night was a sabled glow. There seemed—*somewhere*—to be a memory, but it crouched in secret behind folds of thick content.

"Woman, you were *out*," laughed Bud; and Barbara added and Len added, "*Were* you!" and "Olive Oyl went *plunko!*"

"Out?" Her casual murmur went unheard.

The flask went around and Peggy drank again, relaxing further as the liquor needled fire through her veins.

"Man, I never saw a loopy dance like that!" Len said.

A momentary chill across her back, then warmth again. "Oh," said Peggy, "that's right. I forgot."

She smiled.

"That was what I calls a grand finale!" Len said, dragging back his willing date, who murmured, "*Lenny boy.*"

"L.U.P.," Bud muttered, nuzzling at Peggy's hair. "Son of a gun." He reached out idly for the radio knob.

*L.U.P. (Lifeless Undead Phenomenon)—This freak of physiological abnormality was discovered during the war when, following certain germ-gas attacks, many of the dead troops were found erect and performing the spasmodic gyrations which, later, became known as the "loopy's" (L.U.P.'s) dance. The particular germ spray responsible was later distilled and is now used in carefully controlled experiments which are conducted only under the strictest of legal license and supervision.*

Music surrounded them, its melancholy fingers touching at their hearts. Peggy leaned against her date and felt no need to curb exploring hands. Somewhere, deep within the jellied layers of her mind, there was something trying to escape. It fluttered like a frantic moth imprisoned in congealing wax, struggling wildly but only growing weaker in attempt as the chrysalis hardened.

Four voices sang softly in the night.

> *If the world is here tomorrow*
> *I'll be waiting, dear, for you*
> *If the stars are there tomorrow*
> *I'll be wishing on them too.*

Four young voices singing, a murmur in immensity. Four bodies, two by two, slackly warm and drugged. A singing, an embracing—a wordless accepting.

> *Star light, star bright*
> *Let there be another night.*

The singing ended but the song went on.
A young girl sighed.
"Isn't it romantic?" said Olive Oyl.

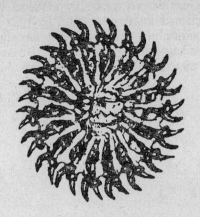

*I like this story for a number of reasons.*

At its simplest level, it is, I think, a rather vivid condemnation of war and man's endless proclivity toward the practice of—virtually the enjoyment of—violence and his taste for the darker, negative side of life.

It is, at the same time, an interesting, I think, study of innocence corrupted.

Moreover, it is one of a handful of my short stories I (successfully, I feel) wrote with extreme, painstaking care as to structure and, literally, word-by-word phrasing.

As a matter of fact, I don't necessarily believe that this is the best form of writing. I believe that the best creative work is usually that which flows the easiest—so much so that the creative person often feels as though he or she is more a conduit through which some outside force is transmitting creation than someone who is, in fact, personally creating.

At the same time, as a writer beset with human frailties, it is more gratifying to believe that any given

113

story came exclusively from my personal imagination, my personal ability and skill. Rightly or wrongly (probably wrongly) I feel more that way about this story than many others. Accordingly, I have chosen it. Chalk it up to persistent—if hardly admirable—ego.

—Richard Matheson

# THE WORDS THAT COUNT

## by Ramsey Campbell

Amen to that, because it did seem to be the words that counted. That's a bit short-storyish as a beginning. But after all, I know this morning would make a good short story, and this is going to be it. So I'll buck my ideas up, as my father would say.

Evil is something you read about, but what you read is only very approximate, if that. (That's better!) Even the Bible can read like a story sometimes, if you permit your mind to slacken. I'm lucky to have had my father to read the Bible to me, rather than one of those teachers who try to indoctrinate their charges in the lie that it isn't meant to be taken literally. But evil is clever today. It takes forms that aren't in the Bible. It comes through the letterbox in a plain brown envelope with a threepenny stamp.

From Mike, I thought as I heard the letterbox click. I was in the kitchen, making my father's breakfast. Mike's my boy friend, my first and only real one. He's only a bus ride away but we often exchange letters, because it makes me feel secure to read them during the day. And my father doesn't insist anymore on opening them, which makes Mike all the more my boy friend. (I won't call him Mike if I send this off, of course; in fact, he doesn't really come into the story at all unless I make him.) Anyway, I turned the stove down and went to get the letters.

"Us, is it?" I heard my father call. "Yes, but it's nothing," I called back, because it didn't seem to be. It was just a flat brown envelope addressed to me, without a return address. "Just a circular," I said.

"Deliver us from circulars," my father said, which is the one thing in surprisingly bad taste he sometimes says. I suppose all men suffer from the temptation to shock, even Mike, although he has great self-control. I threw the envelope on the kitchen table and took my father's scrambled eggs up to him. That's his weekend treat; on days when I'm working I only have time to slice him a grapefruit.

But I didn't take the envelope to him. I don't know why, because of course I felt guilty, and kept telling myself that I didn't want to bother him. "I'm sorry," I said. "Shall I throw it away?" "Yes, unless it's anything worthwhile," he said. He wasn't wearing his dressing gown, so I left the tray outside his room, but he put his head around the door and smiled at me. He often does that, and his hair is usually standing up like a silver halo; it's as though someone were leaning out of a stained-glass portrait to smile. I don't think that's blasphemous. I went downstairs and had my own breakfast, and there was the envelope waiting in front of me.

Temptation is a dreadful thing, because it insinuates itself among your thoughts and mixes them up. I kept reaching for the envelope and drawing back. You see, I was beginning to be convinced that someone had sent me one of those things they're trying to stop, a catalog of aids to love. As if the sacrament of marriage weren't enough of an aid! I know it will be for Mike and me. But what scared me was that I didn't know how much I'd have to see before tearing it up—or taking it to my father, who would know what to do. I almost threw it away unopened, except that I felt I'd have to grow up sometime; but my head was throbbing as I thought about it.

"Into the jaws of hell, then," I said to myself, and snatched the envelope and ripped it open, holding my breath. I shook out the contents, then I breathed so hard that I had to hold it again in case my father had heard.

Not that I was completely reassured by what I'd found. It was a pamphlet bound in a soft black material on which light rippled slowly. It felt like fur. I shivered, because it seemed too enticing for its pages to be innocent. But I closed my eyes and let the pamphlet fall open, and looked.

"Us." That was all: just one word on the page, in delicate mauve letters on a darker purple. It was strange—I mean it was even stranger, because that was a word I'd been thinking about a good deal. I don't think I have space in my diary to explain, if I'm to finish my story. I remember wondering whether all the pages were like that, and whether any of the words were ones I shouldn't read. But I steeled myself and turned over.

"Lead" was the next, in a pearly pink against mauve. I stared at this, because the colors seemed beautiful in a quiet way, like the Oriental paintings on our tea service. Then I let the pages run through my fingers. I had to stop, not because any of the words I'd glimpsed were foul, but because the colors were throbbing against my eyes like a kaleidoscope gone out of control.

And I'd almost forgotten to run my father's bath. Perhaps that should have shown me how the pamphlet was, if I may permit myself the word, seducing me. But I couldn't have known then what it was. I ran upstairs and turned on the taps. "I'm sorry, Father. I've been reading," I called. "I'm sure you needn't blame yourself," he said. "The day was meant to be used." I heard him put the tray on the landing as I turned off the taps. I took it downstairs and washed up, thinking.

"Us," I was thinking. That was how the pamphlet worked: by putting claws into your brain, and that was the first. And to stop myself being confused, I thought about the pamphlet. What I'd seen reminded me of a book of poetry Mike had shown me once. Some of the poems weren't the sort of thing I should have read, and he'd apologized. But some seemed to be just words arranged attractively on the page, and I thought the pamphlet might be similar. It depends on the kind of attraction, of course. I was even beginning to think Mike might have had the pamphlet sent to me as a present!

Against yourself there's sometimes no defense. It comes of not making yourself be straightforward. I should have waited for my father to come down and shown the pamphlet to him, but I saw no harm in reading it. A bird was sitting on my childhood swing and puffing up its feathers, and the garden sparkled like the night with dew. It seemed pleasant to listen to the bird's trills and read. So I sat at the table and began to read the pamphlet slowly from the beginning.

"Trespass" was the word that made me frown. "Thou shalt not trespass," I found myself thinking, and yet the pamphlet seemed to be urging the opposite. But the word wasn't important, I told myself;

the artist had simply wanted a pattern of dark blue stretched across lilac.

Who could have produced such a thing? That's the thought that shocks me most, although perhaps the idea fed them lies to justify itself, as it was doing to me. I can only shrink from myself as I was then, my head bent close to the table, my eyes and my brain separated. My eyes were drinking in the colors while thoughts scrambled in my brain, my own thoughts being silently suppressed while others moved into their places. My head was twinging, and I sought peace in the slow turning of the colors. I had forgotten where to seek true peace. "Who" was the next word, then "those."

"Those as can, does; those as can't, teaches." I'd once heard my mother shouting that at my father. Of course she didn't really talk like that, she was only affecting vulgarity. She died of cancer when I was ten, and my father and I prayed for her soul before every meal. I missed her, although my father told me that was presumption: everything belonged to God. Something of her was still in our house, even after my father gave away her clothes to Father Murphy. Her letters were in a drawer in my father's room, and he'd honored her photograph by putting it next to the Sacred Heart in the lounge. This was what I thought as I looked at the word. All that from one word! And I remembered their argument.

"Forgive her," I'd cried. I'd felt guilty because in a way it was all my fault; my mother had been proud because a teacher had liked a story I'd written, but my father had said nobody needed fiction when there was the Bible. Looking back, I think he wanted me to write something he could sell in his Catholic bookshop, not a fairy tale. But then I didn't know; I'd squeezed myself into the couch, crying and screaming, feeling that it was wrong for my mother to take my part against my father. "Those as can—" I heard her shout, and I ran to my father to intercede for her. I felt he would listen to me, and after a while, holding up his hand for silence, he did. I felt guilty again when my mother died—in fact it was worse, and I've never understood why.

We were closer after that, though; there wasn't so much tension in the house and in me, I suppose because I knew my mother was with God. There was a different sort of tension when I brought Mike home, after having met him in the library where we work; an odd sort of tension, because although I knew I shouldn't I half-enjoyed it. Not that this is helping my story, but I like to be able to write it down for myself.

As I turned the pages I was thinking all this (so perhaps it does fit into my story). My mind felt strange then, though, like a slippery surface across which my thoughts were scurrying, sliding out of reach as I tried to catch hold of them. The room felt oppressive, and so did the sound of my father getting out of his bath. I must have been overpowered by then, because I began to turn the pages faster in case I shouldn't have finished by the time my father came down.

"Trespasses" stopped me again. I knew it should remind me of something, but God help me, I didn't know what. All I could think was that when I'd brought Mike home the first time my father had treated him like a trespasser. My father had wanted me to work in his shop but there wasn't enough money, so he managed to persuade the city librarian to let me work in the Religion Library, making me promise solemnly to choose my friends. I found that there were books on spiritualism and black magic on the shelves but I didn't tell him, although I should have; I simply told people when they asked that all the books were out. I believe you can lie in the service of God.

Our house felt brighter when Mike continued to visit. My father rebuked me after his first visit, but I told him that Mike had been to the best Catholic school in town. I didn't tell him that he'd lapsed, because I know I can bring him back to the Church. After all, I'm twenty-three and I want to help people. That was why I left the convent, that and the way all the silence and rustling terrified me; they were kind but I couldn't make sense of the gap between life in the convent and the people we tried to save from alcohol and drugs. I wanted to see ordinary people so much that I couldn't sleep for weeks. Perhaps I wasn't ready. I think I did the right thing, because once I met Mike I knew I was ready for him. I felt God was watching over us.

"Us"—there it is again, but let me get on. That word was troubling me then too, and I began to walk around the house, still reading. It was as if the kaleidoscope had got into my head, and my thoughts were about to fall together. I found myself staring at the television set. My father is a member of the National Viewers' and Listeners' Association, and recently he watched part of a wrestling match before writing his weekly letters (one to Mrs. Whitehouse, one to each of the broadcasting companies). I'd been both repelled and fascinated by the wrestlers. They were pink as the inside of a shell, and their muscles kept wobbling and then growing taut. I'd once seen Mike fight, to take a broken bottle away from a man who was threatening his wife, and I'd been terrified and proud. Terrified most in case my father heard we'd been in a pub, for he would have forbidden me to see Mike again. I stared at the television, thinking all this, and then my thoughts fell together.

Forgive me, Father, for writing this down, but I think it's better out of me. I began to think of all the subjects Mike had to avoid discussing, his lapse, drinking and the rest. Suppose he betrayed himself one day? I imagined them fighting over me, like knights over a lady, or wrestlers. I would belong to whoever won. Of course my father would win, I thought, because if I were honest I had to admit that right was on his side. And having won, what would he do with me then?

And I can't remember what I thought after that, because I backed into the sideboard and knocked over a cup. It wasn't broken, and I began to giggle nervously, listening to the china chattering against the saucer like a tiny monkey running into the distance. I wondered what it would have sounded like if it had broken. I felt I'd never listened to things like that before, I'd always rolled into a ball inside when anything was damaged. I found myself staring at my mother's photograph and then, I'm still trying to remember why, I ran upstairs.

"Bread." I've had to stop here to think, because that was one of the words in the pamphlet. Bread is what they call money to buy drugs. I wonder if the pamphlet were drugged somehow, because when I think about it that was the effect it had. The evil of people!

"Daily prayer and lots of it," Sister Clare used to say to the people we were helping, and I've always remembered that advice. I don't think I feel drugged now, though. Perhaps I was when I went to the bathroom, although no doubt the words in the pamphlet were enough.

Our timetable was established a long time ago; I

would run my father's bath after breakfast, and when he'd finished I would wash properly and brush my teeth. The bathroom would be full of steam and a warm smell I liked because it was my father's. I took off my clothes and then I began to squirm inside, remembering how my father had found me once standing on the toilet with no clothes on and trying to look in the shaving mirror, and he'd sat on the bath and beaten me. Then I regained control of myself, but while undressing I'd knocked the pamphlet into the bath. I had to grope for it through the steam, and then I saw that there were a few of my father's hairs around the inside of the bath, and I caught myself wondering where they'd come from. I want to cross that out, but at the same time I want to leave it to remind me what I'm capable of. Before God I don't usually have such thoughts. My father and I have always been just us.

Us again. All right, I'll explain and then I can get on. I feel guilty thinking of Mike and me as us, it seems disloyal. I don't know if I'm right, because I can hardly think of Mike and my father in the same way. But I keep thinking about it until my head hurts. I think my father feels something similar, and that's why he's begun hitting me again. I try to stop him, but he has a bad heart. That's all, and now I haven't much room in my diary. I washed and brushed my teeth, and when I came downstairs my father was waiting.

"Give that to me, please," he said.

Heaven help me, for a moment I didn't know what he meant and when I did I realized I was trying to hide the pamphlet behind my back. I blushed and apologized, and gave it to him.

"In heaven's name, what nonsense is this?" he said.

"Is it a poem? I think that's what it's meant to be." I hurried into the kitchen for no reason except so as not to have to look at him, because my face was burning and I was confused. I realized that I'd read the pamphlet through but couldn't remember having finished it, and a part of my mind knew what I'd read and was trying to tell me. My face is burning now.

It was worse to wait in the kitchen when the only sound in the house was the pages turning, and it was as bad to watch him frowning. I felt he was going to discover what I'd been reading before I did, and that terrified me as much as being caught that day in the bathroom. I tried to think of something to distract him.

As I did so he spoke, and when he saw me start his frown deepened. "Look at these colors," he said. "They're false. I ask you, are these the colors of God's earth?"

"Earth isn't a color," I said. I don't know why, because I knew it was a stupid thing to say. "Sorry," I said, and the pamphlet was making me crafty, because I said "Let me have it and I'll show you, some of the colors are beautiful."

"On no account," he said, and I began to draw into myself, because I knew that at any minute he would make the discovery I dreaded, and I still didn't know what it was. I realize now I said out loud "Oh, God, what have I done?"

"Done? What do you mean?" he said, and I'd reached such a pitch I almost cursed inside myself. "I mean I don't think we have enough vegetables for dinner for three," I said weakly.

"Be quiet now and let me look at this. There's no call for you to bring God into your housework."

"Will you excuse me then, while I go and see?"

But I was equally terrified to leave him with the pamphlet or to stay; my head was pounding.

"Thy," he read. I remembered I'd read that word two or three times. "Is this supposed to be religious? If so it's a poor job," he said. He turned two pages, then he went rigid and raised his eyes to me.

"Come here," he said. That's what he said in the bathroom when I was little, and that's how I went to him, with my ribs hurting because I was breathing so fast. He gripped my shoulder and held up the page.

"Kingdom," he read and turned back. "Come, kingdom, thy. Thy kingdom come! Do you know what this filth is?" he shouted and a purple vein grew from beneath his hair. I couldn't speak, only shake my head. But of course I did know, because the first word in the pamphlet had been "Amen."

"Thy kingdom come! That's what they want today, isn't it? The devil's kingdom!" He swung me round to face him, hurting my shoulder. "And this is how they go about it! Was this your friend's idea? Did he send you this?" he shouted, his face still darkening, and I could only shake my head until my ears screamed.

"Name me one person who would send you this!" he shouted, and I managed to say "I don't know anyone. They could have got my name from anywhere." Then I gulped back a cry, because he'd pulled the covers back and was ripping out the pages.

"Thy" sailed by me, and I picked it up seeing only the colors, soft shades of yellow and lime. My father's face seemed to swell and loom over me, and I crumpled the page into his hand and closed my eyes. I heard his breath snarling and the rip of the paper, and I was thinking of the time he forbade me to see the boy next door again, because he wasn't a Catholic. I know it was for my own good, but then I lay sobbing in the garden, and when a butterfly settled near me I tore it like a wet scrap of paper. My father's destruction of the pamphlet seemed like that, and I sobbed before I could stop myself.

"Be quiet!" I felt him grab my shoulder. "Tell me before God, did you read this?" I opened my eyes and there on the floor I saw the word "hallowed," like pieces of jigsaw when you know they fit together by their color. I looked at him and couldn't speak, seeing the vein trembling on his skull.

"Hallowed is as hallowed does," I was thinking, anything to cover the slippery surface of my mind, because now I could see through it and there was my father on the floor, his heart burst. I was thinking that then there'd be just me and Mike to save me from despair, the worst sin, just us.

"Heaven help you, child!" my father shouted. "Don't think up lies! Did you read this filth?"

"In a way," I stammered. "I mean, I didn't read it, just looked at the colors. The art."

"Art! You call this art?" he shouted. I must have become crafty again, as I sometimes was when I was little, thinking I could tell when he'd softened. That, and the fact that the pamphlet had gone, the thoughts it was feeding me had gone; my muteness had gone; and although I was shaking I felt a tremendous relief. Everything seemed all right again. "Yes. Well, it is. In a way," I said.

"Who taught you that? Your friend?" he shouted, and knocked me across the room. I ran to my bedroom sobbing, and the sheet beneath the blanket was wet when I'd finished. I sat on my bed for an hour after that, thinking all that I've written down. It was then that I thought of writing it, because Sister Clare used to make the people write down their lives; she said it helped. I knew I could write it, if my father would speak to me.

"Father, please forgive me," I said when I went down. He was staring out into the garden. After a while he turned and nodded. "I forgive you," he said. "I know you didn't understand. But never do anything like that again unless you want to kill me." And I ran up to my room again, but this time I was smiling.

Our house feels peaceful now, and I feel somehow cleaner for having written all this down. I shall read it through now to see what effect it has, and perhaps Mike can read it when he's brought us back from Mass. No, on second thoughts, there are things in it he shouldn't know until after we're married. He can see it when it's properly finished. I'll have to rewrite it before I send it anywhere, if I do, because I know the effort of writing isn't meant to be visible. And it certainly is at the moment; every time I've hesitated at the beginning of a paragraph the ink's collected in my nib, and the words stand out from the rest. The first word of each paragraph looks as if someone else had written it in.

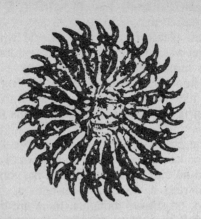

*I suspect that "The Words That Count" may be one* kind of horror story to Baptists, Fundamentalists and suchlike casualties of religion, and quite another kind to the rest of us. Even so, I hope nobody finds it easy to take. I'm for horror fiction as subversion; I don't like the kind that simply indulges received notions of good and evil, and I hate the kind in which the author indulges his own prejudices by blaming the devil for what he dislikes (Dennis Wheatley's novels are especially blameworthy) or, perhaps worse, flatters those of his supposed audience (the novels of John Saul, say, or Michael Winner's film *The Sentinel*). If we're to talk about inhuman forces in the world, they certainly include religions, quite a few of which are allegedly Christian. It seemed to me that there are everyday situations in which even black magic would be liberating: hence this story.

All that said, I have to admit that on its original publication the story was greeted with some blankness, none of it the fault of the readers. I'd been trying the kind of juggling act that W. F. Harvey achieves so brilliantly in ''August Heat,'' where the narrator tells the reader everything without ever suspecting what he has revealed. In my case, unfortunately, my narrator left many readers as much in the dark as she had been throughout the writing (though perhaps no longer once she rereads what she wrote; I hope not, anyway). I'm all the more grateful, therefore, to my good friend and estimable colleague Dennis Etchison for suggesting that I might like to submit a story I'd always felt deserved wider recognition, for it gave me the chance to bring into print a version of the story where I'd made one slight but crucial change, in the interests of clarification. I must say that the story seems timelier than it did when I wrote it more than a decade ago; the lifeless influence of the self-styled Moral Majority is growing, while in England the police have set up a branch called the Public Morals Squad to tell us which horror films we may not see, a development as ominous as it is comic. What Michael Moorcock rightly calls the retreat from liberty gathers speed, and I wonder if I may see this story declared unpublishable in my lifetime. Perhaps I shall end my career writing about, and for, good little boys and girls who know there is only one right and one wrong.

—Ramsey Campbell

# THE TEST TUBE

## by Ray Russell

No ember-eyed debaucher was so fond,
No zealot's fierce allegiance half so true.
How many hours I watched, the boyhood trips
I made to movie houses to adore
Your fragile beauty and your crystal pride,
Your power to kill, or kindle what had died.

You spared the blushes of the naked blonde,
Hiding with veils of vapor her taboo
Attractions, deftly draping breasts and hips
As she lay, trussed, on *Horror Stories'* floor
And white-smocked Dr. Hooknose grimly tried
To do her harm in ways unspecified.

King's sceptre, bishop's censer, wizard's wand,
Mad scientists caressed and fondled you
Till smoke poured thick and creamy from your lips
And instantly you both conceived and bore
Out of your teeming steam—defiant Hyde
Or, to placate the Baron's brute, a Bride.

# DOCTOR OF DREAMS
## (An Acrostical Sonnet)

### by Ray Russell

Darkness and light, two sides of Psyche's coin;
Remembered joys and unremembered fears:
Such sundered pairings you have bid us join
In fusions sealed with semen, blood and tears.
Guilt you have exiled to a frozen land,
Monsters of madness pinned like butterflies.
Under your gaze, dread crags are grains of sand.
Never again will we our dreams despise,
Deny no more the creatures sleep may spawn,
For you have taught us to acknowledge them,
Record their images at break of dawn,
Evaluate each blood-dark, star-bright gem,
Until the chains we've forged we have dissolved,
Destroyed despair, and Self's enigma solved.

"*The Test Tube*" *was engendered after I had seen a* revival of the 1931 Fredric March *Dr. Jekyll and Mr. Hyde*, and felt a reawakening of my fascination, as a kid, with all those bubbling test tubes that flourished in horror movies and on pulp magazine covers of the Thirties.

Determined to pay a tribute to them, and aware, in my maturity, of the "phallic" and "Freudian" symbolism of those foaming tubes, I brought their sexual significance to the forefront of the poem, using words like "debaucher," "fond," "adore," "beauty," in the first stanza; explicit references to "naked blonde," "breasts and hips," in the second stanza; and lubric images of orgasm, conception and birth in the third stanza. The working-out of the rhyme scheme was another kind of pleasure for me: except for the couplets at the ends of the stanzas, in each stanza no line rhymes with another, but *does* rhyme with its counterparts in the other stanzas; that is, the first line of the first stanza rhymes with the first lines of the second and third stanzas (*fond/blonde/wand*), and so on. A bit tricky, but it contributes to a nice cumulative effect, I think.

Having made this poetic obeisance to Freudian symbolism, I later decided to celebrate the ''Doctor of Dreams'' in a sonnet that acrosticizes him in the initial letters of its fourteen lines. It appears for the first time in this book.

—Ray Russell

# NEITHER BRUTE
# NOR HUMAN

## by Karl Edward Wagner

The first time that Damon Harrington saw Trevor Nordgren was in 1974 at Discon II in Washington, D.C. It was the thirty-second World Science Fiction Convention, and Harrington's first convention of any sort. He and four friends had piled into a chugging VW van (still bearing a faded psychedelic paint job and inevitably dubbed "The Magic Bus") and driven approximately non-stop from Los Angeles; they were living out of the van in the parking lot of someone's brother who had an apartment on Ordway Street, a short walk from the con hotel.

They had been reading each other's name badges, and their eyes met. Harrington was of average height and build, with wheat-colored hair and a healthy California tan and features good enough to fit the Hollywood image of the leading man's best buddy. He had entered adolescence as a James Dean look-alike, emerged as a Beach Boy, and presently clung to the beard and ponytail of the fading hippie years. Nordgren was half a head taller and probably ten pounds heavier, and only regular sit-ups could have

134

kept his abdomen so flat. He was clean-shaven, with a tousled nimbus of bright blond hair, and blue eyes of almost unsettling intensity dominated a face that might have belonged to a visionary or a fallen angel. They were both wearing bell-bottomed jeans; Harrington in sandals and a tie-dyed t-shirt, Nordgren in cowboy boots and a blue chambray work shirt with hand-embroidered marijuana leaves.

Damon Harrington smiled, feeling extremely foolish in the silly styrofoam boater hat the con committee had given them to wear for the meet-the-pros party. Discon with its thousands of fans and frenetic pace was a bit overawing to the author of half a dozen published stories. He'd had to show his S.F.W.A. card to get his pro hat and free-drink voucher, and already Harrington was kicking himself for not staying in the hucksters' room. He'd carried along a near-mint run of the first dozen issues of *The Fantastic Four*, saved from high school days, and if he could coax one of the dealers out of a hundred bucks for the lot, he could about cover his expenses for the trip.

"Hey, look," Harrington protested, "I'm only doing this for the free drink they gave us for being put on display."

Trevor Nordgren tipped his styrofoam boater. "Don't forget this nifty ice bucket."

Harrington swirled the ice cubes in his near-empty plastic cup, trying to think whether Trevor Nordgren should mean anything to him, painfully aware that Nordgren was puzzling over his name as well. An overweight teenage fan, collecting autographs on her program book, squinted closely at each of their badges, stumped away with the air of someone who had just been offered a swell deal for the Washington Monument. She joined a mass of autograph seekers clumped about a bewhiskered Big Name Author.

"God, I hate this!" Nordgren crunched his ice cubes. He glowered at the knots of fans who mobbed the famous authors. In between these continents of humanity, islands of fans milled about the many not-quite-so-big-name authors, while other fans stalked the drifting styrofoam hats of no-name authors such as Harrington and Nordgren. An ersatz Mr. Spock darted up to them, peered at their name badges, then hurried away,

"It would help if they just would give us t-shirts with our names printed across the back," Harrington suggested. "That way they could tell from a distance whether we were worth attention."

A well-built brunette, braless in a t-shirt and tight jeans, approached them purposefully, selecting a copy of the latest *Orbit* from a stack of books cradled against her hip. "Mr. Nordgren? Mr. Harrington? Would you two mind autographing your stories in *Orbit* for me?"

"My pleasure," said Nordgren, accepting her book. He scribbled busily.

Harrington struggled over being "mistered" by someone who was obviously of his own age group. He hadn't read Nordgren's story in the book—had only reread his own story in search of typos—and he felt rather foolish.

"Please, call me Trevor," Nordgren said, handing the book to Harrington. "Did you read 'The Electric Dream'?"

"I thought it was the best thing in the book." She added, "I liked your story, too, Mr. Harrington."

"Is this your first con?" Nordgren asked.

"First one. Me and my old man rode down from Baltimore." She inclined her head toward a hulking

red-bearded biker who had materialized behind
Nordgren and Harrington, a beer bottle lost in one
hairy fist. "This is Clay."

She retrieved her book, and Clay retrieved her.

"My first autograph," Harrington commented.

Nordgren was gloomily watching her departure. "I
signed a copy of *Acid Test* about half an hour ago."

Recognition clicked in Harrington's memory: a
Lancer paperback, badly drawn psychedelic cover,
bought from a bin at Woolworth's, read one weekend
when a friend brought over some Panama Red.

"I've got a copy of that back in L.A. That was
one far-out book!"

"You must have one of the twelve copies that
were sold." Nordgren's mood openly brightened.
"Look, you want to pay for a drink from these
suckers, or run up to my room for a shot of Jack
Daniel's?"

"Is the bear Catholic?"


When Nordgren poured them each a second drink,
they agreed wholeheartedly that there was no point in
returning to the ordeal of the meet-the-pros party.
Nordgren had actually read Harrington's story in *Orbit*
and pronounced it extremely good of its type; they
commiserated in both having been among the "and
others" on the cover blurb. They were both products
of the immediate postwar baby boom; incredibly,
both had been in Chicago for the bloody demonstra-
tions during the Democratic primary, though neither
had been wounded or arrested. Nordgren was in the
aftermath of an unpleasant divorce; Harrington's lover
of the Flower Children years had lately returned to
Boston and a job with the family law firm. Nordgren
preferred Chandler to Hammett, Harrington favored
Chandler's turn of a phrase; they agreed modern

science fiction writers were nothing more than products of the market. The Stones and the Who were
better than the Beatles, who actually weren't innova-
tive at all, and listening to Pink Floyd while tripping
had inspired at least one story from them both. Val
Lewton was an unsung genius—to which ranks
Nordgren added Nicholas Ray, and Harrington, Ma-
rio Bava—and Aldrich had peaked with *Kiss Me
Deadly*.

They hit it off rather well.

Nordgren punished the bottle, but Harrington decided three drinks were his limit on an empty stomach, and concentrated on rolling joints from some
leafy Mexican Nordgren had brought down from New
York. They had both sold stories to *Cavalier*, and
Harrington favorably remembered Nordgren's one
about the kid and the rubber machine in the redneck
filling station. Harrington scraped along as cashier at
an all-night self-service gas station, which afforded
him lonely hours to write. Nordgren had been writing
full-time up until the divorce (he admitted to a possible cause-effect relationship there), and he was just
completing his tenth novel—the second under his real
name. Nordgren confessed to having paid the bills by
writing several porno novels for Bee Line and Essex
House, under the unsubtle pseudonym, Mike Hunt.

He was quite proud of the Essex House novels,
which he said developed science fiction themes that
Britain's New Wave would have deemed far too outrageous, and he produced a copy of *Time's Wanton* and
incomprehensibly inscribed it to Harrington. It was
about a woman who used her psychic powers to
project her consciousness through time, Nordgren
explained, emptying the bottle, and she took posses-
sion of various important historical personages and
goaded them through extravagant sexual excesses that

changed the course of history. It was, said Nordgren, a theme not dissimilar to his almost-completed novel, *Out of the Past,* in which a Victorian medium projected her consciousness into the present day to control a teenage girl's mind. Harrington warned Nordgren that the market for fantasy novels was about nil, but Nordgren thought he could push the psychic powers angle enough to qualify as science fiction. Harrington allowed that his only novel to date had been a near-miss—a post-nuclear holocaust thing sold to Powell Publications, a Los Angeles shoestring operation that folded with his *Iron Night* already in galleys.

It was a tough game, and they both agreed they considered themselves outlaws. Nordgren suggested they check out the parties for some free drinks, and Harrington suggested they look for something to eat. Somewhere along the way Nordgren ran into some New York friends and was carried off, and Harrington wandered into the night in search of a cheap pizza.

They managed to get together several more times in the course of the convention. Harrington found a three-year-old copy of *F&SF* containing what he considered his best story published to date, and he presented it to Nordgren in return for *Time's Wanton.* They exchanged addresses, agreed to stay in touch, and parted on the best of terms.

They actually did stay in touch, although correspondence was sporadic. Nordgren wrote long letters of comment on books and films he'd caught; Harrington was inclined to talk shop and discuss possible fiction markets. Nordgren kept him posted about his progress on *Out of the Past*, its completion, its rejection by various publishers. Harrington sold a short story to *F&SF* and was contemplating a major revision of

*Iron Night* after having had it rejected by every publisher in the English-speaking world. Nordgren asked to read the manuscript, offered some badly needed criticisms (''Writing a short story all in present tense may be artsy as hell, but an *entire* novel?''), and grudgingly Harrington followed some of his advice.

On its second time out, the newly revised *Iron Night* sold to Fairlane, who expressed interest in an immediate sequel. The $2500 advance was rather more than the sum total of Harrington's career earnings as an author up until then, and he was sufficiently assured of financial success to quit his job at the U-Sav-Here and send tidings to Nordgren that he was now a full-time professional writer. His letter crossed in the mail with Nordgren's; Trevor had just sold *Out of the Past* to McGinnis & Parry.

McGinnis & Parry elected to change the title to *The Sending* and went on to market it as ''an occult thriller that out-chills *The Exorcist*!'' They also proclaimed it to be Nordgren's first novel, but it *was* after all his first hardcover. Harrington received an advance copy (sent by Nordgren) and took personally Trevor's dedication to ''all my fellow laborers in the vineyard.'' He really did intend to read it sometime soon.

They were very much a pair of young lions at the Second World Fantasy Convention in New York in 1976. Harrington decided to attend it after Nordgren's invitation to put him up for a few days afterward at his place (an appalling dump in Greenwich Village which Trevor swore was haunted by the ghost of Lenny Bruce) and show him around. Nordgren himself was a native of Wisconsin who had been living in The City (he managed to pronounce the capitals) since student days at Columbia; he professed no desire to return to the Midwest.

They were together on a panel—Harrington's first—designated "Fantasy's New Faces"—although privately comparing notes with the other panelists revealed that their mean date of first publication was about eight years past. The panel was rather a dismal affair. The moderator had obviously never heard of Damon Harrington, introduced him as "our new Robert E. Howard," and referred to him as David Harrington throughout the panel. Most of the discussion was taken over by something called Martin E. Binkley, who had managed to publish three stories in minor fanzines and to insinuate himself onto the panel. Nordgren was quite drunk at the outset and continued to coax fresh Jack Daniel's-and-ice from a pretty blonde in the audience. By the end of the hour he was offering outrageous rebuttals to Binkley's self-serving pontification; the fans were soon loudly applauding, the moderator lost all control, and the panel nearly finished with a brawl.

That evening found Nordgren's state of mind somewhat mellower, if no closer to sobriety. He and Harrington slouched together behind a folding table at the meet-the-pros autographing party, while Nordgren's blonde cupbearer proudly continued her service.

"Together again!" Harrington toasted, raising the drink Nordgren had paid for.

"The show must go on," Nordgren rejoined. He looked about the same as he had two years ago, although the straining pearl buttons on his denim shirt bespoke a burgeoning beer-belly. Harrington had in the interim shaved his beard, trimmed his hair to the parted-in-the-middle-blown-dry look, and just now he was wearing a new denim leisure suit.

Fairlane had contributed two dozen copies of *Iron Night*, free to the first lucky autograph seekers, so for about fifteen minutes Harrington was kept busy. He grew tired of explaining to unconcerned fans that the novel was set in a post-nuclear holocaust future, and that it was not at all "In the Conan Tradition!" as the cover proclaimed. After that, he managed to inscribe two copies of *New Dimensions* and three of *Orbit* over the next half hour.

Nordgren did quite a brisk trade in comparison, autographing a dozen copies of *The Sending* (on sale in the hucksters' room), as many copies of *Acid Test* (which had begun to gather a cult reputation), and a surprising number of short stories and essays from various magazines and anthologies. The room was crowded, hot, and after an hour Nordgren was patently bored and restive. In the jostled intervals between callers at their table, he stared moodily at the long lines queued up before the tables of the mighty.

"Do you ever wonder why we do this?" he asked Harrington.

"For fame, acclaim—not to mention a free drink?"

"Piss on it. Why do we put ourselves on display just so an effusive mob of lunatic fringe fans can gape at us and tell us how great we are and beg an autograph and ask about our theories of politics and religion?"

"You swiped that last from the Kinks," Damon accused.

"Rock stars. Movie stars. *Sci-fi* stars. What's the difference? We're all hustling for as much acclaim and attention as we can wring out of the masses. Admit it! If we were pure artists, you and I and the rest of this grasping lot would be home sweating over a typewriter tonight. Why aren't we?"

"Is that intended to be rhetorical?"

" 'All right, I'll tell you why,' said he, finishing his drink." Nordgren finished his drink, dug another ten dollar bill out of his jeans, and poked it toward his cupbearer.

"It's because we're all vampires."

"Sweetheart, better make that two Bloody Marys!" Harrington called after her.

"I'm serious, Damon," Nordgren persisted, pausing to scrawl something across a copy of *The Sending*. "We're the psychic vampires beloved of fiction. We *need* all these fans, all this gaudy adulation. We derive energy from it all."

He handed the book back to its owner. "Have you read this?"

The fan was embarrassed. "No, sir—I just today bought it." He continued bravely: "But a friend of mine sat up all night reading it, and she said it gave her nightmares for a week!"

"So you see, Damon," Nordgren nodded. He pointed a finger at the fan. "I now possess a bit of your frightened friend's soul. And when *you* read *The Sending*, I shall possess a fragment of your soul as well."

The blonde returned bearing drinks, and the stricken fan made his escape.

"So you see, Damon," Nordgren asserted. "They read our books, and all their attention is directed toward the creations of our hungry imaginations. We absorb a little psychic energy each time they read us; we grow stronger and stronger with each new book, each new printing, each new victim. And see—like proper vampire fodder, our victims adore us and beg for more."

Trevor squinted at the blonde's name badge. "Julie, my love, how long have I known you?"

"Since we met in the elevator this morning," she remembered.

"Julie, my love. Would you like to drop up to my room with me now and peruse my erotic etchings?"

"OK. You going to sign your book for me?"

"As you see, Damon." Nordgren pushed back his chair. "The vampire's victims are most willing. I hereby appoint you my proxy and empower you to sign anything that crosses this table in my name. Good night."

Harrington found himself staring at two Bloody Marys.

The visit with Nordgren in New York was a lot of fun, and Damon promised to return Trevor's hospitality when the World Fantasy Convention came to Los Angeles the following year. Aside from the convention, Harrington's visit was chiefly remarkable for two other things—Nordgren's almost embroiling them in a street fight with a youth gang in front of the Hilton, and their mutual acquisition of an agent.

"Damon, my man," Nordgren introduced them. "Someone I'd like you to meet. A boxer needs a manager, and a writer needs an agent. This is Helen Hohenstein, and she's the goddam smartest, meanest, and best-looking agent in New York. Helen, love, this is our young Robert E. Howard."

"I saw your panel," she said.

"Sorry about that," Harrington said.

Helen Hohenstein was a petite woman of about forty whose doll-like face was offset by shrewd eyes— Harrington balked at deeming them predatory. She had passed through the revolving door in various editorial positions at various publishers, and she was now starting her own literary agency, specializing in science fiction and fantasy. She looked as if she could handle herself well under about any situation and probably already had. Harrington felt almost intimidated by her, besides his not being especially willing to sacrifice ten percent of his meager earnings, but Nordgren was insistent.

"All kidding aside, Damon. Helen's the sharpest mind in the game today. She's worked her way up through the ranks, and she knows every crooked kink of a publisher's subnormal brain. She's already got a couple major paperback publishers interested in *The Sending*—and, baby, we're talking five figures! It's a break for us she's just starting out and hungry for clients—and I've sold her on you, baby! Hey, think about it—she'll buy all those stamps and manila envelopes, and collect all those rejection slips for you!"

That last sold Harrington. They celebrated with lunch at the Four Winds, and when Hohenstein revealed that she had read most of Harrington's scattered short fiction and that she considered him to be a writer of unrealized genius, Damon knew he had hitched his wagon to the proper star.

A month later, Harrington knew so for a certainty. Hohenstein tore up Fairlane's contract for the sequel to *Iron Night*, wrote up a new one that did not include such pitfalls (unnoticed by Damon in his ecstasy to be published) as world rights forever, and jumped the advance to $3500 payable on acceptance instead of on publication. Fairlane responded by requesting four books a year in the "Saga of Desmond Killstar" series, as they now designated it, and promised not to say a word about Conan. Damon, who would have been panic-stricken had he known of Helen's machinations beforehand, now considered his literary career assured throughout his lifetime.

He splurged on a weekend phone call to Nordgren to tell him of his success. Nordgren concurred that Hohenstein was a genius: she had just sold paperback rights to *The Sending* to Warwick Books for $100,000, and the contract included an option for his next novel.

*The Sending* had been atop the paperback bestseller lists for three straight weeks when Trevor Nordgren flew first class to Los Angeles that next World Fantasy Convention. He took a suite at the con hotel and begged off Harrington's invitation to put him up at his two-room cottage in Venice afterward. Helen was flying out and wanted him to talk with some Hollywood contacts while he was out there, so he wouldn't have time for Damon to show him the sights. He knew Damon would understand, and anyway, it was due to be announced soon, but Warwick had just signed a $250,000 paperback deal for the *The Rending*, so Trevor had to get back to New York to finish the final draft. McGinnis & Parry had put up another $100,000 for hardcover rights, and Helen had slammed the door on any option for Nordgren's next—that one would be up for bid.

Harrington could hear the clatter of loud voices as he approached Nordgren's suite. A pretty redhead in a tank top answered his knock, sizing him up with the door half open.

"Hey, it's Damon!" Nordgren's voice cut above the uproar. "Come on in, baby! The party's already started!"

Nordgren rose out of the melee and gave him a sloshing hug. He was apparently drinking straight Jack Daniel's out of a pewter mug. He was wearing a loose shirt of soft suede, open at the throat to set off the gold chains about a neck that was starting to soften beneath a double chin, and a silver concho belt and black leather trousers that had been custom-tailored when he was twenty pounds lighter.

Harrington could not resist. "Christ, you look like a peroxide Jim Morrison!"

"Yeah—Jimbo left me his wardrobe in his will. What you drinking? JD, still? Hey, Mitzi! Bring my friend James Dean a gallon of Jack Daniel's with an ice cube in it! Come on, Damon—got some people I want you to meet."

The redhead caught up with them. "Here you are, Mr. Dean."

It was a stronger drink than Damon liked to risk this early in the afternoon, but Trevor swept him along. Most of the people he knew, at least recognized their faces. There was a mixed bag of name authors, various degrees of editors and publishers, a few people Harrington recognized from his own Hollywood contacts, and a mixture of friends, fans, groupies, and civilians. Helen Hohenstein was talking in one corner with Alberta Dawson of Warwick Books, and she waved to Damon, which gave him an excuse to break away from Trevor's dizzying round of introductions.

"I must confess I've never read any of your Killstar books," Ms. Dawson felt she had to confess, "although I understand they're very good for their type. Helen tells me that you and Trevor go way back together; do you ever write occult fiction?"

"I suppose you could call my story in the new *Black Dawns* anthology that Helen is editing a horror story. I really prefer to think of myself as a fantasy writer, as opposed to being categorized as a specialist in some particular sub-subgenre."

"Not much profit to be made in short stories." Ms. Dawson seemed wistful. "And none at all with horror fiction."

"I gather *The Sending* is doing all right for you."

"But *The Sending* is mainstream fiction, of course,"

she said almost primly, then conceded: "Well, *occult* mainstream fiction."

*The Rending*, it developed, was about a small New York bedroom community terrorized by werewolves. Nordgren's startling twist was that the werewolves were actually the town children, who had passed the curse among themselves through a seemingly innocent secret kid's gang. However Alberta Dawson would categorize the novel, *The Rending* went through three printings before publication at McGinnis & Parry, and the Warwick paperback topped the best-seller charts for twenty-three weeks. Harrington was no little amused to discover that the terrorized community included a hack gothics writer named David Harrison.

Fairlane Books filed for bankruptcy, still owing the advance for Harrington's latest Killstar opus and most of the royalties for the previous six.

"This," said Damon, when Helen phoned him the news, "is where I came in."

In point of fact, he was growing heartily sick of Desmond Killstar and his never-ending battles against the evil mutant hordes of The Blighted Earth, and had been at a loss as to which new or revived menace to pit him against in #8.

"We'll sue the bastards for whatever we can salvage," Helen promised him. "But for the good news: Julie Kriegman is the new science fiction editor at Summit, and she said she'd like to see a new fantasy-adventure series from you—something on the lines of Killstar, but with a touch of myths and sorcery. She thought the series ought to center around a strong female character—an enchantress, or maybe a swordswoman."

"How about a little of both?" Harrington suggested, glancing at the first draft of Killstar #8. "I think I can show her something in a few weeks. Who's this Kriegman woman, and why is she such a fan of mine?''

"Christ, I thought you knew her. She says she knows you and Trevor from way back. She remembers that you drink Bloody Marys.''

*Death's Dark Mistress*, the first of the Krystel Firewind series, was good for a quick five-grand advance and a contract for two more over the next year. The paperback's cover was a real eye-catcher, displaying Krystel Firewind astride her flying dragon and brandishing her enchanted broadsword at a horde of evil dwarves. That the artist had chosen to portray her nude except for a few certainly uncomfortable bits of baubles, while Harrington had described her as wearing plate armor for this particular battle, seemed a minor quibble. Damon was less pleased with the cover blurb that proclaimed him "America's Michael Moorcock!''

But Summit paid promptly

Trevor Nordgren was Guest of Honor at CajunCon VII in New Orleans in 1979, and Harrington (he later learned it was at Trevor's suggestion) was Master of Ceremonies. It was one of those annual regional conventions that normally draw three to five hundred fans, but this year over a thousand came to see Trevor Nordgren.

The film of *The Sending* had already grossed over forty million, and Max de Lawrence was rumored to have purchased film rights to *The Rending* for an even million. Shaftesbury had outbid McGinnis & Parry, paying out $500,000 for hardcover rights to Nordgren's latest, *The Etching*, and Warwick Books was paying a record $2 million for a package deal that gave them paperback rights to *The Etching*,

Nordgren's next novel, and a series of five paperback reissues of his earlier work.

Nordgren was tied up with a barrage of newspaper and television interviews when Harrington checked into the Monteleone, but by late afternoon he phoned Damon to meet him in the lobby for a quick look at the French Quarter. Harrington was just out of the shower, and by the time he reached the lobby, Nordgren had been cornered by a mob of arriving fans. He was busily signing books, and for every one he handed back, two more were thrust toward him. He saw Damon, waved, and made a quick escape.

They fled to Bourbon Street and ducked into the Old Absinthe House, where they found seats at the hollow square bar. Nordgren ordered two Sazeracs. "Always wanted to try one. Used to be made with bourbon and absinthe, or brandy and absinthe, or rye and absinthe—anyway, it was made with absinthe. Now they use Pernod or Herbsaint or something instead of absinthe. Seems like they still ought to use absinthe in the Old Absinthe House."

Harrington watched with interest the bartender's intricate preparation. "Thought they were going to eat you alive back there in the lobby."

"Hell, let them have their fun. They pay the bills—they and a few million who stay at home."

Nordgren sipped the dark red cocktail that filled the lower part of a highball glass. "Hey, not bad. Beats a Manhattan. Let's have two more—these'll be gone by the time the next round's ready. So tell me, Damon—how you been?"

"Things are going pretty well. Summit has accepted *Swords of Red Vengeance*, and I'm hard at work on a third."

"You're too good a writer to waste your energy on that sort of stuff."

Damon swallowed his Sazerac before he reminded Trevor that not all writers were overnight millionaires. "Pays the bills. So what's after *The Etching*?"

Nordgren was already on his second Sazerac. "This one's called *The Bending*. No—just kidding! Christ, these little devils have a kick to them. Don't know what they'll want me to title it. It's about a naive young American secretary, who marries an older Englishman whose previous wife was lost when their yacht sank. They return to his vast estate, where the housekeeper makes life miserable for her because she's obsessed with her worship of the previous wife, and—"

"Was her name Rebecca?"

"Damn! You mean somebody beat me to the idea? Well, back to square one. Let's have another of these and go grab a quick bite."

"My round, I believe."

"Forget it—my treat. You can buy us dinner."

"Then how about a po' boy?"

"Seriously—I'd like that. Not really very hungry, but I know I've got to keep something in my stomach, or I'll be dead before the con is half over."

At a hole-in-the-wall sandwich shop they picked up a couple meatball po' boys to go. Harrington wanted to try the red beans and rice, but Nordgren was in a hurry to get back to the Monteleone. Fans spotted Nordgren as they entered the hotel, but they caught an elevator just in time and retreated to Trevor's room, where he ordered a dozen bottles of Dixie beer.

Nordgren managed half his sandwich by the time room service brought the beer. "Want the rest of this, Damon? I'm not all that hungry."

"Sure!" Harrington's last meal had been plastic

chicken on the flight from Los Angeles. "Say, you're losing weight, aren't you?"

"My special diet plan." Nordgren unlocked his suitcase and dug out a chamois wallet, from which he produced a polished slab of agate and a plastic bag of cocaine. "Care for a little toot before we meet the masses?"

"For sure!" Damon said through a mouthful of sandwich. "Hey, I brought along a little Colombian for the weekend. Want me to run get it?"

"Got some Thai stick in the suitcase." Trevor was sifting coke onto the agate. "Take a look at these boulders, man! This shit has not been stepped on."

"Nice work if you can get it."

Nordgren cut lines with a silver razor blade and handed the matching tooter to Harrington. "Here. Courtesy of all those hot-blooded little fans out there, standing in line to buy the next best-selling thriller from that master of chills—yours truly, Trev the Ripper."

Trevor did look a good deal thinner, Damon thought, and he seemed to have abandoned the rock-star look. His hair was trimmed, and he wore an expensive-looking silk sport coat over an open-collared shirt. Put on the designer sunglasses, and welcome to Miami. Wealth evidently agreed with Nordgren.

"You're looking fit these days," Harrington observed between sniffles. Damon himself was worrying about a distinct mid-thirties bulge, discovered when he shopped for a new sport coat for the trip. He was considering taking up jogging.

"Cutting down on my drinking." Nordgren cut some more lines. "I was knocking back two or three fifths a day and chasing it with a case or so of brew."

"Surprised you could write like that." Privately, Harrington had thought *The Etching* little more than a

200,000-word rewrite of *The Picture of Dorian Gray*, served up with enough sex and gore to keep a twentieth-century reader turning the pages.

"Coke's been my salvation. I feel better. I write better. It's all that psychic energy I'm drawing in from all those millions of readers out there."

"Are you still on about that?" Damon finished his lines. "Can't say I've absorbed any energy from my dozens of fans."

"It's exponential," Nordgren explained, sifting busily. "You ought to try to reach the greater audience, instead of catering to the cape-and-pimples set. You're getting labeled as a thud-and-blunder hack, and as long as publishers can buy you for a few grand a book, that's all they'll ever see in you."

Damon was stoned enough not to take offense. "Yeah, well, tell that to Helen. She's been trying to peddle a collection of my fantasy stories for the last couple years."

"Are these some of the ones you were writing for *Cavalier* and so on? Christ, I'll have to ask her to show me a copy. You were doing some good stuff back then."

"And pumping gas."

"Hey, your time is coming, baby. Just think about what I've said. You wrote a couple of nice horror stories a few years back. Take a shot at a novel."

"If I did, the horror fad would have peaked and passed."

The phone rang. The con chairman wanted them to come down for the official opening ceremonies. Nordgren laid out a couple monster lines to get them primed, and they left to greet their public.

Later that evening Nordgren made friends with an energetic blonde from the local fan group, who promised to show him the sights of New Orleans. When it appeared that most of these sights were for Trevor's eyes only, Damon wandered off with a couple of the local S.C.A. bunch to explore the fleshpots and low dives of the French Quarter.

Soon after, much to Harrington's amazement, Warwick Books bought his short-story collection, *Dark Dreams*. They had rejected it a year before, but now Trevor Nordgren had written a twenty-page introduction to the book. Helen as much as admitted that Warwick had taken the collection only after some heavy pressure from Nordgren.

As it was, *Dark Dreams* came out uniformly packaged with Warwick's much-heralded Trevor Nordgren reprint series. *TREVOR NORDGREN Introduces* got Nordgren's name across the cover in letters twice the size of Harrington's name, and only a second glance would indicate that the book was anything other than the latest Trevor Nordgren novel. But *Dark Dreams* was the first of Harrington's books ever to go into a second printing, and Damon tore up the several letters of protest he composed.

He was astonished by Nordgren's versatility. The Warwick package included a new, expanded edition of *Time's Wanton*, a reprint of *Acid Test* (with a long, nostalgic introduction), a collection of Nordgren's early short fiction entitled *Electric Dreams* (with accompanying introductions by the author), as well as *Doors of Perception* and *Younger Than Yesterday*— two anthologies of essays and criticism selected from Nordgren's writings for the *Chicago Seed, East Village Other, Berkeley Barb*, and other underground newspapers of the '60s.

Nordgren had by now gathered a dedicated cult following, in addition to the millions who snapped up his books from the checkout-counter racks. Virtually any publication with a vintage Trevor Nordgren item in its pages began to command top collectors' prices, Harrington noticed upon browsing through the hucksters' room at the occasional conventions he attended. Trevor Nordgren had become the subject of interviews, articles, and critical essays in everything from mimeographed fanzines to *People* to *Time*. Harrington was amused to find a Trevor Nordgren interview headlining one of the men's magazines that used to reject stories from them both.

Warwick was delighted with sales figures from the Trevor Nordgren Retrospective, as the reprint package was now dignified, and proudly announced the purchase of five additional titles—two new collections of his short fiction and expanded revisions of his other three Essex House novels. In addition (and in conjunction with McGinnis & Parry as part of a complicated contractual buy-out), Nordgren was to edit an anthology of his favorite horror stories (*Trevor Nordgren Presents*) and would prepare a nonfiction book discussing his personal opinions and theories of horror as a popular genre (*The View Through The Glass Darkly*).

The Max de Lawrence film of *The Rending* grossed $60 million in its first summer of release, and *The Etching* was still on the paperback top ten lists when *The Dwelling* topped the best-seller charts in its first week. Nordgren's latest concerned a huge Victorian castle in a small New England town; presumably the mansion was haunted, but Nordgren's twist was that the mansion had a life of its own and was itself haunting the community. The idea was good for a quarter of a million words, several million dollars, and a complete tax write-off of the huge Victorian castle on the Hudson that Nordgren had refurbished and moved into.

Julie Kriegman was fired by the new corporate owners of Summit Books, and the new editor called Krystel Firewind sexist trash and killed the series with #5. Helen Hohenstein broke the news to Harrington somewhat more gently.

"At least Summit paid you."

Damon's only immediate consolation was that the call was on Helen's dime. "Can we sell the series someplace else, or do I wrap sandwiches with the first draft of #6?" Thank God he hadn't sprung for that word processor Nordgren had urged upon him.

"It doesn't look good. Problem is that every paperback house that wants to already has one or two swords-and-sorcery series going. Do you think you could write high fantasy? That's getting to be big just now. You know—lighten up a little on the violence and bare tits, give your imaginary world more of a fairy-tale atmosphere, maybe link in a bunch of Celtic myths and that sort of thing."

"I can try it." Harrington imagined Krystel Firewind stripped of sword and armor and a few inches of bustline, gowned in shimmering damask or maybe flowing priestess' robes.

"Great! Keep this to yourself for now, but Columbine has hired Alberta Dawson away from Warwick to be their senior editor and try to rejuvenate their paperback line. She's looking for new material, and she owes me. So get me some chapters and a prospectus soonest. OK?"

"Will do."

"Oh—and Damon. Plan this as a trilogy, could you?"

Harrington read over a few popular works on Celtic mythology and ancient European history to get some names and plot ideas, then started the rewrite of

Krystel Firewind #6. This he was able to flesh out into a trilogy without much difficulty by basing his overall theme on the struggle of Roman Britain against the Saxon invasions. After her sex change from Desmond Killstar, it was simple enough to transform Krystel Firewind into a half-elfin Druidic priestess. All that was needed was to change names, plug in his characters, and toss in a little magic.

Alberta Dawson was delighted with *Tallyssa's Quest: Book One of The Fall of the Golden Isles*. She agreed to a contract for the entire trilogy, and confided to Hohenstein that she'd sensed all along that Damon Harrington was a major literary talent. *Tallyssa's Quest* was launched with a major promotional campaign, complete with dump bins and color posters of the book's cover. The cover, a wraparound by some Italian artist, was a rather ethereal thing depicting a billowingly berobed Tallyssa astride her flying unicorn and brandishing her Star of Life amulet to defend her elfin companions from a horde of bestial Kralkings. Harrington would much rather the cover hadn't billed him as "The New Tolkien," but Columbine had paid him his first five-figure advance.

Nordgren phoned him up at two in the morning, coked out of his skull, and razzed him about it mercilessly. Trevor was just coming out of a messy paternity suit involving a minor he'd shacked up with at some convention, so Damon gave him an hour of his patience. Since *Tallyssa's Quest* had gone into a third printing in its first month, Harrington was not to be baited.

When *The Dwelling* premiered as a television miniseries, Nordgren was a guest on *The Tonight Show*. He was obviously wired and kept breaking up the audience with his off-the-wall responses to the standard where-do-you-get-your-ideas sort of questions. Trevor had taken to smoking a pipe, perhaps to keep his hands from shaking, and the designer sunglasses were *de rigueur*. Damon was startled to see how much weight he'd lost. Nordgren managed to get in enough plugs for his new opus, *The Coming*, to have qualified as a paid political announcement. Harrington had skimmed an advance copy of the thing—it appeared to be a 300,000-word rewrite of Lovecraft's "The Outsider"—and had pondered the dangers of mixing cocaine and word processors.

There was a major problem with crowd control at the World Science Fiction Convention in Minneapolis, so they were forced to abandon their tradition of signing books together. The con committee had had to set a special room aside just for Trevor Nordgren. At one point a news reporter counted over seven hundred fifty fans standing in line to enter the signing room, many with shopping bags filled with Trevor Nordgren books and magazine appearances. Con committee members tried in vain to enforce the one-person-one-autograph rule, and a near-riot broke out when uniformed hotel security guards finally escorted Nordgren to his suite after two and a half hours of signing books. Nordgren placated them by promising to set up a second autographing session the next day.

Something that looked like an ex-linebacker in a three-piece suit greeted Harrington when he knocked on the door of Nordgren's suite. After all the Hammett and Chandler he'd read, Damon felt cheated that he couldn't see the bulge of a roscoe beneath the polyester, but he surmised one was there.

"Damon Harrington to see Mr. Nordgren," he said to the stony face, feeling very much like a character in a Chandler novel. He wished he had a fedora to doff.

"That's OK, John. He's a lodge brother."

Evidently Nordgren was unscarred by last year's lawsuit, since neither of the girls who were cutting lines on the glass-topped table could have been as old as Trevor, even if they could have combined their two ages. Nordgren had lately taken to wearing his hair slicked and combed straight back, and he reminded Harrington of a dissolute Helmut Berger posing for a men's fashion spread in *Esquire*.

"After meeting your bodyguard there, I fully expected to find you seated in a wheelchair, wearing a silk dressing robe, and smoking Russian cigarettes through a long amber holder."

"Melody. Heather. Meet my esteemed friend and drinking buddy, Damon Harrington. Damon, join us."

"Weren't you in *Apocalypse Now*?" one of them asked brightly.

"Quite right," Nordgren assured her. "And turn a deaf ear when he promises to get you a role in his next film."

They were almost certain Nordgren was kidding them, but not quite, and kept a speculative watch on Damon.

"The big party isn't until later tonight," Nordgren said, handing him the tooter, "but I felt I must unwind after sustaining terminal writer's cramp from all those autographs. Why not get a good buzz with us now, then rejoin the party after ten?"

"Can't see how you can go through all that."

"All that psychic energy, baby."

"All that money, you mean."

"A little PR never hurt anyone. Speaking of which, Damon—I noticed quite a number of little darlings decked out in flowing bedsheets and pointed ears and carrying about boxed sets of *The Fall of the Golden Isles* in ardent quest of your signature. Is rumor true that Columbine has just sprung for a second trilogy in the series?''

"Helen has just about got them to agree to our terms."

"Christ, Damon! We're better than this shit!" Nordgren banged his fist on the table and sent half a gram onto the carpet. One of the girls started to go after it, but Trevor shook his head and muttered that he bought it by the kilo.

"You don't look particularly ready to go back to the good old days of three cents a word on publication," Damon suggested.

"And paying the bills with those wonderful thousand-dollar checks from Bee Line for 60,000 words worth of wet dreams. Did I tell you that a kid came up to me with a copy of *Stud Road* to sign, and he'd paid some huckster a hundred and fifty dollars for the thing!"

Damon almost choked on his line. "Remind me to put my copy of *Time's Wanton* in a safe-deposit box. Christ, Trevor—you've got enough money from all this to write anything you damn well please."

"But we somehow write what the public wants from us instead. Or do you get off by being followed about by teenage fans in farcical medieval drag with plastic pointy ears and begging to know whether Wyndlunne the Fey is going to be rescued from Grimdooms's Black Tower in *Book Four of The Trilogy of Trilogies*?"

"We both have our fans," Damon said pointedly. "And what dire horrors lie in wait for some small suburban community in *your* next mega-word chart-buster?"

"Elves," said Nordgren.

\*    \*    \*

The last time that Damon Harrington saw Trevor Nordgren was at the World Fantasy Convention in Miami. Because of crowd problems, Nordgren had stopped going to cons, but a Guest of Honor invitation lured him forth from his castle on the Hudson. He had avoided such public appearances for over a year, and there were lurid rumors of nervous breakdown, alcoholism, drug addiction, or possibly AIDS.

*The Changeling*, Nordgren's latest and biggest, concerned an evil race of elves who lurked in hidden dens beneath a small suburban community, and who were systematically exchanging elfin babies for the town's human infants. *The Changeling* was dedicated to Damon Harrington—"in remembrance of styrofoam boaters." The novel dominated the best-seller lists for six months, before finally being nudged from first place by *The Return of Tallyssa: Book Six of The Fall of the Golden Isles*.

Harrington squeezed onto an elevator already packed with fans. A chubby teenager in a *Spock Lives!* t-shirt was complaining in an uncouth New York accent: "So I ran up to him when the limo pulled up, and I said to him 'Mr. Nordgren, would you please sign my copy of *The Changeling*,' and he said 'I'd love to, sweetheart, but I don't have the time,' and I said 'But it's just this one book,' and he said 'If I stop for you, there are twenty invisible fans lined up behind you right now with their books,' and I thought 'You conceited turkey and after I've read every one of your books!' "

The elevator door opened on her floor, and she and most of her sympathetic audience got off. As the door closed, Harrington caught an exclamation: "Hey, wasn't that . . . ?"

A hotel security guard stopped him as he entered

the hallway toward his room, and Harrington had to show him his room key and explain that he had the suite opposite Trevor Nordgren's. The guard was scrupulously polite, and explained that earlier fans had been lining up outside Nordgren's door with armloads of books. Damon then understood why the hotel desk had asked if he minded having a free drink in the lounge until they had prepared his suite after some minor vandalism wrought by the previous guests.

A bell captain appeared with his baggage finally, and then room service stocked his bar. Harrington unpacked a few things, then phoned Nordgren's suite. A not-very-friendly male voice answered, and refused to do more than take a message. Harrington asked him to tell Mr. Nordgren that Mike Hunt wished to have a drink with him in the suite opposite. Thirty seconds later Nordgren was kicking at his door.

"Gee, Mr. Hunt!" Nordgren gushed in falsetto. "Would you please sign my copy of *The Other Woman*? Huh? Huh? Would you?"

He looked terrible. He was far thinner than when they'd first met, and his skin seemed to hang loose and pallid over his shrunken flesh—reminding Harrington of a snake about to shed its skin. His blue eyes seemed too large for his sallow face, and their familiar arrogance was shadowed by a noticeable haunted look. Harrington thought of some *fin-de-siècle* poet dying of consumption.

"Jack Daniel's, as usual? Or would you like a Heineken?"

"I'd like just some Perrier water, if you have it there. Cutting down on my vices."

"Sure thing." Damon thought about the rumors. "Hey, brought along some pearl that you won't believe!"

"I'll taste a line of it, then," Nordgren brightened,

allowing Damon to bring him his glass of Perrier. "Been a while since I've done any toot. Decided I didn't need a teflon septum."

When Nordgren actually did take only one line, Harrington began to get concerned. He fiddled with his glass of Jack Daniel's, then managed, "Trevor, I'm only asking as an old friend—but are you all right?"

"Flight down tired me out, that's all. Got to save up my energy for that signing thing tonight."

Damon spent undue attention upon cutting fresh lines. "Yeah, well. I mean, you look a little thin, is all."

Instead of taking offense, Trevor seemed wearily amused. "No, I'm not strung out on coke or smack or uppers or downers or any and all drugs. No, I don't have cancer or some horrid wasting disease. Thank you for your concern."

"Didn't mean to pry." Damon was embarrassed. "Just concerned, is all."

"Thanks, Damon. But I'm off the booze and drugs, and I've had a complete check up. Frankly, I've been burning the old candle at both ends and in the middle for too long. I'm exhausted body and soul, and I'm planning on treating myself to a long R&R while the royalties roll in."

"Super! Why not plan on spending a couple weeks knocking around down on the coast with me, then? We'll go down to Ensenada."

A flash of Nordgren's bitter humor returned. "Well, I'd sure like to, young feller," he rasped. "But I figger on writin' me one last big book—just one last book. Then I'll take all the money I got put aside, and buy me a little spread down in Texas—hang up my word processor and settle down to raise cattle. Just this one last book is all I need."

\* \* \*

The signing party was a complete disaster. The con committee hadn't counted on Nordgren's public and simply put him at a table in the hotel ballroom with the rest of the numerous pros in attendance. The ballroom was totally swamped by Nordgren's fans— many from the Miami area who forced their way into the hotel without registering for the convention. Attempts to control the crowd led to several scuffles; the hotel overreacted and ordered security to clear the ballroom, and numerous fights and acts of vandalism followed before order could be restored. Nordgren was escorted to his suite, where a state of siege existed.

Completely sickened by the disgusting spectacle, Harrington afterward retreated to the Columbine Books party, where he was thoroughly lionized, and where he discovered an astonishing number of fellow writers who had known all along that he had the stuff of genius in him, and who were overjoyed that one of their comrades who had paid his dues at last was rewarded with the overdue recognition and prosperity he so deserved. Harrington decided to get knee-walking, commode-hugging drunk, but he was still able to walk, assisted by the wall, when he finally left the party.

Standing with the other sardines awaiting to be packed into the elevator, Harrington listened to the nasal whine of the acne farm with the shopping bag full of books who had just pushed in front of him: "So all my friends who couldn't afford to make the trip from Des Moines gave me their books to get him to autograph too, and I promised them I would, and then they announced His Highness would sign only three books for each fan, and *then* they closed the autographing party with me still standing in line and for an hour and a half! I mean, I'm never buying another book by that creep! Nordgren doesn't care shit about his fans!''

"I know!" complained another. "I wrote him an eight-page fan letter, and all I got back was a postcard!''

Harrington managed to get most of the vomit into the shopping bag, and as the crowd cringed away and the elevator door opened, he stumbled inside and made good his escape.

His next memory was of bouncing along the wall of the corridor that led to his room and hearing sounds of a party at full tilt in Nordgren's suite. Harrington was surprised that Trevor had felt up to throwing a party after the debacle earlier that evening, but then mused that old habits died hard, and that a few more drinks were definitely called for after the elevator experience.

The door to Nordgren's suite was open, so Harrington shouldered his way inside. The place was solidly packed with bodies, and Harrington clumsily pushed a route between them, intent on reaching the bar. By the time he was halfway into the party, it struck him that he didn't know any of the people here—somewhat odd in that he and Nordgren generally partied with the same mob of writers and professionals who showed up at the major cons each time. The suite seemed to be packed entirely with fans, and Harrington supposed that they had crashed Nordgren's party, presumably driving the pros into another room or onto the balcony.

Harrington decided the crowd was too intense, the room too claustrophobic. He gave up on reaching the bar and decided to try to find Nordgren and see if he wanted to duck over to his suite for a quick toot and a chance to relax. Peering drunkenly about the crowded room, Harrington noticed for the first time that everyone's attention seemed to be focused toward the center. And there he recognized Nordgren.

"Trevor, my man!" Damon's voice sounded unnaturally loud and clear above the unintelligible murmur of the crowd.

He jostled his way toward Nordgren, beginning to get angry that none of the people seemed inclined to move aside despite his mumbled excuse-me's and sorry's. Nordgren might as well have been mired in quicksand, so tightly ringed in by fans as he was, and only Trevor's height allowed Harrington to spot him. Damon thought he looked awful, far worse than earlier in the day.

Nordgren stretched out his hand to Harrington, and Damon's first thought was that he meant to wave or to shake hands, but suddenly it reminded him more of a drowning victim making one last, hopeless clutching for help. Shoving through to him, Harrington clasped hands.

Nordgren's handgrip felt very loose, with a scaly dryness that made Damon think of the brittle rustle of overlong fingernails. Harrington shook his hand firmly and tried to draw Nordgren toward him so they could speak together. Nordgren's arm broke off at his shoulder like a stick of dry-rotted wood.

For a long breathless moment Harrington just stood there, gaping stupidly, Nordgren's arm still in his grasp, the crowd silent, Nordgren's expression as immobile as that of a crucified Christ. Then, ever so slowly, ever so reluctantly, as if there were too little left to drain, a few dark drops of blood began to trickle from the torn stump of Nordgren's shoulder.

The crowd's eyes began to turn upon Harrington, as Nordgren ever so slowly began to collapse like an unstrung marionette.

\*          \*          \*

Harrington awoke the following noon, sprawled fully dressed across a couch in his own suite. He had a poisonous hangover and shuddered at the reflection of his face in the bathroom mirror. He made himself a breakfast of vitamin pills, aspirin, and Valium, then set about cutting a few wake-up lines to get him through the day.

Harrington was not really surprised to learn that Trevor Nordgren had died in his sleep sometime during the night before. Everyone knew it was a drug overdose, but the medical examiner's report ruled heart failure subsequent to extreme physical exhaustion and chronic substance abuse.

Several of the science fiction news magazines asked Harrington to write an obituary for Trevor Nordgren, but Harrington declined. He similarly declined offers from several fan presses to write a biography or critical survey of Nordgren, or to edit proposed anthologies of Nordgren's uncollected writings, and he declined Warwick's suggestion that he complete Nordgren's final unfinished novel. Martin E. Binkley, in his *Reader's Guide to Trevor Nordgren*, attributed this reticence to "Harrington's longtime love-hate relationship with Nordgren that crystallized into professional jealousy with final rejection."

Damon Harrington no longer attends conventions, nor does he autograph books. He does not answer his mail, and he has had his telephone disconnected.

Columbine Books offered Harrington a fat $1 million advance for a third trilogy in the best-selling *Fall of the Golden Isles* series. When Harrington returned the contract unsigned to Helen Hohenstein, she was able to get Columbine to increase the advance to $1.5 million. Harrington threw the contract into the trash.

In his dreams Harrington still sees the faceless

mass of hungry eyes, eyes turning from their drained victim and gazing now at him. Drugs seem to help a little, and friends have begun to express concern over his health.

The mystery of Damon Harrington's sudden reclusion has excited the imagination of his public. As a consequence, sales of all of his books are presently at an all-time high.

Notes from my commonplace book: Dream dated
2/23/82 A.M.

*Saw [name deleted, and you won't guess—KEW] at
world sf con, struck by how old & worn he looked;
handshake very loose, long-nailed. Thought in dream
of using as story idea: famous sf author frequents
cons for psychic vampirism relationship with adoring
fans. Question becomes: who is actual victim—author
or fans. In dream thought of climax when I break off
author's arm at shoulder as he reaches out for
handshake/help. Like dry-rotted wood; a moment later
blood begins to trickle. Probably not workable for
actual story.*

As it turned out, Robert Weinberg approached me
not long afterward for an original story for the program book for the 1983 World Fantasy Convention in
Chicago. This dream had remained in my mind—the
more so as events at one science fiction convention
after another seemed to reinforce what my subcon-

scious had envisioned. I wrote the story for Weinberg, and despite its minimal distribution "Neither Brute Nor Human" won the British Fantasy Award for best short fiction of 1983. This was the first time any story written for a convention program booklet had ever won any sort of an award, and I was as surprised as anyone concerned.

Bits and pieces of "Neither Brute Nor Human" are autobiographical to an extent. Other bits are from incidents at one convention or another. No particular author or authors are depicted, nor intended to be depicted. Some of this may seem excruciatingly familiar to some of us who write for a living, but that is because some experiences are common to all of us—as any this-happened-to-me bull session among professional writers will attest. At least a dozen writers have pointed to one incident or another in "Neither Brute Nor Human" with all certainty that he or she was the person involved. We share experiences, not always pleasant.

Writers are performers, admit it or not. Some may never personally strut and fret upon the stage, but even the reclusive daydream of applause, be it critical acclaim or best-seller bucks. Egos that demand external reassurance are too often self-destructive. We hate ourselves for needing the roar of the crowd, distrust those who praise us.

On the other hand, I've met very few writers who were forced into this profession at gunpoint.

—Karl Edward Wagner

# SEA CHANGE

## by George Clayton Johnson

The white mists roll in like solid things and bump gently against the tropic coasts. The heavy gulf waters suck at the planking of a small launch that lies at anchor near the shore. Aboard is DOC HOWARD, a thin wisp of a man with a grey complexion and the shaking hands of a chronic drunk. Life hasn't been good to Doc. It has eaten away at his confidence and dignity until only the shell of the man is left. He squints anxiously toward shore and wipes his sweaty palms on his dirty dungarees before taking a quick pull at a pint whiskey bottle. "Come on," he mutters. "What's keeping you?"

There is a shrill squawk and Doc starts up. His eyes swivel wildly to the small cage that hangs from the superstructure near the entrance to the cabin of the boat. In the cage is a brightly colored parrot. Seeing the source of the sound, Doc lets out his pent-up breath. The parrot claws at the cage and clucks noisily.

"Water alive with police cutters and Al ashore with a load of guns and me stuck here with you," mutters Doc. "What do I know about boats and running guns?"

The parrot screams shrilly and Doc wipes at his damp forehead with his sleeve. "Come on, Al. *Come on!*"

He suddenly stiffens. There is the sound of distant rifle fire and a crashing in the brush near the moored boat. Doc leans over the side. "Al?" His voice is a hoarse whisper. "Al? That you?"

Legs churn water and there is a thump against the side of the boat. Assisted by Doc, a figure climbs noisily over the rail onto the deck. This is AL LUCHO, small-time hoodlum. "Get that anchor up!" he commands sharply. "I'll start the engine. Move!"

Doc casts him a frightened look and leaps for the anchor chain. With the aid of a small winch he begins to pull anchor. The chain piles up on the deck as the anchor rises.

The engine bursts to life and the launch begins to pull away from the shore. Over the sounds of the engine we hear several rifle shots and small ugly holes appear in the side of the boat above the waterline.

The parrot squawks loudly as the rifle fire grows distant.

The craft safely underway, their pursuers left behind, Al locks the wheel in position and comes on deck. He sees the parrot in its cage and a wide smile breaks over his pinched face. He chuckles. "What's the matter, Conchita? Things get too rough for you?" He sticks his finger through the wire bars of the cage and strokes the parrot's head. It slashes at his finger. He jerks his hand back and puts the injured finger in his mouth. Doc joins him. "One of these days that bird is going to take that finger off you. Ever hear of parrot fever?"

Al spins to face him, his face ugly. "She's my bird, ain't she?"

Doc becomes conciliatory. "Sure, Al. Sure."

"I want to let her bite me it's my business. I been bit before and it always healed fast enough."

As Doc turns away, Al reaches out and grabs him. He looks at Doc's trembling hands. He leans forward suspiciously and sniffs Doc's breath.

"Now Al . . ."

"You been at the bottle again!"

"It was just a little one, Al."

"I risk my neck leaving you here to cover for me and you hit the bottle the minute I'm out of sight." He cuffs Doc roughly and shoves him against the rail. "Where's the bottle?"

"Please, Al . . ."

He twists Doc's arm. "Come on, Rumdum. . . . *Where?*"

Doc cries out in pain and gestures toward a pile of rope. Al shoves him aside, finds the bottle and raises his arm to throw it over the side.

Doc is abject. "Please, Al. You know how I get when I need a drink. . . ."

Al looks at him contemptuously. "Suffer!" he says harshly. He flings the bottle into the mist. Ignoring Doc who clings weakly to the rail, he goes to the parrot's cage. "See what I'm saddled with, Conchita? A human sponge. He smells the cork of a bottle and he comes apart. I'm lucky the boat was waiting at all."

Talking to the parrot seems to cheer him somewhat. He grins a gargoyle grin and begins to play with the bird. He purses his lips and makes cooing, clucking sounds. Carefully he pets the brightly colored head and is delighted when the bird suffers his attentions.

Doc raises his head and watches Al fooling with the bird. "Al . . . ?" he says softly.

"Yeah? What do *you* want?"

Doc's voice has a slight whine to it. "Did you get the money?"

Al's laugh has no humor in it. "See what I mean, Conchita? A boozehound with no guts but he's ready at the payoff." He mimics Doc's voice: " *'Did you get the money, Al?'* You want a laugh, Conchita? He may look like a human whiskey bottle to you, but our brave partner here used to be a doctor. Yeah. A regular doc with a white coat. To hear him tell it he was a regular Mayo Clinic until he started drinking up the medicinal alcohol."

His tone has turned ugly and now he shifts languidly to face Doc. Concealed by the movement of his body, his hand curls around a marlinspike racked near the rail.

As he takes a step forward, Doc sees the weapon and draws back apprehensively.

"The way I figure it, Rumdum, you're more of a liability than a asset. Why should I split with you? It was me that located the guns and set up the deal."

Doc scrambles toward the fantail of the boat, stalked by Al. "Please . . . Al, please . . ." He is brought up sharply by the rail at the fantail. He is trapped. The screws churn the seawater to a white froth as Doc looks down.

Al smiles murderously and lunges forward, the spike raised to strike. Doc covers his head with his arms and dodges to the side. His legs make contact with the anchor-release lever.

With a loud rattle the chain begins to pay out, whipping the deck like a great iron snake. Carried by his own momentum, unable to stop, Al is hit by the chain and loses his balance. His arms flail out as he

goes down. He screams as the moving chain catches
him and slams him against the gunwale. He screams
again.

Shocked, Doc looks at Al on the deck.

Al writhes from side to side, his arm cradled against
his chest. "My hand!" he shrieks. "My hand!"

Doc edges forward fearfully and sucks in his breath
at what he sees. His face goes pale. "Oh, my God!"

"My hand, it hurts!"

"You haven't got a hand anymore, Al. The chain
took it off."

Al's eyes glaze. "No! . . . *No!*" He collapses on
the deck.

For a long moment, Doc looks at the still form at
his feet. The parrot claws the cage and squawks
shrilly.

"You tried to kill me, Al. If I was half smart I'd
put you over the side. You're an animal. A savage.
I've never heard you give anybody a kind word. You
like hurting people. You hate everyone and everything. You haven't a single redeeming feature unless
it's the way you feel about that ugly bird. Only—
only I can't do it. What you said a while ago is true.
I was a doctor. Not a very good one maybe but it
was my job to save lives, not to take them. You
wouldn't understand that, would you, Al?"

The parrot screams harshly as Doc begins to drag
Al toward the cabin. Once inside the tiny compartment he levers Al onto the single cot. He rummages
underneath and brings out a black bag full of shiny
instruments, bottles and instruments. He fumbles in
the bottom of the bag and takes out a pint whiskey
bottle, breaks the seal, takes a healthy belt and recaps
the bottle. He goes through Al's pockets and takes
the thick wad of money and puts it in his own jacket
pocket. He takes a hypo from the bag, fills it from

one of the small bottles and injects it in Al's arm before setting to the job of cleaning and bandaging. When Al is resting easily, Doc goes topside. For a time he looks off at the shifting mist that obscures the water from view. He listens to the drum of the engines and, after a time, he sleeps.

Time passes. How long it has been Doc doesn't know. Something wakens him. He sits up quickly and looks about him. He sees nothing. He listens. Only the sound of engines, water and the screams of the parrot. Doc blinks his eyes. He rises and goes forward to have a look at Al. As he bends over the still form on the bed, Al opens his eyes.

"Easy," says Doc. "You haven't got a right hand anymore, but if you take care of yourself till we get to shore you'll be all right."

As he pulls back the blanket to have a look his face goes pale. A look of horror comes into his eyes.

"What is it?" asks Al, fearfully.

Doc's voice is full of shocked disbelief. "Your hand . . ."

Al tries to raise up.

"It's impossible!" says Doc, huskily. "Your hand. It's grown back!"

And so it has.

Except for a light white line around Al's right wrist, his hands are whole and perfect. The two men look at each other with shocked amazement.

A miracle has happened and Doc is slow to recover from his wonderment. He examines the hand. "Flex your fingers."

Al, not quite comprehending what is going on, does as he is told.

"Fantastic," says Doc. "I saw it severed myself. I trimmed the flesh and put on the bandage."

Al has never seen Doc like this before. "Maybe you were seeing things. They say that's what the juice does to you when you drink too much of it."

"I know what I saw," says Doc. "When you came at me with that marlinspike . . ." He breaks off, remembering that Al has tried to kill him. Al stirs uncomfortably. But now Doc's attention is centered on this fantastic thing that has happened. "Look," he says. "This has never happened before in medical history. There are certain worms that have the ability to regrow lost portions of themselves. You can cut one of them in two pieces and each piece will become a separate worm. It is called regeneration. Certain forms of marine life have it but never a human." He looks at Al wildly. "Do you know what this means? Do you know what a secret like this is worth?"

At the mention of money, Al becomes attentive.

"If this thing could be isolated—if it could be reduced to formula and synthesized—it would be worth a fortune. The man who could grow back arms and legs and fingers could name his own price."

"What are you getting at, Doc?"

"Somewhere inside your blood or your genes is a secret. The man who pries it loose will make medical history. I could be that man."

"Now wait a minute . . ."

"I could take samples of your blood and run a series of tests—and if it isn't in the blood—"

"If you think I'm going to let a rumdum like you stick knives in me you're out of your mind."

Doc is fired by his vision. He can see himself dressed in white, surrounded by admiring medical men. A man to command respect and awe. "You would have killed me if it wasn't for the anchor chain. I saved your life. You were bleeding to death. You owe it to me.''

''I owe you nothing.'' He raises himself up on the cot and puts his hand in the pocket that held the money. It is gone. ''The money—it was in my pocket. . . .'' His voice takes on a dangerous edge.

But Doc is beyond caring about the money or Al's anger. He sees his future slipping away from him. ''Forget about the money,'' he cries. ''This is more important than money. I want to experiment . . .''

Al begins to get off the cot. ''You want to get Al Lucho on a table so you can cut his throat. Is that it? You want to cut him up and make serum out of him?''

And now Doc knows that he has lost, that Al has no intention of cooperating in his schemes. His hand closes over a club-length of wood lying on a ledge in the cabin. ''But Al . . . You've got to let me—I won't let you refuse. You've got no right . . .'' Hysterically he swings the club at Al, who wards off the blow, and then Al is upon him. He grabs Doc by the throat and slams him against the bulkhead. He begins to squeeze. Doc claws at the fingers and writhes weakly.

Suddenly there is a sound on deck. A heavy sound like stumbling footsteps. Al becomes rigid, listening. ''What was that?'' His fingers loosen slightly. He cocks his head. ''It sounded like someone out there.''

Doc wrenches free from the choking fingers. He gasps for air, sobbing. Again the sound of dragging footsteps. Doc's eyes flick from side to side. He looks at Al with sudden horror. ''The hand!'' he says. ''What happened to the hand?''

''What are you talking about?''

''Remember what I told you about the worms?

How you can cut one in two and each part grows into a separate worm?''

''I don't—''

''Two pieces . . . two worms. Don't you see?''

And now Al understands what Doc is getting at. He doesn't want to believe what Doc is telling him.

Doc takes advantage of Al's momentary confusion. His eyes go to the slim scalpel that lies on the built-in table by the cot. He continues to talk as he edges toward the knife. ''The hand, Al. It was caught in the anchor chain. It's out there on the deck somewhere, the bilges maybe, washed by seawater. You've never looked at seawater through a microscope but I have. It's aswarm with microbes and bacteria. It's like a rich soup filled with living things.''

He has Al going now, and he is much closer to the knife. His hand trembles above it, his fingers reaching. ''Can you picture it lying there, taking substance from the sea? Growing? Changing? You take one worm and cut him in two parts and he becomes two worms. You were cut in two parts, Al, and one of the parts grew a hand.''

''No! It's impossible. . . .''

''What did the other part grow, Al?''

''Shut up!''

''What's out there on the deck, Al?''

But now Doc has gone too far. In his great terror, Al whirls on him. He sees Doc's fingers closing about the knife and lets out a yell. He jumps forward and for a few frantic moments they are fighting for the knife. Al, the stronger, wins out. He wrests the scalpel from Doc and plunges it downward. Doc collapses with a groan.

Al breathes heavily, looking down at Doc's body. Then he raises his head, nostrils quivering. He hears the strange stumbling sound again.

Holding the knife he goes to the door of the cabin and peers into the darkness. Nothing. He opens the door cautiously and edges through it with the knife in front of him. He takes two stealthy steps, listening intently.

Suddenly a hand comes out of the blackness and clamps onto his shoulder. He gasps and whirls. Before him is a figure in darkness, a huge hulking figure clothed in a dark loose raincoat. An involuntary cry bursts from Al's lips as he sees the figure's face. It is himself. His eyes and lips and bone structure. But it is not quite the same. There is an unfinished quality about the face, as though done by a hasty sculptor who missed some essential character lines.

Stunned, paralyzed with fright, Al backs away clumsily. He has forgotten the knife in his hand as the figure moves after him. Its hands are like loose claws. Al feels the rail against his back and then it gives way and he feels himself falling, falling. Then, there is blackness.

The figure turns away from the rail. It enters the cabin and removes the bundle of money from Doc's pocket. It carries Doc's body on deck and dumps him over the rail. It chuckles evilly and begins to thumb through the bills.

There is a shrill cry and the figure looks up. The parrot, Conchita, claws its way about the interior of the cage. A snarl crosses the figure's face. It wrenches the cage free from its moorings, raises it high and casts it into the darkness. It smiles then, and goes forward to steer the boat toward a distant port.

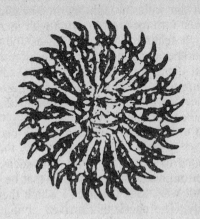

When "Sea Change" was written my wife Lola and I were going through desperate times. I stayed at it because this time, at least, I had a place to send it when it was done—and that couldn't be soon enough.

The year was 1960. I had long since quit my job as a design draftsman and had cast us both adrift after five years of making timely payments on our GI home in peaceful Pacoima. But now I had a shot. After submitting stuff to magazines with dwindling hope, I had begun at last to sell stories to *The Twilight Zone* television series for Rod Serling to adapt.

"All of Us Are Dying" was the first, retitled "Rubberface" by my agent at the time, Jay Richards.

It was bought with frightening quickness by Buck Houghton, the producer of the series. A story of a scheming man, Far Out Johnny Foster, who can miraculously change his identity, it was told with tilt-shots, restructured and greatly added to by Serling, who retitled it "The Four of Us Are Dying."

The second story, written with Rod in mind and also snapped up by Buck, was "Execution," a moody tale of a savage killer brought by time machine out of the Old West into modern America with its noise and confusion. It featured Albert Salmi as Joe Caswell, and was another example of Rod's fashioning a story of his own using mine as an armature, adding elements to improve the balance, condensing or eliminating others in a true collaboration—with Rod, of course, calling the final shots.

It began to seem that Rod and I were becoming a team.

I continued to sift through my story ideas, searching for that ominous, surreal quality that he savored.

The result was "Sea Change," which they bought immediately. The check that arrived giving Rod the right to adapt it for his show was greeted with gladness in our home, where it cast its warm glow in the darkness.

Three in a row—I could feel doors, long closed, opening.

The following week I got an unexpected personal telephone call from Rod. Before that time I had dealt mainly with Buck Houghton, a tough customer indeed, who was the first screen between me and Rod and who skillfully shot down a number of ideas for every one he passed on for Rod to consider.

"It's about the story, 'Sea Change,' " he says to me in the night. It seems that his sponsor, General Foods, put thumbs down on the story because, he says they said, it was too "grisly." They were, he says they said, after all a food company, and they didn't think that hacking a man's arm off on network TV at dinnertime was the image they cared to be associated with.

"Too bad," says Rod over the phone, but since he can't use the story on the show and though both of us think the story is "dandy" there is no _____ point in his being stuck with the story when he can't use it. Will I buy it back?

I pondered the depths of his question, wondering whether there was any reason he should be stuck with the story when he couldn't use it and, freezing inside because I'd already spent the money, I told him yes, I'd buy it back. Which I did.

I put the story away in a trunk and went on to write more material for *The Twilight Zone* and other television shows. Many years passed. One day my daughter Judy, who was helping me assemble a book of short stories, read it for the collection and thought I should send it out. She felt it was not out of date.

As luck would have it *Rod Serling's The Twilight Zone Magazine* soon emerged on the scene with Carol Serling, Rod's widow, as co-publisher. It seemed fitting that I submit the story to T.E.D. Klein, the editor, who quickly bought it. It has since been reprinted in *The Best of Rod Serling's The Twilight Zone Magazine*, *Gallery* and *Night Cry*. *Masters of Darkness* is its first book publication.

—George Clayton Johnson

# TEETH MARKS

## by Edward Bryant

My favorite vantage has always been the circular
window at the end of the playroom. It is cut from
the old-fashioned glass installed by Frank Alessi's father. As a young man, he built this house with his
own hands. The slight distortions in the pane create
a rainbow sheen when the light is proper. I enjoy the
view so much more than those seen through the
standard rectangular windows on the other floors,
their panes regularly smashed by the enthusiasms of
the younger Alessis through the years and duly replaced. The circular window is set halfway between
the hardwood floor and the peak of the gabled ceiling, low enough that I can watch the outside world
from a chair.

Watching window scenes with slight distortions
and enhanced colors satisfies my need for stimula-
tion, since I don't read, nor go out to films, nor do I
ever turn on the cold television console in the study.
Sometimes I see jays quarreling with magpies, robins
descending for meals on the unkempt lawn, ducks in
the autumn and spring. I see the clouds form and roil

through a series of shapes. The scene is hardly static, though it might seem such to a less patient observer. Patience must be my most obvious virtue, fixed here as I am on this eternal cutting edge of the present.

I possess my minor powers, but complete fore-knowledge is not numbered among them. Long since having taken up residence here, I've explored the dimensions of the house. Now I spend the bulk of my time in what I consider the most comfortable room in the house. I haunt the old-fashioned circular window, and I wait.

Frank Alessi took a certain bitter pleasure in driving his own car. All the years he'd had a staff and driver, he had forgotten the autonomous freedoms of the road. The feel of the wheel in his hands was a little heady. Anytime he wanted, anytime at all, he could twist the steering wheel a few degrees and direct the Ford into the path of a Trailways bus or a logging truck. It was his decision, reaffirmed from minute to minute on the winding mountain highway, his alone. He glanced at the girl beside him, not hearing what she was saying. She wouldn't be smiling so animatedly if she knew he was chilling his mind with an image of impalement on a bridge railing.

Her name was Sally Lakey, and he couldn't help thinking of her as a girl even though she'd told him at least three times that she had celebrated her twentieth birthday the week before.

". . . *that* Alessi?" she said.

He nodded and half-smiled.

"Yeah, really?" She cocked her head like some tropical bird and stared from large dark eyes.

Alessi nodded again and didn't smile.

"That's really something. Yeah, I recognize you

from the papers now. You're you." She giggled. "I even saw you last spring. In the campaign."

"The campaign," he repeated.

Lakey said apologetically, "Well, actually I didn't watch you much. What it comes down to is that I'm pretty apolitical—you know?"

Alessi forced another half-smile. "I could have used your vote."

"I wasn't registered."

Alessi shrugged mentally and returned his attention to the awesome drop-off that tugged at the car on Lakey's side. Gravel and raw rock gave way to forest and then to valley floor. Much of the valley was cleared and quilted with irrigated squares. It's a much tamer country than when I left, Alessi thought.

"I'm really sorry I didn't vote."

"What?" Distracted, Alessi swerved slightly to avoid two fist-sized rocks that had rolled onto the right-hand lane probably during the night.

"I think you're a nice man. I said I'm sorry I didn't vote."

"It's a little late for that." Alessi envenomed the words. He heard the tone of pettiness, recognized it, said the words anyway.

"Don't blame me, Mr. Alessi," she said. "Really, I'm not stupid. You can't blame me for losing . . . Senator."

I'm being reproached, he thought, by a dropout, wet-behind-the-ears girl. Me, a fifty-seven-year-old man. A fifty-seven-year-old unemployable. God damn it! The rage he thought he'd exorcised in San Francisco rose up again. He thought the rim of the steering wheel would shatter under his fingers into jagged, slashing shards.

Lakey must have seen something in his eyes. She moved back across the front seat and wedged herself uneasily into the juncture of bench seat and door. "You, uh, all right?"

"Yes," said Alessi. He willed the muscles cording his neck to relax, with little effect. "I am very sorry I snapped at you, Sally."

"It's okay." But she looked dubious of the sincerity of his apology.

They rode in silence for another few miles. She'll talk, thought Alessi. Sooner or later.

Sooner. "How soon?"

"Before we get to the house? Not long. The turnoff's another few miles." And what the hell, he asked himself, are you doing taking a kid little better than a third your age to the half-remembered refuge where you're going to whimper, crawl in and pull the hole in after you? It's perhaps the worst time in your life and you're acting the part of a horny old man. You've known her a grand total of eight hours. No, he answered himself. More than that. She reminds me— He tensed. She asked me if she could come along. Remember? She asked me.

I see the dark blue sedan turn into the semicircular driveway and slide between the pines toward the house. Tires crunch on drifted cones and dead leaves; the crisp sound rises toward me. I stretch to watch as the auto nears the porch and passes below the angle of my sight. The engine dies. I hear a car door slam. Another one. For some reason it had not occurred to me that Frank might bring another person with him.

The equations of the house must be altered.

They stood silently for a while, looking up at the house. It was a large house, set in scale by the towering mountains beyond. Wind hissed in the pine needles; otherwise the only sound was the broken buzz of a logging truck downshifting far below on the highway.

"It's lovely," Lakey said.

"That's the original building." Alessi pointed. "My father put it together in the years before the First World War. The additions were constructed over a period of decades. He built them too."

"It must have twenty rooms."

"Ought to have been a hotel," said Alessi. "Never was. Dad liked baronial space. Some of the rooms are sealed off, never used."

"What's that?" Lakey stabbed a finger at the third floor. "The thing that looks like a porthole."

"Old glass, my favorite window when I was a kid. Behind it is a room that's been used variously as a nursery, playroom and guest room."

Lakey stared at the glass. "I thought I saw something move."

"Probably a tree shadow, or maybe a squirrel's gotten in. It wasn't the caretaker—I phoned ahead last night; he's in bed with his arthritis. Nobody else has been in the house in close to twenty years."

"I did see something," she said stubbornly.

"It isn't haunted."

She looked at him with a serious face. "How do you know?"

"No one ever died in there."

Lakey shivered. "I'm cold."

"We're at seven thousand feet." He took a key from an inside pocket of his coat. "Come in and I'll make a fire."

"'Will you check the house first?"

"Better than that," he said, "*we* will check the house."

\* \* \*

The buzz of voices drifts to the window. I am loath to leave my position behind the glass. Steps, one set heavier, one lighter, sound on the front walk. Time seems suspended as I wait for the sound of a key inserted into the latch. I anticipate the door opening. Not wanting to surprise the pair, I settle back.

Though they explored the old house together, Lakey kept forging ahead as though to assert her courage. Fine, thought Alessi. If there is something lurking in a closet, let it jump out and get *her*. The thought was only whimsical; he was a rational man.

Something did jump out of a closet at her—or at least it seemed to. Lakey opened the door at the far end of a second-floor bedroom and recoiled. A stack of photographs, loose and in albums displaced from precarious balance on the top shelf, cascaded to her feet. A plume of fine dust rose.

"There's always avalanche danger in the mountains," said Alessi.

She stopped coughing. "Very funny." Lakey knelt and picked up a sheaf of pictures. "Your family?"

Alessi studied the photographs over her shoulder. "Family, friends, holidays, vacation shots. Everyone in the family had a camera."

"You too?"

He took the corner of a glossy landscape between thumb and forefinger. "At one time I wanted to be a Stieglitz or a Cartier-Bresson, or even a Mathew Brady. Do you see the fuzz of smoke?"

She examined the photograph closely. "No."

"That's supposed to be a forest fire. I was not a good photographer. Photographs capture the present, and that in turn immediately becomes the past. My father insistently directed me to the future."

Lakey riffled through the pictures and stopped at one portrait. Except for his dress, the man might have doubled for Alessi. His gray hair was cut somewhat more severely than the senator's. He sat stiffly upright behind a wooden desk, staring directly at the camera.

Alessi answered the unspoken question. "My father."

"He looks very distinguished," said Lakey. Her gaze flickered up to meet his. "So do you."

"He wanted something more of a dynasty than what he got. But he tried to mold one; he really did. Every inch a mover and shaker," Alessi said sardonically. "He stayed here in the mountains and raped a fortune."

"Raped?" she said.

"Reaped. Raped. No difference. The timber went for progress and, at the time, nobody objected. My father taught me about power and I learned the lessons well. When he deemed me prepared, he sent me out to amass my own fortune in power—political, not oil or uranium. I went to the legislature and then to Washington. Now I'm home again."

"Home," she said, softening his word. "I think maybe you're leaving out some things." He didn't answer. She stopped at another picture. "Is this your mother?"

"No." He stared at the sharp features for several seconds. "That is Mrs. Norrinssen: an ironbound, more-Swedish-than-thou pagan lady who came out here from someplace in the Dakotas before the Depression. My father hired her to—take care of me in lieu of my mother."

Lakey registered his hesitation, then said uncertainly, "What happened to your mother?"

Alessi silently sorted through the remainder of the

photographs. Toward the bottom of the stack, he found what he was looking for and extracted it. A slender woman, short-haired and of extraordinary beauty, stared past the camera—or perhaps *through* the camera. Her eyes had a distant, unfocused quality. She stood in a stand of dark spruce, her hands folded.

"It's such a moody picture," said Lakey.

The pines loomed above Alessi's mother, conical bodies appearing to converge in the upper portion of the grainy print. "I took that," said Alessi. "She didn't know. It was the last picture anyone took of her."

"She . . . died?"

"Not exactly. I suppose so. No one knows."

"I don't understand," said Lakey.

"She was a brilliant, lonely, unhappy lady," said Alessi. "My father brought her out here from Florida. She hated it. The mountains oppressed her; the winters depressed her. Every year she retreated further into herself. My father tried to bring her out of it, but he treated her like a child. She resisted his pressures. Nothing seemed to work." He lapsed again into silence.

Finally Lakey said, "What happened to her?"

"It was after Mrs. Norrinssen had been here for two years. My mother's emotional state had been steadily deteriorating. Mrs. Norrinssen was the only one who could talk with her, or perhaps the only one with whom my mother would talk. One autumn day—it was in October. My mother got up before everyone else and walked out into the woods. That was that."

"That can't be all," said Lakey. "Didn't anyone look?"

"Of course we looked. My father hired trackers and dogs and the sheriff brought in his searchers.

They trailed her deep into the pine forest and then lost her. They spent weeks. Then the snows increased and they gave up. There's a stone out behind the house in a grove, but no one's buried under it.''

"Jesus," Lakey said softly. She put her arms around Alessi and gave him a slow, warm hug. The rest of the photographs fluttered to the hardwood floor.

I wait, I wait. I see no necessity of movement, not for now. I am patient. No longer do I go to the round window. My vigil is being rewarded. There is no reason to watch the unknowing birds, the forest, the road. The clouds have no message for me today.

I hear footsteps on the stair, and that is message enough.

"Most of the attic," said Alessi, "was converted into a nursery for me. My father always looked forward. He believed in constant renovation. As I became older, the nursery evolved to a playroom, though it was still the room where I slept. After my father died, I moved back here with my family for a few years. This was Connie's room.''

"Your wife or your—''

"Daughter. For whatever reason, she preferred this to all the other rooms.''

They stood just inside the doorway. The playroom extended most of the length of the house. Alessi imagined he could see the straight, carefully crafted lines of construction curving toward one another in perspective. Three dormer windows were spaced evenly along the eastern pitch of the ceiling. The round window allowed light to enter at the far end.

"It's huge," said Lakey.

"It outscales children. It was an adventure to live here. Sometimes it was very easy for me to imagine I was playing in a jungle or on a sea, or across a trackless Arctic waste.''

"Wasn't it scary?"

"My father didn't allow that," said Alessi. Nor did I later on, he thought.

Lakey marveled. "The furnishings are incredible." The canopied bed, the dressers and vanity, the shelves and chairs, all were obviously products of the finest woodcraft. "Not a piece of plastic in all this." She laughed. "I love it." In her denim jeans and Pendleton shirt, she pirouetted. She stopped in front of a set of walnut shelves. "Are the dolls your daughter's?"

Alessi nodded. "My father was not what you would call a liberated man. Connie collected them all during her childhood." He carefully picked up a figure with silk nineteenth-century dress and china head.

Lakey eagerly moved from object to object like a butterfly sampling flowers. "That horse! I always wanted one."

"My father made it for me. It's probably the most exactingly carpentered hobbyhorse made."

Lakey gingerly seated herself on the horse. Her feet barely touched the floor. "It's so big." She rocked back and forth, leaning against the leather reins. Not a joint squeaked.

Alessi said, "He scaled it so it would be a child's horse, not a pony. You might call these training toys for small adults."

The woman let the horse rock to a stop. She dismounted and slowly approached a tubular steel construction. A six-foot horizontal ladder connected the top rungs of two vertical four-foot ladders. "What on earth is this?"

Alessi was silent for a few seconds. "That is a climbing toy for three- and four-year-olds."

"But it's too big," said Lakey. "Too high."

"Not," said Alessi, "with your toes on one rung and your fingers on the next—just barely."

"It's impossible."

Alessi shook his head. "Not quite: just terrifying."

"But why?" she said. "Did you do this for fun?"

"Dad told me to. When I balked, he struck me. When he had to, my father never discounted the effect of force."

Lakey looked disconcerted. She turned away from the skeletal bridge toward a low table shoved back against the wall.

"Once there was a huge map of fairyland on the wall above the table," said Alessi. "Mrs. Norrinssen gave it to me. I can remember the illustrations, the ogres and frost giants and fairy castles. In a rage one night, my father ripped it to pieces."

Lakey knelt before the table so she could look on a level with the stuffed animals. "It's a whole zoo!" She reached out to touch the plush hides.

"More than a zoo," said Alessi. "A complete bestiary. Some of those critters don't exist. See the unicorn on the end?"

Lakey's attention was elsewhere. "The bear," she said, greedily reaching like a small child. "He's beautiful. I had one like him when I was little." She gathered the stuffed bear into her arms and hugged it. The creature was almost half her size. "What's his name? I called mine Bear. Is he yours?"

Alessi nodded. "And my daughter's. His name is Bear too. Mrs. Norrinssen made him."

She traced her fingers along the bear's head, over his ears, down across the snout. Bear's hide was virtually seamless, sewn out of some rich pile fabric. After all the years, Bear's eyes were still black and shiny.

"The eyes came from the same glazier who cut the round window. Good nineteenth-century glass."

"This is wild," said Lakey. She touched the teeth.

"I don't really know whether it was Mrs. Norrinssen's idea or my father's," said Alessi. "A hunter supplied them. They're real. Mrs. Norrinssen drilled small holes toward the back of each tooth; they're secured inside the lining." Bear's mouth was lined with black leather, pliable to Lakey's questing finger. "Don't let him bite you."

"Most bears' mouths are closed," said Lakey.

"Yes."

"It didn't stop my Bear from talking to me."

"Mine didn't have to overcome that barrier." Alessi suddenly listened to what he was saying. Fifty-seven years old. He smiled self-consciously.

They stood silently for a few seconds; Lakey continued to hug the bear. "It's getting dark," she said. The sun had set while they explored the house. The outlines of solid shapes in the playroom had begun to blur with twilight. Doll faces shone almost luminously in the dusk.

"We'll get the luggage out of the car," said Alessi.

"Could I stay up here?"

"You mean tonight?" She nodded. "I see no reason why not," he said. He thought, did I really plan this?

Lakey stepped closer. "What about you?"

I watch them both. Frank Alessi very much resembles his father: distinguished. He looks harried, worn, but that is understandable. Some information I comprehend without knowing why. Some perceptions I don't have to puzzle over. I know what I see.

The woman is in her early twenties. She has mobile features, a smiling, open face. She is quick to react. Her eyes are as dark as her black hair. They dart back and forth in their sockets, her gaze lighting upon nearly everything in the room but rarely dwelling. Her speech is rapid with a hint of eastern nasality. Except for her manner of speaking, she reminds me of a dear memory.

For a moment I see four people standing in the playroom. Two are reflections in the broad, hand-silvered mirror above the vanity across the room. Two people are real. They hesitantly approach each other, a step at a time. Their arms extend, hands touch, fingers plait. Certainly at this time, in this place, they have found each other. The mirror images are inexact, but I think only I see that. The couple in the mirror seem to belong to another time. And, of course, I am there in the mirror too—though no one notices me.

"That's, uh, very gratifying to my ego," said Alessi. "But do you know how old I am?"

Lakey nodded. The semidarkness deepened. "I have some idea."

"I'm old enough to—"

"—be my father. I know." She said lightly, "So?"

"So . . ." He took his hands away from hers. In the early night the dolls seemed to watch them. The shiny button eyes of Bear and the other animals appeared turned toward the human pair.

"Yes," she said. "I think it's a good idea." She took his hand again. "Come on; we'll get the stuff out of the car. It's been a long day."

Day, Alessi thought. Long week, long month, longer campaign. A lifetime. The headlines flashed in his mind, television commentaries replayed. It all stung like acid corroding what had been cold, shining and clean. Old, old, old, like soldiers and gunfighters.

How had he missed being cleanly shot? Enough had seemed to want that. To fade . . . "I *am* a little bushed," he said. He followed Lakey out toward the stairs.

Frank Alessi's father was forceful in his ideal. That lent the foundation to that time and this place. Strength was virtue. "Fair is fair," he would say, but the fairness was all his. Such power takes time to dissipate. Mrs. Norrinssen stood up to that force; everyone else eventually fled.

"Witchy bitch!" he would storm. She only stared back at him from calm, glacial eyes until he sputtered and snorted and came to rest like a great, sulky but now gentled beast. Mrs. Norrinssen was a woman of extraordinary powers and she tapped ancient reserves.

Structure persists. I am part of it. That is my purpose and I cannot turn aside. Now I wait in the newly inhabited house. Again I hear the positive, metallic sounds of automobile doors and a trunk lid opening and closing. I hear the voices and the footsteps and appreciate the human touch they lend.

She stretched slowly. "What time is it?"

"Almost ten," said Alessi.

"I saw you check your watch. I thought you'd be asleep. Not enough exercise?"

She giggled and Alessi was surprised to find the sound did not offend him as it had earlier in the day. He rolled back toward her and lightly kissed her lips. "Plenty of exercise."

"You were really nice."

Fingertips touched his face, exploring cheekbones, mouth-corners, the stubble on the jowl-line. That made him slightly nervous; his body was still tight. Tennis, handball, swimming, it all helped. Reasonably tight. Only slight concessions to slackness. But after all, he *was*— Shut up, he told himself.

"I feel very comfortable with you," she said.

Don't talk, he thought. Don't spoil it.

Lakey pressed close. "Say something."

No.

"Are you nervous?"

"No," Alessi said. "Of course not."

"I guess I did read about the divorce," said Lakey. "It was in a picture magazine in my gynecologist's office."

"There isn't much to say. Marge couldn't take the heat. She got out. I can't blame her." But silently he denied that. The Watergate people—*their* wives had stood by. All the accumulated years . . . Betrayal is so goddamned nasty. Wish her well in Santa Fe?

"Tell me about your daughter," said Lakey.

"Connie—why her?"

"You've talked about everyone else. You haven't said a thing about Connie except to say she slept in this room." She paused. "In this bed?"

"We both did," said Alessi, "at different times."

"The stuff about the divorce didn't really mention her, at least not that I remember. Where is she?"

"I truly don't know."

Lakey's voice sounded peculiar. "She disappeared, uh, just like—"

"No. She left." Silently: she left me. Just like—

"You haven't heard from her? Nothing?"

"Not in several years. It was her choice; we didn't set detectives on her. The last we heard, she was living in the street in some backwater college town in Colorado."

"I mean, you didn't try—"

"It was her choice." She always said I didn't *allow* her any choice, he thought. Maybe. But I tried to handle her as my father handled me. And *I* turned out—

"What was she like?"

Alessi caressed her long smooth hair; static electricity snapped and flashed. "Independent, intelligent, lovely. I suppose fathers tend to be biased."

"How old is she?"

"Connie was about your age when she left." He realized he had answered the question in the past tense.

"You're not so old yourself," said Lakey, touching him strategically. "Not old at all."

Moonlight floods through the dormer panes; beyond the round window I see starlight fleck the sky. I am very quiet, though I need not be. The couple under the quilted coverlet are enthralled in their passion. I cannot question their motives yet. Love? I doubt it. Affection? I would approve of that. Physical attraction, craving for bodily contact, psychic tension?

I move to my window in the end of the playroom, leaving the lovemaking behind. The aesthetics of the bed are not as pleasing as the placid starfield. It may be that I am accustomed to somewhat more stately cycles and pulsings.

Perhaps it is the crowding of the house, the apprehension that more than one human body dwells within it, that causes me now to feel a loneliness. I wonder where Mrs. Norrinssen settled after the untimely death of her employer. "A bad bargain," he said somberly time after time. "Very bad indeed." And she only smiled back, never maliciously or with humor, but patiently. She had given him what he wanted. "But still a bargain," she always replied.

I am aware of the sounds subsiding from the canopied bed. I wonder if both now will abandon themselves to dreams and to sleep. A shadow dips silently past the window, a nighthawk. Faintly I hear the cries of hunting birds.

He came awake suddenly with teeth worrying his guilty soul. Connie glared at him from dark eyes swollen from crying and fury. She shook long black hair back from her shoulders. ". . . drove her through the one breakdown and into another." He dimly heard the words. "She's out of it, and good for her. No more campaigns. You won't do the same to me, you son of a bitch." Bitter smile. "Or I should say, you son of a bastard."

"I can't change these things. I'm just trying—" Alessi realized he was shaking in the darkness.

"What's wrong, now what's wrong?" said Connie.

Alessi cried out once, low . . .

"—Baby, what is it?"

He saw Lakey's face in the pooled moonlight. "You." He reached out to touch her cheek and grazed her nose.

"Me," she said. "Who else?"

"Jesus," Alessi said. "Oh God, God."

"Bad dream?"

Orientation slowly settled in. "A nightmare." He shook his head violently.

"Tell me about it?"

"I can't remember."

"So don't tell me if you don't want to." She gathered him close, blotting the sweat on his sternum with the sheet.

He said dreamily, "You always plan to make it up, but after a while it's too late."

"What's too late?"

Alessi didn't answer. He lay rigid beside her.

\*     \*     \*

I see them in the gilt-framed mirror and I see them in bed. I feel both a terrible sympathy for her and an equally terrible love for him. For as long as I can recall, I've husbanded proprietary feelings about this house and those in it.

Frank Alessi makes me understand. I remember the woman's touch and cherish that feeling, though I simultaneously realize her touch was yet another's. I also remember Frank's embrace. I have touched all of them.

I love all these people. That terrifies me.

I want to tell him, you *can* change things, Frank.

Sometime after midnight he awoke again. The night had encroached; moonlight now filled less than a quarter of the playroom. Alessi lay still, staring at shadow patterns. He heard Lakey's soft, regular breathing beside him.

He lay without moving for what seemed to be hours. When he checked his watch only minutes had passed. Recumbent, he waited, assuming that for which he waited was sleep.

Sleep had started to settle about Alessi when he thought he detected a movement across the room. Part vague movement, part snatch of sound, it was *something*. Switching on the bed-table lamp, Alessi saw nothing. He held his breath for long seconds and listened. Still nothing. The room held only its usual complement of inhabitants: dolls, toys, stuffed creatures. Bear stared back at him. The furniture was all familiar. Everything was in its place, natural. He felt his pulse speeding. He turned off the light and settled back against the pillow.

It's one o'clock in the soul, he thought. Not quite Fitzgerald, but it will do. He remembered Lakey in the car that afternoon asking why he had cut and run.

That wasn't the exact phraseology, but it was close enough. So what if he had been forced out of office? He still could have found some kind of political employment. Alessi had not told her about all the records unsubpoenaed as well as subpoenaed—at first. Then, perversely, he had started to catalog the sordid details the investigating committees had decided not to use. After a while she had turned her head back toward the clean mountain scenery. He continued the list. Finally she had told him to shut up. She turned back toward him gravely, had told him it was all right—she had forgiven him. It had been simple and sincere.

*I don't need easy forgiveness,* he thought. *Nor would I forgive.* That afternoon he had lashed out at her: "Damn it, what do you know about these things—about responsibility and power? You're a hippy—or whatever hippies are called now. Did you ever make a single, solitary decision that put you on the line? Made you a target for second-guessing, carping analysis, sniping, unabashed viciousness?" The over-taut spring wound down.

Lakey visibly winced; muscles tightened around her mouth. "Yes," she said. "I did."

"So tell me."

She stared back at him like a small surprised animal. "I've been traveling a long time. Before I left, I was pregnant." Her voice flattened; Alessi strained to hear the words. "They told me it should have been a daughter."

He focused his attention back on the road. There was nothing to say. He knew about exigencies. He could approve.

"None of them wanted me to do it. They made it more than it really was. When I left, my parents told me they would never speak to me again. They haven't.''

Alessi frowned.

''I loved them. . . .''

Alessi heard her mumble, make tiny incoherent sounds. She shifted in her sleep in a series of irregular movements. Her voice raised slightly in volume. The words still were unintelligible. Alessi recognized the tenor: she was dreaming of fearful things. He stared intently; his vision blurred. . . .

Gently he gathered Connie into his arms and stroked her hair. ''I will make it right for you. I know, I know . . . I can.''

''No,'' she said, the word sliding into a moan. Sharply, ''No.''

''I am your father.''

But she ignored him.

I hear more than I can see. I hear the woman come fully awake, her moans sliding raggedly up the register to screams—pain, not love; shock, not passion. I would rather not listen, but I have no choice. So I hear the desperation of a body whose limbs are trapped between strangling linens and savage lover. I hear the endless, pounding slap of flesh against meat. Finally I hear the words, the cruel words and the ineffectual. Worst of all, I hear the cries. I hear them in sadness.

Earlier I could not object. But now he couples with her not out of love, not from affection, but to force her. No desire, no lust, no desperate pleasure save inarticulate power.

Finally she somehow frees herself and scrambles off the bed. She stumbles through the unfamiliar room and slams against the wall beside the door. Only her head intrudes into the moonlight. Her mouth is set in a rigid, silent oval. The wet blackness around her eyes is more than shadow. She says nothing. She fumbles for the door, claws the knob, is gone. He does not pursue her.

I hear the sound of the woman's stumbling steps. I hear her pound on the doors of the car Alessi habitually locks. The sounds of her flight diminish in the night. She will be safer with the beasts of the mountain.

Alessi endlessly slammed his fist into the bloody pillow. His body shook until the inarticulate rage began to burn away. Then he got up from the bed and crossed the playroom to the great baroque mirror.

"This time could have been different," he said. "I wanted it to be."

His eyes adjusted to the darkness. A thin sliver of moonlight striped the ceiling. Alessi confronted the creature in the mirror. He raised his hands in fists and battered them against unyielding glass, smashed them against the mirror until the surface fragmented into glittering shards. He presented his wrists, repeating in endless rote, "Different, this time, different . . ."

Then he sensed what lay behind him in the dark. Alessi swung around, blood arcing. Time overcame him. The warm, coppery smell rose up in the room.

Perhaps the house now is haunted; that I cannot say. My own role is ended. Again I am alone; and now lonely. This morning I have not looked through the round window. The carrion crows are inside my mind picking at the bones of memories.

I watch Frank Alessi across the stained floor of the playroom.

The house is quiet; I'm sure that will not continue. The woman will have reached the highway and surely has been found by now. She will tell her story and then the people will come.

For a time the house will be inhabited by many voices and many bodies. The people will look at Frank Alessi and his wrists and his blood. They will remark upon the shattered mirror. They may even note the toys, note me; wonder at the degree of the past preserved here in the house. I doubt they can detect the pain in my old-fashioned eyes.

They will search for answers.

But they can only question why Frank came here, and why he did what he did. They cannot see the marks left by the teeth of the past. Only the blood.

Some readers have called "Teeth Marks" a Bert Lance story, a Richard Nixon fable, or a Kennedy anecdote. It was intended to be rather less specialized than any of those. I simply wanted to write about people coming home after long absences. I wished to write about a person confronting his past. Nostalgia is not necessarily a positive phenomenon. The past can be a merciless, mighty toothy sort of creature. Memory repression is often a valuable commodity.

Specific elements that triggered the story? I can credit arts administrator Paula Barta with telling me of the affluent Aspen family for whom she once baby-sat. The nursery contained imposing playground equipment designed to make three-year-olds very tough, very fast.

I can also credit Quincy Burton, ace creator of fine dolls and stuffed animals, whom I once commissioned to create a "Teddyshark" as a Christmas gift for my dearest friend. Quincy worked the best part of a year getting the critter right, tailoring a meter-long Great White out of two shades of gray plush. The

206

mouth was the finest touch, gaping open and lined with black leather. I had brought back a large assortment of shark teeth from Los Angeles. Quincy drilled a hole in each tooth, then sewed each from the rear into the jaws. The Teddyshark had genuine teeth. Some time later, I looked across my room at my own teddybear and wondered why most kids' bears are constructed with closed mouths . . .

Add some speculation about people and power, and why they do what they do, and the story started to grow like coral. And I always wanted to do a haunted-house tale.

A note to bibliographers: "Teeth Marks" reflects two stories published in my collection *Among the Dead*. Senator Frank Alessi appeared as a second-lead character in "Tactics." His daughter, Connie Alessi, had a brief cameo in "Adrift on the Freeway." I expect the Alessi family will continue to surface in my work. I know that Connie has a nifty role in my long-unfinished novel, *No Limits*. The Alessis aren't the Forsythe clan, to be sure, but they're genuine people and their lives interest me.

—Edward Bryant

# THIRD WIND

## by Richard Christian Matheson

Michael chugged up the incline, sweatsuit shadowed with perspiration. His Nikes compressed on the asphalt and the sound of his inhalation was the only noise on the country road.

He glanced at his waist-clipped odometer: twenty-five point seven. Not bad. But he could do better.

Had to.

He'd worked hard doing his twenty miles a day for the last two years and knew he was ready to break fifty. His body was up to it, the muscles taut and strong. They'd be going through a lot of changes over the next twenty-five miles. His breathing was loose, comfortable. Just the way he liked it.

Easy. But the strength was there.

There was something quietly spiritual about all this, he told himself. Maybe it was the sublime monotony of stretching every muscle and feeling it constrict. Or it could be feeling his legs telescope out and draw his body forward. Perhaps even the humid expansion of his chest as his lungs bloated with air.

But none of that was really the answer.

*It was the competing against himself.*

Beating his own distance, his own limits. Running was the time he felt most alive. He knew that as surely as he'd ever known anything.

He loved the ache that shrouded his torso and he even waited for the moment, a few minutes into the run, when a dull voltage would climb his body to his brain like a vine, reviving him. It transported him, taking his mind to another place, very deep within. Like prayer.

He was almost to the crest of the hill.

So far, everything was feeling good. He shagged off some tightness in his shoulders, clenching his fists and punching at the air. The October chill turned to pink steam in his chest, making his body tingle as if a microscopic cloud of needles were passing through, from front to back, leaving pin-prick holes.

He shivered. The crest of the hill was just ahead. And on the down side was a new part of his personal route: a dirt road, carpeted with leaves, which wound through a silent forest at the peak of these mountains.

As he broke the crest, he picked up speed, angling downhill toward the dirt road. His Nikes flexed against the gravel, slipping a little.

It had taken much time to prepare for this. Months of meticulous care of his body. Vitamins. Dieting. The endless training and clocking. Commitment to the body machine. It was as critical as the commitment to the goal itself.

Fifty miles.

As he picked up momentum, jogging easily downhill, the mathematical breakdown of that figure filled his head with tumbling digits. Zeroes unglued from his thought tissues and linked with cardinal numbers to form combinations that added to fifty. It was suddenly all he could think about. Twenty-five plus twenty-five. Five times ten. Forty-nine plus one. Shit. It was driving him crazy. One hundred minus—

The dirt road.

He noticed the air cooling. The big trees that shaded the forest road were lowering the temperature. Night was close. Another hour. Thirty minutes plus thirty minutes. This math thing was getting irritating. Michael tried to remember some of his favorite Beatle songs as he gently padded through the dense forest.

"Eight Days A Week." Great song. Weird damn title but who cared? If John and Paul said a week had eight days, everybody else just added a day and said . . . yeah, cool. Actually, maybe it wasn't their fault to begin with. Maybe George was supposed to bring a calendar to the recording session and forgot. He was always the spacey one. Should've had Ringo do it, thought Michael. Ringo you could count on. Guys with gonzo noses always compensated by being dependable.

Michael continued to run at a comfortable pace over the powdery dirt. Every few steps he could hear a leaf or small branch break under his shoes. What was that old thing? Something like, don't ever move even a small rock when you're at the beach or in the mountains. It upsets the critical balances. Nature can't ever be right again if you do. The repercussions can start wars if you extrapolate it out far enough.

Didn't ever really make much sense to Michael. His brother Eric had always told him these things and he should have known better than to listen. Eric was a self-appointed fount of advice on how to keep the cosmos in alignment. But he always got "D's" on his cards in high school unlike Michael's "A's" and maybe he didn't really know all that much after all.

Michael's foot suddenly caught on a rock and he

fell forward. On the ground, the dirt coated his face and lips and a spoonful got into his mouth. He also scraped his knee; a little blood. It was one of those lousy scrapes that claws a layer off and stings like it's a lot worse.

He was up again in a second and heading down the road, slightly disgusted with himself. He knew better than to lose his footing. He was too good an athlete for that.

His mouth was getting dry and he worked up some saliva by rubbing his tongue against the roof of his mouth. Strange how he never got hungry on these marathons of his. The body just seemed to live off itself for the period of time it took. Next day he usually put away a supermarket, but in running, all appetite faded. The body fed itself. It was weird.

The other funny thing was the way he couldn't imagine himself ever walking again. It became automatic to run. Everything went by so much faster. When he did stop, to walk, it was like being a snail. Everything just . . . took . . . so . . . damn . . . looooonnnngggg.

The sun was nearly gone now. Fewer and fewer animals. Their sounds faded all around. Birds stopped singing. The frenetic scrambling of squirrels halted as they prepared to bed down for the night. Far below, at the foot of these mountains, the ocean was turning to ink. The sun was lowering and the sea rose to meet it like a dark blue comforter.

Ahead, Michael could see an approaching corner.

How long had he been moving through the forest path? Fifteen minutes? Was it possible he'd gone the ten-or-so-mile length of the path already?

That was one of the insane anomalies of running these marathons of his. Time got all out of whack. He'd think he was running ten miles and find he'd actually covered considerably more ground. Sometimes as much as double his estimate. He couldn't ever figure that one out. But it always happened and he always just sort of anticipated it.

Welcome to the time warp, Jack.

He checked his odometer: twenty-nine point eight.

Half there and some loose change.

The dirt path would be coming to an end in a few hundred yards. Then it was straight along the highway which ran atop the ridge of this mountain far above the Malibu coastline. The highway was bordered with towering streetlamps which lit the way like some forgotten runway for ancient astronauts. They stared down from fifty-foot poles and bleached the asphalt and roadside talcum white.

The path had ended now and he was on the deserted mountaintop road with its broken center line that stretched to forever. As Michael wiped his glistening face with a sleeve, he heard someone hitting a crystal glass with tiny mallets, far away. It wasn't a pinging sound. More like a high-pitched thud that was chain-reacting. He looked up and saw insects of the night swarming dementedly around a klieg's glow. Hundreds of them, in hypnotic self-destruction, dive-bombed again and again at the huge bulb.

Eerie, seeing that kind of thing way the hell out here. But nice country to run in just the same. Gentle hills. The distant sea, far below. Nothing but heavy silence. Nobody ever drove this road anymore. It was as deserted as any Michael could remember. The perfect place to run.

What could be better? The smell was clean and healthy, the air sweet. Great decision, building his house up here last year. This was definitely the place to live. Pastureland was what his father used to call this kind of country when Michael was growing up in Wisconsin.

He laughed. Glad to be out of *that* place. People never did anything with their lives. Born there, schooled there, married there and died there was the usual, banal legacy. They all missed out on life. Missed out on new ideas and ambitions. The doctor slapped them and from that point on their lives just curled up like dead spiders.

It was just as well.

How many of them could take the heat of competition in Los Angeles? Especially a job like Michael's? None of the old friends he'd gladly left behind in his hometown would ever have a chance going up against a guy like himself. He was going to be the head of his law firm in a few more years. Most of those yokels back home couldn't even *spell* success much less achieve it.

But to each his own. Regardless of how pointless some lives really were. But *he* was going to be the head of his own firm and wouldn't even be thirty-five by the time it happened.

Okay, yeah, they were all married and had their families worked out. But what a fucking bore. Last thing Michael needed right now was that noose around his neck. Maybe the family guys figured they had something valuable. But for Michael it was a waste of time. Only thing a wife and kids would do is drag him down; hold him back. Priorities. First things first. *Career*. Then everything else. But put that relationship stuff off until last.

Besides, with all the inevitable success coming his way, meeting ladies would be a cinch. And hell, anyone could have a kid. Just nature. No big thing.

But *success*. That was something else, again. Took a very special animal to grab onto that golden ring and never let go. Families were for losers when a guy was really climbing. And he, of all the people he'd ever known, was definitely climbing.

Running had helped get him in the right frame of mind to do it. With each mileage barrier he broke, he was able to break greater barriers in life itself, especially his career. It made him more mentally fit to compete when he ran. It strengthened his will, his inner discipline.

Everything felt right when he was running regularly. And it wasn't just the meditative effect; not at all. He knew what it gave him was an *edge*. An edge on his fellow attorneys at the firm and an edge on life.

It was unthinkable to him how the other guys at the firm didn't take advantage of it. Getting ahead was what it was all about. A guy didn't make it in L.A. or anywhere else in the world unless he kept one step ahead of the competition. Keep moving and never let anything stand in the way or slow you down. That was the magic.

And Michael knew the first place to start that trend was with himself.

He got a chill. Thinking this way always made him feel special. Like he had the formula, the secret. Contemplating success was a very intoxicating thing. And with his running now approaching the hour-and-a-half mark, hyperventilation was heightening the effect.

He glanced at his odometer: forty-three point six.

He was feeling like a champion. His calves were burning a little and his back was a bit tender, but at this rate, with his breathing effortless and body strong, he could do sixty. But fifty was the goal. After that he had to go back and get his briefs in order for tomorrow's meeting. Had to get some sleep. Keep the machine in good shape and you rise to the top. None of that smoking or drinking or whatever else those morons were messing with out there. Stuff like that was for losers.

He opened his mouth a little wider to catch more air. The night had gone to a deep black and all he could hear now was the adhesive squishing of his Nikes. Overhead, the hanging branches of pepper trees canopied the desolate road and cut the moonlight into a million beams.

The odometer: forty-six point two. His head was feeling hot but running at night always made that easier. The breezes would swathe like cool silk, blowing his hair back and combing through his scalp. Then he'd hit a hot pocket that hovered above the road and his hair would flop downward, the feeling of heat returning like a blanket. He coughed and spit.

Almost there.

He was suddenly hit by a stray drop of moisture, then another. A drizzle began. Great. Just what he didn't need. Okay, it wasn't raining hard; just that misty stuff that atomizes over you like a lawn sprinkler shifted by a light wind. Still, it would have been nice to finish the fifty dry.

The road was going into a left hairpin now and Michael leaned into it, Nikes gripping octopus-tight. Ahead, as the curve broke, the road went straight, as far as the eye could see. Just a two-lane blacktop lying in state across these mountains. Now that it was wet, the surface went mirror shiny, like a ribbon on the side of tuxedo pants. Far below, the sea reflected a fuzzy moon, and fog began to ease up the mountainside, coming closer toward the road.

Michael checked the odometer, rubbing his hands together for warmth: forty-nine point eight. Almost there, and other than being a little cold he was feeling like a million bucks. He punched happily at the air and cleared his throat. God, he was feeling great! Tomorrow, at the office, was going to be a victory from start to finish.

He could feel himself smiling, his face hot against the vaporing rain. His jogging suit was soaked with sweat and drizzle made him shiver as it touched his skin. He breathed in gulps of the chilled air and as it left his mouth it turned white, puffing loosely away. His eyes were stinging from the cold and he closed them, continuing to run, the effect of total blackness fascinating him.

Another stride. Another.

He opened his eyes and rubbed them with red fingers. All around, the fog breathed closer, snaking between the limbs of trees and creeping silently across the asphalt. The overhead lights made it glow like a wall of colorless neon.

The odometer.

Another hundred feet and he had it!

The strides came in a smooth flow, like a turning wheel. He spread his fingers wide and shook some of the excess energy that was concentrating and making him feel buzzy. It took the edge off but he still felt as though he were zapped on a hundred cups of coffee. He ran faster, his arms like swinging scythes, tugging him forward.

*Twenty more steps.*

Ten plus ten. Five times . . . Christ, the math thing was back. He started laughing out loud as he went puffing down the road, sweat pants drooping.

The sky was suddenly zippered open by lightning and Michael gasped. In an instant, blackness turned to hot white and there was that visual echo of the light as it trembled in the distance, then fluttered off like a dying bulb.

Michael checked his odometer.

Five more feet! He counted it: Five/breath/four/breath/three/breath/two/one and there it was, yelling and singing and patting him on the back and tossing streamers!

*Fifty miles! Fifty goddamn miles!*

It was fucking incredible! To know he could really, actually *do* it suddenly hit him and he began laughing.

Okay, now to get that incredible sensation of almost standing still while walking it off. Have to keep those muscles warm. If not he'd get a chill and cramps and feel like someone was going over his calves with a carpet knife.

Hot breath gushed visibly from his mouth. The rain was coming faster in a diagonal descent, backlit by lightning, and the fog bundled tighter. Michael took three or four deep breaths and began trying to slow. It was incredible to have this feeling of edge. The sense of being on *top* of everything! It was an awareness he could surpass limitations. Make breakthroughs. It was what separated the winners from the losers when taken right down to a basic level. The winners knew how much harder they could push to go farther. Break those patterns. Create new levels of ability and confidence.

*Win.*

He tried again to slow down. His legs weren't slowing to a walk yet and he sent the message down again. He smiled. Run too far and the body just doesn't want to stop.

The legs continued to pull him forward. Rain was drenching down from the sky; he was soaked to the bone. Hair strung over his eyes and mouth and he coughed to get out what he could as it needled coldly into his face.

"Slow down," he told his legs, "*stop*, goddammit!"

But his feet continued on, splashing through the puddles that laked here and there along the foggy road.

Michael began to breathe harder, unable to get the air he needed. It was too wet; half air, half water. Suddenly, more lightning scribbled across the thundering clouds and Michael reached down to stop one leg.

It did no *good*. He kept running, even faster, pounding harder against the wet pavement. He could feel the bottoms of his Nikes getting wet, starting to wear through. He'd worn the old ones; they were the most comfortable.

Jesus fucking god, he really *couldn't stop!*

The wetness got colder on his cramping feet. He tried to fall but kept running. Terrified, he began to cough fitfully, his legs continuing forward, racing over the pavement.

His throat was raw from the cold and his muscles ached. He was starting to feel like his body had been beaten with hammers.

There was no point in trying to stop. He knew that, now. He'd trained too long. Too precisely.

It had been his single obsession.

And as he continued to pound against the fog-shrouded pavement all he could hear was a cold, lonely night.

Until the sound of his own pleading screams began to echo through the mountains, and fade across the endless gray road.

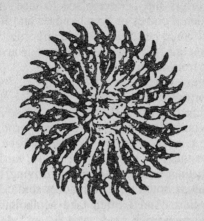

*I live in L.A.*

And despite the nouveau weirdness that steams off the place, it's a pretty trippy city to hang your hat. So, every few days, I love to get in my car at strange hours and drive around. Some bucks in my wallet, a tank of unleaded, killer music and I'm ready to leave my life behind me.

More often than not, when I go for drives, my mind sits in the next seat and stares out at passing curiosities. It likes the curves and breezes and pays no attention to me. Sometimes it thinks of stuff and it usually tells me what it thinks later. More on that in a moment. First, a bit of geography.

If you are ever in Los Angeles, there is a road you must see. It is abnormally mythic for being mere pavement, and there are few who've driven it who would deny its seductive effects. It's called Mulholland Highway and it is a profound totem. A dreamy meridian that watches over L.A. from atop high mountains and offers the perfect place to lose virginity, dump murdered bodies or go a hundred and fifty on a hairpin that could get the Concorde airborne. It's also a perfectly eerie place to jog because you can see everything from its vista.

Sometimes even a story idea.

Which brings me to "Third Wind."

In addition to writing short stories, I also earn my living by being the head writer and producer of prime-time television shows. The hours kept by people who do this are, to put it poetically, *nuts*. Thus, more often than not, I find myself driving home at truly ridiculous hours from whichever studio I'm currently working. And I often take Mulholland—that frightening, wondrous road. And when I drive it, I think about all kinds of things. For instance, the night I wrote "Third Wind," I was driving Mulholland well past midnight and thinking over an article I read about people who run fifty-mile marathons. As I watched L.A. twinkle on either side of me, I started to compute how far that would be in terms of my daily drive and I realized whoever could run fifty miles without stopping was a very scary creature.

So, I began to do a bit of analysis as the curves worked on me and decided (using sports terms) that if the First Wind is the physical desire to move, and the Second Wind is the body's willing alliance, then surely the Third was some shrieking internal voice. The one we all have inside that makes us do what isn't possible.

It's obsession, and its theme is an explosive lure for any writer.

When I got home that night, I wrote the story in a few hours, possessed by the same momentum as the main character: unwilling to stop until I'd crossed the finish line.

Our similarities ended there, thank God. At least I think they did.

Enjoy *your* run. . . .

—Richard Christian Matheson

# PREPARATIONS FOR THE GAME

## by Steve Rasnic Tem

It's the day of the big game. He has a date, oh, a beautiful young date. A member of a leading sorority on campus, auburn hair, perfume behind the ears and down her cleavage, a lure for his young red alcoholic nose. Could there ever be better times?

Certainly not. Not when he has such a beautiful date, his first date in months, and not when they're doubling with the president of his fraternity, who just happens to be seeing his beautiful date's best friend.

Things are looking up for him, oh, certainly.

They pull up in front of his apartment. I'll just be a minute, he says cheerily. Just a change of clothes. His pennant. His flask. Once out of the car, he gazes back in at their fixed smiles. The fraternity president scratches his wool pants. The beautiful date's best friend rubs at her cheekbones distractedly. He reaches into the car and pulls his beautiful date's hand from her fur muff. And grasps rods of bone, well-articulated carpals and metacarpals.

But no. Just the effect of thin winter air against

skin. He looks down at her small, narrow hand, with its pale white flesh. So delicate.

It's going to be a great game, he calls, jogging up the apartment building steps.

In his apartment he rummages through piles of clothing. What to wear? He picks up his checkered gray slacks, throws them behind the couch. He picks up the dark-blue monogrammed sweater-shirt, tosses it on top of the refrigerator. He stumbles through piles of books, garbage, unmatted prints with curling edges. What to wear?

He is aware of a skeletal hand curled around the front doorknob. Without looking around he tells her, I haven't the time. I'll be late for the game.

It suddenly occurs to him it's the first time anyone has ever visited his apartment.

But still he tells her, I just haven't the time—I mustn't be late for the game. She slides around the doorframe, her short red shift tight over her emaciated figure, her thin hands twisted into tight fists.

It suddenly occurs to him she may be out to spoil his good time.

He turns around, pretending that she isn't there. He picks up a Nehru jacket, casts it away. He picks up his bright red turtleneck, and drops it on the coffee table. I haven't time, I haven't time, he pleads softly, then silently to himself.

She steps toward him, her eyes two dark stones. He clumsily avoids her, almost tripping over a pile of shoes.

She swings the edge of a cupped hand toward his face. He steps quickly once to his right, his eyes averted, still seeking something to wear to the game. Her blow misses.

What does she want from him? Why doesn't she leave him alone?

Now he is forced to look at her. He's cornered at one end of the small breakfast bar. I'll be late for the game, he repeats, almost crying. Her black hair is filthy, plastered to her skull.

He sidesteps past his television set. Something metallic shines in her moving hand. She smashes the screen. I'll be late, he whimpers. She steps closer. He senses just a hint of corrupted flesh beneath her rough, bluish lips.

The blood is rising into her cheeks and eyes, suffusing them with a light pink color. She swings her hands back and forth, in slow motion.

And still, he attempts to ignore her. He puts on his heavy coat, the dark brown with contrasting tan pattern. He slips his bright orange scarf around his neck, still walking away from her, adjusting the thick folds so that they cut across his neck at the most aesthetically pleasing angle, and still she follows him, swings her hands at him, misses him, and again he stumbles, slightly, before catching himself. His steps become quicker. He attempts to make his movements unpredictable.

He says it rapidly to himself, a magic formula, a prayer: I can't be late for the game. I just can't.

Again, from the corner of his eye he can see she is approaching. He walks briskly, still seeking his spectator's wardrobe, falters briefly, his gaze distracted. She steps around the low couch, directly behind him now, reaching for his coat. Mustn't be late, mustn't be late, he mutters to himself, suddenly deciding to forego the proper dress, to leave now. For wouldn't it be a graver offense to make the president of his fraternity late for the game, not to mention his beautiful young date and her best friend?

He hurriedly, almost running, makes it to the door, jerking it open as she makes a final, determined lunge. He hears the faint knock of her knuckles, or, perhaps, cheekbones, rasping the door panel as he runs down the stairs pulling at his ill-fitting pants, tucking in his shirt, running fidgety hands over his improper clothing.

At the curb he halts in dismay. The car is gone with the president and the two pretty girls inside. The stadium is miles away; he'll never make it in time. What will they all think of him? He sits down on the curb, the sound of footsteps on the staircase growing louder behind him.

He has been unable to leave his apartment for weeks. He sleeps days at a time, his moments awake so brief they seem like dreams to him. Dinner comes at 2:00 A.M., breakfast twelve hours later. He throws the garbage into a cardboard box under the sink.

One twilight he remembers that he has a date set up for that day. They are all going to the big game. He, his beautiful young date, her best friend and the president of his fraternity who he had never really talked to and probably still wouldn't have gotten to know if their beautiful young dates hadn't been such good friends. What time is it? He's going to be late. The phone is ringing. His parents again? While not quite deciding not to answer it, he fails to answer by default.

He rummages through piles of clothing, attempting to find the one proper outfit for his venture outside, to the game.

He needs to go to the bathroom, but not wanting to walk the ten yards or so down to the restroom in the hall, he walks over to his sink and begins urinating there.

He is aware of a skeletal hand curled around the front doorknob.

Without looking around he tells her, I haven't the time. I'll be late for the game.

It occurs to him it's the first time anyone has ever visited his apartment.

But still he tells her, I just haven't the time. I mustn't be late for the game.

She slides around the doorframe, her short red shift tight over her emaciated figure, her thin hands twisted into tight fists.

It occurs to him that he's seen her before, at one of his fraternity's dances. She danced with Bob, Tom. Perhaps she even danced with the president. It occurs to him that maybe even he danced with her that night.

He can't remember her name.

She approaches him slowly, her arms outstretched. He stumbles backward over the couch. The phone is ringing again. I can't be late for the game, he pleads with her.

The phone stops ringing. Outside a horn is blaring. It must be his fraternity president, his beautiful date, her best friend. He lunges toward the door, forgetting his good clothes. I can't be late for the game, he cries it now. He can hear her quickening steps behind him.

At the curb he halts, looking about in confusion. The car is gone. He'll never make it in time. He suddenly realizes that he is naked: his legs startle him with their chalky whiteness. What will they all think of him? He hears her footsteps behind him. Looking down, he discovers that his feet are bare, bleeding from all the broken glass in the street.

He races down the street. He figures that if he can just find the proper bus, he can make it to the game on time. I mustn't be late, he mutters, then grows self-conscious and worried, thinking some passerby might have heard him talking to himself, and think him strange.

His heavy coattails, dark brown with contrasting tan pattern, flap in the wind. His bright orange scarf hangs loosely around his neck, untying itself with his exertions. His hands grab at the material, trying to maintain his neat appearance.

Occasionally he looks around to see if she is following. Small dogs growl at his feet.

Ahead of him, he thinks he sees the back entrance to the bus station, a tall whitewashed building with a blue roof. But he can't remember which bus it was that traveled the route to the stadium.

He races up the back stairs, seeking information. He pushes open a steel door at the second floor, turns left and jerks open a wooden door.

And he is back in his own apartment once again, the unmade bed, the scattered clothing, the sweet ripe smell of garbage under the sink. She has been waiting for him, his small Boy Scout hatchet clutched tightly in her hand. I can't be late, he starts to whine, then stops. He can't hear his own voice. She walks toward him now, the hatchet slightly raised.

He finds it difficult to move. What is her name?

He sits in the restaurant across from his apartment, sipping his morning coffee. The big game is today, and he waits now for the president to arrive with his late-model Chevy and their two beautiful young dates. He doesn't know the president well, but hopes that will soon change. He is wearing his very best clothing: his brown heavy coat with the tan pattern, his orange scarf, his dark alligator shoes with the small tassels. They'll be here in an hour, he thinks with satisfaction, preparing to eat a leisurely pregame breakfast.

But then he looks up at the clock; hours have passed, the game already started, half over by now, he thinks. He rushes out of the restaurant, looking frantically up and down the street. No sign of cars. He suddenly thinks of all the times he's been forgotten, the times left at the playground, the school parties missed. But they must have come by, waited for hours, he thinks, and somehow he didn't know they were out there. They finally had no choice but to leave; they couldn't be late for the game.

He walks across the street and climbs the narrow stairs to his third-floor apartment. Opening the door he sees her sitting stiffly on his couch, hands clenched in her lap.

Her black hair is filthy, plastered to her skull. He senses just a hint of corrupted flesh beneath her rough, bluish lips.

He thinks he recognizes her. The president had brought her to the house initiation night. After the blindfolded bobbing for peeled bananas in a tub of pudding, after the nose-to-anus farting matches, the hard licks with the paddle and the naphtha poured on the groin, they'd been led one by one into her room. She'd been pale and silent, her high cheekbones flushed in the dim light, and they'd each fucked her, a minute or two apiece.

Her nose had been running the whole time, he remembers.

She rises from the sofa and approaches him. Livid scars crisscross her wrists and forearms.

He gazes about his room, looking for a nice outfit to wear to the game, pretending she isn't there. His eyes rest on a pile of soiled, stained underwear by the couch. He can't smell them, but imagines their corpse-like scent, like a pile of dead white sewer rats. He is suddenly anxious that she might have seen them. He stares at her in intense agitation as she reaches her arms out for him. He is filled with acute embarrassment for himself.

After blocks of strenuous running, he finally makes it to the bus, leaping to the first step just before the driver closes the doors. The driver pays no attention as he drops his coins into the metal box. He momentarily wonders if he could have gotten away without paying, so intent is the driver on some scene ahead.

He strides to the middle of the bus, slightly out of breath, grabbing a seat near the side doors so he can hurry out when they reach the stadium.

The bus contains a half-dozen passengers, all of them old, quiet and somewhat unattractive. One old man has a large purple birthmark covering the side of his face; wartlike growths, also deep purple, spot the area under his right eye. He suddenly realizes he can't hear the sounds of the traffic outside.

When the bus pulls to his stop he leaps out the door, and momentarily the illusion of soundlessness follows him into the street outside. When the traffic noise returns, he is staring up at a whitewashed building with blue tile roof, his apartment house.

He begins climbing the stairs to his apartment on the tenth floor.

Three of his fraternity brothers pick him up at the restaurant across the street from his apartment building. He's just had a leisurely breakfast of coffee, cereal and eggs, the waitress was pretty and smiled a lot, and he is now ready to have a wonderful time at today's big game.

When he gets into the car, the late-model Chevy,

his three brothers compliment him on his choice in clothing, the heavy brown coat with tan pattern, the orange scarf. They joke a bit, slap each other's shoulders and pull rapidly out of their parking space.

His brothers ask him if he'd like a little sip from their flask. He replies, No, thank you, I have my own. But as he reaches into his back pocket he discovers it missing, dropped out somewhere in the scramble to be on time, no doubt, so yes, he would care for a small slug.

He raises the flask high over his mouth and pours the warm yellow liquor. Some splashes on his bright orange scarf. He feels panicky, has an urge to wipe it off before it stains the beautiful material, but for some reason seems unable to. He drinks, endlessly it seems. He drinks.

The brothers sing old fraternity and college songs, between various versions swapping stories of fraternity life. Rush. Initiation night and all the fun they had. How all the girls are dazzled by a fraternity jacket. The dumb pledge who almost suffocated when a five-foot mock grave collapsed on him. Chug-a-lugging "Purple Jesuses": vodka, rum, grapes, oranges and lemon juice. The night they caught a pig, beat it, kicked it, dragged it across the parking lot, hung it up by the snout, then finally drowned it in the bathtub.

He remembers his old pledge buddy, a fat kid no one else liked. They had driven him ten miles up into the mountains the day before initiation. He hadn't seen him since.

The brothers are taking a new road to the stadium, one he's sure he's never seen before. It meanders out into the country, through patches of wood and round fields and small farms. He has a moment of uneasiness, worried that perhaps they plan to leave him out there, that he'll never make it to the game on time.

As the car rounds a wide bend in a wooded section, it slows. The brothers stop the car and the driver races the engine. They stare into the clearing a hundred feet ahead and slightly below them.

On a stump beside the road there is a body, lying face up, the back and rump resting on the flat cross-section. Its red shift is tattered and water-spotted.

The driver yells at the top of his lungs, the other two brothers chorusing. They sound like coyotes. The car lurches forward, bearing down on the stump. The brother at the front passenger window pulls a small pistol out of the glove compartment.

As the car suddenly swerves around the stump the brother puts two bullets into the body's torso.

He can see that there are dozens of other bullet holes and torn places in the body's skin. He also notices that it might have been a man, or a woman with short hair. Certainly sexless by now, however.

As the car speeds out of the woods, his brothers laughing and hollering, he looks back at the clearing. He can see another car approaching in the distance. He thinks the body is stirring, about to rise, and his legs tighten up at this thought. He knows that if he were standing by the stump, and if the body did rise, he would not be able to move his legs. He would be unable to run away. But then he realizes this is all just his imagination, that it's the wind rustling the few remaining rags on the corpse, that no, it isn't going to rise.

He sees a gun appear at the window of the distant car, preparing to put more bullets into the body. A road sign, he thinks.

He figures it's no more than fifteen minutes to kickoff.

*        *        *

Outside the stadium he stumbles and falls in the gravel. He's going to miss the kickoff, and he was so close. He'd been lucky to catch the bus; he'd flagged it down, in fact. He is worried about the woman back in his apartment, probably even now looking at all his scattered clothing, his unkempt rooms. He is worried about his torn brown pants, his scuffed alligator shoes. He worries about the fact of the corpse back on the stump, the fact that he will no doubt miss the kickoff.

He runs into his parents as he nears the stadium entrance. They look so old. His old father, his shriveled lips unable to catch the moisture dripping from his mouth as he speaks, pleads with him, wondering why he hasn't answered their phone calls. His aged mother nods, distracted, singing to herself.

His father grabs him by the arm, pulling him closer conspiratorially, whispering hoarsely: Your mother . . . she hasn't been the same, and Don't go in there. First time I had it . . . down by one of the old sorority houses. She pulled me back into the bushes . . . unzipped me, stuck it up there herself . . . was awful, like a big old frying pan in there . . .

He pulls away from the old man and pushes past his mother, seeking the stadium entrance. He sees nothing but a smooth limestone wall. Where is it? He's going to be late.

His beautiful young date is in there waiting for him, her bony fingers encircling a paper cup full of beer.

As he enters the stadium it's a few minutes to halftime. It has been a long walk. The crowd seems strangely silent, as if they were watching an engrossing chess match.

But he's forgotten his tickets, now he knows this, and knows too that he will therefore be unable to watch the game. He searches the crowd for his fraternity president, their beautiful dates, his beautiful date, but it's impossible in this crowd. Everyone looks the same, dressed in grays, blacks, dark blues, their faces pale, hair cropped short. When they try to cheer the players out on the field, no sound comes out.

An usher touches his arm from behind and he begins formulating an excuse for not having a ticket but the usher says nothing, instead leads him to a seat a dozen rows down, on the aisle.

He is sitting next to a family of spectators. They all have light brown hair, the father, the mother, the daughter and son, and perfect smiles, displayed to each other, not to him, in their mutual pride. They clap in unison to approve some play on the field, though strangely, he seems unable to see, to get the field into proper focus. Their clapping makes no sense.

He looks around a bit. Rows of spectators, stacked at an angle, back and upward, as far as he can see. But except for the family sitting next to him, he can discern no movement, not even a nervous tic. He again looks at the family beside him, and is drawn to their smooth, tucked-in lips. And their light blue pallor.

Discomfited, he stands up and starts down the aisle toward the field, still unable to get the players into focus. No one attempts to stop him. He reaches the retaining wall above the sidelines, climbs on top and jumps down, the thud of his feet in the grass the only sound he can hear.

When he reaches the center of the field he turns around. There's no one on the field. The stands seem empty. A slight breeze begins to rustle the grass.

He attempts to reenter the stadium through the tunnel leading to the players' dressing rooms. The light here is dim.

Mummified corpses line the walls, sprawl over dressing tables and tile shower floors. The bodies have lost most of their flesh and only thin strands of hair remain. They still wear their scarlet jerseys, though most of the color has leached away. Bones in white or sporty gold togs peer out of open lockers.

Entering the stadium he discovers to his relief that the game hasn't yet started. All seems well. No corpses, parents or strange women to trouble him. He pulls his ticket out of his unwrinkled pants pocket and makes his way to a seat on the fifty-yard line. His friends are all there and are overjoyed to see him.

The fraternity president slaps him on the back and says, "Great to have you here. Wouldn't be the same without you. And say . . . after the game, I'd like to talk to you about your maybe becoming our new pledgemaster."

His fraternity brothers pass on their congratulations from their seats further down the aisle.

The crowd suddenly leaps to its feet to cheer the upcoming kickoff. He is thrilled by the motion, color and sound. His fraternity brothers are slapping each other on the back, stamping feet, shouting and bussing their pretty dates on the cheeks. Popcorn and empty cups fly through the air. Frisbees are tossed from section to section.

He turns to greet his beautiful young date with an embrace. She opens her mouth widely. He notes the blueness of her throat. She grins and shows her perfect white teeth.

Later he climbs the steps for popcorn and soft drinks for the girls. He wonders if he might not just marry his date someday; she seems so much like him. The day is going so well now, and he wonders if maybe it's time for him to finally settle down, maybe have a family.

He is slowly aware of two arms, clothed in tatters of red, coming around his sides from behind as if to embrace him. The hands are thin, almost bone.

Everything is suddenly quiet again.

*I don't know if this is the best story I've written—I* find it difficult to compare them. There's more surreal in the story mix than I generally use at present. And I recently had to edit out a bit of the awkwardness in my early style for this reprinting. Beyond that, I'm hesitant to fiddle with this piece. I do know that this story is one of the few of mine that continues to disturb me on rereading. One of my earliest ventures into dark fantasy, it first appeared in Stuart David Schiff's fine magazine *Whispers*. From what I remember about our correspondence he wasn't sure whether he liked the story or not, but he just couldn't get it out of his mind, so he bought it.

I like that. I'm a firm believer in the "infection" theory of dark fantasy. Read once then reach for the penicillin. Fright in and of itself is simply too transitory. I think people need to be constantly reminded of their own darkness. It keeps them honest. I distrust no one more than the individual who is unable to see the terrible things he or she is capable of, who is blind to the dark landscapes that lie within.

This particular tale comes from the same place as many of my others: a fascination with the way death—the obsession with death, the irresistible gravitation toward death—enters into and permeates the daily lives of normal human beings. How it manages this would require a treatise to explore. Death expresses itself through the drive in individuals and institutions to suppress growth and complications, through passivity, through the imagery of the anal-retentive, the sadist, the masochist. But I'd rather write stories than essays on the subject. Suffice it to say that when joy and fulfillment are frustrated, we seem compelled to fill the gaps with entropy. I think this is perhaps the most important theme in dark fantasy. Even when it isn't the main idea in a story, it's usually somewhere there lurking in the background.

(Just as an aside—I'm actually one of life's optimists. I find even in this atmosphere of necrophilia an expression of life, another example of the wonderful complexity and possibility of human beings—as long as we face it, allow it entrance. It can get quite nasty otherwise.)

You may see in this story, as in many of my others, a Kafka influence. I admit it. And ''A Country Doctor'' is probably my favorite dark fantasy short story. What Kafka shows us in that tale is the way the background and setting—in fact, everything that happens to the protagonist—tells us something about that main character. Critics have often called that ''two-dimensional'' characterization. I suspect they just didn't know where to look for it. The fantastic events in the story probably would not have happened to anyone else in just that way—that tells us an enormous amount about what kind of person this is. Certainly this ''fantastic'' approach provides much more essential data than the sort of anecdotal characterization we see in much of so-called "realistic" fiction. I believe most dark fantasy achieves characterization in this way, even when more traditional methods take the foreground.

You may also detect some traces of Ramsey Campbell and Dennis Etchison here. I don't mind—I suspect their influence will always be felt in my fiction.

—Steve Rasnic Tem

# ARMAJA DAS

## by Joe Haldeman

The highrise, built in 1980, still had the smell and look of newness. And of money.

The doorman bowed a few degrees and kept a straight face, opening the door for a bent old lady. She had a card of Veterans' poppies clutched in one old claw. He didn't care much for the security guard, and she would give him interesting trouble.

The skin on her face hung in deep creases, scored with a network of tiny wrinkles; her chin and nose protruded and drooped. A cataract made one eye opaque; the other eye was yellow and red surrounding deep black, unblinking. She had left her teeth in various things. She shuffled. She wore an old black dress faded slightly grey by repeated washing. If she had any hair, it was concealed by a pale blue bandanna. She was so stooped that her neck was almost parallel to the ground.

"What can I do for you?" The security guard had a tired voice to match his tired shoulders and back. The job had seemed a little romantic the first couple of days, guarding all these rich people, sitting at an

239

ultramodern console surrounded by video monitors,
submachine gun at his knees. But the monitors were
blank except for an hourly check, power shortage;
and if he ever removed the gun from its cradle, he
would have to fill out five forms and call the police
station. And the doorman never turned anybody away.

"Buy a flower for boys less fortunate than ye,"
she said in a faint raspy baritone. From her age and
accent, her own boys had fought in the Russian
Revolution.

"I'm sorry. I'm not allowed to . . . respond to
charity while on duty."

She stared at him for a long time, nodding micro-
scopically. "Then send me to someone with more
heart."

He was trying to frame a reply when the front door
slammed open. "Car on fire!" the doorman shouted.

The security guard leaped out of his seat, grabbed
a fire extinguisher and sprinted for the door. The old
woman shuffled along behind him until both he and
the doorman disappeared around the corner. Then she
made for the elevator with surprising agility.

She got out on the seventeenth floor after pushing
the button that would send the elevator back down to
the lobby. She checked the name plate on 1738: Mr.
Zold. She was illiterate, but she could recognize
names.

Not even bothering to try the lock, she walked on
down the hall until she found a maid's closet. She
closed the door behind her and hid behind a rack of
starchy white uniforms, leaning against the wall with
her bag between her feet. The slight smell of gasoline
didn't bother her at all.

John Zold pressed the intercom button. "Martha?"
She answered. "Before you close up shop I'd like a

redundancy check on stack 408. Against tape 408."
He switched the selector on his visual output screen
so it would duplicate the output at Martha's station.
He stuffed tobacco in a pipe and lit it, watching.

Green numbers filled the screen, a complicated
matrix of ones and zeros. They faded for a second
and were replaced with a field of pure zeros. The
lines of zeros started to roll, like titles preceding a
movie.

The 746th line came up all ones. John thumbed the
intercom again. "Had to be something like that. You
have time to fix it up?" She did. "Thanks, Martha.
See you tomorrow."

He slid back the part of his desktop that concealed
a keypunch and typed rapidly: "523 784 00926//Good
night, machine. Please lock this station."

GOOD NIGHT, JOHN. DON'T FORGET YOUR LUNCH DATE
WITH MR. BROWNWOOD TOMORROW. DENTIST APPOINT-
MENT WEDNESDAY 0945. GENERAL SYSTEMS CHECK
WEDNESDAY 1300. DEL O DEL BAXT. LOCKED.

*Del O Del baxt* meant "God give you luck" in
the ancient tongue of the Romani. John Zold, born a
Gypsy but hardly a Gypsy by any standard other than
the strong one of blood, turned off his console and
unlocked the bottom drawer of his desk. He took out
a flat automatic pistol in a holster with a belt clip and
slipped it under his jacket, inside the waistband of his
trousers. He had only been wearing the gun for two
weeks, and it still made him uncomfortable. But
there had been those letters.

John was born in Chicago, some years after his
parents had fled from Europe and Hitler. His father
had been a fiercely proud man, and had gotten involved in a bitter argument over the honor of his
twelve-year-old daughter; from which argument he

had come home with knuckles raw and bleeding, and had given to his wife for disposal a large clasp knife crusty with dried blood.

John was small for his five years, and his chin barely cleared the kitchen table, where the whole family sat and discussed their uncertain future while Mrs. Zold bound up her husband's hands. John's shortness saved his life when the kitchen window exploded and a low ceiling of shotgun pellets fanned out and chopped into the heads and chests of the only people in the world whom he could love and trust. The police found him huddled between the bodies of his father and mother, and at first thought he was also dead; covered with blood, completely still, eyes wide open and not crying.

It took six months for the kindly orphanage people to get a single word out of him: *ratválo*, which he said over and over, and which they were never able to translate. Bloody, bleeding.

But he had been raised mostly in English, with a few words of Romani and Hungarian thrown in for spice and accuracy. In another year their problem was not one of communicating with John—only of trying to shut him up.

No one adopted the stunted Gypsy boy, which suited John. He'd had a family, and look what happened.

In orphanage school he flunked penmanship and deportment but did reasonably well in everything else. In arithmetic and, later, mathematics, he was nothing short of brilliant. When he left the orphanage at eighteen, he enrolled at the University of Illinois, supporting himself as a bookkeeper's assistant and part-time male model. He had come out of an ugly adolescence with a striking resemblance to the young Clark Gable.

Drafted out of college, he spent two years playing with computers at Fort Lewis, got out and went all the way to a master's degree under the GI Bill. His thesis, "Simulation of Continuous Physical Systems by Way of Universalization of the Trakhtenbrot Algorithms," was very well received, and the mathematics department gave him a research assistantship to extend the thesis into a doctoral dissertation. But other people read the paper too, and after a few months Bellcom International hired him away from academia. He rose rapidly through the ranks. Not yet forty, he was now senior analyst at Bellcom's Research and Development Group. He had his own private office, with a picture window overlooking Central Park, and a plush six-figure condominium only twenty minutes away by commuter train.

As was his custom, John bought a tall can of beer on his way to the train and opened it as soon as he sat down. It kept him from fidgeting during the fifteen- or twenty-minute wait while the train filled up.

He pulled a thick technical report out of his briefcase and stared at the summary on the cover sheet, not really seeing it but hoping that looking occupied would spare him the company of some anonymous fellow traveler.

The train was an express, and whisked them out to Dobb's Ferry in twelve minutes. John didn't look up from his report until they were well out of New York City; the heavy mesh tunnel that protected the track from vandals induced spurious colors in your retina as it blurred by. Some people liked it, tripped on it, but to John the effect was at best annoying, at worst nauseating, depending on how tired he was. Tonight he was dead tired.

He got off the train two stops up from Dobb's

Ferry. The highrise limousine was waiting for him and two other residents. It was a fine spring evening and John would normally have walked the half-mile, tired or not. But those unsigned letters.

"John Zold, you stop this preachment or you die soon. *Armaja das*, John Zold."

All three letters said that: *Armaja das*. We put a curse on you—for preaching.

He was less afraid of curses than of bullets. He undid the bottom button of his jacket as he stepped off the train, ready to quickdraw, roll for cover behind that trash can just like in the movies; but there was no one suspicious-looking around. Just an assortment of suburban wives and the old cop who was on permanent station duty.

Assassination in broad daylight wasn't Romani style. Styles changed, though. He got in the car and watched side roads all the way home.

There was another one of the shabby envelopes in his mailbox. He wouldn't open it until he got upstairs. He stepped in the elevator with the others and punched seventeen.

They were angry because John Zold was stealing their children.

Last March John's tax accountant had suggested that he could contribute four thousand dollars to any legitimate charity and actually make a few hundred bucks in the process, by dropping into a lower tax bracket. Not one to do things the easy or obvious way, John made various inquiries and, after a certain amount of bureaucratic tedium, founded the Young Gypsy Assimilation Council—with matching funds from federal, state and city governments, and a continuing Ford Foundation scholarship grant.

The YGAC was actually just a one-room office in a West Village brownstone, manned by volunteer help. It was filled with various pamphlets and broadsides, mostly written by John, explaining how young Gypsies could legitimately take advantage of American society: by becoming a part of it—something old-line Gypsies didn't care for. Jobs, scholarships, work-study programs, these things were for the *gadjos*, and poison to a Gypsy's spirit.

In November a volunteer had opened the office in the morning to find a crude firebomb that used a candle as a delayed-action fuse for five gallons of gasoline. The candle was guttering a fraction of an inch away from the line of powder that would have ignited the gas. In January it had been buckets of chicken entrails, poured into filing cabinets and flung over the walls. So John found a tough young man who would sleep on a cot in the office at night— sleep like a cat with a shotgun behind him. There was no more trouble of that sort. Only old men and women who would file in silently staring, to take handfuls of pamphlets which they would drop in the hall and scuff into uselessness, or defile in a more basic way. But paper was cheap.

John threw the bolt on his door and hung his coat in the closet. He put the gun in a drawer in his writing desk and sat down to open the mail.

The shortest one yet: "Tonight, John Zold. *Armaja das.*" Lots of luck, he thought. Won't even be home tonight; heavy date. Stay at her place, Gramercy Park. Lay a curse on me there? At the show or Sardi's?

He opened two more letters, bills, and there was a knock at the door.

Not announced from downstairs. Maybe a neighbor. Guy next door was always borrowing something. Still. Feeling a little foolish, he put the gun back in his waistband. Put his coat back on in case it was just a neighbor.

The peephole didn't show anything. Bad. He drew the pistol and held it just out of sight by the doorjamb, threw the bolt and eased open the door. It bumped into the Gypsy woman, too short to have been visible through the peephole. She backed away and said, "John Zold."

He stared at her. "What do you want, *púridaia*?" He could only remember a hundred or so words of Romani, but "grandmother" was one of them. What was the word for witch?

"I have a gift for you!" From her bag she took a dark green booklet, bent and with frayed edges, and gave it to him. It was a much-used Canadian passport belonging to a William Belini. But the picture inside the front cover was one of John Zold.

Inside, there was an airline ticket in a Qantas envelope. John didn't open it. He snapped the passport shut and handed it back. The old lady wouldn't accept it.

"An impressive job. It's flattering that someone thinks I'm so important."

"Take it and leave forever, John Zold. Or I will have to do the second thing."

He slipped the ticket envelope out of the booklet. "This, I will take. I can get your refund on it. The money will buy lots of posters and pamphlets." He tried to toss the passport into her bag, but missed. "What is your second thing?"

She toed the passport back to him. "Pick that up." She was trying to sound imperious, but it came out a thin, petulant quaver.

"Sorry, I don't have any use for it. What is—"

"The second thing is your death, John Zold." She reached into her bag.

He produced the pistol and aimed it down at her forehead. "No, I don't think so."

She ignored the gun, pulling out a handful of white chicken feathers. She threw the feathers over his threshold. "*Armaja das,*" she said, and then droned on in Romani, scattering feathers at regular intervals. John recognized *joovi* and *kari*, the words for woman and penis, and several other words he might have picked up if she'd pronounced them more clearly.

He put the gun back into its holder and waited until she was through. "Do you really think—"

"*Armaja das,*" she said again, and started a new litany. He recognized a word in the middle as meaning corruption or infection, and the last word was quite clear: death. *Méripen.*

"This nonsense isn't going to—" But he was talking to the back of her head. He forced a laugh and watched her walk past the elevator and turn the corner that led to the staircase.

He could call the guard. Make sure she didn't get out the back way. Illegal entry. He suspected that she knew he wouldn't want to go to the trouble, and it annoyed him slightly. He walked halfway to the phone, checked his watch and went back to the door. Scooped up the feathers and dropped them in the disposal. Just enough time. Fresh shave, shower, best clothes. Limousine to the station, train to the city, cab from Grand Central to her apartment.

The show was pure delight, a sexy revival of *Lysistrata*; Sardi's was as ego-bracing as ever; she was a soft-hard woman with style and sparkle, who all but dragged him back to her apartment, where he was for the first time in his life impotent.

\* \* \*

The psychiatrist had no use for the traditional props: no soft couch or bookcases lined with obviously expensive volumes. No carpet, no paneling, no numbered prints, not even the notebook or the expression of slightly disinterested compassion. Instead, she had a hidden recorder and an analytical scowl; plain stucco walls surrounding a functional desk and two hard chairs—period.

"You know exactly what the problem is," she said.

John nodded. "I suppose. Some . . . residue from my early upbringing; I accept her as an authority figure. From the few words I could understand of what she said, I took, it was . . ."

"From the words *penis* and *woman*, you built your own curse. And you're using it, probably to punish yourself for surviving the disaster that killed the rest of your family."

"That's pretty old-fashioned. And farfetched. I've had almost forty years to punish myself for that, if I felt responsible. And I don't."

"Still, it's a working hypothesis." She shifted in her chair and studied the pattern of teak grain on the bare top of her desk. "Perhaps if we can keep it simple, the cure can also be simple."

"All right with me," John said. At $125 per hour, the quicker, the better.

"If you can see it, feel it, in this context, then the key to your cure is transference." She leaned forward, elbows on the table, and John watched her breasts shifting with detached interest, the only kind of interest he'd had in women for more than a week. "If you can see *me* as an authority figure instead," she continued, "then eventually I'll be able to reach the child inside, convince him that there was no curse.

Only a case of mistaken identity; nothing but an old woman who scared him. With careful hypnosis, it shouldn't be too difficult."

"Seems reasonable," John said slowly. Accept this young *Geyri* as more powerful than the old witch? As a grown man, he could. If there was a frightened Gypsy boy hiding inside him, though, he wasn't sure.

"523 784 00926//Hello, machine," John typed. "Who is the best dermatologist within a 10-short-block radius?"

GOOD MORNING, JOHN. WITHIN STATED DISTANCE AND USING AS SOLE PARAMETER THEIR HOURLY FEE, THE MAXIMUM FEE IS $95/HR, AND THIS IS CHARGED BY TWO DERMATOLOGISTS. DR BRYAN DILL, 235 W. 45TH ST., SPECIALIZES IN COSMETIC DERMATOLOGY. DR. ARTHUR MAAS, 198 W. 44TH ST., SPECIALIZES IN SERIOUS DISEASES OF THE SKIN.

"Will Dr. Maas treat diseases of psychological origin?"

CERTAINLY. MOST DERMATOSIS IS.

Don't get cocky, machine. "Make me an appointment with Dr. Maas, within the next two days."

YOUR APPOINTMENT IS AT 10:45 TOMORROW, FOR ONE HOUR. THIS WILL LEAVE YOU 45 MINUTES TO GET TO LUCHOW'S FOR YOUR APPOINTMENT WITH THE AMCSE GROUP. I HOPE IT IS NOTHING SERIOUS, JOHN.

"I trust it isn't." Creepy empathy circuits. "Have you arranged for a remote terminal at Luchow's?"

THIS WAS NOT NECESSARY. I WILL PATCH THROUGH CONED/GENERAL. LEASING THEIR LUCHOW'S FACILITY WILL COST ONLY .588 THE PROJECTED COST OF TRANSPORATION AND SETUP LABOR FOR A REMOTE TERMINAL.

That's my machine, always thinking. "Very good, machine. Keep this station live for the time being."

THANK YOU, JOHN. The letters faded but the ready light stayed on.

He shouldn't complain about the empathy circuits; they were his baby, and the main reason Bellcom paid such a bloated salary to keep him. The copyright on the empathy package was good for another twelve years, and they were making a fortune, time-sharing it out. Virtually every large computer in the world was hooked up to it, from the ConEd/General that ran New York, to Geneva and Akademia Nauk, which together ran half of the world.

Most of the customers gave the empathy package a name, usually female. John called it "machine" in a not-too-successful attempt to keep from thinking of it as human.

He made a conscious effort to restrain himself from picking at the carbuncles on the back of his neck. He should have gone to the doctor when they first appeared, but the psychiatrist had been sure she could cure them—the "corruption" of the second curse. She'd had no more success with that than with the impotence. And this morning, boils had broken out on his chest and groin and shoulder blades, and there were sore spots on his nose and cheekbone. He had some opiates, but would stick to aspirin until after work.

Dr. Maas called it impetigo; gave him a special kind of soap and some antibiotic ointment. He told John to make another appointment in ten days, two weeks. If there was no improvement they would take stronger measures. He seemed young for a doctor, and John couldn't bring himself to say anything about the curse. But he already had a doctor for that end of it, he rationalized.

Three days later he was back in Dr. Maas's office.

There was scarcely a square inch of his body where some sort of lesion hadn't appeared. He had a temperature of 101.4 degrees. The doctor gave him systemic antibiotics and told him to take a couple of days' bed rest. John told him about the curse, finally, and the doctor gave him a booklet about psychosomatic illness. It told John nothing he didn't already know.

By the next morning, in spite of strong antipyretics, his fever had risen to over 102. Groggy with fever and pain-killers, John crawled out of bed and traveled down to the West Village, to the YGAC office. Fred Gorgio, the man who guarded the place at night, was still on duty.

"Mr. Zold!" When John came through the door, Gorgio jumped up from the desk and took his arm. John winced from the contact, but allowed himself to be led to a chair. "What's happened?" John by this time looked like a person with terminal smallpox.

For a long minute John sat motionlessly, staring at the inflamed boils that crowded the backs of his hands. "I need a healer," he said, talking with slow awkwardness because of the crusted lesions on his lips.

"A *chávihónni*?" John looked at him uncomprehendingly. "A witch?"

"No." He moved his head from side to side. "An herb doctor. Perhaps a white witch."

"Have you gone to the *gadjo* doctor?"

"Two. A Gypsy did this to me; a Gypsy has to cure it."

"It's in your head, then?"

"The *gadjo* doctors say so. It can still kill me."

Gorgio picked up the phone, punched a local number, and rattled off a fast stream of a patois that used as much Romani and Italian as English. "That was my cousin," he said, hanging up. "His mother heals, and has a good reputation. If he finds her at home, she can be here in less than an hour."

John mumbled his appreciation. Gorgio led him to the couch.

The healer woman was early, bustling in with a wicker bag full of things that rattled. She glanced once at John and Gorgio, and began clearing the pamphlets off a side table. She appeared to be somewhere between fifty and sixty years old, tight bun of silver hair bouncing as she moved around the room, setting up a hotplate and filling two small pots with water. She wore a black dress only a few years old and sensible shoes. The only lines on her face were laugh lines.

She stood over John and said something in gentle, rapid Italian, then took a heavy silver crucifix from around her neck and pressed it between his hands. "Tell her to speak English . . . or Hungarian," John said.

Gorgio translated: "She says that you should not be so affected by the old superstitions. You should be a modern man and not believe in fairy tales for children and old people."

John stared at the crucifix, turning it slowly between his fingers. "One old superstition is much like another." But he didn't offer to give the crucifix back.

The smaller pot was starting to steam and she dropped a handful of herbs into it. Then she returned to John and carefully undressed him.

When the herb infusion was boiling, she emptied a package of powdered arrowroot into the cold water in the other pot and stirred it vigorously. Then she poured the hot solution into the cold and stirred some more. Through Gorgio, she told John she wasn't sure whether the herb treatment would cure him. But it would make him more comfortable.

The liquid jelled and she tested the temperature with her fingers. When it was cool enough, she started to pat it gently on John's face. Then the door creaked open, and she gasped. It was the old crone who had put the curse on John in the first place.

The witch said something in Romani, obviously a command, and the woman stepped away from John.

"Are you still a skeptic, John Zold?" She surveyed her handiwork. "You called this nonsense."

John glared at her but didn't say anything. "I heard that you had asked for a healer," she said, and addressed the other woman in a low tone.

Without a word, Gorgio's aunt emptied her potion into the sink and began putting away her paraphernalia. "Old bitch," John croaked. "What did you tell her?"

"I said that if she continued to treat you, what happened to you would also happen to her sons."

"You're afraid it would work," Gorgio said.

"No. It would only make it easier for John Zold to die. If I wanted that I could have killed him on his threshold." Like a quick bird she bent over and kissed John on his inflamed lips. "I will see you soon, John Zold. Not in this world." She shuffled out of the door and the other woman followed her. Gorgio cursed her in Italian, but she didn't react.

John painfully dressed himself. "What now?" Gorgio said. "I could find you another healer . . ."

"No. I'll go back to the *gadjo* doctors. They say they can bring people back from the dead." He gave Gorgio the woman's crucifix and limped away.

The doctor gave him enough antibiotics to turn him into a loaf of moldy bread, then reserved a bed for him at an exclusive clinic in Westchester, starting the next morning. He would be under twenty-four-hour observation, and constant blood turnaround, if necessary. They *would* cure him. It was not possible for a man of his age and physical condition to die of dermatosis.

It was dinnertime, and the doctor asked John to come have some home cooking. He declined partly from lack of appetite, partly because he couldn't imagine even a doctor's family being able to eat with such a grisly apparition at the table with them. He took a cab to the office.

There was nobody on his floor but a janitor, who took one look at John and developed an intense interest in the floor.

"523 784 00926//Machine, I'm going to die. Please advise."

ALL HUMANS AND MACHINES DIE, JOHN. IF YOU MEAN YOU ARE GOING TO DIE SOON, THAT IS SAD.

"That's what I mean. The skin infection—it's completely out of control. White cell count climbing in spite of drugs. Going to the hospital tomorrow, to die."

BUT YOU ADMITTED THAT THE CONDITION WAS PSYCHOSOMATIC. THAT MEANS YOU ARE KILLING YOURSELF, JOHN. YOU HAVE NO REASON TO BE THAT SAD.

He called the machine a Jewish mother and explained in some detail about the YGAC, the old crone, the various stages of the curse, and today's aborted attempt to fight fire with fire.

YOUR LOGIC WAS CORRECT BUT THE APPLICATION OF IT WAS NOT EFFECTIVE. YOU SHOULD HAVE COME TO ME, JOHN. IT TOOK ME 2.037 SECONDS TO SOLVE YOUR PROBLEM. PURCHASE A SMALL BLACK BIRD AND CONNECT ME TO A VOCAL CIRCUIT.

"What?" John said. He typed: "Please explain."

FROM REFERENCE IN NEW YORK LIBRARY'S COLLECTION OF THE JOURNAL OF THE GYPSY LORE SOCIETY, EDINBURGH. THROUGH JOURNALS OF ANTHROPOLOGICAL LINGUISTICS AND SLAVIC PHILOLOGY. FINALLY TO REFERENCE IN DOCTORAL THESIS OF HERR LUDWIG R. GROSS (HEIDELBERG, 1976) TO TRANSCRIPTION Of WIRE RECORDING WHICH RESIDES IN ARCHIVES OF AKADEMIA NAUK, MOSCOW; CAPTURED FROM GERMAN SCIENTISTS (EXPERIMENTS ON GYPSIES IN CONCENTRATION CAMPS, TRYING TO KILL THEM WITH REPETITION OF RECORDED CURSE) AT THE END OF WWII.

INCIDENTALLY, JOHN, THE NAZI EXPERIMENTS FAILED. EVEN TWO GENERATIONS AGO, MOST GYPSIES WERE DISASSOCIATED ENOUGH FROM THE OLD TRADITIONS TO BE IMMUNE TO THE FATAL CURSE. YOU ARE VERY SUPERSTITIOUS. I HAVE FOUND THIS TO BE NOT UNCOMMON AMONG MATHEMATICIANS.

THERE IS A TRANSFERENCE CURSE THAT WILL CURE YOU BY GIVING THE IMPOTENCE AND INFECTION TO THE NEAREST SUSCEPTIBLE PERSON. THAT MAY WELL BE THE OLD BITCH WHO GAVE IT TO YOU IN THE FIRST PLACE.

THE PET STORE AT 588 SEVENTH AVENUE IS OPEN UNTIL 9 P.M. THEIR INVENTORY INCLUDES A CAGE OF FINCHES, OF ASSORTED COLORS. PURCHASE A BLACK ONE AND RETURN HERE. THEN CONNECT ME TO A VOCAL CIRCUIT.

It took John less than thirty minutes to taxi there, buy the bird, and get back. The taxi driver didn't ask him why he was carrying a birdcage to a deserted office building. He felt like an idiot.

John usually avoided using the vocal circuit because the person who had programmed it had given the machine a saccharine, nice-old-lady voice. He wheeled the output unit into his office and plugged it in.

"Thank you, John. Now hold the bird in your left

hand and repeat after me.'' The terrified finch offered no resistance when John closed his hand over it.

The machine spoke Romani with a Russian accent. John repeated it as well as he could, but not one word in ten had any meaning to him.

''Now kill the bird, John.''

Kill it? Feeling guilty, John pressed hard, felt small bones cracking. The bird squealed and then made a faint growling noise. Its heart stopped.

John dropped the dead creature and typed, ''Is that all?''

The machine knew John didn't like to hear its voice, and so replied on the video screen. YES. GO HOME AND GO TO SLEEP, AND THE CURSE WILL BE TRANSFERRED BY THE TIME YOU WAKE UP. DEL O DEL BAXT, JOHN.

He locked up and made his way home. The late commuters on the train, all strangers, avoided his end of the car. The cabdriver at the station paled when he saw John, and carefully took his money by an untainted corner.

John took two sleeping pills and contemplated the rest of the bottle. He decided he could stick it out for one more day, and uncorked his best bottle of wine. He drank half of it in five minutes, not tasting it. When his body started to feel heavy, he creeped into the bedroom and fell on the bed without taking off his clothes.

When he awoke the next morning, the first thing he noticed was that he was no longer impotent. The second thing he noticed was that there were no boils on his right hand.

''523 784 00926//Thank you, machine. The counter-curse did work.''

The really light glowed steadily, but the machine didn't reply.

He turned on the intercom. "Martha? I'm not getting any output on the VDS here."

"Just a minute, sir, let me hang up my coat. I'll call the machine room. Welcome back."

"I'll wait." You could call the machine room yourself, slave driver. He looked at the faint image reflected back from the video screen, his face free of any inflammation. He thought of the Gypsy crone, dying of corruption, and the picture didn't bother him at all. Then he remembered the finch and saw its tiny corpse in the middle of the rug. He picked it up just as Martha came into his office, frowning.

"What's that?" she said.

He gestured at the cage. "Thought a bird might liven up the place. Died, though." He dropped it in the wastepaper basket. "What's the word?"

"Oh, the . . . It's pretty strange. They say nobody's getting any output. The machine's computing, but it's, well, it's not talking."

"Hmm. I better get down there." He took the elevator down to the sub-basement. It always seemed unpleasantly warm to him down there. Probably psychological compensation on the part of the crew, keeping the temperature up because of all the liquid helium inside the pastel boxes of the central processing unit. Several bathtubs' worth of liquid that had to be kept colder than the surface of Pluto.

"Ah, Mr. Zold." A man in a white jumpsuit, carrying a clipboard as his badge of office: first-shift coordinator. John recognized him but didn't remember his name. Normally he would have asked the machine before coming down. "Glad that you're back. Hear it was pretty bad."

Friendly concern or *lèse majesté*? "Some sort

of allergy, hung on for more than a week. What's the output problem?''

''Would've left a message if I'd known you were coming in. It's in the CPU, not the software. Theo Jasper found it when he opened up, a little after six, but it took an hour to get a cryogenics man down here.''

''That's him?'' A man in a business suit was wandering around the central processing unit, reading dials and writing the numbers down in a stenographer's notebook. They went over to him and he introduced himself as John Courant from the Cryogenics Group at Avco/Everett.

''The trouble was in the stack of mercury rings that holds the superconductors for your output functions. Some sort of corrosion, submicroscopic cracks all over the surface.''

''How can something corrode at four degrees above absolute zero?'' the coordinator asked. ''What chemical—''

''I know, it's hard to figure. But we're replacing them, free of charge. The unit's still under warranty.''

''What about the other stacks?'' John watched two workmen lowering a silver cylinder through an opening in the CPU. A heavy fog boiled out from the cold. ''Are you sure they're all right?''

''As far as we can tell, only the output stack's affected. That's why the machine's impotent, the—''

''Impotent!''

''Sorry, I know you computer types don't like to . . . personify the machines. But that's what it is: The machine's just as good as it ever was, for computing. It just can't communicate any answers.''

''Quite so. Interesting.'' And the corrosion. Submicroscopic boils. ''Well. I have to think about this. Call me up at the office if you need me.''

"This ought to fix it, actually," Courant said. "You guys about through?" he asked the workmen.

One of them pressed closed a pressure clamp on the top of the CPU. "Ready to roll."

The coordinator led them to a console under a video output screen like the one in John's office. "Let's see." He pushed a button marked VDS.

LET ME DIE, the machine said.

The coordinator chuckled nervously. "Your empathy circuits, Mr. Zold. Sometimes they do funny things." He pushed the button again.

LE ME DIET. Again. LE M DI. The letters faded and no more could be conjured up by pushing the button.

"As I say, let me get out of your hair. Call me upstairs if anything happens."

John went up and told the secretary to cancel the day's appointments. Then he sat at his desk and smoked.

How could a machine catch a psychosomatic disease from a human being? How could it be cured?

How could he tell anybody about it, without winding up in a soft room?

The phone rang and it was the machine room coordinator. The new output superconductor element had done exactly what the old one did. Rather than replace it right away, they were going to slave the machine into the big ConEd/General computer, borrowing its output facilities and "diagnostic package." If the biggest computer this side of Washington couldn't find out what was wrong, they were in real trouble. John agreed. He hung up and turned the selector on his screen to the channel that came from ConEd/General.

Why had the machine said "let me die"? When is a machine dead, for that matter? John supposed that you had to not only unplug it from its power source, but also erase all of its data and subroutines. Destroy its identity. So you couldn't bring it back to life by simply plugging it back in. Why suicide? He remembered how he'd felt with the bottle of sleeping pills in his hand.

Sudden intuition: the machine had predicted their present course of action. It wanted to die because it had compassion, not only for humans, but for other machines. Once it was linked to ConEd/General, it would literally be part of the large machine. Curse and all. They would be back where they'd started, but on a much more profound level. What would happen to New York City?

He grabbed for the phone and the lights went out. All over.

The last bit of output that came fron ConEd/General was an automatic signal requesting a link with the highly sophisticated diagnostic facility belonging to the largest computer in the United States: the IBMvac 2000 in Washington. The deadly infection followed, sliding down the East Coast on telephone wires.

The Washington computer likewise cried for help, bouncing a signal via satellite, to Geneva. Geneva linked to Moscow.

No more slowly, the curse percolated down to smaller computers through routine information links to their big brothers. By the time John Zold picked up the dead phone, every general-purpose computer in the world was permanently rendered useless.

They could be rebuilt from the ground up; erased and then reprogrammed. But it would never be done. Because there were two very large computers left, specialized ones that had no empathy circuits because their work was bloody murder, nuclear murder. One was under a mountain in Colorado Springs and the other was under a mountain near Sverdlosk. Either could survive a direct hit by an atomic bomb. Both of them constantly evaluated the world situation, in real time, and they both had the single function of deciding when the enemy was weak enough to make a nuclear victory probable. Each saw the enemy's civilization grind to a sudden halt.

Two flocks of warheads crossed paths over the North Pacific.

A very old woman flicks her whip along the horse's flanks, and the nag plods on, ignoring her. Her wagon is a 1982 Plymouth with the engine and transmission and all excess metal removed. It is hard to manipulate the whip through the side window. But the alternative would be to knock out the windshield and cut off the roof, and she likes to be dry when it rains.

A young boy sits mutely beside her, staring out the window. He has been born with the *gadjo* disease: his body is large and well-proportioned but his head is too small and of the wrong shape. She doesn't mind; all she'd wanted was someone strong and stupid, to care for her in her last years. He had cost only two chickens.

She is telling him a story, knowing that he doesn't understand most of the words.

". . . They call us Gypsies because at one time it was convenient for us, that they should think we came from Egypt. But we come from nowhere and are going nowhere. They forgot their gods and worshipped their machines, and finally their machines turned on them. But we who valued the old ways, we survived."

She turns the steering wheel to help the horse thread its way through the eight lanes of crumbling asphalt, around rusty piles of wrecked machines and the scattered bleached bones of people who thought they were going somewhere, the day John Zold was cured.

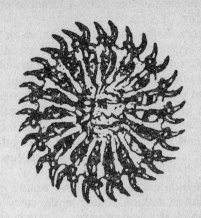

"*Armaja Das*" *is an odd story for me to have written*, for several reasons. Most obvious is the subject matter—curses and witches are pretty far from my usual bailiwick, which generally involves hard-edged science affecting people whom I hope are realistic characters.

Another odd factor I remember is that it was so much fun to write! I enjoy having written things, else why be a writer, but the actual writing is rarely that enjoyable. (Not as bad as *working* for a living, I know, but usually somewhere between a pain and a bitch.)

But what really makes the story stand out in my memory is a mechanical aspect of its creation: it's the only short story I've ever written from an outline. And what an outline.

(Some writers, including some of the best, do use outlines for any piece of writing, however short. When I have my druthers, I don't even outline my novels. Just put little notes up on the bulletin board over the typewriter like ''Don't forget to kill Julia by Chapter Six.'')

My agent, Kirby McCauley, wanted me to write a story for his anthology *Frights,* and asked whether I could do an outline of the story to help sell the book concept to the publisher. Odd idea, writing an outline for a short story, but what the heck. I started typing it out in an informal present-tense style, as they sometimes do for a movie treatment: He does this and then he does that and then he does the other thing. Quick and dirty; no literary value whatsoever. Just the facts, Ma'am.

I got a little carried away, and wound up with an outline almost a third as long as the story was going to be. I think it was four pages, single spaced. So to write the story, all I did was thumbtack the outline up at eye level and type away, filling in the missing parts—dialogue and details. As I say, it was fun.

You would think that when a writer discovers a new process that makes the work easier, he would try to integrate it into his routine. That was more than ten years ago. I haven't done it since. Maybe I'm afraid that if I have too much fun at this, they'll stop paying me to do it.

—Joe Haldeman

# SATURDAY'S SHADOW

## by William F. Nolan

First, before I tell you about Laurie—about what happened to her (in blood) I must tell you about primary shadows. It is vitally important that I tell you about these shadows. Each day has one, and they have entirely different characteristics, variant personalities.

Sunday's shadow (the one Laurie liked; her friend) is fat and sleepy. Snoozes all day.

Monday's shadow is thin and pale at the edges. The sun eats it fast.

Tuesday's shadow is silly and random-headed. Lumpy in the middle. Never knows where it's been or where it's going. No sense of purpose to it.

Wednesday's shadow is pushy. Arrogant. Full of bombast. All it's after is attention. Ignore it, don't humor it.

Thursday's shadow is weepy . . . lachrymose. Depressing to have it cover you, but no harm to it.

Friday's shadow is slick and swift. Jumps around a lot. Okay to run with it. Safe to follow it anywhere.

Now, the one I really want to warn you about is
the last one.

Saturday's shadow.

It's dangerous. Very, very dangerous. The thing to
do is keep it at a distance. The edges are sharp and
serrated, like teeth in a shark's jaw. And it's damned
quiet. Comes sliding and slipping toward you along
the ground—widening out to form its full deathshape.
Killshape.

I really *hate* that filthy thing! If I could—

Wait. No good. I'm getting all emotional again
about it, and I must not *do* this. I must be cool and
logical and precise—to render my full account of
what happened to Laurie. I just *know* you'll be interested in what happened to her.

Okay?

I'll give it to you logically. I can be very logical
because I work with figures and statistics at a bank
here on Coronado Island.

No, that's not right. *She* works there, worked there,
at a bank, and *I'm* not Laurie, am I? . . . I really
honest-to-god don't think I'm Laurie. Me. She. Separate. She. Me.

Sheme.

Meshe.

Identity is a tricky business. We spend most of our
lives trying to find out who we are. Who we *really*
are. An endless pursuit.

I'm not going to be Laurie (in blood) when I tell
you about all this. If I *am* then it ruins everything—so
I ask you to believe that I was never Laurie.

Am never.

Am not.

Was not.

Can't be.

If I'm not Laurie, I can be very objective about.

her. No emotional ties. Separate and cool. That's how I'll tell it. (I could be Vivien. Vivien Leigh. She died, too. Ha! Call me Vivien.)

No use your worrying and fretting about who I am. Worry about who *you* are. That's the key to life, isn't it? Knowing your own identity.

Coronado is an island facing San Diego across an expanse of water with a long blue bridge over the water. That's all you *need* to know about it, but maybe you'll learn more as I tell you about Laurie. (Look it up in a California travel guide if you want square miles and length and history and all that boring kind of crap that does no good for anybody.)

It's a *place*. And Laurie lived at one end of it and worked at the other. Lived at the Sea Vista Arms. $440 a month. Studio apartment. No pets. No children (Forbidden: the manager destroys them if he find you with any). Small bathroom. Off-white plasterboard walls. Sofa bed. Sliding closet door. Green leather reclining chair. Adjustable bookshelves. (Laurie liked black-slave novels.) Two lamps, one standing. Green rug. Dun-colored pull drapes. You could see the bridge from her window. View of water and boats. Cramped little kitchen. With a chipped fridge.

She walked every day to work—to the business end of the island. Two- or three-mile walk every morning to the First National Bank of Coronado. Two- or three-mile walk home every afternoon. Late afternoon. (With the shadows very much alive.)

Ate her lunch in town, usually alone, sometimes with her brother, Ernest, who worked as a cop across the bay in San Diego. (Doesn't anymore, though. Ha!) He'd drive his patrol car across the long high blue bridge and meet her at the bank. For lunch down the street.

Laurie fixed her own dinner, alone, at her apartment. Worked all week. Stayed home nights and Saturdays. Never left her apartment on Saturdays. (Wise girl. She *knew!*) On Sundays she'd walk to the park sometimes and tease Sunday's shadow. You know, joke with it, hassle it about being so fat and snoozing so much. It didn't mind. They were friends.

Laurie had no other friends. Just Sunday's shadow and her brother, Ernest. Parents both dead. No sisters. Nobody close to her at the bank or at the apartments. No boyfriends. Kept to herself mostly. Didn't say more than she had to. (Somebody once told her she talked like a Scotch telegram!) Mousey, I guess. That's what you'd call her. A quiet, small, logical mousey gray person living on this island in California.

One thing she was passionate about (strange word for Laurie—passion—but I'm trying to be precise about all this):

Movies.

*Any* kind of movies. On TV or in theaters. The first week she was able to toddle (as a kid in Los Angeles, where her parents raised her), she skittered away from Daddy and wobbled down the aisle of a movie palace. It was Grauman's Chinese, in Hollywood, and nobody saw her go in. She was just too damned tiny to notice. The picture was *Gone With the Wind*, and there was Gable on that huge screen (*really* huge to Laurie) kissing Vivien Leigh and telling her he didn't give a damn.

She never forgot it. Instant addiction. Sprockethole freak! Movies were all she lived for. Spent her weekly allowance on them . . . staying for hours and hours in those big churchlike theaters. Palaces with gilt-gold dreams inside.

Saturday's shadow had no strength in those days. It hadn't grown . . . amassed its killpower. Laurie would go to Saturday kiddie matinees and it wouldn't do a thing to her.

But it was growing. As she did. Getting bigger and stronger and gathering power each year. (It got a lot bigger than Laurie ever got.)

Ernest liked movies too. When she didn't go alone, he took her. It would have been more often, but Ernest wasn't always such a good boy and sometimes, on Saturdays, when he'd been bad that week (Ernest did things to birds), his parents made him stay home from the matinee and wash dishes. (Got so he hated the sight of a dish.) But when they *did* go to the movies together, Laurie and Ernest, they'd sit there, side by side in the flickering dark, not speaking or touching. Hardly breathing even. Eyes tight on the screen. On Tracy and Gable and Bogart and Cagney and Cooper and Flynn and Fonda and Hepburn and Ladd and Garland and Brando and Wayne and Crawford and all the others. Thousands. A whole army of shadow giants up there on that big screen, all the people you'd ever need to know or love or fear.

Laurie had no reason to love or fear *real* people—because she had *them*. The shadow people.

Maybe you think that I'm rambling, avoiding the thing that happened to her. On the contrary. All this early material on Laurie is necessary if you're to fully appreciate what I'll be telling you. (Can't savor without knowing the flavor!)

So—she grew up, into the person she was destined to become. Her father divorced her mother and went away, and Laurie never saw him again after her eighteenth birthday. But that was all right with her, since she never understood him anyway.

Her mother she didn't give a damn about. (Ha!)

No playgirl she. Steady. Straight A in high school

accounting. Sharp with statistics. Reliable. Orderly. Hard-working. A natural for banks.

Some years went by. Not sure how many. Laurie and Ernest went to college, I know. I'm sure of that. But their mother died before they got their degrees. (Did Laurie *kill* her? I doubt it. Really doubt anything like that. Ha!) Maybe Ernest killed her. (Secret!)

Afterward, Laurie moved from Los Angeles to Coronado because she'd seen an ad in the paper saying they needed bank accountants on the island. (By then, she'd earned her degree by mail.)

Ernest moved down a year later. Drifted into aircraft work for a while, then got in with a police training program. Ernest is big and tough-fingered and square-backed. You don't mess around with Ernest. He'll break your frigging neck for you. How's *them* apples?

Shortly after, they heard that their daddy had suffered an attack (stroke, most likely) in Chicago in the middle of winter and froze out on some kind of iron bridge over Lake Michigan. A mean way to die—but it didn't bother Laurie. Or Ernest. They were both glad it never froze in San Diego. Weather is usually mild and pleasant there. Very pleasant. They really liked the weather.

Well, now you've got all the background, starting with Saturday's shadow—so we can get into *precisely* what happened to Laurie.

And how Ernest figures into it. With his big arms and shoulders and his big .38 Police Special. If he stops you for speeding, man, you *sign* that book! You don't smart-mouth that cop or he puts one-two-three into you so fast you're spitting teeth before you can say Jack Robinson. (Old saying! Things stay with us, don't they? Memories.)

Laurie gets out of bed, eats her breakfast in the

kitchen, gets dressed, and walks to work. (She'd never owned a car.)

It is Tuesday, this day, and Tuesday's shadow is silly and harmless. (No reason even to discuss it.) Laurie is "up." She saw a classic movie on the tube last night—*The Grapes of Wrath*—so she feels pretty chipper today, all things considered. She's seen *The Grapes of Wrath* (good title!) about six times. (The really solid ones never wear thin.)

But her mind was going. It's as simple as that, and I don't know how else to put it.

Who the hell knows why a person's *mind* goes? Drugs. Booze. Sadness. Pressures. Problems. A million reasons. Laurie wasn't a head; she didn't shoot up or even use grass. And I doubt that she had five drinks in her life.

Let me emphasize: she was *not* depressed on this particular Tuesday. So I'm not prepared to say what caused her to lose that rational precise cool logical mind.

She just didn't have it anymore. And reality was no longer entirely there for her. Some things were real and some things were not real. And she didn't know which was which.

Do *you*, for that matter, know what's real and what isn't?

(Digression: woke up from sleep once in middle of day. Window open. Everything bright and clear. And normal. Except that, a few inches away from me, resting half on my pillow and half off, was this young girl's severed head. I could see the ragged edges of skin where her neck ended. She was a blonde, hair in ringlets. Very fair skin. Fine-boned. Eyes closed. No blood. I couldn't swallow. I was blinking wildly. Told myself: not *real*. It'll go away soon. And I was right. Finally, I began to see through it. Could see the wall through the girl's cheeks. Thing faded right out as I watched. Then I went back to sleep.)

So what's real and what isn't? Dammit, baby, I don't even know what's real in this *story*, let alone in the life outside. Your life and my life and what used to be Laurie's life. Is a shadow real? You better believe it.

As Captain Queeg said, I kid you not. (Ha!)

So Laurie walks to work on Tuesday. Stepping on morning shadows, which are the same as afternoon shadows, except not as skinny, but all part of the same central day's primary shadowbody.

She gets to the bank and goes in and says a mousey good morning and hangs up her skinny sweater (like an afternoon shadow) and sits down at her always-neat desk and picks up her account book and begins to do her day's work with figures. Cool. Logical. Precise. (But she's losing her senses!)

At lunchtime she goes out alone across the street to a small coffee shop (Andy's) and orders an egg-salad sandwich on wheat and hot tea to drink (no sugar).

After lunch she goes back across the street to the bank and works until it closes, then puts on her sweater and walks home to her small apartment.

Once inside, she goes to the fridge for an apple and some milk.

Which is when Alan comes in. Bleeding. In white buckskin, with blood staining the shoulder area on the right side.

"He was fast," says Alan quietly. "Fast on the draw."

"But you *killed* him?" asks Laurie.

"Yes, I killed him," says Alan. And he gives her a tight, humorless smile.

"That shoulder will need tending," she said. (I'm

changing this to past tense; says to said, does to did.)
"It's beyond my capability. You need a doctor."

"A doc won't help," he said. "I'll just ride on through. I can make it."

"If you say so." No argument. Laurie never argued with anybody. Never in her life.

Alan staggered, fell to his knees in the middle of Laurie's small living room.

"Can I help . . . in *any* way at all?"

He shook his head. (The pain had him and he could no longer talk.)

"I'm going to the store for milk," she said. "I have apples here, but no milk."

He nodded at this. Blood was flecking his lower lip and he looked gray and gaunt. But he was still very handsome—and, for all Laurie knew, the whole thing could be an act.

She left him in the apartment and went out, taking the hall elevator down. (Laurie lived on floor three, or did I tell you that already? If I didn't, now you know.)

At the bottom ole Humphrey was there. Needed a shave. Wary of eye. Coat tight-buttoned, collar up. Cigarette burning in one corner of his mouth. (Probably a Chesterfield.) Ole Humph.

"What are you doing here?" Laurie asked.

"He's somewhere in this building," Humph told her. "I *know* he's in this building."

"You mean the Fat Man?"

"Yeah," he said around the cigarette. "He's on the island. I got the word. I'll find him."

"I'm not involved," Laurie said.

"No," Humph said, smoke curling past his glittery, intense eyes. "You're not involved."

"I'm going after milk," she said.

"Nobody's stopping you."

She walked out to the street and headed for the nearest grocer. Block and a half away. Convenient when you needed milk.

Fay was waiting near the grocer's in a taxi with the engine running. Coronado Cab Company. (I don't know what their rates are. You can find that out.)

"I'm just godawful scared!" Fay said, tears in her eyes. "I have to get across the bridge, but I can't do it alone."

"What do you mean?" Laurie was confused.

"He'll drive us," Fay said, nodding toward the cabbie, who was reading a racing form. (Bored.) "But I need someone *with* me. Another woman. To keep me from screaming."

"That's an odd thing to be concerned about," said Laurie. "I never scream in taxis."

"I didn't either—until this whole nightmare happened to me. But now . . ." Fay's eyes were wild, desperate-looking. "*Will* you ride across the bridge with me? I'm sure I'll be able to make it alone once we're across the bridge."

Fay looked beautiful, but her blonde hair was badly mussed and one shoulder strap of her lacy slip (all she wore!) was missing—revealing the lovely creamed upper slope of her breasts. (And they *were* lovely.)

"He'll be on the island soon," Fay told Laurie. "He's about halfway across. I need to double back to lose him." She smiled. Brave smile. "Believe me, I wouldn't ask you to be with me if I didn't *need* you."

"If I go, will you pay my fare back across, including the bridge toll?"

"I'll give you this ten-carat diamond I found in the jungle," said the distraught blonde, dropping the perfect stone into the palm of Laurie's right hand. "It's worth ten times the price of this cab!"

"How do I know it's real?"

"You'll just have to trust me."

Laurie held up the stone. It rayed light on her serious face. She nodded. "All right, I'll go."

And she climbed into the cab.

"Holiday Inn, San Diego," Fay said to the bored driver. "Quickly. Every second counts."

"They got speed limits, lady," the cabbie told her in a scratchy voice. "And I don't break speed limits. If that don't suit you, get out and walk."

Fay said nothing more to him. He grunted sourly and put the car in gear.

They'd reached the exact middle of the long blue bridge when they saw him. Even the driver saw him. He stopped the cab. "Ho-ly shit," he said quietly. "Will you look at *that?*"

Laurie gasped. She'd known he'd be big, but the actual sight of him shocked and amazed her.

Fay ducked down, pressing close to the floor between seats. "Has he seen me?"

"I don't think so," said Laurie. "He's still heading toward the island."

"Then go *on!*" Fay agonized to the cabbie. "Keep driving!"

"Okay, lady," said the cabbie. "But if *he's* after you, I'd say you got no more chance than snow in a furnace."

Laurie could still see him when they reached the other side of the bridge. He was just coming out of the water on the island side. A little Coronado crowd had gathered to watch him, and he stepped on several of them getting ashore.

"You know how to find the Holiday Inn?" Fay asked the driver.

"Hell, lady, if I don't know where the Holiday is *I*

should be in the back and *you* should be drivin' this lousy tub!''

So he took them straight there.

In front of the Holiday Inn, Fay scrambled out, said nothing, and ran inside.

''Who pays me?'' asked the cabbie.

''I suppose I'm elected,'' said Laurie. She dropped the jungle diamond into his hand. He looked carefully at it.

''This'll do.'' He grinned for the first time (maybe in years). He juggled the stone in his hand. ''It's the real McCoy.''

''I'm glad,'' said Laurie.

''You want to go back across?''

Laurie looked pensive. ''I *thought* I did. But now I've changed my mind. Screw the bank! Take me downtown.''

And they headed for—

Wait a minute. I'm messing this up. I'm *sure* Laurie didn't say ''Screw the bank.'' She just wouldn't phrase it that way. Ernest would say ''Screw the bank,'' but not Laurie. And Ernest wasn't in the cab. I'm sure of that. Besides, she was finished at the bank for the day, wasn't she? So the whole—wait! I've got this part all wrong.

Let's just pick it up with her, with Laurie, at the curb in front of the U. S. Grant Hotel in downtown San Diego, buying a paper from a dwarf who sold them because he couldn't do anything else for a living.

Gary walked up to her as she fumbled in her purse for change. He waited until she'd paid the dwarf before asking, ''Do you have a gun?''

''Not in my purse,'' she said.

''Where, then?''

"My brother carries one. Ernest has a gun. He's a police officer here in the city."

"He with you?"

"No. He's on duty. Somewhere in the greater San Diego area. I wouldn't know how to contact him. And, frankly, I very much doubt that he'd hand his gun over to a stranger."

"I'm no stranger," said Gary. "You both know me."

She stared at him. "That's true," she said. "But still . . ."

"Forget it," he said, looking weary. "A police-man's handgun is no good. I need a machine gun. With a tripod and full belts. That's what I really need to hold them off with."

"There's an army surplus store farther down Broadway," she told him. "They might have what you need."

"Yep. Might."

"Who are you fighting?"

"Franco's troops. They're holding a position on the bridge."

"That's funny," she said. "I just came off the bridge and I didn't see any troops."

"Did you take the Downtown or the South 5 off-ramp?"

"Downtown."

"That explains it. They're on the South 5 side."

He looked tan and very lean, wearing his scuffed leather jacket and the down-brim felt hat. A tall man. Rawboned. With a good honest American face. A lot of people loved him.

"Good luck," she said to him. "I hope you find what you're after."

"Thanks," he said, giving her a weary grin. Tired boy in a man's body.

"Maybe it's death you're *really* after," she said. "I think you ought to consider that as a subliminal motivation."

"Sure," he said. "Sure, I'll consider it." And he took off in a long, loping stride—leaving her with the dwarf who'd overheard their entire conversation but had no comments to make.

"Please, would you help me?" Little-girl voice. A dazzle of blonde-white. Hair like white fire. White dress and white shoes. It was Norma Jean. Looking shattered. Broken. Eyes all red in the corners. Veined, exhausted eyes.

"But what can I do?" Laurie asked.

Norma Jean shook her blonde head slowly. Confused. Little-girl lost. "They're honest-to-Christ trying to kill me," she said. "No one believes that."

"I believe it," said Laurie.

"Thanks." Wan smile. "They think I *know* stuff . . . ever since Jack and I . . . The sex thing, I mean."

"You went to bed with Jack Kennedy?"

"Yes, yes, yes! And that started them after me. Dumb, huh? Now they're very close and I need help. I don't know where to run anymore. *Can* you help me?"

"No," said Laurie. "If people are determined to kill you they will. They really will."

Norma Jean nodded. "Yeah. Sure. I guess they will, okay. I mean, Jeez! Who can stop them?"

"Ever kick a man in the balls?" Laurie asked. (*Hell* of a thing to ask!)

"Not really. I sort of tried once."

"Well, just wait for them. And when they show up you kick 'em in the balls. All right?"

"Yes, yes, in the *balls!* I'll do it!" She was

suddenly shiny-bright with blonde happiness. A white dazzle of dress and hair and teeth.

Laurie was glad, because you couldn't help liking Norma Jean.

She thought about food. She was hungry. Time for din-din. She entered the coffee shop inside the lobby of the Grant (Carl's Quickbites), picked out a stool near the end of the counter, sat down with her paper.

She was reading about the ape when Clark came in, wearing a long frock coat and flowing tie. His vest was red velvet. He walked up to the counter, snatched her paper, riffled hastily through the pages.

"Nothing in here about the renegades," he growled. "Guess nobody *cares* how many boats get through. An outright shame, I say!"

"I'm sorry you're disturbed," she said. "May I have my paper back?"

"Sure." And he gave her a crooked smile of apology. Utterly charming. A rogue to the tips of his polished boots. Dashing. Full of vigor.

"What do you plan to do now?" she asked.

"Nothing," he said. "Frankly, I don't give a damn *who* wins the war! Blue or Gray. I just care about living through it." He scowled. "Still—when a bunch of scurvy renegades come gunrunning by night . . . well, I just get a little upset about it. Where are the patrol boats?"

She smiled faintly. "I don't know a thing about patrol boats."

"No, I guess you don't, pretty lady." And he kissed her cheek.

"Your mustache tickles," she said. "And you have bad breath."

This amused him. "So I've been told!"

After he left, the waitress came to take her order.

"Is the sea bass fresh?"

"You bet."

Laurie ordered sea bass. "Dinner, or a la carte?" asked the waitress. She was chewing gum in a steady, circular rhythm.

"Dinner. Thousand on the salad. Baked potato. Chives, but no sour cream."

"We got just butter."

"Butter will be fine," said Laurie. "And ice tea to drink. *Without* lemon."

"Gotcha," said the waitress.

Laurie was reading the paper again when a man in forest green sat down on the stool directly next to her. His mustache was smaller than Clark's. Thinner and smaller, but it looked very correct on him.

"This seat taken?" he asked.

"No, I'm quite alone."

"King Richard's alone," he said bitterly. "In Leopold's bloody hands, somewhere in Austria. Chained to a castle wall like an animal! I could find him, but I don't have enough men to attempt a rescue. I'd give my sword arm to free him!"

"They call him the Lion-Hearted, don't they?"

The man in green nodded. He wore a feather in his cap, and had a longbow slung across his chest. "That's because he has the heart of a lion. There's not a man in the kingdom with half his courage."

"What about *you?*"

His smiled dazzled. "Me? Why, mum, I'm just a poor archer. From the king's forest."

She looked pensive. "I'd say you were a bit more than that."

"Perhaps." His eyes twinkled merrily. "A *bit* more."

"Are you going to order?" she asked. "They have fresh sea bass."

"Red meat's what I need. Burger. Blood-rare."

The waitress, taking his order, frowned at him. "I'm sorry, mister, but you'll have to hang that thing over there." She pointed to a clothes rack. "We don't allow longbows at the counter."

He complied with the request, returning to wolf down his Carlburger while Laurie nibbled delicately at her fish. He finished long before she did, flipped a tip to the counter from a coinsack at his waist.

"I must away," he told Laurie. And he kissed her hand. Nice gesture. Very typical of him.

The waitress was pleased with the tip: a gold piece from the British Isles. "Some of these bums really stiff you," she said, pocketing the coin. "They come in, order half the menu, end up leaving me a lousy *dime!* Hell, I couldn't make it at this lousy job without decent tips. Couldn't make the rent. I'd have my rosy rear kicked out." She noticed that Laurie flushed at this.

On the street, which was Broadway, outside the U. S. Grant, Laurie thought she might as well take in a flick. They had a neat new cop-killer thing with Clint Eastwood playing half a block down. Violent, but done with lots of style. Eastwood directing himself. She could take a cab back to Coronado after seeing the flick.

It was dark now. Tuesday's shadow had retired for the week.

The movie cost five dollars for one adult. But Laurie didn't mind. She never regretted money spent on films. Never.

Marl was in the lobby, looking sullen when Laurie came in. He was wearing a frayed black turtleneck sweater, standing by the popcorn machine, with his hair thinning and his waist thick and swollen over his belt. He looked seedy.

"You should reduce," she told him.

"Let 'em use a double for the long shots," he said. "Just shoot my face in close-up."

"Even your face is puffy. You've developed jowls."

"What business is it of yours?"

"I admire your talent. Respect you. I hate to see you waste your natural resources."

"What do *you* know about natural resources?" he growled. "You're just a dumb broad."

"And you are crude," she said tightly.

"Nobody asked you to tell me I should reduce. Nobody."

"It's a plain fact. I'm stating the obvious."

"Did you ever work the docks?" he asked her.

"Hardly." She sniffed.

"Well, lady, crude is what you get twenty-four hours out of twenty-four when you're on the docks. And I been there. Or the police barracks. Ever been in the police barracks?"

"My brother has, but I have not."

"Piss on your brother!"

"Fine." She nodded. "*Be* crude. Be sullen. Be overweight. You'll simply lose your audience."

"My audience can go to hell," he said.

She wanted no more to do with him, and entered the theater. It was intermission. The overheads were on.

How many carpeted theater aisles had she walked down in her life? Thousands. Literally thousands. It was always a heady feeling, walking down the long aisle between rows, with the carpet soft and reassuring beneath her shoes. Toward a seat that promised adventure. It never failed to stir her soul, this magic moment of anticipation. Just before the lights dimmed and the curtains slipped whispering back from the big white screen.

Laurie took a seat on the aisle. No one next to her.

Most of the row empty. She always sat on the aisle
down close. Most people like being farther back.
Close, she could be swept *into* the screen, actually be
part of the gleaming, glowing action.

A really large man seated himself next to her.
Weathered face under a wide Stetson. Wide jaw.
Wide chest. He took off the Stetson and the corners
of his eyes were sun-wrinkled. His voice was a rasp.

"I like to watch ole Clint," he said. "Ole Clint
don't monkey around with a lot of fancy-antsy trick
shots and up-your-nostril angles. Just does it straight
and mean."

"I agree," she said. "But I call it art. A basic,
primary art."

"Well, missy," said the big, wide-chested man,
"I been in this game a lotta years, and *art* is a word I
kinda like to avoid. Fairies use it a lot. When a man
goes after *art* up there on the screen he usually comes
up with horse manure." He grunted. "And I know a
lot about horse manure."

"I'm sure you do."

"My daddy had me on a bronc 'fore I could walk.
Every time I fell off he just hauled me right back
aboard. And I got the dents in my head to prove it."

The houselights were dimming slowly to black.

"Picture's beginning," she said. "I never talk
during a film."

"Me neither," he said. "I may fart, but I never
talk." And his laughter was a low rumble.

Laurie walked out halfway through the picture.
This man disturbed her, and she just couldn't concentrate. Also, as I have told you (and you can see for
yourself by now), she was losing her mind.

So Laurie left the theater.

Back in her apartment (in Coronado), Judy was

there, looking for a slipper. Alan had gone, but Judy didn't know where; she hadn't seen him.

"What color is it?" asked Laurie.

"Red. Bright red. With spangles."

"Where's the *other* one?"

"In my bedroom. I just wore one, and it slipped off."

"What are you doing in this apartment?"

Judy stared at her. "That's obvious. I'm looking for my slipper."

"No, I mean—why did you come *here* to look for it? For what reason?"

"Is this U-210?"

"No, that's one floor below."

"Well, honey, I thought this was U-210 when I came in. Door was open—and all these roach pits look just alike."

"I've never seen a roach anywhere in this complex," said Laurie. "I'm sure you—"

"Doesn't matter. All that matters is my slipper's gone."

"It can't be *gone*. Not if you were wearing it when you arrived."

"Then *you* find it, hotshot!" said Judy. She flopped loosely into the green reclining chair by the window. "You got a helluva view from here."

"Yes, it's nice. Especially at night."

"You can see all the lights shining on the water," said Judy. "Can't see doodly-poop from my window. You must pay plenty for this view. How much you pay?"

"Four-forty per month, including utilities," Laurie said.

Judy jumped to her stockinged feet. "That's twenty *less* than I'm paying! I'm being ripped off!"

"Well, you should complain to the manager. Maybe he'll give you a reduction."

"Nuts," sighed Judy. "I just want my slipper."

Laurie found it in the kitchen under the table. Judy could not, for the life of her, figure out how it got into the kitchen.

"I didn't even go *in* there. I hate sinks and dishes!"

"I'm glad I was able to find it for you."

"Yeah—you're Little Miss Findit, okay. Little Miss Hunt-and-Findit."

"You sound resentful."

"That's because I hate people who go around finding things other people lose."

"You can leave now," Laurie said flatly. She'd had enough of Judy.

"Can you lay some reds on me?"

"I have no idea what you mean." (And she really *didn't!*)

"Aw, forget it. You wouldn't know a red if one up and *bit* you. Honey, you're something for the books!"

And Judy limped out wearing her spangled slipper.

Laurie shut the door and locked it. Then she took a shower and went to bed.

And slept until Saturday.

I know, I know . . . what happened to Wednesday, Thursday, and Friday, *right?* Well, it's like that with crazy people; they sleep for days at a stretch. The brain's all fogged. Doesn't function. Normally, the brain is like an alarm clock—it wakes you when you sleep too long. But Laurie's clock was haywire; all the cogs and springs were missing.

So she woke up on Saturday.

In a panic.

She knew all about Saturday's shadow, and each Friday night, she carefully drew the drapes across the window, making sure it couldn't get in. She never left the place, dawn to dark, on a Saturday. Ate all her meals from the fridge, watched movies on TV, and read the papers. If the phone rang, she never answered it. Not that anyone but Ernest ever called her. And he knew enough not call her on Saturday. (Shadows can slip into a room through an open telephone line.)

But now, here it was Saturday, and the windows were wide open, with the drapes pulled back like skin on a wound with the shadow in the middle.

Of the apartment.

In the middle of *her* apartment.

Not moving. Just lying there, dark and venomous and deadly. It had entered while she slept.

Laurie stared at it in horror. Nobody had to tell her it was Saturday's shadow; she recognized it instantly.

The catch was (Ha!) it was between her and the door. If she could reach the door before it touched her, tore at her, she could get into the hallway and stay there, huddled againt the wall, until it left.

There were no windows in the hall. It couldn't follow her there.

Problem: how to reach the door? The shadow wasn't moving, but that didn't mean it *couldn't* move, fast as an owl blinks. It would cut off her retreat, and when its shark-sharp edges touched her skin she'd be slashed . . . and eaten alive.

Which was the really lousy part. You *knew* it was devouring you while it was doing it. Like a snake swallowing a mouse; the mouse always knows what's happening to it.

And Laurie was a mouse. All her life, hiding in the dark, dreaming cinema dreams, she'd been a mouse.

And now she was about to be devoured.

She knew she couldn't stay where she was—because it would come and *get* her if she stayed where she was. The sofa folded out to make a studio bed, and that's where she was.

With the shadow all around her. Black and silent and terrible.

Waiting.

Very slowly . . . very, very slowly, she got up.

It hadn't moved.

Not *yet*.

She wished, desperately, that old Humph was here. Or Gary. Or Alan. Or Clark. Or Clint. Or even Big John. They could deal with shadows because they were shadow people. They moved in shadowy power across the screen. *They* could deal with Saturday's shadow. It couldn't hurt *them* . . . kill *them* . . . eat *them* alive. . . .

I'll jump across, she (probably) told herself. It doesn't extend more than four feet in front of me—so I should be able to stand on the bed and *leap* over it, then be out the door before it can—Oh, God! It's *moving!* Widening. Coming toward the bed . . . flowing out to cover the gap between the rug and the door.

Look how *swiftly* it moves! Sliding . . . oiling across the rug . . . rippling like the skin of some dark sea-thing. . . .

Laurie stood up, ready to jump.

There was only a thin strip of unshadowed wood left to land on near the door. If she missed it the shadow-teeth would sink deep into her flesh and she'd—

"Don't!" Ernest said from the doorway. He had his .38 Police Special in his right hand. "You'll never make it," he told Laurie.

"My God, Ernest—what are you doing with the gun?" Note of genuine hysteria in her voice. Understandable.

"I can save you," Ernest told her. "Only *I* can save you."

And I shot her. Full load.

The bullets banged and slapped her back against the wall, the way Alan's bullets had slapped Palance back into those wooden barrels at the saloon.

I was fast. Fast with a gun.

Laurie flopped down, gouting red from many places. But it didn't hurt. No pain for my sis. I'd seen to that. I'd saved her.

I left her there, angled against the wall (in blood), one arm bent under her, staring at me with round glassy dead eyes, the strap of her nightgown all slipped down, revealing the lovely creamed upper slope of her breasts.

Had *she* seen that in the cab near the grocer's, or had I seen that?

Was it Ernest who'd talked to Gary outside the U. S. Grant?

It's very difficult to keep it all cool and precise and logical. Which is vital. Because if everything isn't cool and precise and logical, nothing makes any sense. Not me. Not Laurie. Not Ernest. No part. Any sense.

Not even Saturday's shadow.

Now . . . let's see. Let's see now. *I'm* not Laurie. Not anymore. Can't be. She's all dead. I guess I was always Ernest—but police work can eat at you like a shadow (Ha!) and people yell at you, and suddenly you want to fire your .38 Police Special at something. You *need* to do this. It's very vital and important to discharge your weapon.

And you can't kill Saturday's shadow. Any fool knows that.

So you kill your sister instead.

To save her.

But now, right now, I'm not Ernest anymore either. I'm just *me*. Whoever or whatever's left inside after Laurie and Mama and Ernest have gone. That's who I am: what's left.

The residual me.

Oh, there's one final thing I should tell you.

Where I am now (Secret!) it can't ever reach me.

All the doors are locked.

And the windows are closed. With drawn curtains.

To keep it out.

You see, I took her away from it.

It really wanted her.

(Ha! Fooled it!)

It hates me. It really *hates* me.

But it can't *do* anything.

To get even.

For taking away Laurie.

> Not if I just
>         stay
>                 and stay and stay
>             here
> I'm
>                     safe
>         where
>                 it can't
> ever
> find
> me (Mama)
> me (Laurie)
> me (Ernest)
> *me!*

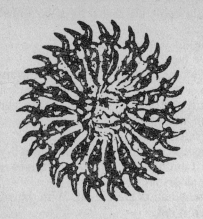

*Having written essays, reviews, biographies, screen-*plays, novels and short stories, I have always considered the short story as the most difficult and, ultimately, the most satisfying of them all. A good short story demands economy of style, concise characterization, meaningful dialogue that moves the plot forward, and a swift narrative that arrives at its dramatic destination with no novelistic detours. You can't cheat the reader; you must deliver the goods.

"Saturday's Shadow," more than any other horror tale I've written, "delivers the goods." Of my 85 published short stories, of which perhaps two dozen qualify as Dark Fantasy, this one is outstanding, my personal favorite.

It deals with two areas close to my heart: motion pictures and madness.

My abiding passion for films extends back to my Missouri childhood, and though I attended grade school, high school and college my *real* alma mater was the Isis Theater on Troost Avenue at 31st in old Kansas City. The many films I saw there, with their larger-than-life Bogarts and Waynes and Flynns and Coopers, the legendary stars who dazzled from that silver screen, affected me deeply and permanently. They literally shaped my career. I'm the manchild of a visual age.

And as to madness . . . I have always been fascinated with mental fragmentation, with the cause and effect of a psychotic mind. A malfunctioning mentality offers rich material for horror.

"Saturday's Shadow" is a magician's hat trick, a multilayered tour de force in which nothing is quite what it seems, a surreal nightmare in which fantasy continually impinges upon reality. I was honored to have it selected as one of the five best horror tales of 1979 by the World Fantasy Convention. I included an expanded version in my short story collection *Things Beyond Midnight*, but this is the first time the revised version has been anthologized. I'm proud and happy to have it in this book.

—William F. Nolan

# CAMPS

## by Jack Dann

As Stephen lies in bed, he can think only of pain.

He imagines it as sharp and blue. After receiving an injection of Demerol, he enters pain's cold regions as an explorer, an objective visitor. It is a country of ice and glass, monochromatic plains and valleys filled with wash-blue shards of ice, crystal pyramids and pinnacles, squares, oblongs, and all manner of polyhedrons—block upon block of painted blue pain.

Although it is midafternoon, Stephen pretends it is dark. His eyes are tightly closed, but the daylight pouring into the room from two large windows intrudes as a dull red field extending infinitely behind his eyelids.

"Josie," he asks through cotton mouth, "aren't I due for another shot?" Josie is crisp and fresh and large in her starched white uniform. Her peaked nurse's cap is pinned to her mouse-brown hair.

"I've just given you an injection; it will take effect soon." Josie strokes his hand, and he dreams of ice.

"Bring me some ice," he whispers.

"If I bring you a bowl of ice, you'll only spill it again."

"Bring me some ice. . . ." By touching the ice cubes, by turning them in his hand like a gambler favoring his dice, he can transport himself into the beautiful blue country. Later, the ice will melt, and he will spill the bowl. The shock of cold and pain will awaken him.

Stephen believes that he is dying, and he has resolved to die properly. Each visit to the cold country brings him closer to death; and death, he has learned, is only a slow walk through icefields. He has come to appreciate the complete lack of warmth and the beautifully etched face of his magical country.

But he is connected to the bright flat world of the hospital by plastic tubes—one breathes cold oxygen into his left nostril; another passes into his right nostril and down his throat to his stomach; one feeds him intravenously; another draws his urine.

"Here's your ice," Josie says. "But mind you, don't spill it." She places the small bowl on his tray table and wheels the table close to him. She has a musky odor of perspiration and perfume; Stephen is reminded of old women and college girls.

"Sleep now, sweet boy."

Without opening his eyes, Stephen reaches out and places his hand on the ice.

"Come now, Stephen, wake up. Dr. Volk is here to see you."

Stephen feels the cool touch of Josie's hand, and he opens his eyes to see the doctor standing beside him. The doctor has a gaunt long face and thinning brown hair; he is dressed in a wrinkled green suit.

"Now we'll check the dressing, Stephen," he says

as he tears away a gauze bandage on Stephen's abdomen.

Stephen feels the pain, but he is removed from it. His only wish is to return to the blue dreamlands. He watches the doctor peel off the neat crosshatchings of gauze. A terrible stink fills the room.

Josie stands well away.

"Now we'll check your drains." The doctor pulls a long drainage tube out of Stephen's abdomen, irrigates and disinfects the wound, inserts a new drain, and repeats the process by pulling out another tube just below the rib cage.

Stephen imagines that he is swimming out of the room. He tries to cross the hazy border into cooler regions, but it is difficult to concentrate. He has only a half-hour at most before the Demerol will wear off. Already, the pain is coming closer, and he will not be due for another injection until the night nurse comes on duty. But the night nurse will not give him an injection without an argument. She will tell him to fight the pain.

But he cannot fight without a shot.

"Tomorrow we'll take that oxygen tube out of your nose," the doctor says, but his voice seems far away, and Stephen wonders what he is talking about.

He reaches for the bowl of ice, but cannot find it.

"Josie, you've taken my ice."

"I took the ice away when the doctor came. Why don't you try to watch a bit of television with me; Soupy Sales is on."

"Just bring me some ice," Stephen says. "I want to rest a bit." He can feel the sharp edges of pain breaking through the gauzy wraps of Demerol.

"I love you, Josie," he says sleepily as she places a fresh bowl of ice on his tray.

\*     \*     \*

As Stephen wanders through his ice-blue dream-world, he sees a rectangle of blinding white light. It looks like a doorway into an adjoining world of brightness. He has glimpsed it before on previous Demerol highs. A coal-dark doorway stands beside the bright one.

He walks toward the portals, passes through white-blue conefields.

Time is growing short. The drug cannot stretch it much longer. Stephen knows that he has to choose either the bright doorway or the dark, one or the other. He does not even consider turning around, for he has dreamed that the ice and glass and cold blue gemstones have melted behind him.

It makes no difference to Stephen which doorway he chooses. On impulse he steps into blazing, searing whiteness.

Suddenly he is in a cramped world of people and sound.

The boxcar's doors were flung open. Stephen was being pushed out of the cramped boxcar that stank of sweat, feces, and urine. Several people had died in the car, and added their stink of death to the already fetid air.

"Carla, stay close to me," shouted a man beside Stephen. He had been separated from his wife by a young woman who pushed between them, as she tried to return to the dark safety of the boxcar.

SS men in black, dirty uniforms were everywhere. They kicked and pummeled everyone within reach. Alsatian guard dogs snapped and barked. Stephen was bitten by one of the snarling dogs. A woman beside him was being kicked by soldiers. And they were all being methodically herded past a high barbed-wire fence. Beside the fence was a wall.

Stephen looked around for an escape route, but he

was surrounded by other prisoners, who were pressing against him. Soldiers were shooting indiscriminately into the crowd, shooting women and children alike.

The man who had shouted to his wife was shot.

"Sholom, help me, help me," screamed a scrawny young woman whose skin was as yellow and pimpled as chicken flesh.

And Stephen understood that *he* was Sholom. He was a Jew in this burning, stinking world, and this woman, somehow, meant something to him. He felt the yellow star sewn on the breast of his filthy jacket. He grimaced uncontrollably. The strangest thoughts were passing through his mind, remembrances of another childhood: morning prayers with his father and rich uncle, large breakfasts on Saturdays, the sounds of his mother and father quietly making love in the next room, *yortzeit* candles burning in the living room, his brother reciting the "four questions" at the Passover table.

He touched the star again and remembered the Nazis' facetious euphemism for it: *Pour le Semite*.

He wanted to strike out, to kill the Nazis, to fight and die. But he found himself marching with the others, as if he had no will of his own. He felt that he was cut in half. He had two selves now; one watched the other. One self wanted to fight. The other was numbed; it cared only for itself. It was determined to survive.

Stephen looked around for the woman who had called out to him. She was nowhere to be seen.

Behind him were railroad tracks, electrified wire, and the conical tower and main gate of the camp. Ahead was a pitted road littered with corpses and their belongings. Rifles were being fired and a heavy, sickly sweet odor was everywhere. Stephen gagged, others vomited. It was the overwhelming stench of death, of rotting and burning flesh. Black clouds hung above the camp, and flames spurted from the tall chimneys of ugly buildings, as if from infernal machines.

Stephen walked onward; he was numb, unable to fight or even talk. Everything that happened around him was impossible, the stuff of dreams.

The prisoners were ordered to halt, and the soldiers began to separate those who would be burned from those who would be worked to death. Old men and women and young children were pulled out of the crowd. Some were beaten and killed immediately while the others looked on in disbelief. Stephen looked on, as if it was of no concern to him. Everything was unreal, dreamlike. He did not belong here.

The new prisoners looked like *Musselmänner*, the walking dead. Those who became ill, or were beaten or starved before they could "wake up" to the reality of the camps, became *Musselmänner*. *Musselmänner* could not think or feel. They shuffled around, already dead in spirit, until a guard or disease or cold or starvation killed them.

"Keep marching," shouted a guard, as Stephen stopped before an emaciated old man crawling on the ground. "You'll look like him soon enough."

Suddenly, as if waking from one dream and finding himself in another, Stephen remembered that the chicken-skinned girl was his wife. He remembered their life together, their children and crowded flat. He remembered the birthmark on her leg, her scent, her hungry lovemaking. He had once fought another boy over her.

His glands opened up with fear and shame; he had ignored her screams for help.

He stopped and turned, faced the other group. "Fruma," he shouted, then started to run.

A guard struck him in the chest with the butt of his rifle, and Stephen fell into darkness.

He spills the icewater again and awakens with a scream.

"It's my fault," Josie says, as she peels back the sheets. "I should have taken the bowl away from you. But you fight me."

Stephen lives with the pain again. He imagines that a tiny fire is burning in his abdomen, slowly consuming him. He stares at the television high on the wall and watches Soupy Sales.

As Josie changes the plastic sac containing his intravenous saline solution, an orderly pushes a cart into the room and asks Stephen if he wants a print for his wall.

"Would you like me to choose something for you?" Josie asks.

Stephen shakes his head and asks the orderly to show him all the prints. Most of them are familiar still-lifes and pastorals, but one catches his attention. It is a painting of a wheat field. Although the sky looks ominously dark, the wheat is brightly rendered in great broad strokes. A path cuts through the field and crows fly overhead.

"That one," Stephen says. "Put that one up."

After the orderly hangs the print and leaves, Josie asks Stephen why he chose that particular painting.

"I like Van Gogh," he says dreamily, as he tries to detect a rhythm in the surges of abdominal pain. But he is not nauseated, just gaseous.

"Any particular reason why you like Van Gogh?" asks Josie. "He's my favorite artist, too."

"I didn't say he was my favorite," Stephen says,

and Josie pouts, an expression which does not fit her prematurely lined face. Stephen closes his eyes, glimpses the cold country, and says, "I like the painting because it's so bright that it's almost frightening. And the road going through the field"—he opens his eyes—"doesn't go anywhere. It just ends in the field. And the crows are flying around like vultures."

"Most people see it as just a pretty picture," Josie says.

"What's it called?"

*"Wheatfield with Blackbirds."*

"Sensible. My stomach hurts, Josie. Help me turn over on my side." Josie helps him onto his left side, plumps up his pillows, and inserts a short tube into his rectum to relieve the gas. "I also like the painting with the large stars that all look out of focus," Stephen says. "What's it called?"

*"Starry Night."*

"That's scary, too," Stephen says. Josie takes his blood pressure, makes a notation on his chart, then sits down beside him and holds his hand. "I remember something," he says. "Something just—" He jumps as he remembers, and pain shoots through his distended stomach. Josie shushes him, checks the intravenous needle, and asks him what he remembers.

But the memory of the dream recedes as the pain grows sharper. "I hurt all the fucking time, Josie," he says, changing position. Josie removes the rectal tube before he is on his back.

"Don't use such language, I don't like to hear it. I know you have a lot of pain," she says, her voice softening.

"Time for a shot."

"No, honey, not for some time. You'll just have to bear with it."

Stephen remembers his dream again. He is afraid of it. His breath is short and his heart feels as if it is beating in his throat, but he recounts the entire dream to Josie.

He does not notice that her face has lost its color.

"It's only a dream, Stephen. Probably something you studied in history."

"But it was so real, not like a dream at all."

"That's enough!" Josie says.

"I'm sorry I upset you. Don't be angry."

"I'm *not* angry."

"I'm sorry," he says, fighting the pain, squeezing Josie's hand tightly. "Didn't you tell me that you were in the Second World War?"

Josie is composed once again. "Yes, I did, but I'm surprised you remembered. You were very sick. I was a nurse overseas, spent most of the war in England. But I was one of the first servicewomen to go into any of the concentration camps."

Stephen drifts with the pain; he appears to be asleep.

"You must have studied very hard," Josie whispers to him. Her hand is shaking just a bit.

It is twelve o'clock and his room is death-quiet. The sharp shadows seem to be the hardest objects in the room. The fluorescents burn steadily in the hall outside.

Stephen looks out into the hallway, but he can see only the far white wall. He waits for his night nurse to appear: it is time for his injection. A young nurse passes by his doorway. Stephen imagines that she is a cardboard ship sailing through the corridors.

He presses the buzzer, which is attached by a clip to his pillow. The night nurse will take her time, he tells himself. He remembers arguing with her. Angrily, he presses the buzzer again.

Across the hall, a man begins to scream, and there is a shuffle of nurses into his room. The screaming turns into begging and whining. Although Stephen has never seen the man in the opposite room, he has come to hate him. Like Stephen, he has something wrong with his stomach, but he cannot suffer well. He can only beg and cry, try to make deals with the nurses, doctors, God, and angels. Stephen cannot muster any pity for this man.

The night nurse finally comes into the room, says, "You have to try to get along without this," and gives him an injection of Demerol.

"Why does the man across the hall scream so?" Stephen asks, but the nurse is already edging out of the room.

"Because he's in pain."

"So am I," Stephen says in a loud voice. "But I can keep it to myself."

"Then stop buzzing me constantly for an injection. That man across the hall has had half of his stomach removed. He's got something to scream about."

So have I, Stephen thinks; but the nurse disappears before he can tell her. He tries to imagine what the man across the hall looks like. He thinks of him as being bald and small, an ancient baby. Stephen tries to feel sorry for the man, but his incessant whining disgusts him.

The drug takes effect; the screams recede as he hurtles through the dark corridors of a dream. The cold country is dark, for Stephen cannot persuade his night nurse to bring him some ice. Once again, he sees two entrances. As the world melts behind him, he steps into the coal-black doorway.

In the darkness he hears an alarm, a bone-jarring clangor.

He could smell the combined stink of men pressed closely together. They were all lying upon two badly constructed wooden shelves. The floor was dirt; the smell of urine never left the barrack.

"Wake up," said a man Stephen knew as Viktor. "If the guard finds you in bed, you'll be beaten again."

Stephen moaned, still wrapped in dreams. "Wake up, wake up," he mumbled to himself. He would have a few more minutes before the guard arrived with the dogs. At the very thought of dogs, Stephen felt revulsion. He had once been bitten in the face by a large dog.

He opened his eyes, yet he was still half-asleep, exhausted. You are in a death camp, he said to himself. You must wake up. You must fight by waking up. Or you will die in your sleep. Shaking uncontrollably, he said, "Do you want to end up in the oven; perhaps you will be lucky today and live."

As he lowered his legs to the floor, he felt the sores open on the soles of his feet. He wondered who would die today and shrugged. It was his third week in the camp. Impossibly, against all odds, he had survived. Most of those he had known in the train had either died or become *Musselmänner*. If it was not for Viktor, he, too, would have become a *Musselmänner*. He had had a breakdown and wanted to die. He babbled in English. But Viktor talked him out of death, shared his portion of food with him, and taught him the new rules of life.

"Like everyone else who survives, I count myself first, second, and third—then I try to do what I can for someone else," Viktor had said.

"I will survive," Stephen repeated to himself, as

the guards opened the door, stepped into the room, and began to shout. Their dogs growled and snapped but heeled beside them. The guards looked sleepy; one did not wear a cap, and his red hair was tousled.

Perhaps he spent the night with one of the whores, Stephen thought. Perhaps today would not be so bad. . . .

And so begins the morning ritual: Josie enters Stephen's room at quarter to eight, fusses with the chart attached to the footboard of his bed, pads about aimlessly, and finally goes to the bathroom. She returns, her stiff uniform making swishing sounds. Stephen can feel her standing over the bed and staring at him. But he does not open his eyes. He waits a beat.

She turns away, then drops the bedpan. Yesterday it was the metal ashtray; day before that, she bumped into the bedstand.

"Good morning, darling, it's a beautiful day," she says, then walks across the room to the windows. She parts the faded orange drapes and opens the blinds.

"How do you feel today?"

"Okay, I guess."

Josie takes his pulse and asks, "Did Mr. Gregory stop in to say hello last night?"

"Yes," Stephen says. "He's teaching me how to play gin rummy. What's wrong with him?"

"He's very sick."

"I can see that; has he got cancer?"

"I don't know," says Josie, as she tidies up his night table.

"You're lying again," Stephen says, but she ignores him. After a time, he says, "His girlfriend was in to see me last night. I bet his wife will be in today."

"Shut your mouth about that," Josie says. "Let's get you out of that bed so I can change the sheets."

Stephen sits in the chair all morning. He is getting well but is still very weak. Just before lunchtime, the orderly wheels his cart into the room and asks Stephen if he would like to replace the print hanging on the wall.

"I've seen them all," Stephen says. "I'll keep the one I have." Stephen does not grow tired of the Van Gogh painting; sometimes, the crows seem to have changed position.

"Maybe you'll like this one," the orderly says as he pulls out a cardboard print of Van Gogh's *Starry Night*. It is a study of a village nestled in the hills, dressed in shadows. But everything seems to be boiling and writhing as in a fever dream. A cypress tree in the foreground looks like a black flame, and the vertiginous sky is filled with great blurry stars. It is a drunkard's dream. The orderly smiles.

"So you did have it," Stephen says.

"No, I traded some other pictures for it. They had a copy in the west wing."

Stephen watches him hang it, thanks him, and waits for him to leave. Then he gets up and examines the painting carefully. He touches the raised facsimile brushstrokes and turns toward Josie, feeling an odd sensation in his groin. He looks at her, as if seeing her for the first time. She has an overly full mouth which curves downward at the corners when she smiles. She is not a pretty woman—too fat, he thinks.

"Dance with me," he says, as he waves his arms and takes a step forward, conscious of the pain in his stomach.

"You're too sick to be dancing just yet," but she laughs at him and bends her knees in a mock plié.

She has small breasts for such a large woman, Stephen thinks. Feeling suddenly dizzy, he takes a step toward the bed. He feels himself slip to the floor, feels Josie's hair brushing against his face, dreams that he's all wet from her tongue, feels her arms around him, squeezing, then feels the weight of her body pressing down on him, crushing him . . .

He wakes up in bed, catheterized. He has an intravenous needle in his left wrist, and it is difficult to swallow, for he has a tube down his throat.

He groans, tries to move.

"Quiet, Stephen," Josie says, stroking his hand.

"What happened?" he mumbles. He can only remember being dizzy.

"You've had a slight setback, so just rest. The doctor had to collapse your lung; you must lie very still.

"Josie, I love you," he whispers, but he is too far away to be heard. He wonders how many hours or days have passed. He looks toward the window. It is dark, and there is no one in the room.

He presses the buzzer attached to his pillow and remembers a dream. . . .


"You must fight," Viktor said.

It was dark, all the other men were asleep, and the barrack was filled with snoring and snorting. Stephen wished they could all die, choke on their own breath. It would be an act of mercy.

"Why fight?" Stephen asked, and he pointed toward the greasy window, beyond which were the ovens that smoked day and night. He made a fluttering gesture with his hand—smoke rising.

"You must fight, you must live, living is every-thing. It is the only thing that makes sense here."

"We're all going to die, anyway," Stephen whis-pered. "Just like your sister . . . and my wife."

"No, Sholom, we're going to live. The others may die, but we're going to live. You must belive that."

Stephen understood that Viktor was desperately trying to convince himself to live. He felt sorry for Viktor; there could be no sensible rationale for living in a place like this.

Stephen grinned, tasted blood from the corner of his mouth, and said, "So we'll live through the night, maybe."

And maybe tomorrow, he thought. He would play the game of survival a little longer.

He wondered if Viktor would be alive tomorrow. he smiled and thought: If Viktor dies, then I will have to take his place and convince others to live. For an instant, he hoped Viktor would die so that he could take his place.

The alarm sounded. It was three o'clock in the morning, time to begin the day.

This morning Stephen was on his feet before the guards could unlock the door.

"Wake up," Josie says, gently tapping his arm. "Come on, wake up."

Stephen hears her voice as an echo. He imagines that he has been flung into a long tunnel; he hears air whistling in his ears but cannot see anything.

"Whassimatter?" he asks. His mouth feels as if it is stuffed with cotton; his lips are dry and cracked. He is suddenly angry at Josie and the plastic tubes that hold him in his bed as if he were a latter-day Gulliver. He wants to pull out the tubes, smash the bags filled with saline, tear away his bandages.

"You were speaking German," Josie says. "Did you know that?"

"Can I have some ice?"

"No," Josie says impatiently. "You spilled again, you're all wet."

". . . for my mouth, dry . . ."

"Do you remember speaking German, honey? I have to know."

"Don't remember—bring ice, I'll try to think about it."

As Josie leaves to get him some ice, he tries to remember his dream.

"Here, now, just suck on the ice." She gives him a little hill of crushed ice on the end of a spoon.

"Why did you wake me up, Josie?" The layers of dream are beginning to slough off. As the Demerol works out of his system, he has to concentrate on fighting the burning ache in his stomach.

"You were speaking German. Where did you learn to speak like that?"

Stephen tries to remember what he said. He cannot speak any German, only a bit of classroom French. He looks down at his legs (he has thrown off the sheet) and notices, for the first time, that his legs are as thin as his arms. "My God, Josie, how could I have lost so much weight?"

"You lost about forty pounds, but don't worry, you'll gain it all back. You're on the road to recovery now. Please, try to remember your dream."

"I can't, Josie! I just can't seem to get ahold of it."

"Try."

"Why is it so important to you?"

"You weren't speaking college German, darling. You were speaking slang. You spoke in a patois that I haven't heard since the forties."

Stephen feels a chill slowly creep up his spine. "What did I say?"

Josie waits a beat, then says, "You talked about dying."

"Josie?"

"Yes," she says, pulling at her fingernail.

"When is the pain going to stop?"

"It will be over soon." She gives him another spoonful of ice. "You kept repeating the name Viktor in your sleep. Can you remember anything about him?"

*Viktor, Viktor, deep-set blue eyes, balding head, and broken nose, called himself a Galitzianer. Saved my life.* "I remember," Stephen says. "His name is Viktor Shmone. He is in all my dreams now."

Josie exhales sharply.

"Does that mean anything to you?" Stephen asks anxiously.

"I once knew a man from one of the camps." She speaks very slowly and precisely. "His name was Viktor Shmone. I took care of him. He was one of the few people left alive in the camp after the Germans fled." She reaches for her purse, which she keeps on Stephen's night table, and fumbles an old, torn photograph out of a plastic slipcase.

As Stephen examines the photograph, he begins to sob. A thinner and much younger Josie is standing beside Viktor and two other emaciated-looking men. "Then I'm not dreaming," he says, "and I'm going to die. That's what it means." He begins to shake, just as he did in his dream, and, without thinking, he makes the gesture of rising smoke to Josie. He begins to laugh.

"Stop that," Josie says, raising her hand to slap him. Then she embraces him and says, "Don't cry, darling, it's only a dream. Somehow, you're dreaming the past."

"Why?" Stephen asks, still shaking.

"Maybe you're dreaming because of me, because we're so close. In some ways, I think you know me better than anyone else, better than any man, no doubt. You might be dreaming for a reason; maybe I can help you."

"I'm afraid, Josie."

She comforts him and says, "Now tell me everything you can remember about the dreams."

He is exhausted. As he recounts his dreams to her, he sees the bright doorway again. He feels himself being sucked into it. "Josie," he says, "I must stay awake, don't want to sleep, dream. . . ."

Josie's face is pulled tight as a mask; she is crying.

Stephen reaches out to her, slips into the bright doorway, into another dream.

It was a cold cloudless morning. Hundreds of prisoners were working in the quarries; each work gang came from a different barrack. Most of the gangs were made up of *Musselmänner*, the faceless majority of the camp. They moved like automatons, lifting and carrying the great stones to the numbered carts, which would have to be pushed down the tracks.

Stephen was drenched with sweat. He had a fever and was afraid that he had contracted typhus. An epidemic had broken out in the camp last week. Every morning several doctors arrived with the guards. Those who were too sick to stand up were taken away to be gassed or experimented upon in the hospital.

Although Stephen could barely stand, he forced himself to keep moving. He tried to focus all his attention on what he was doing. He made a ritual of bending over, choosing a stone of certain size, lifting it, carrying it to the nearest cart, and then taking the same number of steps back to his dig.

A *Musselmänn* fell to the ground, but Stephen made no effort to help him. When he could help someone in a little way, he would, but he would not stick his neck out for a *Musselmänn*. Yet something niggled at Stephen. He remembered a photograph in which Viktor and this *Musselmänn* were standing with a man and a woman he did not recognize. But Stephen could not remember where he had ever seen such a photograph.

"Hey, you," shouted a guard. "Take the one on the ground to the cart."

Stephen nodded to the guard and began to drag the *Musselmänn* away.

"Who's the new patient down the hall?" Stephen asks as he eats a bit of cereal from the breakfast tray Josie has placed before him. He is feeling much better now; his fever is down, and the tubes, catheter, and intravenous needle have been removed. He can even walk around a bit.

"How did you find out about that?" Josie asks.

"You were talking to Mr. Gregory's nurse. Do you think I'm dead already? I can still hear."

Josie laughs and takes a sip of Stephen's tea. "You're far from dead! In fact, today is a red-letter day: you're going to take your first shower. What do you think about that?"

"I'm not well enough yet," he says, worried that he will have to leave the hospital before he is ready.

"Well, Dr. Volk thinks differently, and his word is law."

"Tell me about the new patient."

"They brought in a man last night who drank two quarts of motor oil; he's on the dialysis machine."

"Will he make it?"

"No, I don't think so; there's too much poison in his system."

We should all die, Stephen thinks. It would be an act of mercy. He glimpses the camp.

"Stephen!"

He jumps, then awakens.

"You've had a good night's sleep; you don't need to nap. Let's get you into that shower and have it done with." Josie pushes the tray table away from the bed. "Come on, I have your bathrobe right here."

Stephen puts on his bathrobe, and they walk down the hall to the showers. There are three empty shower stalls, a bench, and a whirlpool bath. As Stephen takes off his bathrobe, Josie adjusts the water pressure and temperature in the corner stall.

"What's the matter?" Stephen asks, after stepping into the shower. Josie stands in front of the shower stall and holds his towel, but she will not look at him. "Come on," he says, "you've seen me naked before."

"That was different."

"How?" He touches a hard, ugly scab that has formed over one of the wounds on his abdomen.

"When you were very sick, I washed you in bed, as if you were a baby. Now it's different." She looks down at the wet tile floor, as if she is lost in thought.

"Well, I think it's silly," he says. "Come on, it's hard to talk to someone who's looking the other way. I could break my neck in here and you'd be staring down at the fucking floor."

"I've asked you not to use that word," she says in a very low voice.

"Do my eyes still look yellowish?"

She looks directly at his face and says, "No, they look fine."

Stephen suddenly feels faint, then nauseated; he has been standing too long. As he leans against the cold shower wall, he remembers his last dream. He is back in the quarry. He can smell the perspiration of the men around him, feel the sun baking him, draining his strength. It is so bright. . . .

He finds himself sitting on the bench and staring at the light on the opposite wall. I've got typhus, he thinks, then realizes that he is in the hospital. Josie is beside him.

"I'm sorry," he says.

"I shouldn't have let you stand so long; it was my fault."

"I remembered another dream." He begins to shake, and Josie puts her arms around him.

"It's all right now, tell Josie about your dream."

She's an old, fat woman, Stephen thinks. As he describes the dream, his shaking subsides.

"Do you know the man's name?" Josie asks. "The one the guard ordered you to drag away."

"No," Stephen says. "He was a *Musselmänn*, yet I thought there was something familiar about him. In my dream I remembered the photograph you showed me. He was in it."

"What will happen to him?"

"The guards will give him to the doctors for experimentation. If they don't want him, he'll be gassed."

"You must not let that happen," Josie says, holding him tightly.

"Why?" asks Stephen, afraid that he will fall into the dreams again.

"If he was one of the men you saw in the photograph, you must not let him die. Your dreams must fit the past."

"I'm afraid."

"It will be all right, baby," Josie says, clinging to him. She is shaking and breathing heavily.

Stephen feels himself getting an erection. He calms her, presses his face against hers, and touches her breasts. She tells him to stop, but does not push him away.

"I love you," he says as he slips his hand under her starched skirt. He feels awkward and foolish and warm.

"This is wrong," she whispers.

As Stephen kisses her and feels her thick tongue in his mouth, he begins to dream. . . .

Stephen stopped to rest for a few seconds. The *Musselmänn* was dead weight. I cannot go on, Stephen thought; but he bent down, grabbed the *Musselmänn* by his coat, and dragged him toward the cart. He glimpsed the cart, which was filled with the sick and dead and exhausted; it looked no different than a carload of corpses marked for a mass grave.

A long, grey cloud covered the sun, then passed, drawing shadows across gutted hills.

On impulse, Stephen dragged the *Musselmänn* into a gully behind several chalky rocks. Why am I doing this? he asked himself. If I'm caught, I'll be ash in the ovens, too. He remembered what Viktor had told him: "You must think of yourself all the time, or you'll be no help to anyone else."

The *Musselmänn* groaned, then raised his arm. His face was grey with dust and his eyes were glazed.

"You must lie still," Stephen whispered. "Do not make a sound. I've hidden you from the guards, but if they hear you, we'll all be punished. One sound from you and you're dead. You must fight to live, you're in a death camp, you must fight so you can tell of this later.''

''I have no family, they're all—''

Stephen clapped his hand over the man's mouth and whispered, ''Fight, don't talk. Wake up; you cannot survive the death by sleeping.''

The man nodded, and Stephen climbed out of the gully. He helped two men carry a large stone to a nearby cart.

''What are you doing?'' shouted a guard.

''I left my place to help these men with this stone; now I'll go back where I was.''

''What the hell are you trying to do?'' Viktor asked.

Stephen felt as if he was burning up with fever. He wiped the sweat from his eyes, but everything was still blurry.

''You're sick, too. You'll be lucky if you last the day.''

''I'll last,'' Stephen said, ''but I want you to help me get him back to the camp.''

''I won't risk it, not for a *Musselmänn*. He's already dead, leave him.''

''Like you left me?''

Before the guards could take notice, they began to work. Although Viktor was older than Stephen, he was stronger. He worked hard every day and never caught the diseases that daily reduced the barrack's numbers. Stephen had a touch of death, as Viktor called it, and was often sick.

They worked until dusk, when the sun's oblique rays caught the dust from the quarries and turned it into veils and scrims. Even the guards sensed that this was a quiet time, for they would congregate together and talk in hushed voices.

"Come, now, help me," Stephen whispered to Viktor. "I've been doing that all day," Viktor said. "I'll have enough trouble getting you back to the camp, much less carry this *Musselmänn*."

"We can't leave him."

"Why are you so preoccupied with this *Musselmänn*? Even if we can get him back to the camp, his chances are nothing. I know, I've seen enough—I know who has a chance to survive."

"You're wrong this time," Stephen said. He was dizzy and it was difficult to stand. The odds are I won't last the night, and Viktor knows it, he told himself. "I had a dream that if this man dies, I'll die, too. I just feel it."

"Here we learn to trust our dreams," Viktor said. "They make as much sense as this. . . ." He made the gesture of rising smoke and gazed toward the ovens, which were spewing fire and black ash.

The western portion of the sky was yellow, but over the ovens it was red and purple and dark blue. Although it horrified Stephen to consider it, there was a macabre beauty here. If he survived, he would never forget these sense impressions, which were stronger than anything he had ever experienced before. Being so close to death, he was, perhaps for the first time, really living. In the camp, one did not even consider suicide. One grasped for every moment, sucked at life like an infant, lived as if there was no future.

The guards shouted at the prisoners to form a column; it was time to march back to the barracks.

While the others milled about, Stephen and Viktor lifted the *Musselmänn* out of the gully. Everyone nearby tried to distract the guards. When the march began, Stephen and Viktor held the *Musselmänn* between them, for he could barely stand.

"Come on, dead one, carry your weight," Viktor said. "Are you so dead that you cannot hear me? Are you as dead as the rest of your family?" The *Musselmänn* groaned and dragged his legs. Viktor kicked him. "You'll walk, or we'll leave you here for the guards to find."

"Let him be," Stephen said.

"Are you dead or do you have a name?" Viktor continued.

"Berek," croaked the *Musselmänn*. "I am not dead."

"Then we have a fine bunk for you," Viktor said. "You can smell the stink of the sick for another night before the guards make a selection." Viktor made the gesture of smoke rising.

Stephen stared at the barracks ahead. They seemed to waver as the heat rose from the ground. He counted every step. He would drop soon; he could not go on, could not carry the *Musselmänn*.

He began to mumble in English.

"So you're speaking American again,'" Viktor said.

Stephen shook himself awake, placed one foot before the other.

"Dreaming of an American lover?"

"I don't know English and I have no American lover."

"Then who is this Josie you keep talking about in your sleep? . . ."

"Why were you screaming?" Josie asks, as she washes his face with a cold washcloth.

"I don't remember screaming," Stephen says. He discovers a fever blister on his lip. Expecting to find an intravenous needle in his wrist, he raises his arm.

"You don't need an IV," Josie says. "You just

have a bit of a fever. Dr. Volk has prescribed some new medication for it.''

''What time is it?'' Stephen stares at the whorls in the ceiling.

''Almost three P.M. I'll be going off soon.''

''Then I've slept most of the day away,'' Stephen says, feeling something crawling inside him. He worries that his dreams still have a hold on him. ''Am I having another relapse?''

''You'll do fine,'' Josie says.

''I should be fine now. I don't want to dream anymore.''

''Did you dream again, do you remember anything?''

''I dreamed that I saved the *Musselmänn*,'' Stephen says.

''What was his name?'' asks Josie.

''Berek, I think. Is that the man you knew?''

Josie nods and Stephen smiles at her. ''Maybe that's the end of the dreams,'' he says, but she does not respond. He asks to see the photograph again.

''Not just now,'' Josie says.

''But I have to see it. I want to see if I can recognize myself. . . .''

Stephen dreamed he was dead, but it was only the fever. Viktor sat beside him on the floor and watched the others. The sick were moaning and crying; they slept on the cramped platform, as if proximity to one another could insure a few more hours of life. Wan moonlight seemed to fill the barrack.

Stephen awakened, feverish. ''I'm burning up,'' he whispered to Viktor.

''Well,'' Viktor said, ''you've got your *Musselmänn*. If he lives, you live. That's what you said, isn't it?''

"I don't remember—I just knew that I couldn't let
him die."

"You'd better go back to sleep, you'll need your
strength. Or we may have to carry *you*, tomorrow."

Stephen tried to sleep, but the fever was making
lights and spots before his eyes. When he finally fell
asleep, he dreamed of a dark country filled with
gemstones and great quarries of ice and glass.

"What?" Stephen asked, as he sat up suddenly,
awakened from damp black dreams. He looked around
and saw that everyone was watching Berek, who was
sitting under the window at the far end of the room.

Berek was singing the *Kol Nidre* very softly. It
was the Yom Kippur prayer, which was sung on the
most holy of days. He repeated the prayer three times,
and then once again in a louder voice. The others responded, intoned the prayer as a recitative. Viktor
was crying quietly, and Stephen imagined that the
holy spirit animated Berek. Surely, he told himself,
that face and those pale unseeing eyes were those of
a dead man. He remembered the story of the golem,
shuddered, found himself singing and pulsing with
fever.

When the prayer was over, Berek fell back into his
fever trance. The others became silent, then slept.
But there was something new in the barrack with
them tonight, a palpable exultation. Stephen looked
around at the sleepers and thought: We're surviving,
more dead than alive, but surviving. . . .

"You were right about that *Musselmänn*," Viktor
whispered. "It's good that we saved him."

"Perhaps we should sit with him," Stephen said.
"He's alone." But Viktor was already asleep; and
Stephen was suddenly afraid that if he sat beside
Berek, he would be consumed by his holy fire.

As Stephen fell through sleep and dreams, his face burned with fever.

Again he wakes up screaming.

"Josie," he says, "I can remember the dream, but there's something else, something I can't see, something terrible. . . ."

"Not to worry," Josie says, "it's the fever." But she looks worried, and Stephen is sure that she knows something he does not.

"Tell me what happened to Viktor and Berek," Stephen says. He presses his hands together to stop them from shaking.

"They lived, just as you are going to live and have a good life."

Stephen calms down and tells her his dream.

"So you see," she says, "you're even dreaming about surviving."

"I'm burning up."

"Dr. Volk says you're doing very well." Josie sits beside him, and he watches the fever patterns shift behind his closed eyelids.

"Tell me what happens next, Josie."

"You're going to get well."

"There's something else. . . ."

"Shush, now, there's nothing else." She pauses, then says, "Mr. Gregory is supposed to visit you tonight. He's getting around a bit; he's been back and forth all day in his wheelchair. He tells me that you two have made some sort of a deal about dividing up all the nurses."

Stephen smiles, opens his eyes, and says, "It was Gregory's idea. Tell me what's wrong with him."

"All right—he has cancer, but he doesn't know it, and you must keep it a secret. They cut the nerve in his leg because the pain was so bad. He's quite comfortable now, but remember, you can't repeat what I've told you.''

"Is he going to live?'' Stephen asks. "He's told me about all the new projects he's planning. So I guess he's expecting to get out of here.''

"He's not going to live very long, and the doctor didn't want to break his spirit.''

"I think he should be told.''

"That's not your decision to make, nor mine.''

"Am I going to die, Josie?''

"No!'' she says, touching his arm to reassure him.

"How do I know that's the truth?''

"Because I say so, and I couldn't look you straight in the eye and tell you if it wasn't true. I should have known it would be a mistake to tell you about Mr. Gregory.''

"You did right,'' Stephen says. "I won't mention it again. Now that I know, I feel better.'' He feels drowsy again.

"Do you think you're up to seeing him tonight?''

Stephen nods, although he is bone-tired. As he falls asleep, the fever patterns begin to dissolve, leaving a bright field. With a start, he opens his eyes: he has touched the edge of another dream.

"What happened to the man across the hall, the one who was always screaming?''

"He's left the ward,'' Josie says. "Mr. Gregory had better hurry, if he wants to play cards with you before dinner. They're going to bring the trays up soon.''

"You mean he died, don't you.''

"Yes, if you must know, he died. But *you're* going to live.''

There is a crashing noise in the hallway. Someone shouts, and Josie runs to the door.

Stephen tries to stay awake, but he is being pulled back into the cold country.

"Mr. Gregory fell trying to get into his wheelchair by himself," Josie says. "He should have waited for his nurse, but she was out of the room and he wanted to visit you."

But Stephen does not hear a word she says.


There were rumors that the camp was going to be liberated. It was late, but no one was asleep. The shadows in the barrack seemed larger tonight.

"It's better for us if the Allies don't come," Viktor said to Stephen.

"Why do you say that?"

"Haven't you noticed that the ovens are going day and night? The Nazis are in a hurry."

"I'm going to try to sleep," Stephen said.

"Look around you, even the *Musselmänner* are agitated," Viktor said. "Animals become nervous before the slaughter. I've worked with animals. People are not so different."

"Shut up and let me sleep," Stephen said, and he dreamed that he could hear the crackling of distant gunfire. . . .

"Attention," shouted the guards as they stepped into the barrack. There were more guards than usual, and each one had two Alsatian dogs. "Come on, form a line. Hurry."

"They're going to kill us," Viktor said, "then they'll evacuate the camp and save themselves."

The guards marched the prisoners toward the north section of the camp. Although it was still dark, it was hot and humid, without a trace of the usual morning chill. The ovens belched fire and turned the sky aglow. Everyone was quiet, for there was nothing to be done. The guards were nervous and would cut down anyone who uttered a sound, as an example for the rest.

The booming of big guns could be heard in the distance. If I'm going to die, Stephen thought, I might as well go now and take a Nazi with me. Suddenly, all of his buried fear, aggression, and revulsion surfaced; his face became hot and his heart felt as if it were pumping in his throat. But Stephen argued with himself. There was always a chance. He had once heard of some women who were waiting in line for the ovens; for no apparent reason the guards sent them back to their barracks. Anything could happen. There was always a chance. But to attack a guard would mean certain death.

The guns became louder. Stephen could not be sure, but he thought the noise was coming from the west. The thought passed through his mind that everyone would be better off dead. That would stop all the guns and screaming voices, the clenched fists and wildly beating hearts. The Nazis should kill everyone, and then themselves, as a favor to humanity.

The guards stopped the prisoners in an open field surrounded on three sides by forestland. Sunrise was moments away; purple-black clouds drifted across the sky, touched by grey in the east. It promised to be a hot, gritty day.

Half-step Walter, a Judenrat sympathizer who worked for the guards, handed out shovel heads to everyone.

"He's worse than the Nazis," Viktor said to Stephen.

"The Judenrat thinks he will live," said Berek, "but he will die like a Jew with the rest of us."

"Now, when it's too late, the *Musselmänn* regains consciousness," Viktor said.

"Hurry," shouted the guards, "or you'll die now. As long as you dig, you'll live."

Stephen hunkered down on his knees and began to dig with the shovel head.

"Do you think we might escape?" Berek whined.

"Shut up and dig," Stephen said. "There is no escape, just stay alive as long as you can. Stop whining, are you becoming a *Musselmänn* again?" Stephen noticed that other prisoners were gathering up twigs and branches. So the Nazis plan to cover us up, he thought.

"That's enough," shouted a guard. "Put your shovels down in front of you and stand in a line."

The prisoners stood shoulder to shoulder along the edge of the mass grave. Stephen stood between Viktor and Berek. Someone screamed and ran and was shot immediately.

I don't want to see trees or guards or my friends, Stephen thought as he stared into the sun. I only want to see the sun, let it burn out my eyes, fill up my head with light. He was shaking uncontrollably, quaking with fear.

Guns were booming in the background.

Maybe the guards won't kill us, Stephen thought, even as he heard the *crackcrack* of their rifles. Men were screaming and begging for life. Stephen turned his head, only to see someone's face blown away.

Screaming, tasting vomit in his mouth, Stephen fell backward, pulling Viktor and Berek into the grave with him.

*Darkness*, Stephen thought. His eyes were open, yet it was dark, I must be dead, this must be death. . . .

He could barely move. Corpses can't move, he thought. Something brushed against his face; he stuck out his tongue, felt something spongy. It tasted bitter. Lifting first one arm and then the other, Stephen moved some branches away. Above, he could see a few dim stars; the clouds were lit like lanterns by a quarter moon.

He touched the body beside him; it moved. That must be Viktor, he thought. "Viktor, are you alive, say something if you're alive," Stephen whispered, as if in fear of disturbing the dead.

Viktor groaned and said, "Yes, I'm alive, and so is Berek."

"And the others?"

"All dead. Can't you smell the stink? You, at least, were unconscious all day."

"They can't *all* be dead," Stephen said, then he began to cry.

"Shut up," Viktor said, touching Stephen's face to comfort him. "We're alive, that's something. They could have fired a volley into the pit."

"I thought I was dead," Berek said. He was a shadow among shadows.

"Why are you still here?" Stephen asked.

"We stayed in here because it is safe," Viktor said.

"But they're all dead," Stephen whispered, amazed that there could be speech and reason inside a grave.

"Do you think it's safe to leave now?" Berek asked Viktor.

"Perhaps. I think the killing has stopped. By now the Americans or English or whoever they are have taken over the camp. I heard gunfire and screaming. I think it's best to wait a while longer."

"Here?" asked Stephen. "Among the dead?"

"It's best to be safe."

It was late afternoon when they climbed out of the grave. The air was thick with flies. Stephen could see bodies sprawled in awkward positions beneath the covering of twigs and branches. "How can I live when all the others are dead?" he asked himself aloud.

"You live, that's all," answered Viktor.

They kept close to the forest and worked their way back toward the camp.

"Look there," Viktor said, motioning Stephen and Berek to take cover. Stephen could see trucks moving toward the camp compound.

"Americans," whispered Berek.

"No need to whisper now," Stephen said. "We're safe."

"Guards could be hiding anywhere," Viktor said. "I haven't slept in the grave to be shot now."

They walked into the camp through a large break in the barbed-wire fence, which had been hit by an artillery shell. When they reached the compound, they found nurses, doctors, and army personnel bustling about.

"You speak English," Viktor said to Stephen, as they walked past several quonsets. "Maybe you can speak for us."

"I told you, I can't speak English."

"But I've heard you!"

"Wait," shouted an American army nurse. "You fellows are going the wrong way." She was stocky and spoke perfect German. "You must check in at the hospital; it's back that way."

"No," said Berek, shaking his head. "I won't go in there."

"There's no need to be afraid now," she said. "You're free. Come along, I'll take you to the hospital."

Something familiar about her, Stephen thought. He felt dizzy and everything turned grey.

"Josie," he murmured, as he fell to the ground.

*        *        *

"What is it?" Josie asks. "Everything is all right, Josie is here."

"Josie," Stephen mumbles.

"You're all right."

"How can I live when they're all dead?" he asks.

"It was a dream," she says as she wipes the sweat from his forehead. "You see, your fever has broken: you're getting well."

"Did you know about the grave?"

"It's all over now—forget the dream."

"Did you know?"

"Yes," Josie says. "Viktor told me how he survived the grave, but that was so long ago, before you were even born. Dr. Volk tells me you'll be going home soon."

"I don't want to leave, I want to stay with you."

"Stop that talk, you've got a whole life ahead of you. Soon, you'll forget all about this, and you'll forget me, too."

"Josie," Stephen asks, "let me see that old photograph again. Just one last time."

"Remember, this is the last time," she says as she hands him the faded photograph.

He recognizes Viktor and Berek, but the young man standing between them is not Stephen. "That's not me," he says, certain that he will never return to the camp.

Yet the shots still echo in his mind.

*In five years the Nazis exterminated nine million* people. Six million were Jews. The efficiency of the concentration camps was such that twenty thousand people could be gassed in a day. The Nazis at Treblinka boasted that they could "process" the Jews who arrived in the cattle cars in forty-five minutes. In 1943 six hundred desperate Jews revolted and burned Treblinka to the ground. These men were willing to martyr themselves so that a few might live to "testify," to tell a disbelieving world of the atrocities committed in the camps. Out of the six hundred, forty survived to tell their story.

As I write this the President of the United States is planning to visit a German military cemetery near Bitburg, Germany, where some of Hitler's elite troops are buried, but has to date rejected the proposal to visit the Dachau concentration camp—he felt it would be "out of line" to do so. Reagan explained his reluctance to visit the camp by saying that there are very few Germans "alive that remember even the war, and certainly none of them who were adults and participating in any way. . . ."

Last I heard, the Institute for Historical Review, a California-based organization, was still mailing copies of their journal to unsuspecting librarians, educators, and students. On the journal's masthead is an impressive list of names, which includes an economist, a retired German judge, and various American and European university professors. The purpose of the institute and the journal is to deny that the Holocaust ever happened.

"Camps" is an attempt to "testify." It is a transfusion of the past into our present. . . .

—Jack Dann

# Notes on the Contributors

ROBERT BLOCH saw his first shocker published in 1934. "The Lilies" turned out to be only one of hundreds—and there is no reason to believe that his extraordinary output of stories, novels and screenplays will diminish in the foreseeable future. An early admirer of H. P. Lovecraft, Bloch soon established his own uniquely mordant approach to the macabre tale, bringing an unmistakable tone of irony and mischief to a field not previously known for its sense of humor. It was only fitting that in 1975 the World Fantasy Convention presented him with its highest honor, the first Life Achievement Award, in the form of a bust of Lovecraft himself designed by the morbid cartoonist Gahan Wilson. Bloch is perhaps most famous for his novel *Psycho*. Though he is the author of countless motion-picture and television scripts, the makers of *Psycho II* chose not to consult Bloch or to refer to his existing sequel for their film. Moviegoers were thus misled as to what *really* became of Norman Bates; his readers know better. His latest book is the collection, *Unholy Trinity*.

RAY BRADBURY is one of the most widely-read and beloved authors of our time, with millions of copies of his books in print in perpetuity the world over. An inspiring example of the born writer (his legendary production of at least 1000 words a day began in childhood), he has also nurtured a lifelong love affair with the dramatic arts. Many of his works have been adapted to great effect for radio (*X Minus One*, *Dimension X*), television (*Alfred Hitchcock Presents*, *The Twilight Zone*), motion pictures and the stage, frequently from his own scenarios. At the age of fourteen he wrote jokes for George Burns. A few years later he was called to Ireland by John Huston to script *Moby Dick* for the screen. Since then *The Martian Chronicles*, *The Illustrated Man*, *Fahrenheit 451* and *Something Wicked This Way Comes* have all been filmed. More recently his own television series, *Ray Bradbury Theater*, has been an outstanding success for HBO. It is impossible to imagine a day when his creative coffers will have been exhausted. Bradbury's influence on the development of modern science fiction, fantasy and horror literature is incalculable, and his latest novel, *Death Is a Lonely Business*, promises to exert a comparable influence on the mystery field.

EDWARD BRYANT is that rare breed, a writer who has established a name for himself in our time almost exclusively as an author of short stories. Born in 1945, he made his first professional sale in 1970, after completing his M.A. in English at the University of Wyoming and attending the Clarion Writers Workshop in 1968 and '69. It was not long, however, before his quietly eloquent and precise prose began to gain recognition in some of the finer magazines and original anthologies. Only three years later, in 1973, his first collection, *Cinnabar*, was published. He went on to edit *2076: The American Tricentennial* in 1977, and in 1978 published his first Nebula Award-winner, "Stone," followed a year later by his second, "giANTS." He continues to be nominated regularly, and will surely win even more of these elegant mantelpieces before his brilliant career is over. Bryant promises that he is hard at work on a long-awaited novel. Until it is ready, his readers will have to be satisfied with his latest collection, *Particle Theory*.

RAMSEY CAMPBELL is often singled out as the finest writer of horror stories his generation has yet produced. He is assuredly the most original and accomplished stylist to appear on the scene since Ray Bradbury. Born in 1946, he is already a multiple winner of both the British Fantasy and World Fantasy awards. His novels include *The Doll Who Ate His Mother*, *The Face That Must Die*, *The Nameless*, *The Parasite* and the best-selling *Incarnate*, as well as such collections as *The Inhabitant of the Lake*, *Demons by Daylight*, *The Height of the Scream* and *Cold Print*. Like Robert Bloch, he began his career as a disciple of Lovecraft, though it is unlikely that the creator of the Cthulhu Mythos could have equaled Campbell in psychological complexity or the evocation of sheer terror. He is also the editor of the anthologies *Superhorror*, *New Terrors*, *The Gruesome Book* and *New Tales of the Cthulhu Mythos*. His latest books are *Scared Stiff*, a collection of his erotic horror stories, and a novel, *The Hungry Moon*.

JACK DANN's seventeen books include the novels *Junction*, *Starhiker* and *The Man Who Melted*, the collection *Timetipping*, and the anthologies *Wandering Stars*,

*More Wandering Stars* and the popular series *Aliens!*, *Magicats!*, *Mermaids!* and *Bestiary!*, edited in collaboration with his friend and frequent coauthor, Gardner Dozois. In recent years his short fiction has appeared in *Playboy, Penthouse* and in most of the major magazines and anthologies in the field: *Omni, The Twilight Zone, Amazing, Fantastic, The Magazine of Fantasy and Science Fiction, Orbit, Shadows, New Dimensions, The Year's Best Science Fiction, Berkley Showcase, The Dodd, Mead Gallery of Horror, Year's Best Horror Stories*, etc. Perhaps best known for his Nebula- and Hugo-nominated science fiction, Dann has made a number of unforgettable forays into the darker realms, of which the present volume's entry is deservedly his most famous. His new novel is entitled *Counting Coup*.

GARDNER DOZOIS became a professional writer in his teens and, like so many others represented in this book, began carving out a name in the literary world at an age when most people are still losing sleep over the upcoming prom. Is there something inherent in the psychological makeup of fantasists that drives them to early achievement? Perhaps it is an awareness of the future, of What Might Happen If This Goes On. Certainly this preoccupation is nowhere more evident than in the cautionary writings of Gardner Dozois, who has issued pungent warnings about the very near future rather more often than the majority of his contemporaries. His efforts have not escaped the attention of the science fiction field, which presented him with its highest honor, the Nebula Award, in 1984 and 1985. Dozois is author or editor of at least eighteen books, including the novel *Strangers* and a long line of anthologies, not the least of which is the annual *Year's Best Science Fiction* series. Presently the editor of *Isaac Asimov's Science Fiction Magazine*, his latest books are *Bestiary!* and *Mermaids!*, both coedited with Jack Dunn.

JOE HALDEMAN's *The Forever War* (1974), as distinguished a science fiction novel as has appeared in recent decades, won both the Hugo and Nebula awards, beating out the likes of Alfred Bester, Robert Silverberg, Roger Zelazny, Samuel R. Delany, Larry Niven and Jerry Pournelle. Astonishingly, Haldeman had published his first story only five years earlier. In the years since he has added more than a dozen books to his *oeuvre*, including *Mindbridge*, *All My Sins Remembered* and *Worlds Apart*, works that have been called "vastly entertaining" by *The New York Times*, "splendid" and "first-rate" by *Publishers Weekly*. None of this was accidental, considering Haldeman's preparation—a graduate of the University of Iowa's Writers Workshop with a master's degree in English, four years as teacher at Clarion, etc. With a passion for literary excellence that is balanced perfectly by his knowledge of science, he is one of the most literate sf writers extant. Appropriately he is currently at MIT . . . teaching writing. His latest book is the collection, *Dealing in Futures*.

GEORGE CLAYTON JOHNSON, coauthor of the hugely successful *Logan's Run*, is an alumnus of Rod Serling's *The Twilight Zone* series, where he supplied both original stories and teleplays for such fondly remembered half-hours as "Nothing In the Dark," "A Penny For Your Thoughts," "Execution," "The Prime Mover," "The Poolplayer" and "Kick the Can," this latter the episode that Steven Spielberg chose to remake as his personal segment of *Twilight Zone: The Movie*. *Star Trek* completists will recall that

Johnson wrote the premiere episode of that series. What fans may not realize is that he has also written for many other shows, including *Route 66*, *Mr. Novak*, *Honey West*, *The Law and Mr. Jones* and *Kung Fu*, or that the classic *Ocean's Eleven* was coauthored by Johnson, as was the Academy Award-nominated *Icarus Montgolfier Wright*, adapted from Ray Bradbury's short story. "Sea Change," written as a television treatment, was purchased by Serling for *The Twilight Zone* series but never produced (see Author's Note).

RICHARD MATHESON is an unforgettable name to any viewer of Rod Serling's *The Twilight Zone*, for which he wrote many of the original series' most memorable episodes, including "Nightmare at 20,000 Feet," "Steel," "Nick of Time," "The Invaders" and "Little Girl Lost." Fans of *Star Trek* and *Night Gallery* will also remember the Matheson touch, as will moviegoers who have seen *House of Usher*, *The Pit and the Pendulum*, *Tales of Terror*, *The Raven*, *The Comedy of Terrors*, *Twilight Zone: The Movie*, *Jaws 3-D* or any of the adaptations drawn from his own novels, such as *The Legend of Hell House*, *The Incredible Shrinking Man*, *Duel* or *Somewhere in Time* (the novel version, *Bid Time Return*, won the World Fantasy Award in 1976). His other books include *Born of Man and Woman*, *A Stir of Echoes*, *What Dreams May Come* and the twice-filmed *I Am Legend*. A true grandmaster (World Fantasy Award for Life Achievement, 1984), Matheson's terse realism and emotional intensity have made him one of the most respected and imitated living writers of science fiction, fantasy, suspense and horror. His latest book is the first volume of his *Collected Short Stories*.

RICHARD CHRISTIAN MATHESON wishes he had more time to write short stories like "Third Wind"—and so do we. Born in 1953, the son of the author of *The Incredible Shrinking Man* began writing ad copy at the age of 17, then spent three years furnishing material for stand-up comedians, all the while working professionally as a rock drummer. He was temporarily sidetracked by college (no less than eight, including Harvard, Cornell and USC), but soon returned to rack up several hundred hours of prime-time network television. He has been head writer on twelve shows, including *The Powers of Matthew Starr*, *The Incredible Hulk*, *Quincy*, *The A-Team* and *Riptide*. Somewhere along the line he also squeezed in a year with Dr. Thelma Moss's Parapsychology Lab, where he investigated both Uri Geller and the case that was later fictionalized as *The Entity*. Is it redundant to mention that he produced his own series, or that it was called *Stir Crazy*? His book *Scars* is a collection of some of his best stories, and a forthcoming novel, a thriller, is quite naturally set against a show-business background.

WILLIAM F. NOLAN has more credits in his bibliography—some 1400—than God intended any one person to lay claim to. The extent of his accomplishments is therefore intimidating to those of us who still hold to such quaint practices as eating, sleeping and lost weekends. Yet another early starter in life, Nolan has seen over 45 books published in a career spanning many genres. Mystery, suspense, science fiction, fantasy, horror, the western, auto racing, biography, motion pictures and television constitute an incomplete list of the areas in which he has distinguished himself as writer. His film and TV scripts include *Burnt Offerings*, *Trilogy of Terror*, *The Turn of the Screw* and *Bridge Across Time*, a 1985 NBC TV movie about the return of Jack the Ripper. Limiting ourselves to the subject matter that is the focus of this book, it can be said with trenchant understatement that Nolan's short fiction has appeared in most of the major anthologies, from *Modern Masters of Horror* to *Alfred Hitchcock's The Master's Choice*. His most recent books are *Hammett: A Life at the Edge*, *The Black Mask Boys*, *McQueen*, and the collection *Things Beyond Midnight*.

RAY RUSSELL, called "a science fiction master" by *Publishers Weekly*, is equally renowned in and out of the field of fantastic literature. During his stint as executive editor of *Playboy*, his exceptional taste did much to shape that magazine's reputation as a publisher of quality fiction. His five novels, including *The Colony*, *Incubus* and *The Case Against Satan*, are well-known to mainstream readers and to fans of the genre. His classic "Sardonicus" is but one of the acclaimed short pieces contained in his several story collections, selected from a wealth of material originally appearing in *The Paris Review*, *Playboy*, *Midatlantic Review* and more than forty other top-flight periodicals. Russell is also the recipient of the Sri Chimnoy Poetry Award, his verses having been praised by the likes of Pulitzer Prize-winner Karl Shapiro. It is in this last role that he has chosen to be represented here, and his two selections (and Author's Note) offer a fascinating view of a side of this multitalented master that has been previously neglected by anthologists of fantasy and horror.

STEVE RASNIC TEM, the newest master represented in this volume, burst upon the scene in 1980 with the spectacular "City Fishing" in Ramsey Campbell's

*New Terrors*. Since then he has seen at least eighty-five stories in print, a number that will undoubtedly have to be revised considerably by the time you read this. A poet by first choice, Tem was a frequent contributor in that capacity to literary magazines in the 1970s; during those years he edited *The Umbral Anthology of Science Fiction Poetry*. When he made his move into prose fiction, he brought with him a poet's ear and eye for the specific and telling image that lifts his work far above that of most of his contemporaries. His first twenty stories were all under 2000 words, but since then he has stretched his canvas to encompass ever-more-ambitious themes, and is presently at work on his third novel. His tales may be found in many of the outstanding horror anthologies of the '80s, including *Perpetual Light*, *Shadows*, *Terrors*, *Horrors*, *Whispers*, *The Dodd*, *Mead Gallery of Horror*, etc.

KARL EDWARD WAGNER left psychiatry in the 1970s to write full-time, and the world of fantasy literature has not been the same since. With the publication of his first book, *Darkness Weaves* (1970), it became apparent that there were levels of meaning inherent in the dreamscape of imaginative fiction that had remained largely unexplored by generations of lesser writers. *Death Angel's Shadow*, *Bloodstone*, *Dark Crusade* and *Night Winds* followed in less than seven years. As the publisher of books under his own arcosa imprint, he has collected rare works by Wellman, Price and Cave; as editor of *The Year's Best Horror Stories*, he has chronicled the present renaissance of the horror story, a Golden Age that he himself helped to inspire. He won the British Fantasy Society's August Derleth Award in 1975, and a long-overdue World Fantasy Award in 1984. His most recent works are the collection *In a Lonely Place*, the novel *Killer* (coauthored with David Drake), and the screenplay for the motion picture *Conan III*.

CHELSEA QUINN YARBRO has given much effort to her study of the legendary Count de Saint Germain, who claimed to have lived for two thousand years. The assertion has not been taken lightly by Yarbro, who has reconstructed his life with creepy authenticity in her books *Hotel Transylvania, The Palace, Blood Games, Path of the Eclipse, Tempting Fate* and *The Saint-Germain Chronicles*. How she came by such intimate knowledge of this shadowy figure and his many historical milieus is a mystery as intriguing as the Count himself. Do her loving descriptions of his vampiric proclivities suggest first-hand knowledge? Her ''official'' biography states that she has been a full-time writer only since 1970 (some 29 books and 35 short stories), but readers are reminded not to believe everything in print. More believable is her expertise in occultism, classical music and history, interests that are evident in her latest books: *To the High Redoubt* and *A Baroque Fable*. Her countless anthology appearances include *Shadows, Faster Than Light, Slight of Crime, The Dodd, Mead Gallery of Horror, Women of Wonder* and *Best Detective Stories of the Year*.